THE PATH TO BETRAYAL

BY

PHILLIP TUCKER

www.philliptucker.com.au

ACKNOWLEDGEMENT

A wise old lady once told me, that everyone has a book in them waiting to be written. This is mine. I'd like to thank the many friends, who encouraged me to write, especially Mary, Fiona, Nigel, Gayle and Michelle, my editor, who showed me that even a person with appalling grammar can write. All it takes is imagination and a computer with spell check and good friends. But most of all I thank my family, especially my wife, Michelle, for putting up with me during this time.

COPYRIGHT © PHILLIP TUCKER 2009

CONTENTS

NEW YORK PRESENT DAY

As the lift groaned and shuddered to a halt, a metallic voice announced the twelfth floor.

"Whatever you do, don't screw up!" Nigel whispered to himself, as he led his team out of the lift. It was his first assignment as a senior agent, and he wanted to make a good impression. Hoping he took the right direction, Nigel led his team down the seemingly endless corridor, wondering if he should have pushed harder for backup.

When given the assignment briefing he had asked for backup; his Section Chief had firmly told him to stop complaining, it was a low priority assignment. Nigel had capitulated, his boss knew better. Now, here with only his three men, he started to wonder if saving money was his the Chief's main consideration.

Ever since 9-11, New York had a habit of swallowing the FBI's funds and resources. The FBI had been in a heightened state of readiness, fielding calls from crackpots and concerned citizens alike. Most were just a waste of time and money that the Bureau didn't have or, like this one, a low priority. Observing his team, Nigel realised that they didn't inspire him with much confidence. Allan and Ian, who walked confidently behind him in their off the rack suits, had been out of the academy for only three months. With no street experience, both thought this assignment was shit hot.

Mind you, Nigel reminded himself, he'd only been here for a year himself. In that period he'd spent six months on the streets, the minimum time for leading a team like this. Bill, on the other hand, was an interesting case. He'd been on the street for more than ten years and looked every inch a seasoned agent.

Studying Bill, Nigel asked himself, 'Why isn't he leading this team?' Bill's suit, unlike the others, was old and well worn, fraying at the sleeves. His shirt collar was unbuttoned behind his tie, to allow extra space for his oversized neck. 'He must have fucked up pretty badly, to be here taking orders from me,' Nigel assumed, getting closer and apprehensive.

"What's this guy wanted for again Nigel?" Bill asked suddenly, startling him.

"Entered the country twice but only left once. They didn't pick it up until after he'd left the airport, because of some glitch with the computer. So, partner, we're here to drag his arse downtown for questioning." Nigel answered lightheartedly, eliciting smiles from Allan and Ian.

"Do you know anything else about him? Like did you even bother to do a background check?" Bill asked gruffly, not amused by Nigel's sense of humour.

"Of course I did! I even asked for backup, but the agency didn't think it was warranted!" Nigel responded, putting Bill in his place.

"Sorry Nigel, but we know squat about this guy. It worries me." Bill shrugged, as they pulled up outside the room.

Unknown to the others, it was an assignment like this that had led to Bill's demotion. He and his partner had been sent to pick up a known drug dealer for questioning. Arriving at his home, they'd interrupted a drug deal between the dealer and two of his associates. In the following shootout, all three dealers had been shot along with Bill's partner, and some poor bastard who'd been walking past at the time. Bill had been left to take the fall for the whole mess. It had made him very cautious.

"Well you're right about one thing Bill; it doesn't hurt to go in with a bit of care. Ian, you knock, while Bill backs you up on the right side. Allan can cover this side, and I'll cover his back." Nigel suggested. Personally, he thought it was over the top, but it was his way of apologising for coming down hard on Bill. As they moved into position, Ian fronted up to the door excitedly and banged loudly.

"FBI, open up!" Ian said in a clear voice. Silence followed.

"FBI, open up!" he repeated, louder this time, thinking the occupant hadn't heard him, but again there was no answer. As he turned with shrugged shoulders to get advice from Nigel, a metallic sound came from the apartment.

"Get away from the door!" Bill screamed, going for his gun. The terror in Bill's voice, made them dive away from the door. A jackhammer-like noise erupted inside the apartment, as a series of holes appeared along the bottom of the door. Crumbling, unable to withstand the damage, the door exploded out into the hallway. On the opposite side of the hallway appeared a neat matching line of holes, except for the one space where Ian's leg had been.

Nigel and Allan lay dazed though unhurt on their side of the hallway. Their eyes were glued to the bloody mess that Ian's leg had become. Bill dragged the now screaming agent further down the hallway. Remembering his training, Nigel jumped to his feet, pulling out his automatic. With a mixture of fear and anger, he emptied a full clip into the remains of the apartment door then jumped away. Allan managed to get into position, as Nigel reloaded. They prepared for the worst but hoped he'd shot the bastard.

A crash inside the apartment gave them hope. He'd either clipped the offender or made him take cover. Either way, it gave them breathing space as they backed further away from the door. Looking down the corridor, Nigel saw that Bill had taken off his belt and wrapped it tightly around Ian's leg, as he tried to stem the bleeding. He'd also had his radio out; it was lying beside him on the floor. 'Thank God! He's radioed for backup!' Nigel realised something he hadn't even thought of yet.

"Shit I'm glad Bill came!" Nigel said to Allan.

In return, he received a dazed look from the still rattled agent, as they both faced the door, weapons ready. As the seconds ticked by in the hallway, Nigel's hearing started to return, filtering through other sounds from the building. He could hear the screams of ordinary people running away from the danger the gunshots signified. The fire alarm activating in the hallway meant someone was trying to evacuate the remaining people away from the danger on the twelfth floor.

Eventually, an eerie silence returned to the hallway, punctuated by moaning from Ian. Fifteen minutes seemed like fifteen hours to the agents as the adrenalin rush, which had been fuelled by fear wore off. The agents were left gasping for air, as fatigue gripped them. Shaking like a druggie waiting for his next hit, Nigel gripped his weapon unsteadily in his sweat-drenched hands.

"Where the fuck is the backup?" Nigel cursed loudly, his eyes glued to the assailant's door. No answer came from the others, as Nigel realised he was speaking just for the hell of it. Finally, after what seemed like an eternity, the clatter of weapons and body armour heralded the arrival of the Swat team.

"Bloody hell, it's about time!" Bill grumbled as the first Swat member approached, giving him the finger as a reply. Bill smiled, as the heavily armed police officers quickly moved into place. Having been given the well-done signal, Nigel and his men moved cautiously away.

After receiving no answer to the command to surrender, a

tremendous series of explosions echoed down the hallway. The Swat unit stormed through the doorway into room 1217, expecting the worst. Instead, they found the unconscious shooter with a bullet wound to the leg, plus a graze on the side of his head. The danger over, medics now rushed down the hallway. One team attended to Ian's injuries, the other stabilised the shooter. As normality returned, a series of 'well done' slaps rained down on the four agents, who had somehow become heroes.

Pulling himself together, Nigel followed Ian's stretcher on unsteady legs back down the long hallway with his men silently behind him. To his surprise, ordinary cops and firemen clapped their hands and cheered his group, as they quietly passed.

"My God all I want is to get out of here," Nigel said softly to the others, as the medics and his team crowded into a lift.

Exiting on the ground floor, the agents were swamped by a sea of people. The crowd cheered as the media yelled questions; Nigel and his men shyly waved back. Dodging microphones that sprouted from the mob like corn, they were forced to push their way through the jubilant, relieved crowd. Making slow progress, the group followed Ian's stretcher to the ambulance, making sure he was safely inside, as cameras snapped wildly. The local police came to their rescue forming an honour guard, escorting Nigel's team out to their vehicle. Bill jumped behind the wheel, driving slowly through the crowd, away from the hotel. Near breaking point, the three agents sat quietly letting their tension slowly fade as they drove back to their headquarters.

"My first assignment, what a fuckup," Nigel muttered to himself.

FBI HEADQUARTERS NEW YORK

Back at headquarters Nigel, Bill and Allan were subjected to a two-hour debriefing. When the interrogation was finished, they gathered in the canteen feeling dejected. Badly shaken, exhausted and smelling of dry sweat, the agents were given the rest of the week off. Still, no one wanted to leave, without first finding out how Ian was doing at the hospital.

Sitting there in silence, Nigel looked up to see the Head of the FBI, John Wilson stroll into the room. He was followed by a large group of reporters and "yes" men, including Nigel's Section Chief, the same man who'd told him he wouldn't need backup.

For the next ten minutes, Wilson shook hands with the three agents, telling all "these fine men had gone above and beyond the call of duty to arrest the suspected terrorist." While this was happening, Wilson's staff manoeuvred the camera crews around the room, trying to get the perfect picture of their boss with his men. As quickly as it had started, it was over, leaving the three agents wondering if they'd dreamt the whole thing. Silence settled again over the room, broken eventually by Nigel.

"If it weren't for you Bill, we'd all be dead!"

"Don't be stupid!" Bill retorted "It was just Ian's bad luck. Hey, did you notice how low the scumbag shot? I don't think he was trying to kill anyone."

"Still I shouldn't have been in charge, I lacked experience."

"Forget it, Nigel, what's done is done. And no one will accuse you of having no experience again!" Bill smiled, hoping to lift the mood, but failing. Nigel's ringing phone brought them all to alert. Ian was okay and would gain the full use of his leg in a couple of weeks. Relieved, they shook each other's hands as they got to their feet. Departing on their weeks leave, they forgot all about that day's events and their discussion of the shooter's aim.

Two days after the shooting, the man from room 1217 opened his eyes and looked around the room. He was apparently in hospital. The only difference between this room and the hundreds of other rooms in the complex, were the six heavily armed guards watching him like hawks, as he lay handcuffed to the bed. Seeing him stir, one of the guards spoke into his headset. Moments later, two more men entered the room. Although not armed, the shooter knew that these were the men who could do him the most harm.

"Good morning Mr Brown. It would appear you've been a bad boy." One of the new arrivals told him. "Your passport shows you're an American citizen from Nevada, but under the anaesthetic, you were speaking Arabic. We then checked your prints with Interpol and were bombarded with requests for your extradition from the Israelis. Care to make a statement, Mr Brown?"

"It will be a lot easier for you if you co-operate," the other man put forward, a slight smile on his lips. He gave the impression of being a friend, though his eyes told another story. This continued day and night for the next week, as the FBI's top two interrogators did their best to break him. Unfortunately, he showed about as much reaction to questioning as a rock, so they tried another tactic.

"Who trained you, Mr Brown? You allowed yourself to get trapped in a room by four rookie agents! Then you were stupid enough to get hit by a stray bullet! Who trained you? Some Mountain Afghani?" the interrogator asked smiling.

This caused the guards in the room to start chuckling, as they tried not to laugh at Mr Brown's embarrassment.

"The room was not my idea smartarse! And I was trained by your CIA at Fort Bragg, you little shit!" Mr Brown shouted angrily, silencing the room. Smiling confidently to each other, the interrogators thought their ploy had delivered their first break, just as the man posing to be Mr Brown had intended.

THE WHITE HOUSE, WASHINGTON DC

The Oval office had always fascinated John Wilson. As he sat with the other Department Heads, waiting for the President, he was amazed at how the President's desk dominated the room. Of course, when it was originally built, it was designed for that exact purpose. It had been skillfully engineered to give their President an advantage when having meetings with overseas politicians and dignitaries. Its oval shape, with the President's desk in the centre to the side, meant that anyone sitting in the room was isolated from the man next to him. The President, on the other hand, looked at everyone at the same time, dominating them.

It also worked well at staff meetings like this one, and Wilson knew he would soon feel that isolation. Looking around the room, he caught Don Brooks, the Head of the CIA, staring at him over the top of his rimmed glasses. It wasn't much of a secret in Washington that Wilson and Brooks loathed each other. Wilson figured that Brooks gleefully thought that today was the day that he would get the axe. Catching Wilson watching him, Brooks busied himself with a folder of documents. Moments later his unblinking eyes returned to Wilson, this time with a confident smile on his lips. From the side door, two Secret Service Agents slipped into the room, announcing the arrival of the President, as all made ready to stand.

"Sit down everyone. Now Wilson, can you explain why the Israeli President call me a liar when I told him that this "Mr Brown" fellow had died of his injuries. Care to elaborate?"

"Well, the Israeli agents watching the hospital must've guessed that it was a lie. We had to say something to get the press of our backs," Wilson replied casually. The President looked taken aback by the statement.

"You idiot Wilson, you've made the President lie to one of our allies. You should be dismissed!" Brooks screamed. The rest of the Department Heads sat stunned into absolute silence. It wasn't caused by Wilson's statement, but by the way, Brooks had venomously attacked him. No one knew what to say, but they had to agree with Brooks on one thing, John Wilson looked to be leaving office and soon. Brooks, sensing the mood in the room, was about to continue hammering Wilson when the President raised his hand for silence.

"You'd better have a good excuse for lying to me Wilson, and I want to hear it right now!" the President commanded angrily.

"We can't hand him over, Sir. He's one of ours," Wilson signed, letting the gravity of the statement flow over him.

"Oh my God!" The President whispered, his eyes never leaving Wilson's face. Silence settled over the room, as the President considered his options. "Let's hear it, John, though it's my understanding that this Mr Brown is over fifty. That's a bit old for the Army isn't it?"

"Sir, it's my belief, and we have several records from Army Intelligence to prove it, that Mr Brown, better known as Ali Moustaffer, was part of a unit set up in the eighties. It was made up of Foreign Special Forces troops to take care of targets around the world under the orders of the CIA. This continued, until several years ago, when the CIA lost control of the unit. It then became a force for hire."

"You're crazy Wilson! You can't prove any of this!" Brooks yelled angrily, before being silenced by a raised hand from the President.

"Everyone except Wilson and Brooks out of the room!" the President ordered flatly. "And not a word of this leaves this office. Am I understood?" the President ordered. The Department Heads quickly nodded their agreement, before fleeing the room.

"Brooks, the fact that you said Wilson couldn't prove it, instead of denying it was true, means I believe him. So now I want the whole truth. You start Wilson, we've got all night." The President suggested getting comfortable; he knew this would be a long story. Sipping a glass of water, he began.

"Well Sir, it started in early nineteen eighty-two!"

NORTHERN NSW AUSTRALIA
6 MONTHS EARLIER

Steve and Ken sat in a corner booth at their local pub doing what they did best, drinking. Steve's boss, Ken, sat facing away from the crowd, while Steve as always sat watching the crowd around him. Dressed in their matching farm work clothes - blue shorts, blue shirts and brown farm boots, it was evident to everyone present that looking for female company was the last thing on their minds.

'Friday night, the end of the work week' Steve thought, as he looked around the overcrowded room, checking for danger, spotting none. It was a big night, and the Alstonville Station Pub was filled to the brim, overflowing with a colourful mix of locals, tourists and drunks. Crushed together, the crowd stood around talking loudly over each other, trying to squeeze some joy into their miserable, lonely lives.

"Maybe it's just me?" Steve mumbled to himself, as he scanned the room trying to spot something or someone to lift his spirit. Just when he was about to give up, he spotted Justine the barmaid and signalled for two more drinks. Poor Justine! In her late twenties, good looks and a knockout figure, it was always going to be hard working as a barmaid. At least she was a friendly face in a sea of nobodies, and it cheered him up slightly. Weaving her way towards their table, Steve noticed Justine was wearing her usual frozen smile. She'd learnt to do this while trying to ignore the comments made by drunken men about her body. Navigating her way through an ocean of chatter, Justine delivered their drinks, placing them carefully on the table.

"Thanks, Justine," Steve said paying for the beers and giving her a good tip for her trouble. For this small act of kindness, he received a genuine smile.

Picking up their empty glasses, Justine turned and made her way back to the bar, her frozen smile in place. Looking back at Steve from behind the bar Justine wished that this mystery man had been a little younger, there was something about him that she found attractive. She liked Steve and Ken; they had been coming to the pub on and off for over a year and in that time had caused no problems. Apart from the fact that no one knew anything about Steve, for some reason he aroused her.

"Maybe age isn't that important?" Justine said smiling.

"How about a beer or something else sexy!" a sneering voice asked, from behind Justine. It was followed by wolf whistles and hoots from the man's friends. Looking around at the new arrivals with loathing, Justine snapped back to reality.

"You know my name, Derrick. Either behave or leave." Justine angrily replied. Derrick stared back at her silently, a malicious smile on his lips. Pouring his beer, she collected his money, all the time standing her ground.

"You'll keep bitch," Derrick whispered, before turning and walking outside. As she served his friends, Justine watched him go, containing the fear she felt. Derrick and his gang of dropouts had plagued the area for several years. Unlike the other members of his group, Derrick's family were wealthy, giving him a form of protection from the law. Drugs and drinking to excess was their trademark, though assaulting the less fortunate was what they got off on.

There were rumours that Derrick's father had beaten him as a child. Though unproven Justine guessed it was close to the truth. It explained why he usually targeted the elderly, somehow punishing them for his childhood.

Witnessing Justine's altercation with Derrick, a feeling of impending danger settled over the hotel staff. Steve also sensed trouble; his instincts warned him that it was time to go before he became involved. Turning to Ken, he was just about to suggest leaving, when Ken began to speak.

"My wife's leaving me, Steve, why is she leaving me?" Ken babbled, looking into his glass for answers. Ken was right to look there, for in the last three months he had spent almost every night here, instead of at home with his wife. Ken was an alcoholic or close to it and had given up caring about anything else.

"You fool! To throw away love so easily, what I'd give to have my wife back!" Steve murmured to himself, as his mind flooded with visions of his wife. She was dressed as he remembered her best, in her long black dress, blonde hair spilling down over her shoulders. It had been the night he made up his mind to marry her rather than be separated a minute longer. His eyes blurred as her image danced before him making his heart fill with love for her, and thump rapidly with longing.

A sudden sob from Ken interrupted his thoughts causing the vision to vanish, leaving him back in the bar feeling gutted and angry. Looking closely at Ken, Steve saw tears running down his face, which surprised him. 'He really loved her. Why did he let her go?' Steve asked himself. 'He didn't get her killed like you did!' a voice laughed in his head, tormenting him, causing his anger surface.

"Come on Ken, you've had enough, let's go!" Steve growled, starting to stand, hoping to get as far away as possible before he exploded. Ken looked up and saw the black anger in Steve's eyes and knew what it meant, his demon had returned. Ken had found Steve to be hard working and completely reliable, but he was a mystery. Ken knew nothing of his past only that he had children and a demon that possessed him when he became enraged.

Only once had he seen this anger take control of Steve. His hand had become caught in a Chipper while he was working. Unable to free it, he'd become consumed with rage, repeatedly hitting the machine. Ken had just stood there too scared to approach, for fear of being hit. In the end, he'd waited until Steve collapsed from exhaustion before approaching him.

He'd thought of firing Steve over the incident, but he was good company, and since then it hadn't happened again, until now.

"Okay Steve take it easy, I'll just finish my drink!" Ken smiled nervously, as he quickly downed his drink. Unsteadily Ken got to his feet, before walking erratically towards the front door. Turning to make sure Steve was following; he collided with two of the troublemakers from the bar. The smashing of glasses raised a cheer from the crowd, as Ken disentangled himself from the two young men.

"Sorry about that, I'll get you some more drinks," Ken said pleasantly, realising it was his mistake.

"Fucking greybacks! You old timers should be in a fucking retirement home, not out drinking!" Derrick snarled, looking murderously at Ken.

"I said I was sorry, I'll get those drinks. I don't want any trouble." Ken blurted out, fear in his voice. Moving backwards, Ken collided with Steve, as he tried to put some distance between them and the growing group of young men.

"It's too late for that old man, you and your mate need sorting out!" Derrick declared, getting support from the watching crowd.

"He said he'd replace your drinks big mouth, now how about backing off!" Steve growled dangerously. Silence settled over the crowd at Steve's defiance. Even Derrick felt a touch of foreboding from Steve's reply. But with his friends behind him and the crowd support, he moved forward.

"Steve for God's sake, take it easy, help me get their drinks!" Ken begged, worried that his friend wanted this confrontation to release his anger.

"Too late for that grandpa!" Derrick spat out, as he came in low, punching Ken in the stomach, doubling him over. Like a wild pack of dogs, the group hammered Ken, punching and kicking him to the ground, until he lay unmoving. Sensing Ken was finished they concentrated their blows on Steve. The crowd, enjoying the free entertainment yelled excitedly as the fistfight continued. At first, Steve held back hesitating, hearing Ken's words, knowing he was right. Seeing Ken hit the floor changed everything, as his suppressed anger surfaced and his training took over.

Surging forward, he drove his fist into Derrick's throat, crushing his windpipe, sending him spinning back into the crowd. Blows continued to rain down on him, but forgetting the pain, he concentrated on his opponents. Pivoting to one side, he smashed the legs out from under two young men, clearly breaking the first one's leg, causing him to scream in agony. A chop to the left broke the nose of another poor bastard, blood spraying over the crowd.

Two of the group's more solid members tried to crush him against the wall, only to find him drop to the ground, punching them ruthlessly between the legs. Paralysed, overwhelmed with pain, both men collapsed onto the floor unable even to groan. The crowd screamed their approval at every blow, mesmerised by the action. Baying in like wild animals, they yelled for blood.

The brawl ground on, Steve taking punishment, but giving more back, until gradually a space opened up around Ken and himself. The once cheering crowd stood unmoving, shaken at the carnage inflicted on so many by two old men. Steve, fighting through a wall of pain, grabbed Ken from the floor; before he disdainfully looked around at the sea of faces watching.

"Are you all happy? Did you get to see a fight?" Steve barked, as the effects of his injuries, started to sap his strength. "Someone call a medic," Steve added, as, fighting through his pain, he tried to get

Ken outside, before it started again. They'd almost made it too. While pushing the swinging front door open, while supporting Ken, a glass bottle shattered against the back of Steve's head, knocking him unconscious.

Crashing to the pavement outside, blood from his head wound sprayed over the surprised police officers who were just about to enter. Looking down at the two bleeding middle-aged men, who appeared severely beaten by the cheering mob inside, the police, came to the obvious conclusion,

"The poor old bastards! They really worked them over." A young constable stammered out, as the sound of celebration broke out in the pub.

"Get the mongrels!" yelled their Sergeant, as he called for backup. Needing no encouragement, the police officers drew their batons and charged into the wild and drunken crowd dealing out rough justice. When it was all over thirty-eight people were admitted to the hospital, including four officers. A further twenty were arrested for various offences and popular little hotel, looked like a bomb had hit it. After things had quietened down, the dazed hotel staff slowly emerged from their hiding spots behind the bar. They then forlornly started the job of cleaning up the mess.

"What the hell happened here?" a voice demanded from the door, as Detective Boulton worked his way through the debris to stand in front of the hotel staff.

"We're not really sure. We were all busy serving at the time when it started" Luke answered. Seeing the Detective wanted to hear more, he continued.

"All I saw was two old guys heading for the door. I think one bumped into a couple of young guys, spilling their drinks. Next minute the whole place erupted. Me and the other staff hid behind the bar, other than that we saw nothing." Luke volunteered, getting nods of support from the other staff.

"Are Steve and Ken okay Officer?" Justine asked worried for them.

"They're both in hospital, but they'll be okay. Do you know them miss?" the Detective asked fishing for information.

"Not really," Justine shrugged," They work out on a farm about five kilometres from here to the south. They've been coming here for about a year."

"Cause any trouble before?" The Detective asked, scanning the staff faces.

"What those old guys? You're kidding us, Detective, they must be in their fifties!" Luke answered smiling.

"I know how it sounds, but lots of the witnesses say that one of the old guys inflicted most of the injuries, before trying to walk out. I'm just checking to see if It's true." Detective Boulton replied. Seeing the surprised looks, it was clear no one believed him.

It was three days before Steve regained consciousness and through a wall of pain tried to take stock of his surroundings. His eyes were blurry, but it was definitely a hospital room, by the equipment near the three other beds.

"So you're finally awake?" a friendly voice asked, from the end of his bed. Focusing, Steve recognised Justine sitting with an open book in her hands. He tried desperately to get his mind up to speed to make a reply, but nothing came.

"I've got to tell you, Steve, you don't look too good. But you're certainly better looking than the pub; it looks like a bomb went off there!" Justine exclaimed smiling.

"Bomb! Was it sanctioned?" Steve exclaimed before his mind could focus properly.

"Sanctioned! Now that's an interesting word, what's it mean?" asked a male voice to the right of Justine, out of Steve's line of sight.

"I'm not sure he knows what he is saying, Detective?"

Inside Steve's brain alarm bells started going off, clearing his mind and alerting him to a danger he sensed.

"Hello Justine, how long have I been here?" Steve asked warily, this time hoping for information on what had occurred since the fight. Justine happily told Steve three nights had passed since the fight, giving him a rough outline of the events since then. She even introduced Detective Boulton, the Officer in charge of the Investigation, who was here to protect him.

"Why do I need protecting?"

"Well, it appears several members of the public, who were hurt in the fight, reckon you did all the damage to them and the pub. Several have threatened to get even, so here I am!" replied Detective Boulton, watching Steve.

"I really can't remember a thing detective, only that Ken bumped into some young men spilling their beers. That's about it."

"How silly detective, how could Ken and Steve do so much damage? They were just victims, of some young thugs who'd had too much to drink." Justine pointed out worried they might come after him.

"I suppose your right miss. It would take an incredibly good fighter or trained soldier to fight his way out of a brawl. Wouldn't it Captain?" Boulton smiled, as he turned and walked out the door, leaving Justine staring at Steve.

A week later, Justine helped Steve into his rented cottage. Hobbling inside, Justine made him a cup of tea, as he settled into a lounge chair, and sorted through his pile of mail found on the doorstep. Most were junk mail, two were not. One was from the owner of the cottage giving him three weeks notice, the other was from Ken. It said that he was no longer required on the farm, and included a cheque for two weeks' severance pay. It appeared that the Derrick and his group were leaning on people. Even Ken, his friend, had decided to keep his distance. Seeing his reaction to the letters Justine came over and took them from Steve, reading them.

"They've got no right to treat you like this!" Justine snarled, tears forming in her eyes.

"I'm not a local Justine, just an outsider. The people who own this place and Ken, well they have to live here. This is the only way for them to co-exist with the people that were hurt at the pub." Steve tried to sound logical and accepting, inside he was gutted.

"Still, Ken was your friend, I would've expected better from him!" Justine answered, seeing the sorrow on Steve's face.

"You're a good friend, Justine, though it might be best for your job to keep away from me," Steve said softly.

"You don't have to worry Steve. I quit a couple of days ago after a run-in with the manager. So if it's okay with you, I'll stay here with you for awhile." Justine replied, her eyes getting misty, worried that he might say no.

"Of course you can. I'd love to have you stay with me, but it's a bit cramped, it's only got one bed." Steve answered.

"It's okay Steve I'm sure we'll both fit!" Justine replied, with a mischievous smile on her lips.

Steve lay exhausted staring at Justine's naked body beside him. Having spent most of the afternoon and night making love, he contemplated what this relationship meant to each of them. He felt guilty about Justine's age. 'My own daughters are in their twenties, and Justine is only twenty-nine. I'm just a dirty old man!' Steve thought to himself, smiling at the situation.

On the other hand, he couldn't remember the last time he'd made love, he knew it had been with his wife, for she was the only other woman he'd slept with. It must have been the night before the…He stopped there, remembering was still too painful, and he didn't want to ruin this moment.

Justine lay beside Steve more content and satisfied than she could remember for a long time and at the same time sad, knowing wouldn't last. She knew in her heart that Steve wouldn't be staying with her, it was in his eyes. At first, his lovemaking had been like a caged animal seeking only to satisfy a hunger. As time passed, he had become a more considerate lover wanting her to enjoy it as much as he did. It had been a beautiful experience for her, and she would always treasure it, but he would not be staying.

And there was something about the look in his eyes when the Detective had called him Captain. She sensed that she would be in danger, if she stayed with him, and she knew he would not allow that.

"Why'd the detective call you Captain?" Justine asked softly, rolling over and facing him.

"I was in the Army once. I worked my way up to the rank of Captain before I left." Steve answered defensively. "There's a lot more to the story Justine, but I'm not joking when I tell you that your life could be in danger for knowing it." Steve stammered out, thinking she'd think him slightly crazy.

"Tell me, Steve, I can see it in your eyes you need to tell someone. You can trust me." Hugging him to her, she waited knowing he was desperate to unburden to someone. Looking deeply into her eyes Steve slowly told her of his life and the demons that haunted him.

When he'd finished, he wept and sobbed uncontrollably in Justine's arms, finally releasing the pain he had held in for so long.

"You've got to go to the authorities and tell them, Steve!" Justine said, wiping tears from her eyes.

"I'd be dead as soon as I showed my face. The only thing that stops them at the moment is that I am hard to find. Unfortunately, the detective running a check on me has ruined my staying here." Steve answered, wondering if he was falling in love with this young woman. Time went slowly by as they both lay silently together, trying desperately to find an answer to their problems, and in the end, not finding one.

"I'll miss you, Steve, when you go, but for now I've still got you!" Justine whispered, with a forced smile. Pushing Steve down onto the bed, she decided, to enjoy her time with him as much as possible, before he left.

Superintendent Ken Walker sat at his desk checking his Officer's reports before filing them or passing them onto Sydney. One was missing from Detective Dave Boulton's pile, the one on the pub brawl. Reaching across to the intercom he had his secretary call Detective Boulton. Five minutes later Boulton knocked and entered Walker's office.

"Where's the report on the brawl Dave? I thought it was a simple fight?" Ken asked flatly, indicating he should take a seat.

"So did I, but there's something fishy about Steve Roberts. Here have a look at his file from Sydney," Dave suggested. Ken quickly read through the dossier then turned to Dave.

"What's the problem, Dave? He was in the Army, his wife's deceased and his kids live with his sister. What's the problem? I don't see anything here?" Ken answered confused.

"That's the problem! There's nothing in there, the guys a zero. He hasn't even had a parking ticket, something smells wrong!" Dave exclaimed, suspicious of the file.

"You're wasting time Dave, you've got nothing!" Ken spat out, wondering where this was going.

"Look! I did some checking on this guy through a friend of mine in the Feds. The guy's kids go to the best private school in Sydney. Their money all comes out of trust funds and shares in Australian companies worth millions. Where'd a soldier get that type of money eh? My friend, then got his arse kicked, for checking Roberts' record. The guy's dangerous, I can feel it." Dave explained.

"You might be onto something Dave. But you've got no proof, and it seems he still has friends somewhere. Let it go, Detective. Lean on get him to leave if you want, but let it go." This left Dave no option.

"Okay Sir, I'll finish the report," Dave replied leaving.

Steve and Justine had been at the cabin for about a week, when someone tossed a brick through the window, spraying the room with glass, before driving off into the night. Steve had wanted to let it go, but Justine insisted on calling the police. Detective Boulton arrived the next morning and superficially examined the damage.

"Looks like someone doesn't like you, Captain?" Boulton smiled, as Justine appeared from inside the cabin. Looking from Justine to Steve, at first Boulton appeared surprised, but he'd seen it all before. "Any clue as to who threw the brick?"

"No. But I'm sure you do." Steve replied.

Detective Boulton stood there his smile gone, his anger barely suppressed, as he watched Steve. 'What would happen if I went for my gun and tried to arrest him?' Boulton thought. His anger told him to go for it, but his gut told him he'd never make it. For as relaxed as Roberts looked there was something in his eyes that said he was ready. For the first time in his long career, Dave knew death was looking him in the eye and fear made him hesitate.

"Is there a problem Detective?" Justine asked nervously as both men stood there silently watching each other.

"No I'm finished here, I'll keep you informed," Boulton told him, as he backed away and climbed into his vehicle. Not looking back, Dave drove off down the road. At the club that night, Dave was greeted by two cops from his station, Mick and Adam.

"Did the bricks work?" Adam asked smiling.

"Yeah, I think he'll leave soon, but for other reasons," Boulton replied distantly, as he looked into his glass with an empty expression.

"What's wrong with Dave?" Mick laughed, perplexed by Dave's strange mood.

"Nothing, just the guy worries me."

"You think we should give him another visit?" Adam asked neutrally.

"No, he'll be ready next time," Dave muttered.

"Bloody hell Dave, pull yourself together, what are you worried about? There's two of us, what's he going to do, kill us both?" Adam laughed.

"Trust me, that's exactly what he'll do, so don't go near him, that's an order!" Dave hissed. Finishing his drink, he got up and left without another word, leaving his two friends bewildered.

Steve sat outside on the veranda thinking of a way out of this problem. The detective knew a brick had been used. Justine had told the police that a rock had been thrown, as he'd said her to. The cops were in on it. He knew it was time to go, but he didn't want to leave Justine. He'd just got to really know her, and he had to admit, he was falling in love with her. What should he do? At that moment Justine came out and sat beside him.

"Your thinking of leaving, aren't you?"

"Yes as much as it hurts, I've got to go."

"I knew when you talked to the detective, something had happened between the two of you."

"You were right he did see me as a threat. Another thing you were right about is clearing my name, and I think with luck, I've found a way," Steve said hugging her fiercely, as they sat clinging to each other.

Early the next morning, Steve borrowed Justine's car. He had several things to arrange, starting with finding somewhere for Justine to live. He'd been looking through the paper and seen several units for sale in the seaside town of Ballina. One, in particular, caught his eye. The town's location to Steve was perfect. It had a small airport and scenic riverside harbour. Not only was it beautiful, but Steve also considered it far enough from Alstonville to keep Justine away from any trouble with the locals.

Getting the real estate agent moving was Steve's main problem. In his work clothes, Steve did not lend to the image of someone able to buy a million dollar unit. A quick ring to his bank in Sydney, guaranteeing the total purchase price, suddenly made things happen. Paying the total amount had its advantages. It allowed him to rent the unit, until it was exchanged, complete with furniture.

Next stop on his outing was to buy several suits, travel clothes and baggage. This would fit his businessman image, something his farm shorts and boots would not do. The last purchase was to buy a plane ticket to Sydney, for the following week. Steve hoped very much that one day he would return, but for security, he only purchased a one-way ticket. To Justine the days remaining before Steve left passed by in a heartbreaking rush.

No matter how much time she spent with Steve, or made love to him, it didn't seem enough considering the likelihood of him coming back to her appeared slim. Moving out of the cottage was a sad time for them both as it had become special to them, but Steve assured her he had found somewhere more comfortable for her to stay until he returned.

The shock at arriving at the unit overwhelmed Justine. The cottage had been at the lower end of the rental market, the unit was definitely at the other. With its three bedrooms and incredible views of the ocean from its large balcony, it was a place everyone hoped to live in.

"Steve it's lovely, but I can't stay here the rent would kill you, and I don't know when I'll find a job, while your away to help out!" she explained worriedly.

"I didn't rent it, Justine, I bought it. I want something nice to come home to, as well as you." Steve whispered into her ear, kissing her.

"I don't understand. You worked on a farm and lived in a dumpy cottage. Why?" she asked, pulling away from him.

"I've always been lucky with money. It's hiding from my enemy that has made me live the life I live now." Steve answered hugging her, stopping more questions.

"Well I'm glad you bought it furnished it'll make tonight a lot more fun!" she giggled, removing her clothes as she wandered into the bedroom.

Two days slipped by and departure day arrived. While Steve showered and dressed, Justine tried to put on a brave face to take him to the airport. Coming out of the bathroom dressed in a suit and freshly shaved, Justine was so surprised she couldn't speak. She'd never seen him in anything but shorts and a work shirt before.

"God Steve, you look totally different!" Justine stammered, sounding both amazed and scared by his transformation. Her surprise gave way to fear knowing he might not be coming back. Pulling her to him, Steve held her kissing her forehead.

"I'll be back before you know it. Don't worry my love." He assured her kissing her on the lips, stopping further discussion.

Driving to the airport, Steve told Justine to drop him and keep going. At first, she refused, wanting to come in with him. He warned her not to, surveillance cameras were everywhere, and for safety, he did not want her photographed with him. Handing her a credit card,

Steve brooked no argument when he told her to use it to pay bills and live off until he returned. Instead of complaining, she reached across with tears in her eyes and kissed him passionately. Weak at the knees, Steve dragged himself away from her waving as she sadly drove away.

From the car park, Boulton and his two sidekicks watched as Steve kissed Justine goodbye before entering the airport.

"Bloody hell! That was quite a kiss." Mick smiled, from the back seat.

"He's a bit old for her isn't he?" Adam put in.

"I don't give a shit about her! I just want to make sure he's gone!" Dave mumbled angrily, wondering where Roberts' suit had come from. He looked totally different, 'more confident' he thought. Twenty minutes passed, and Dave checked his watch noting that the flight would be boarding any minute now.

"Nice of you three to see me safely off!" a voice whispered next to Dave's window, making the three officers jump. Looking up, Dave saw Steve standing there, his face devoid of emotion.

"Going to miss your plane if you don't hurry, Captain," Dave smiled a lot calmer than he felt.

"I can understand you guys trying to scare me off with the brick. If I were in your situation, I'd most probably have done the same thing. But believe it or not, I'm no danger to you or anyone else here. Sure I've killed. My unit over the years has killed more people than I could possibly count. That was our job, and we were good at it. So look after my girl while I'm gone my friends, you wouldn't want me to bring my unit back here!" Silence settled over the car as they thought about how Roberts had got to the car without anyone seeing him, it was a clear space between them and the terminal.

"Do you think we should go after him?" Mick suggested, breaking the silence.

"How'd he do that? How did he get next to the car without us seeing him?" Adam asked, rattled.

"It's his training I'd guess, and I'd say he's had a lot of it," Dave answered, getting over the shock. He realised that his gut feeling had been right about Roberts being dangerous, just not to whom. The danger was to who he was sent after, not them.

"Well, I don't think I'll be asking Justine out on a date while he's gone!" Mick said, trying to look serious, and breaking into a grin. At the same time, the three officer laughed, relieving the pressure they all felt at the departure of this anonymous man.

The flight to Sydney passed without incident. Upon arrival, Steve set his plan in motion. Firstly, he booked a one-way ticket to Los Angeles, business class, leaving the following day. He didn't need a visa, as his fake passport showed him as an American returning from a business trip. Booking a room at the Airport Hilton, under his assumed name, Steve settled in for the night. At 3am, Steve reached for the phone and dialled Switzerland, after four rings he hung up and dialled again. This time it was picked up.

"Hello who is it?" a familiar voice asked.

"It's Steve, how are you, Ali?"

"Shit Steve, I thought they'd got you. How long has it been?" Ali was genuinely relieved to hear from him.

"Too long my friend! I'm ringing because I've got a plan to stop running, are you in?"

"Let's hear it first!" Ali replied doubting it could be done. Steve laid out his plan for the mission, giving him the complete rundown of his operation. Finished, he waited for a reply, wondering how desperate Ali was to join him in this operation. After a long pause, Ali answered.

"I've got to tell you Steve it's risky, especially for me, being an Arab." He said nervously pausing again. "Okay, I'm in Steve, though I'm not sure about the others."

"I've put a lot of thought into it, Ali, it's a good plan."

"Look, I'll contact the others, and if they agree or not, I'll meet you in New York in ten days time, at the Waldorf," Ali assured him, hanging up without another word. 'God, I didn't even ask how his wife and kids were,' Steve chastised himself, as he tried to get some sleep.

The next day Steve passed through customs without attracting attention and entered the Business Lounge area, where he settled in to await his departure. Breaking one of his own rules, he bought a mobile phone at a duty-free store, dialling his sister's home.

"Hello who is it?" answered the unmistakable sound of his sister's voice.

"Hello sis, how have you been?"

"Steve, is it really you?" Louise answered, her voice trembling with emotion.

"Yes, it's me! How are you and the kids? Are you all okay?"

"We thought you were surely dead. Where have you been?"

"Not far from where we lived as kid's sis. God, I've missed you!" Tears started to run down his cheeks.

"Everyone's fine, your girls are doing great, come home Steve!" his sister pleaded.

"I can't sis. They're still after me, but with luck, I hope to stop running and come home." Steve croaked out, wiping his eyes before he continued. "Tell them I love them, and I miss you all." Steve sobbed, before cutting the connection, hoping no one was listening or tracking his call. Looking around seeing no danger, Steve quickly wiped his eyes and dumped the phone in the nearest bin. Eyes straight ahead, his expression neutral, Steve walked casually towards the boarding gate, to the outside world showing no emotion whatsoever. Sitting in Business class sipping complimentary champagne, Steve thought back over his life.

'What a mess. How could we have been all have been so stupid?' he thought, as he finishing his drink, he fell into an uneasy sleep.

WESTERN AUSTRALIAN DESERT 1982

Regiment Sergeant Major John MacDonald looked over the twelve men standing to attention in front of him as if he was looking at a bunch of dogs that had crapped on his lawn.

"You bunch of scum! I can't believe the Army is so desperate. Shit! It's amazing that you got this far!" He spat out.

It was the final test for these men to prove that they had what it takes to join Australia's elite fighting force, and they all wanted it badly. For three months they'd been put through hell to break them. Initially, there had been twenty-five men, but the training was brutal, emotionally and physically. MacDonald looked them over carefully, noting that there wasn't an ounce of fat on any of them. They were some of the best recruits he'd seen come from the regular army units since he'd been posted here, and that was a long time. Since Vietnam, the Army had been cutting back, which included elite units as well. The high cost of maintaining these groups meant that only two new positions were available.

"This is your last chance to make it easy for yourselves. Just step back one pace, and there'll be no questions asked," he asked politely. No one moved, which of course he knew would happen, they were good men. "Well don't say you weren't warned," he sneered with an evil smile before continuing. "All you have to do is make it back to the Field Command bunker thirty kilometres to the west of this position, and you've got all of this lovely day and night to do it in. No problems eh!" he laughed, splashing water from his canteen on his face. It was forty degrees centigrade in the shade, and it was just eight in the morning. What would it be like by midday? Each soldier had only one canteen of water.

"Oh I forgot to mention, tough guys, forty our best men dressed like these will be deployed to protect the bunker," MacDonald explained, as ten soldiers materialised from the area around them. They were all wearing camouflaged killer suits, as the American soldiers called them. The suits were made mostly out of hessian, with local vegetation or colours added. It made them very hard to spot, especially when they were stationary.

"You've got twenty-four hours. I suggest you use it wisely. Now get out of my sight!" the RSM bellowed at the recruits, sending them running from the area in twelve different directions. When all the recruits had disappeared from sight, MacDonald loaded up the trucks with the ten Regiment soldiers and headed back towards the base.

Marching into the bunker, the RSM gave his report to Regiment Commander Colonel Stevenson, as the enlisted staff checked their uniforms, all fearing the Sergeant Major's temper.

"What do you think of their chances of making it?" the Colonel asked MacDonald.

"In thirty years only three have made it. But they'll give it their best Sir; they're all good men,"

"Well at least there's three positions now!" the Colonel nodded towards an American Officer, sitting in the corner quietly observing the exercise. "It appears that high command wants one of our new recruits to be incorporated into a unit the Americans are forming, and they get to pick the man themselves!" the Colonel informed him, sounding none too happy about it. He was about to ask the Colonel why when they were interrupted.

"Excuse me, Sir, Recruit Roberts is here." the Radio Operator informed them.

"Which one's Roberts?" the Colonel asked MacDonald, wondering how he'd been caught so quickly.

"That's a surprise, I'd have thought he would be one of the last," MacDonald replied sadly, before continuing. "He's a good soldier, but insolent. I remembered the other day, he'd come into lunch dirty from digging a weapons pit. I'd gone up to him and pointed my pacing stick at him and told him there was shit at the end of my stick. He'd turned around and said it wasn't at his end. I made him run twenty kilometres for that, the cheeky little bugger!" All in hearing range laughed, much to the RSM's embarrassment including the Colonel, until a look from the Staff Sergeant froze everyone.

"Where'd they'd catch him?" the Colonel asked the Radio Operator, changing the subject quickly.

"I'm sorry Sir, you misunderstood me. They didn't catch him; he's outside the door and wants to know if he passed Sir!"

"Get him in here now!" the Colonel exploded, turning to his Sergeant Major. "How did he get back here so quickly?"

"I've no idea Sir. It's impossible!" MacDonald as at a loss and that didn't happen often. At that moment, in walked recruit Roberts wearing a killer suit, minus the headgear. He came to attention, in front of his Commanding Officer.

"How you get here so fast Roberts? Out with it!"

"Well Sir, when the RSM's group started to head back to base, I just put on my killer suit and climbed aboard the vehicle, with the rest of the soldiers. It seemed the easiest way of breaking through the defences, Sir." Robert's answered, to a surprised audience.

"Very clever Roberts, now get your ass on a truck and back out to the start! This time walk here like the others!" the Colonel bellowed, before dismissing him from the bunker. In the corner, the American Officer smiled. 'These guys were the best he'd seen, yet this Private had outfoxed them. I'll have to watch and see how this Recruit Roberts fares.' he thought to himself, writing down the soldier's name.

"One question Sir, is that counted as a pass? He actually did make it." MacDonald asked the Colonel wondering.

"Yes I was thinking the same thing, it was damned clever. But I'd still like to see if he can break through the lines with the others. But I think it's a pass!" the Colonel replied with a smile.

Back out at the starting point Steve was dropped off and left in a cloud of dust, contemplating his options. Starting late meant he'd have to hurry to make it back in time. The others had started at eight, three hours ago, and it was now hotter. The advantage was the regiment's soldiers had been hunting for a long time it might make them careless. Instead of staying in fixed positions they might be moving around, making them easier to spot. He still had until seven tomorrow morning, and darkness was his friend, so without another thought, he headed off towards the target.

THE BUNKER

It was now three thirty in the morning, and outside the bunker, it was as still as a cemetery and as dark. Phantom-like figures silently patrolled the area, waiting for the last recruit. Inside behind blacked out curtains, the command post had become deadly quiet. The staff worked with the minimum of noise necessary to carry out their duties, knowing what was at stake. All the recruits had been caught except one, Roberts. The second last one, only five minutes ago, four hundred metres from this position. Most of the patrols had been pulled in around the bunker's position.

Knowing it was the recruit's destination was a huge advantage, and they figured he must be close. Roberts had been spotted several times in his race to get back quickly. In each case, he had given the soldiers hunting him the slip. No mean feat considering the calibre of the soldiers chasing him. Since darkness had fallen no one had spotted him, which didn't surprise any of the other captured recruits, they had a nickname for him - The Ghost.

"He'll have to make a break for it soon; the sun will be coming up in another hour!" MacDonald pointed out to bunker staff.

"Do you think he'll try? He must have heard the last man get caught a few minutes ago?" the Colonel replied.

"He's got guts and brains, of course, he'll try!" answered the American, startling everyone present. This was because; except for the odd question on the exercise he'd said hardly anything. Looking around the room the Colonel saw nods of agreement from all the enlisted men, they knew from experience what it took to make it. The unauthorised betting, on which new recruit would make it, had Roberts at the top.

"Anyone got money on him?" The Colonel laughed, watching the American out of the corner of his eye.

What's his game, the Colonel thought to himself, and why does he want one of my men? Looking around the Colonel saw two men put their hands up.

"I can't believe it! You bet against our own men, why?" the Colonel asked good-naturedly.

"There's something about him Sir!" a Private answered. "I was out on one of the new recruit's first exercises, a night attack on a coastal position. We were covering a stretch of open ground on the beach, maybe two hundred metres wide, and we were all on alert. He crossed that open ground and killed me and two others. I've never seen anything like it Sir!" the Private admitted as everyone there listened in silence taking in this new information. The American to the side smiled.

"That's why they call him 'The Ghost' Sir," said another Private.

"He sounds formidable. We'll see shortly if he lives up to his nickname. Now back to your post!" MacDonald ordered, getting the men to focus on the job at hand.

Without warning a brilliant flash of light exploded into the sky to the west of the bunker, turning night into day for a half a mile in every direction. Someone out there had triggered a trip flare. They had been placed by the hunters around the approaches to narrow the odds.

"They got him now!" yelled one of the staff, as everyone crowded the windows on the western side of the bunker to watch his capture by the soldiers.

"Blackout those windows you fools!" shouted the RSM, as shouts and the running of feet sounded from the outside of the bunker, as the hunters moved in on their prey. The Colonel stood shaken, at the momentary loss of control by his Command Staff. More so by the presence of an American Officer, who he would now have to apologise to, for this blunder. Looking around he saw the American to one side talking to an enlisted man.

"Private have you got nothing better," was all he got out when he recognised the private. "Roberts what the hell are you doing here?" the Colonel exploded, making everyone in the bunker look around.

"Sorry, Sir. I was just about to report, when the Colonel told me to sit down here and offered me a job!" Recruit Roberts replied, to his speechless Commanding Officer.

CAMPBELLS BARRACKS
SWANBOURNE PERTH, WA

Private Roberts sat in the headquarters waiting room while his future was discussed in the office next door. Earlier at the exercise debriefing, Steve had described how after getting within half a mile of the bunker, he saw that a stealth approach was not going to work. He came up with a plan to create a diversion, using a flare. He'd rigged up a can full of sand with a hole in it, attached to a rock, above a flare. When the sand ran out of the tin, the rock came down on the trip flare, setting it off, giving him enough time to close in on the bunker from the opposite direction.

All went to plan; when the flare went up, he'd merely walked casually to the bunker while the defence units moved west towards the flare. Around him, the Regiments soldiers involved remained silent. They were embarrassed by how easily he'd lead them astray. Others sat amazed by his plan's simplicity and how effective he had been in pulling it off. RSM MacDonald listened silently, then came up and slapped him on the back.

"Well done!" He smiled, giving the others in the room, the 'You're all in trouble look' before continuing. "Remember the English SAS's motto men 'Who dares wins' it works every time," the RSM smiled.

Across in the Colonel's office, Private Roberts' role was discussed with the Americans

"He is still under your control when he isn't helping us out operationally, or training with us." the American Colonel informed him.

"What will he be doing?" Colonel Stevenson asked.

"What he's told to Colonel! Remember this order comes from high up in both our governments, so no more questions!" the American answered sharply. Stevenson realised he'd gone as far as he could, nodded in a sign of acceptance.

"Very well then, travelling orders shall be sent to transfer Private Roberts to America for some special training, goodbye Colonel." The American Colonel concluded, leaving without a backwards glance. Colonel Stevenson sat there fuming. Several minutes after the Americans departure, RSM MacDonald and Private Roberts entered the Colonel's office saluting him.

"Sit down both of you." Colonel Stevenson sat looking at Roberts wondering what would happen to him in America. "I won't beat around the bush! I'll tell you honestly, I'm not happy about you going off and working with the Yanks! But orders are orders, and you'll be able to pass on any training or knowledge you get while with them. Just remember, we can't help you once you go. Are we clear?" The Colonel then waited for any questions.

"Personally I didn't like the American Officer, but Private Roberts has proved himself. I think it's up to him." MacDonald answered quietly.

"Well Sir, I respect your opinion. But he promised I'd be trained by the best, and there'd only be one mission a year. So after the initial training, I can return here to serve with the regiment unless they need me. I think I'd be a fool not to go, Sir," Roberts replied.

"Well, good luck then private. We'll look forward to seeing what you've learned." the Colonel smiled, before dismissing Roberts, and signalling for the RSM to remain. After he left, MacDonald and Stevenson went over the remaining recruits to pick the two who'd join the Regiment. Their thoughts drifted back to Roberts.

"I've got to tell you, I nearly fell over when I saw Roberts sitting next to that Yank," Paul the CO said to John with a grin.

"Not as much as I did, when he arrived here the first time, after hitching a ride in the truck I was in the front of," replied John laughing, at the balls of the guy.

"He's something special isn't he?"

"Yeah, when other soldiers here called him 'The Ghost,' and they are the best, you've got to wonder," John replied as they both sat in silence pondering Roberts's future.

SYDNEY AIRPORT

The flight from Perth to Sydney was long and bumpy, and Steve wondered what the flight to America would be like. He would like to have stayed overnight with his sister Louise and her husband here, but the Army was paying for the flight, so that was it. Wandering around the terminal while waiting to board, Steve noticed a payphone and although it was early, he decided to ring his sister. The phone rang three times before it was picked up.

"Hello who is it?" answered a sleepy male voice.

"In the army, we've been up for two hours," Steve replied smiling, noticing it was eight in the morning on the flight information clock.

"Yeah sure, you would smart ass! Still showering with all those men and trying to get into the super soldier outfit!" Edward chuckled, laughing at his own joke.

"I made it Edward; they're sending me to America for some special training. I just thought I'd ring before I jumped on another plane to America, is sis there?"

"No, your sister is working today, she left early. What do you mean you're going overseas? Nothing happening is it?" Edward replied, concerned for Steve. Edward had served in the English Army before moving to Australia, he knew something was unusual here.

"No it's some special training, I can't tell you any more than that," Steve answered, giving nothing away. 'Edward would make a good cop' Steve thought, knowing he'd applied for the Federal Police Force and was waiting for a reply.

"Well be careful, and ring your sister if you can," Edward advised, still sounding a little suspicious.

Hanging up smiling, Steve turned around to see the boarding call for his flight flashing. Running to the boarding gate, he arrived just as the gate was closing. Entering the plane, he was directed through first class to economy. Reaching the dividing curtain between sections, he pushed through it, colliding with a young air hostess, who had just closed it.

"Sorry miss!" Steve said shyly, as he came face to face with the young woman. She could see he was embarrassed at bumping into her.

"That's okay, I thought everyone was aboard. What's your seat number, Sir?"

"I don't know? I just transferred from another flight from Perth. Then I rang my sister who lives in Sydney, I nearly didn't make it!" Steve babbled shyly, realising what a fool he sounded like.

"Well you can't sit on the floor Sir; I'll see what I can do. What's your name?" the hostess said, with a widening smile at Steve's red face. Leaving Steve standing near the curtain, Michelle walked over to her supervisor explaining Steve's dilemma. The Supervisor then looked at his passenger manifest.

"There's no Steve Roberts, but there's a seat booked by the

American Defence Department, does he sound American?"

"No, he's definitely an Australian, but he does look like a soldier," Michelle replied, eyeing Steve, as he stood waiting.

"Okay I'll talk to him!" the Supervisor replied before approaching Steve. Michelle watched as the Supervisor, and the young man talked. There was something about him that she liked. He was good-looking, and in great shape, but she'd been out with lots of handsome men. No, it was something else, the way he talked about his sister. He was honest she realised, something many of her boyfriends hadn't been. 'At least he'll be nice to talk to on this flight,' she thought with a smile, as she went back to work. Looking up from stowing some gear, Michelle noticed the Supervisor had finished talking to the young man and showed him to a seat. He then returned to Michelle to fill her in.

"Yeah, he's okay, some sort of training with the Americans. They're paying for it for some reason." the Supervisor told her, before hurrying off to solve another problem.

Once in the air, Steve relaxed. He was impressed with how smooth the overseas plane was, compared to domestic ones he'd flown in. Settling in for the flight he quickly dozed off. Opening his eyes, he looked up to see the same hostess looking down at him.

"Sorry, I just wanted to know if you wanted anything" the Hostess exclaimed blushing, disappearing up the hallway. Steve smiled; it appeared he was not the only one who went red.

That evening, as dinner was served, Steve could not help smiling at the hostess, as she tried to serve out meals to the other passengers. Knowing he was watching, Michelle became more and more self-conscious, until she finally dropped a dinner on the floor. Apologising to a customer, she continued serving meals, avoiding looking at Steve. Back at her workstation Michelle tried to pull herself together

"What's going on Michelle? You never make mistakes." Janette, the other hostess in economy, asked.

"It's the guy in seat thirty-A, he keeps smiling at me!" Michelle replied sheepishly, realising how lame it sounded.

"Are you kidding, I wish that's the only thing they did." Janette smiled

"It's just when I was serving lunch earlier today, he was asleep and looked so relaxed and well attractive, that I stood there looking at him. Unfortunately, he woke up suddenly and caught me." Michelle said blushing again.

"Look, Michelle, take your break and sit next to him. The seats not occupied and it appears to me, that you're attracted to him. Work it out or get over it!" Janette suggested, leaving Michelle thinking.

Three hours after dinner and when the movie was finished, the lights were dimmed so people could sleep. Steve, half awake, looked across to see the attractive air hostess sit down next to him.

"Your smiles put me off of my work Mr Roberts. My name is Michelle, what's yours?" she asked, catching him off guard.

"It's Steve, and I was only joking," Steve stammered out, realising just how beautiful she was.

"Well, I've got to admit I was watching you before. You looked so tired and peaceful I couldn't help it."

"Yeah you could be right; I've been training pretty hard lately. I guess it catches up with you." Steve answered honestly. For the rest of the break, Michelle sat with Steve making small talk until she had to leave to return to work. Steve sat there watching her go, wishing he had at least asked for her phone number or something.

"You idiot!" He said out loud, making the other passengers across the aisle from him, turn and regard him suspiciously.

Landing at Los Angeles and feeling like he needed a shower, Steve hung back hoping to talk to Michelle. Unfortunately, as he approached the door and came up to Michelle, the supervisor appeared and asked her to help with a problem in first class. So all he got was a smile and a goodbye before he was herded off the plane with the other passengers. Well, I blew that one, Steve chastised himself, as he joined a queue for Customs.

"What is your reason for travelling here Mr Roberts?" asked the Customs Officer, in an official bored tone. This caused Steve's first problem, as his assignment was secret.

"I'm here to train with your army. Someone is supposed to meet me here."

"My apologies General! We were not informed of your arrival. Now how about opening your bag!" the Customs Officer mocked, watching Steve's reaction. For a split second, he saw something dangerous lurking in those eyes, and fear touched him. Pressing a panic button on the floor beside his foot, he summoned backup. Calming down and knowing he had no other choice Steve slowly started opening his duffel bag. The bag contained his army uniforms, spare clothes, killer suit and webbing, plus his combat knife.

Laying the camouflaged gear on the table, plus the knife, attracted the attention of every passenger on the flight. Seeing people staring two ordinary police officers wandered over as well, backing up the three Customs Officers. Steve could feel the ground starting to slip out from under him.

"Excuse me, is there a problem here?" Michelle inquired having seen Steve's bags being searched.

"Get back in line little girl! This guy claims he's with our army!" the Customs Officer ordered, dismissing her.

"Well your Defence Department paid for his ticket; it was on our passenger manifest!" Michelle shot back, putting the Customs Officer on the defensive. All present took in this new information, looking at each other, as the police turned to leave. Before anyone could move or reply, two Military Policemen and a plain-clothes officer approached from behind the Customs Barrier. After flourishing his badge, the plainclothes officer, promptly dismissed the Customs Officers, before approaching Steve.

"Sorry for this problem Private Roberts, we were only just informed of your flight. If you follow these two men, we'll get you to your next flight," he explained. Turning to thank Michelle for her trouble, Steve bumped his bag, making his gear topple onto the ground revealing his dress uniform and beret with his regiment's insignia. The Officer dived forward blocking the view of the other passengers, while the two MPs helped Steve quickly shove his gear back into his duffel bag. Meanwhile, Michelle continued to stare at Steve. Taking her to the side for some privacy under the watchful eyes of the two MPs of course, Steve tried to explain.

"Michelle," Steve started to say when she cut him off.

"It's okay Steve, two of my brothers were in the Army, I know that insignia is worn by SAS soldiers. I guess you're one of them?"

"Yes your right, though what I'm doing here is kind of secret. So thanks for your help Michelle." Steve replied softly.

"Well best of luck Steve," she whispered, kissing him lightly on the lips and putting a piece of paper in his hand. She then turned and disappeared back into the crowd near the customs line. Turning around a wide grin on his face, he saw the envious looks from the two MPs, as he opened the note and found her phone number and address in Sydney. It was the best moment in his life so far.

An hour later, Steve walked briskly across the tarmac to a Hercules transport plane. He'd been informed that it would take him to Fort Braggs. He was still shadowed by the two MPs but Steve didn't care, he still couldn't believe his luck in getting Michelle's phone number.

"Hey Aussie did yah do the tart back there on the flight, she sure looked like she wanted it?" snorted one of the MPs.

"Are you kidding these Aussie soldiers all sleep together they've no time for a woman!" The other MP replied laughing, as Steve dropped his bag.

On the Hercules, an airman looked out the rear cargo door of the plane, for the tenth time. He'd been waiting for the mystery passenger to appear, so he could then tell his impatient pilot to take off. Looking down he saw a civilian and behind him on the ground lay two MPs.

"You our passenger?" the airman yelled over the engines and got a nod in return. He then signalled for Steve to board. "What happened to them?" the Airman asked, looking down at the two MP's.

"I don't know I didn't see anything!"

"Good enough for me. Let's go!" The Airman grinned, as he closed the rear door and told the pilot to go. Once they were in the air, the airman went to a cupboard and handed Steve a flask of whiskey.

"It's universal Aussie, everyone hates MPs!" as they both settled down for the flight. Ten minutes later someone discovered the MPs, and after they were revived, they headed for the Commanders Office to complain. After the CO heard their version of the story, he phoned the Area Commander to work out what to do.

"To tell you two the truth my friends, nothing can be done. The man in question doesn't exist, so if I were you, I'd let it go," the CO explained, before dismissing the two MPs with a smile on his face, walking back into his office.

"God I'd love to have been there when that Aussie flattened those two big mouths!" the CO exclaimed, laughing hysterically with his staff after the MPs had left. Hearing the laughter from the office behind them, the MPs red with shame and anger headed for the closest phone and rang Fort Braggs to prepare a surprise for the son of a bitch when he arrived.

FORT BRAGG MARCH 1982

Flying into Fort Braggs was an overwhelming experience for Steve. Row upon row of planes of every description lined the runways. Surrounding the planes was a vast complex of hangers, overflowing with aircraft. Beside the airbase was the Army training centre with hundreds of barracks buildings neatly laid out in straight lines. Walking from the plane, after saying his farewells to an intoxicated airman, Steve was greeted by an Army Private, who was assigned to drive him out to the jungle training centre, which he told him, had been abandoned for years.

"What are all you foreigners doing out there anyhow? It's miles from the main base!" the Private asked fishing for information.

"I'll know when I get there!" Steve answered keeping it simple. The rest of the trip was spent in silence. Finally, the jeep stopped just short of a ten foot tall, barb wire fence. The only entrance was protected by four MPs.

"I shouldn't say anything, but the MPs are supposed to be after someone so watch yourself." the Private whispered, before driving off. Steve walked forward towards the gate, watching the reception committee, and gauging his best course of action. Walking up to gate Steve put his gear down and showed his credentials to the MP Sergeant.

"Well we've got ourselves an Aussie to join the rest of the zoo!" the Sergeant barked, getting a laugh from the other three.

"I'm sure the papers are in order Sergeant, can we get past the jokes and let me in; I'm running late!" Steve tried to be civil and avoid trouble.

"Well we're sorry Private, but us nobodies got a job to do too. So when you tell us why you're here, we'll let you in!" the Sergeant grinned. Steve sensed the three other MPs close in behind him.

"I can't do that Sergeant because I'd have to use big words that you wouldn't understand." Steve smiled, picking up his bag and preparing for the worst. At first, nothing happened, the Sergeant actually turned as if in capitulation, to open the barrier across the

39

road. Then with amazing speed, Steve didn't think he was capable of, the Sergeant swung his baton, which was sitting out of sight on the barrier, straight at Steve's head.

Caught momentarily off guard, Steve threw his duffel bag at the sergeant, knocking him backwards, but still received a nasty hit to his shoulder. Having no time to wait Steve turned and lifted his leg kicking the closest MP between the legs, sending him down onto the ground in agony. Charging, he cannoned into the two other MPs ending up on top of both of them on the ground. Headbutting one, and breaking his nose, he then drove a fist into the other's stomach, taking the wind and the fight out of him. Getting to his feet, he didn't even get time to turn around, before the Sergeant belted him across the shoulder with his baton.

Luckily it was badly aimed, or it would have caved in his head. Even so, he still ended up on the ground. Fighting through the pain, he saw the Sergeant running in to finish him with a kick his stomach. Grabbing a handful of dirt, he threw it into the Sergeant's face. Rolling sideways and gaining his feet again, Steve circled the partially blinded Sergeant, before charging in. Delivering a well-aimed blow to the Sergeant's jaw Steve heard a loud crack. Breathing heavily, fighting the pain, he watched the Sergeant drop sideways onto the ground with his men. Feeling slightly concussed Steve staggered to his gear, waiting till the dizziness stopped. Feeling better, he limped through the gateway and into the compound.

Across from the gate in the CO's office, Colonel Dobson and Staff Sergeant Decker stood watching the fight, with interest through the window.

"That's Roberts I'd say, he's the only one not checked in. He's going to have to learn to fight better; he could have been injured out there. Then he'd have been of no use to us!" the Colonel suggested.

"There were four of them Sir, and they had the advantage of surprise." the Sergeant replied, with a slight smile on his lips.

"Now they're all here, we'll have them all fall in an hour. Dismissed!" the Colonel informed him, resuming his work.

"What an arsehole." the Sergeant whispered to himself, as he walked out to meet the last arrival. "Private Roberts I presume?" Sergeant Decker asked, looking Steve over.

"Yes Sergeant," Steve answered, hoping the Sergeant had not

seen the fight.

"Follow me, I'll show you to your barracks and give you a brief rundown on the camps procedures," Decker answered. As they walked along, the Sergeant filled Steve in on what he needed to know about the camp. Reaching the barracks, Decker told him there would be a parade in an hour. Steve thinking his altercation with the MPs hadn't been noticed turned to leave.

"By the way, try to hit me like you did those MPs, and I'll kill you!" Sergeant Decker warned him. Receiving the message loud and clear, Steve remained silent.

At the sound of a klaxon horn, the parade formed up. Steve, lining up with the rest could not believe the different uniforms on parade. He recognised some of the uniforms. To his left, were British SAS soldiers and Paratroops, and French Legionnaires, while on his stood several soldiers from Middle Eastern countries and two Japanese marines. The rest were unknown to him, but they all had something in common, fitness and steely determination.

"Attention!" Decker bellowed across the parade ground.

This brought everyone to attention, as an Officer stepped forward. Steve recognised him as the same Colonel who had offered him the job in Australia.

"Gentlemen, the name's Colonel Dobson. You have been asked by your country to join a Special Force. This unit will help us regain the initiative back from our enemies. You will do it in secrecy and the only thanks you'll get will be from me. For your service to this unit, you will be well rewarded I can assure you. Training starts tomorrow at six hundred hours and from now on you talk to no one outside this compound. You are dismissed." the Colonel shouted, before turning and walking back to his office. The men on parade all stood there wondering what was going on. It was a strange introduction. What was that about being rewarded? Till now money had not been an issue, as they enlisted for the safety of their country.

"Get moving you slackers!" Decker yelled, snapping the men into action, as the men on parade dispersed.

As promised at 600hrs Steve's new life started. He was glad the SAS were sticklers for running, as every day, promptly at six there was a ten-mile run. This was followed by unarmed combat and if you were lucky lunch. The afternoon was weapons training, with more unarmed combat. Just when you thought you'd had enough, there was another run, then dinner, before tactics and logistics exercises. The training was physically gut-wrenching and mentally draining. Steve guessed it was designed this way, to thin out the volunteers into manageable units.

After a week of barely holding his shit together, Steve saw several men he'd team up with fold and leave. Hard as it was he had to admit that some of the instructors were far superior to the ones he'd trained with back home. They'd been brought in from all over America, just for this training. It was a great opportunity to learn from the best.

SIX MONTHS LATER

"How's the training going Sergeant?" Dobson asked Decker, as he entered the Colonel's office.

"Fine Sir, out of the original eighty we're down to four teams of five men each. To cut them further we'll have to do some in-country training, Sir." Decker answered.

"Fine, four hundred miles to our north is a State Park. I've cleared it with the local authorities to allow our men to train there. Remember Sergeant, the fewer who know our presence there, the better!" The Colonel reminded him, before going back to his papers.

"What's going on here?" the Sergeant asked himself, as he left the Colonel's Office. No saluting? He'd been in the regular army for twenty years and quite clearly this Colonel, if he was a Colonel, hadn't. So who was he and what did he want with these foreign troops? Something big was going down, the question was, 'who was going down with it.'

Over the past six months, Steve had worked in many five-man teams. As men were cut during the selection, the teams always merged into units of five men. The team he belonged to now had bonded into a tightly knit group, which used its collective skills to form a formidable unit.

Ali Moustaffer was their thinker; he worked out the logistics of each mission, and planned the operation from start to finish, making him commander of the unit. He had been an up, and coming officer in the Iranian Army in an Elite Guard unit. Trouble caused by the Shah losing control meant he might be better off not going back. At first, Steve had found his strict religious belief worrying. Being a Muslim Ali prayed at least four times a day. As Steve got to know Ali, he knew that he'd never let his beliefs interfere with his role in the unit. More importantly, Steve trusted him completely. Ali had once asked Steve if he was okay with his religion. Steve had told him truthfully, that praying four times a day might someday come in handy in their line of work. This made Ali laugh till he cried.

Sukai was a tough, smart Japanese Marine. He was also the weapons and supplies man. Although short and lean, he carried his share, never complaining; a good man to have at your back. He had an evil sense of humour if you crossed him. Several soldiers in the camp disliked having the two small Japanese Marines compete, thinking them inferior. During an exercise, a paratrooper from Italy, supposedly by mistake, cut a rope while Sukai's friend was climbing, nearly killing him.

The Italian soldier woke that night, to find a rattlesnake in his bed, even though all the windows and doors were locked. The soldier had left the next day, after complaining to Decker who'd deduced what was going on. Ali had commented about Sukai sleepwalking that night from the barracks.

"Just needed to shake my little snake," Sukai chuckled from his bunk. No one threatened him again.

Cody, a Scotsman, belonged to a British Paratrooper Regiment. Big and strong, he was the unit's heavy weapons man; in other words, he carried the machine gun because it was bloody heavy. At first, Cody appeared slow and methodical; many who made this assumption learned to regret it. Underneath his slow outward appearance, lurked a cunning fighter. On one cross-country run, someone had changed a signpost adding ten miles to the distance. Cody had spotted it before they turned, having memorised the route.

Aaron, the fourth member, was a French Paratrooper and a good with a knife. His main role was the medic for the unit. No one had any doubt that sooner or later he'd be needed. The Frenchman was proud of his homeland, and it could be a near fatal mistake to insult his country within his hearing. Wine was his first love; all he talked about was getting his own vineyard after he retired from the army.

As second in command, Steve was the point man or scout. Early on in training, he had proved his superior ability at leading the unit past enemy positions without being spotted. By day he was good, at night he excelled. That's why tonight, as usual, he was out in front, as he carefully glided through the woods, looking for their targets.

The four groups had parachuted in at twenty-kilometre gaps to the four points on a compass. Steve's group was the southern team. The mission of each group was straightforward. Find and eliminate the other enemy units, without getting killed yourself. Each team was equipped with paintball weapons, which fired a non-lethal cartridge of paint. It didn't kill, but it sure did hurt and made a noise.

Noise, was the enemy in this exercise. It gave your position away to the other units, while you were engaged with your target. Steve signalled the others to sit tight as he disappeared ahead, silently moving over the rough ground barely making a sound. This was their second night of closing with the enemy groups, and Steve knew that two of the groups were extremely close. Only the third group's position was unknown.

It was four hundred hours, first light was only hours away, but in this forest, it was pitch black, perfect for Ali's plan. From Steve's earlier reconnaissance he knew one group was in a defensive position in a hollow to the right. One hundred metres to the left was another group, was closing in on the first group. He knew this because he had been leading them here deliberately making the odd noise, which they had cautiously followed.

Ali planned to get the other units to engage while sitting back and finishing off the survivors. The only problem was the third group was not where it should be. Steve didn't understand it, he'd done the same thing to them, led them slowly towards the other two groups, but where were they now? Heading back to his team position, Steve smiled to himself speculating on how jumpy the unit must be by now. Lying motionless in the dark awaiting nervously for their point man to return, and hoping it would be him that did return.

Approaching the position he took this into account and gave two muffled taps to identify himself before entering their location. Steve approached Ali and whispered in his ear how the third group was gone and asked what he thought. Ali sat quietly thinking, before going wide-eyed. He pointed behind them, telling Steve in sign language to check that direction. Moving slowly past the other members of the team, he again disappeared from sight.

Once he'd left, the others took up a defensive position covering the direction Steve had headed. He'd covered about three hundred metres seeing nothing when the breeze changed. The wind now blew into his face, and with it came the slight smell of body odour, making him freeze. They were close, so close that they must be lining me up right now Steve thought, as he painstakingly retraced his steps. With extreme care, Steve silently moved away from the third group, expecting any minute to be hit by a paintball. He'd moved back about half the distance to his unit when he heard movement behind him and realised they were following slowly behind him. They must have spotted me Steve surmised, and by following him now, they hoped to catch his whole team unawares.

Taking a risk Steve doubled his speed through the darkness, knowing there was a chance of making a fatal mistake or noise, but needing the time. Steve came out of the darkness moving swiftly, grabbing Cody across the mouth, stopping him from crying out from Steve's sudden appearance. Whispering in Cody's ear, Steve pointed to some high ground to the north, he then moved to the next unit member. Repeating the instructions, he kept going until he came to Ali. Grabbing Ali, knowing it was too late to talk, he led him to the high ground. Here the others had set up a hasty position. No sooner had they arrived, when the third group, ghosted through their now abandoned position, heading in the direction of the other two enemy groups.

"That was close!" Ali whispered into Steve's ear as the third group disappeared from view, followed by the unmistakable sound of weapons firing in the darkness. The shooting went on for twenty minutes as three confused groups traded shots in the dark, until it slowly subsided, replaced by single shots as survivors were tracked down.

Forming a skirmish line, Steve's unit advanced slowly onto the killing ground, finding two complete units plus two men of the third unit sitting on the ground silently with no weapons. Rules of engagement were, once hit, you play dead. Sensing movement to the side of their position Ali concluded that the remaining group was circling to come round again. Signalling to everyone to take up positions facing the direction they'd come from, the unit waited. With only three members left, the third unit had circled around behind them hoping to surprise Ali's unit. It was a good tactic, but they had made too much noise circling, so when they came in at a rush, they were taken out by Steve's unit without any casualties, much to the other unit's surprise.

THE DEBRIEFING

Sergeant Decker sat through the debriefing listening as each group described what had happened during the exercise, as the instructors present made notes. The first group told how they heard movement and had taken up a defensive position, before opening fire on an advancing unit before being hit by the third unit after inflicting casualties on the first.

The second unit told how they followed movement to the enemy position, before engaging and being overrun by the third unit. The third group explained how they had followed a noise and sensed it could be a trap. They'd then swung away to the north circling around, coming in from the opposite direction. Spotting movement they'd tried to follow it before coming onto the firefight between the first two groups, which they engaged. The engagement over, they had circled the position trying to trap the fourth group and had been wiped out themselves.

Up until this point, everyone there had thought it was just bad luck that each unit had stumbled on each other in the dark, until Ali explained what they had planned, and what Steve had done, including how it had nearly failed. At first, a couple of soldiers chuckled and yelled bullshit at Ali, but the room fell into silence, as everyone realised it was the truth. Sergeant Decker looked across and noticed several instructors sitting spellbound, pencil poised at Ali's explanation of the attack. They were impressed by the planning and skill required, in trapping fifteen elite soldiers.

"Gentlemen you have all proven yourselves to be elite soldiers. Only two teams can go on from this point, they are the third group and Ali's team, the other two groups are dismissed," Decker informed them, before shaking each man's hand wishing them well. Two more hours were spent going over each unit's tactics and execution of their plans. Decker impressed, gave them all two days off, while he appraised the reports. As they went to leave, Decker pulled Ali and Steve to one side.

"That was an excellent plan and well-executed gentlemen. But you were overconfident with the third group. Remember, the enemy is never predictable," Decker explained giving a rare smile.

"Thanks for the advice Sergeant. Any idea, what we'll be doing now?" Steve asked.

"No that's above my pay grade soldier. Whatever you do though, always watch your back." Decker replied softly, before walking into the night.

"What the hell did he mean by that?" Ali asked Steve softly.

"I'm not sure," he answered, as they walked to their barracks, mulling over what the Sergeant had said.

Three days on, Sergeant Decker found himself again in Colonel Dobson's office going over the unit reports. Decker wondered which unit would make the grade and be assigned to this mysterious command.

"It's hard to pick between the two. Private Roberts got lucky spotting the third unit's approach. It could've gone down completely differently," Dobson suggested, after reading the report.

"I think the fact that Ali sent Roberts behind his position to check, shows his units tactics were superior," Decker replied, knowing that had this Colonel ever been in the field, he would've to know that. 'So who is he and how did he get the army to cooperate' Decker wondered.

"Anyway Sergeant, there's one way to find out for sure, and that's to send them on a live mission. I thought this one would do, it was part of a course they did on planning missions. What do you think?" Dobson watched him closely. Reading the report, Decker remembered the planning of such a raid during the course

"Well, it's a good test for both groups, but it's a long way from home if they have casualties!" the Sergeant replied apprehensively.

SINGAPORE 1983

Steve passed through customs at Singapore Airport, using his fake American passport. Because of his accent, his main problem had been, keeping silent as much as possible. The two units would arrive separately, and while here they would have no contact with the other. Sukai had arrived four days earlier than the rest of their unit, as his assignments would take the longest to complete. Travelling to Sukai's hotel, Steve met up with the rest of the team, as Sukai assured them everything was on schedule. He told them to go out sightseeing and act like tourists until they met again that night.

Steve did as advised and took in the sights, hoping he'd get used to the incredible humidity. The heat, hung over the city like its smog, making Steve sweat profusely. Outwardly he appeared calm, enjoying the tour. Inside his gut twisted with the fear, at going on his first mission. Getting back to his room, he quickly showered ahead of the meeting. Wandering down to the lobby, Ali approached him signalling for him to follow him up to his room. Once they were all there, Ali reviewed the mission and discussed what Sukai had been up too.

THE MISSION

During the Vietnam War, several prisoners of war had reported being questioned by a Major Tran Vin, a brutal and effective interrogator in the intelligence section of the North Vietnamese Army. Some were lucky and survived, most died. After the war, General Tran Vin had become a governor of a province in South Vietnam, as a reward for his service to the north. He still continued to torture, mostly citizens, who didn't like their new masters from the north and needed re-educating. Also in his time as governor, he had seized weapons and munitions, left behind by the Americans during their retreat. The General had then embraced capitalism, selling weapons to anyone who was interested and more importantly, had the money.

The target of this mission was twofold. Steve's unit would pay the General a visit at his Colonial-style mansion on the upper reaches of the Mekong River, about forty kilometres inland from the delta. The other unit would take care of the ammo dump, which was still believed to hold large quantities of munitions. His team's mission was to procure a seaworthy vessel in Singapore and travel North across the South China Sea. Once they reached Vietnam, they'd travel up the Mekong River, to a point five kilometres south of the General's home. Located there was a disused wharf complex, which once serviced a US Air Force base.

Here they would camouflage the vessel and wait for the arrival of the second unit at the airstrip. The second unit would fly across in a twin-engine plane, which they would acquire in Singapore. They would signal when they were leaving, so Steve's group could quietly secure the airstrip. Steve's unit would then eliminate the General, while the other unit took care of the dump.

Both groups would then fly west to Thailand. There they would parachute into a remote spot and hike to the coast, before flying home. The vessel would be left in reserve, used only as a backup in case they had trouble with flying out. The mission at first looked complicated. Ali explained that by using simple codes over local marine radio frequencies if at any stage it wasn't successful, the mission could be aborted quickly. Without endangering any of the men involved.

Ali's plan allowed for twelve days sailing time; this left them seven days to procure equipment. Sukai, who had been here for four days already, had located a boat which was his prime objective. It was an old South Vietnamese Navy patrol boat that had made its final trip to Singapore. Its crew and their families hoped for refugee status here. Instead upon arriving, the crew had found themselves imprisoned by their former allies in Singapore. Though it was old and in need of repairs, the twin diesel engines still ran soundly. The best part was as the Vietnamese still used these boats to patrol their waterways, it was ideal for their purpose. Aaron, who before joining up had been a diesel mechanic, volunteered to check the engine as an extra precaution.

Steve was the only member of the unit that hadn't been to sea on a small vessel before, he worried this might prove a problem. Along with Cody and Aaron, he would be confined below deck, for most of the trip, because of their European appearance. The others joked that it would be an experience for him being trapped below deck. He'd decided to get a good supply of motion sickness tablets before they left, just in case. While the travel side details were completed, Ali went over the logistics of the operation.

Assigning Cody and Steve the task of procuring supplies and weapons, he instructed them to order in small amounts to avoid suspicion. Most of the supplies were easy to obtain, as Singapore, being a large maritime port, had a great many trading houses. By the end of their first day they had all their food, and equipment, the problem was the weapons.

The people they would be doing business with were mostly underworld gangs. They dressed in business suits with legitimate company names, but they were criminals just the same. To avoid suspicions about the raid, it had been decided to buy a lot of weapons. Steve pretended to be buying them for the anti-government force in Southern Africa. Instead, they would be stored here in Singapore for future operations. The Colonel had given one other restriction on the purchase of weapons. All weapons used would be made by the Soviets or by one of their allies, nothing was to be American. When Steve had first met the men they'd be dealing with, he sensed that things wouldn't go well and on leaving, Cody confirmed his opinion.

"They're thieves Steve; we're not going to walk out of there with the money or the weapons!" Cody confessed as they hurried to inform the others of the situation. The order had been for two hundred assault rifles, ten machine guns, twenty RPG's (rocket propelled grenade launchers) and an ample supply of ammo for each weapon, plus grenades, explosives and field equipment for 500 men. The second order for a more substantial amount of material was to follow. Steve knew the weapons wouldn't be the problem, the warehouse was overflowing with them, the trick would be to pay the money and leave with them. Even with a second order pending these men could see a business opportunity, in keeping the weapons and supplying nothing ahead of the second order.

At the unit meeting that night, they discussed the issue of the weapons and how to handle it. Three days had passed since Sukai had purchased the vessel. All supplies were loaded, and the timeframe for success meant they must leave in the next two days, or the mission would be behind schedule.

"We need those weapons, especially the explosives, not only our group but for the unit flying in! On the other hand, we can't afford trouble with the authorities before leaving. Anyone got any ideas?" Ali asked looking around the room.

"I had one idea on how it could be done, but it's risky," Steve replied. He then explained an idea he'd had while coming back from his meeting with the gang. After he had run through his plan, the others sat in silence, each weighing the risk. With a little refinement from Ali, Steve's plan was adopted, as their best chance of success, even though Aaron and Cody weren't overjoyed about their part in it.

"Well, we've only got two nights till we depart. To cut down on risk, we'll do it the same night we leave. Get as much sleep as you can." Ali suggested, giving Steve a well-done nod.

THE WEAPONS BUY

Aaron and Cody drove into the warehouse in a beat up old Bedford truck, trying to act as casually as possible. Their only weapons, two Soviet Army combat knifes, that they had purchased at a local market.

"Shit I hope Steve's plan works!" Cody said softly.

"It's a good plan Cody, let's go," Aaron whispered, as he opened his door and climbed down to the warehouse floor.

"Do you have the money, Mr Smith!" The smiling Gang Leader asked Cody.

"Yes, Mr Lou. But we'd like to see our goods and have them placed aboard our vehicle first." Cody replied politely.

"Then the two of you are not carrying the money. That shows distrust Mr Smith," Lou asked, not smiling this time.

"These are terrible times Mr Lou, a man must be watchful. The money is outside with an associate. When the equipment is checked and loaded, he will come inside and pay in full." Cody informed him.

"As you wish Mr Smith, we are all friends here!" Mr Lou replied with a forced grin. Apart from his three associates next to him, plus the four workers for loading, eight men were concealed in the warehouse around them. They waited for the order to open fire, which was the phrase 'Goodbye Mr Smith'.

It took nearly an hour, to check the weapons and equipment, then load it onto the truck. Once done, Aaron climbed up into the truck and pressed the horn twice. This was the signal for Sukai to enter the warehouse, carrying a briefcase containing the payment. One of Mr Lou's associates quickly but expertly checked the money. When the counting was over, they all shook hands, and the three unit members made ready to depart. As Cody, Aaron and Sukai started to climb into their truck, the men around them moved back.

"Goodbye, Mr Smith" Lou said in a loud voice, making the three turn around and wave. Nothing else happened.

"Goodbye, Mr Smith" Lou yelled angrily but still nothing, as Cody waved again, before starting the truck and quickly driving away.

"You stupid fools! Where have you got to!" Lou yelled angrily in Chinese, as turning, he saw two heavily camouflaged soldiers materialised behind him. Lou's associates like him froze, as they came face to face with the two demon-like creatures. Carrying assault rifles, the two apparitions, glided across the floor towards him, as Lou fought for control.

"You didn't kill all my men, did you? One is my nephew, and although stupid, he's is my wife's favourite."

"No most are tied up. Two we had to knock unconscious." Ali answered his weapon's aim, never leaving Lou's body.

"That is good; I am most impressed with your business sense and professionalism. We will look forward to receiving your order for the next shipment!" Lou announced politely as if nothing had happened.

"Thank you, Mr Lou. Doing business with you has been an experience!" Steve answered with a grin, as he and Ali backed out of the warehouse, disappearing into the night.

After Steve and Ali had left, Mr Lou gathered his associates, to discuss the night's developments.

"We should track them down and make an example of them!" shouted one of Lou's associate, named Kai. He felt they had lost face to these men and wanted revenge. He received a roar of support from the others.

"Let's look at the facts gentlemen!" Lou suggested, raising his hands, silencing the others.

"Two men came into this heavily protected warehouse, unarmed. They disabled eight of our best-trained men, without killing anybody, especially ourselves. They then left knowing we had tried to kill their friends. Would you really like to upset them more?" Lou asked the others.

"They weren't unarmed, they had weapons!" Kai barked smugly.

"Taken from our men you fool! Leave the thinking to me Kai, or you can go back to gutting fish for your father at his fish farm!" Lou exploded, continuing. "I'll tell you what we'll do; we'll treat them with every respect, which they deserve. In the future, if someday we need their help, I can assure you, they will prove most useful." Lou assured them, thinking of how close he had come to dying.

"And remember, whoever lost those two weapons must pay for them!" Lou ordered, before walking out, heading for his home, it had been a long day.

Unloading at their own warehouse, the group picked through the weapons and explosives. Taking what they'd needed for the mission, they then drove the truck inside, bolting the door, placing the key behind a loose brick near the front door. Leaving the key behind a brick seemed pretty casual for a warehouse full of weapons. However, inside a trip wire was connected to the front door. Unless you knew that, you were in for a nasty explosion.

This way, any member of their unit or the second unit, could gain access without bringing a key. As long as they remembered the trip wire!

FIRST MISSION

It was midnight by the time they had reached the vessel. While Sukai started up the engines, Steve and the others quickly stowed their gear and weapons below deck, settling in. The sudden forward motion and the increase in engine noise signalled the departure from Singapore. Ali, using the Captain's old cabin for his planning room, poured over the charts with Steve. They'd worked out that at the cruising speed of twenty-two knots they should arrive in position in ten days. It gave them two days to spare, which would be cutting it close.

"If we hit bad weather, or are spotted, it could finish the operation right then and there!" Ali confessed, worried about the things he couldn't plan for.

"Well if we fail it won't be for lack of trying," Steve smiled.

"There's another worry Steve. Once we land, for all our training no one has actually been in combat. Killing for the first time won't be easy, and on this mission, it's mostly knife work. Even blowing up the ammo dump, has to be delayed until after we've left, to give us a better chance of making it across enemy airspace" Ali explained, wondering if everyone on the mission had what it takes to kill.

"The unit's been well trained Ali, they won't let you down. Remember the guy we're after, and his henchmen are dirtbags, they deserve what they're going to get!" Steve replied, meaning it. In his bunk that night, Steve wondered if he had what it took to do this job. It was one thing when the target was a murderer, what happened when the person's only crime was being in the wrong place at the wrong time. It gave him plenty to think about.

Six days passed without incident. Steve's stomach had done some flip-flops. Otherwise, he was surviving. On the seventh day after crossing the southernmost point of Vietnam, their luck ran out. Running on a north-easterly course, one hundred kilometres outside Vietnam's territorial waters, dark clouds approached from the east. The patrol boat they were aboard was twenty metres in length, though the size of the waves rolling towards them, made Steve feel he was in a rowboat.

Day eight came and went, their vessel struggling to make it up the side of these unstoppable juggernauts. Steve, for the hundredth time, wished he was dead, as he tried to empty his stomach again. His head rested in his hands, as he sat on the floor of the galley, utterly miserable.

"Want some more gravy on your chops?" Aaron asked Cody smiling, as they both looked at Steve laughing at his predicament.

"You both think you're funny now, wait till I get to shore!" Steve groaned, as he again vomited into his bucket, making Aaron and Cody burst into laughter.

Day nine was the same, as the storm continued unabated. Ali decided to shelter near a small group of islands, called Con Son. They were located roughly opposite the Mekong Delta, a couple of hundred kilometres out to sea. Once in the shadow of these Islands, the sea subsided enough, for everyone to clean up. After repairs to the vessel were completed, a meeting was held.

"Gentlemen we are now within full days sailing of our target. I would suggest that we hold this position tonight and sail early in the morning. That will bring us into the delta area late tomorrow night. The problem is, we must then scout the other teams landing zone, and the General's home, before four hundred hours the following morning, or the second group's mission will be scrubbed. Is everyone clear so far?" receiving no replies, he continued. "Well get some sleep if you can, especially you Steve. Your yodelling is keeping everyone awake!" Ali added with a smile. Everyone except Steve laughed.

"You guys are a bunch of bastards!" Steve croaked, his voice gone, as he tried to grin, before reaching for his bucket.

The next morning the storm abated to a rain depression, which made travelling a lot more comfortable. It also hid them from the prying eyes. On deck, Ali and Sukai could be seen dressed in Vietnamese Naval uniforms, with Aaron out of sight inside at the helm. At the rear of the boat, the Vietnamese flag flapped in the breeze, completing the picture and hiding their true identity. Entering the Delta region of the Mekong River, small craft covered the entire area, as many had sheltered here from the storm. Most were now either fishing near the mouth or preparing to head out.

In the darkness, all the unit saw, were a few hand waves from fishermen as they passed, too busy to give an old patrol boat a second look. Further up the river, the number of vessels dwindled. At times they were the only one in sight as they cruised on the flat water surface, fast approaching their objective.

Out of the gloom, on the port side of the river, appeared the abandoned docks and rusted cranes of the US Air Force base. Slowly idling in closer to the shore, Aaron at the helm spotted an old drainage ditch beside one of the wharfs. This provided them with a place to camouflage their vessel out of sight from the river, ready for an immediate departure if a problem arose. Steve, whose sea sickness had lessoned gradually since entering the Mekong River, cautiously went ashore with Ali. While they scouted the area, the others hid the vessel using nets and local foliage.

Steve recovered as soon as his feet hit dry land, making him smile. He'd never felt so good in his life to be off the boat and on dry land. Though he wasn't entirely recovered, he felt well enough to help Ali to check the area. Giving each other mutual cover, Ali and Steve worked their way through what had once been a busy supply base. Finding no people or equipment, Steve realised that the place had been stripped bare.

The only reason the cranes were still there was because of their size, everything else had been taken. After carrying out a sweep of the buildings, Steve wondered why no one had made this area into a place to live. With the docks and the warehouses, it was ideal for fishing. It was then that Ali found the bodies. In a ditch on the inland side of the base, Ali found the remains of an extensive collection of bodies. Even in the dark, they could see some were skeletons, and others looked fresh. The smell was overpowering as they stood there silently.

"Looks like we found the General's dumping ground!" Ali said softly, startling Steve, used to only getting hand signs when patrolling.

Arriving back they told the others of their find. Ali warned them to be alert, as the General's men could turn up at any minute to drop off another poor victim. Now the area was secure, Ali and Steve set out in different directions, to check on their individual primary targets. Ali, whose in-country ability, was not as accomplished as Steve, went to check the Airfield and the ammo dump. Steve meanwhile, would check the General's house, before meeting back at the boat.

Two hours of quietly surveying the General's property, by the light of a half-full moon, found Steve wondered why he had bothered being so quiet. Music filled the air, as soldiers silhouetted by the lights of the house strolled around as if they didn't have a care in the world. He was just about to move from the protection of the scrub when a cough sounded from a group of trees to his right, making him freeze. Not everyone was careless Steve scolded himself, as he circled around towards the cough.

Looking up into the trees, Steve spotted a soldier with a sniper rifle sitting quietly about five metres above the ground, on a wooden platform. It gave him a good field of fire into the surrounding bush. Steve cursed himself silently, knowing that if it weren't for that cough, he would have walked right out in front of him. Circling around the entire property this time, Steve found two more positions manned by snipers. These two were on ground level, making an approach to them easier. All up, including the three snipers, Steve counted twelve soldiers, plus those inside. It would not be easy to eliminate them all quietly, but now he knew their positions it was more likely they would succeed.

Retracing his steps around the perimeter Steve was just about to leave when an agonising scream came from the house. It was not a party going on at the General's home, but another night of torture, Steve assumed as he stood there motionless, listening to the screams, as the guards on duty laughed.

Steve arrived back at the same time as Ali.

"Don't explain what happened, we've no time left! Is it possible?" Ali asked softly.

"It won't be easy, but yes it's a go!" Steve answered, realising they had only had minutes left to send the okay signal to the second team. Ali picked up his radio and sent what sounded like a normal weather report from a vessel at sea, in plain English. Knowing that because of its short length it wouldn't be able to be traced. After several seconds another boat gave a different weather report in English, and then it too stopped transmitting.

"Gentlemen we have a go for tomorrow night! Steve, you report first." Ali suggested as they all sat down, to discuss the plan of attack. Steve went over his patrol, telling about the three positions and how he nearly blew it. Finished, he told them about the screaming from the house.

"And the guards laughed did they? They deserve what they're going to get!" Cody replied as the others nodded. Ali looked around the group and knew his worries about the unit being able to kill, had evaporated with Steve's report.

Ali then told them about the airfield. It was being used now to fly out the General's weapons. At the airport, was an old Douglas Dakota transport plane parked in a hangar, and guarded by four soldiers. They were pretty casual and had been playing cards while Ali did his recon, making his job easier. Ali further reported a far more substantial supply of weapons and ammo than expected at the dump.

It looked like the General had been buying weapons from Governors' all over the country and had built up a massive amount of weaponry both American and Russian. At the complex there were at least one hundred soldiers and several Africans, who were most probably from the plane, there to do business. Unlike the airport guards, the guards at the dump were vigilant, Ali warned. They all realised that even with two teams it was going to be tough to complete this dual mission. Ali suggested they all sleep on it and go over it in the morning. In the meantime Aaron would stand watch till daylight, being the best rested.

The group awoke at five and did a quick sweep of the area and then slept again till nine while Sukai stood watch. When they were all awake and had breakfast, Sukai, filled them in on the goings on during his morning watch. Soldiers from the General's house had dropped off five bodies, four young women and an old man. Sukai was upset by what had been done to the bodies and would not talk about it. He made it clear that he wanted to be one of the team members that went tonight to the General's house.

"We'll all be going!" Ali told them, as he went over his revised plan.

Because of the size and scope of the operation, Ali decided that they couldn't afford to wait for the other team, as they wouldn't arrive till one in the morning. Instead, as soon as it was dark enough, they would take out the General. This way if they had any problems, they could signal the second team to abort and take off in the boat. On the other hand, if it proved successful they would take out the guards at the airfield and await the arrival of their support team. They all could then proceed to the dump, lay explosives and depart in the second team's plane from the airfield.

The rest of the day was spent in refining the plan and getting ready for the attack, sleeping when possible; it would be a long night. As the scout Steve decided to make a killer suit, figuring it was the only way to get close to the snipers. If he'd brought his army issued one; it would have saved a lot of trouble, he mused.

THE ATTACK

Ali led the unit cautiously and silently towards their objective. Somewhere ahead, Steve was checking for enemy soldiers. Checking his surroundings, Ali slowly moved forward, followed blindly by the rest of the unit searching for danger. On this raid, the only weapons were their blackened combat knifes and a pair of Russian automatic pistols that Ali and Cody carried as a last resort. They knew if they were used, surprise would be lost for the second part of the mission.

Music could be heard from somewhere up ahead, and faint traces of light filtered through the trees, revealing the house. Ali's nerves started to jump, worried where Steve had got to, and how close he was to the sniper's position. Ali was about to call a halt until Steve returned when two shapes appeared on the ground in front of him. Shocked, Ali, went for his pistol, nearly dropping his knife in the process, when he realised the lumps were two dead soldiers. The sight of the dead men froze the whole group and forgetting where they were, they all stopped to look, mesmerised. Looking up from the two corpses, the team got their second fright, as Steve wearing his killer suit materialised from nowhere.

With his face camouflaged, he looked like some evil creation from hell. Considering the bodies at his feet, it could be an apt description Ali thought to himself. Using hand signals, Steve told them he'd killed these two and two others on the other side, taking care of all the hidden snipers. This left only the visible patrolling guards, which he told them amounted to about eight. At first, the group didn't move, and Steve sensed that they seemed wary of him. He shrugged it off and turned back towards the house, the others spreading out behind him.

Scouting for the remaining guards, it occurred to Steve why they had looked at him so strangely. He had killed and described it as if he'd ordered a pizza; it was far from the truth. When Steve had approached the first enemy position, he began to doubt that he could climb the tower and kill the sniper without being seen. Fate had stepped in, for he had arrived just as the snipers were changing watch. Standing at the bottom of the tree Steve, watched the first sniper climb down. Clearing his mind to concentrate the sniper's relief appeared right in front of him.

Forced into action, he grabbed the startled soldier's mouth and drove his knife in between his ribs, deep into his heart. He had barely slid the first soldier to the ground when the first sniper dropped to the ground on the opposite side of the tree. This gave Steve time to recover and attack him before he could cry out. For several minutes Steve stood frozen in a state of shock, as his hands trembled. Feeling the sniper's body stop convulsing, Steve looked down seeing the man's life flow out of him. 'Forget it move on,' his instincts warned him, as his training took over. Wiping the blood from his hands, he slowly moved towards his next target. Concentrating on the mission, he killed another sniper, before taking care of the last position. He wasn't shaking any longer but felt he was somehow different as if his emotions had been removed from his body, protecting him from his actions.

As the unit split up, Sukai silently approached one of the mobile sentries while he was urinating behind some bushes. He dispatched him quickly, wondering how these men could kill innocent people, hoping he would never become like that. Turning to look for another target, Sukai was just starting to move forward, when a guard appeared out of the trees, in front of him. Seeing Sukai, he began to raise his weapon to fire. Blinking, Sukai saw the soldier's gun hesitate, then start going back down, in the end falling from the guard's grip.

Looking beyond the guard, he saw the undergrowth take shape and become Steve, the Aussie soldier. Shaking with relief, Sukai nearly said thanks out loud, but a signal from the Aussie to be more careful stopped him. Snapping out of it Sukai signalled his thanks, as Steve waved him towards the house and moved off. The team briefly met and reported all the guards had been taken care off before they broke into separate groups and moved towards their next objectives.

Cody and Aaron's job was to cover the two road approaches to the property, while Sukai and Steve headed for the rear kitchen entrance, leaving Ali to cover the front door. Silently they entered the kitchen area, which was deserted. It was evident by how clean it was that the staff who worked here had gone for the night. Muffled voices could be heard coming from the room adjoining the kitchen, so Sukai quietly approached and looked through the crack in the door frame.

He observed two guards, one-half asleep at a table while the other sang along with the music, still blaring outside. Opening the door with great care both took up position behind 'happy' and 'sleepy'. After listening for several seconds for any other voices, they quickly dispatched both men, lowering them to the floor. Steve cautiously searched the ground floor of the double storey house finding no one. Meeting Sukai back near the staircase, he indicated that the ground floor was secure.

Moving upstairs, they divided going down the two short corridors that lead off each side of the staircase. Searching the rooms for any more guards, they met back at the top of the staircase. Sukai quietly whispered in Steve's ear that four Africans were asleep in the bedrooms down his corridor. Steve reported that the General was asleep in the end bedroom, but he had company. Both went straight to the General's room, opening the door and silently approached on both sides of the large king sized bed.

Steve signalled Sukai that he could kill the General, while he stopped the young girl from yelling out. Sukai raised his knife and with a swift thrust into the general's heart finished him quickly. More quickly than he probably deserved, but stealth was everything at the moment. The girl proved easy, as Steve placed some duct tape over her mouth he discovered her hands and feet were already tied. 'She didn't even try to struggle!' Steve thought, as she lay limp in his arms. Wrapping the naked young girl in a blanket and tossing her over his shoulder, Steve and Sukai headed back downstairs.

Signalling Ali to come inside, they quietly discuss the Africans, deciding to let them sleep. They were just about to leave when the girl came to life struggling violently, pointing to a door. Steve thought in his initial search that it was a cupboard. To quieten her, Sukai went to examine it. After descending down a set of stairs, he found where all those screams had come from.

The basement room was like a medieval torture chamber and to one side laid a group of twenty people all naked, bound with ropes and rags stuffed in their mouths. Approaching the group who huddled defensively, Sukai signalled them to be quiet, as he cut the ropes on their feet, pointing towards the door. Getting the message they made their way up in a tight-knit group, emerging to find Ali dressed in black, with his face blackened and Steve in his jungle growth killer suit.

This caused the first three out to collapse on the floor, the others in panic, retreat back down the stairs. Steve quickly removed his headgear and tried to reassure the frightened people. Ali worried about the noise, drew his pistol and moved upstairs to keep watch, in case the four Africans awoke. Grabbing an old man who seemed to know the young girl, Steve pointed him and the other captives towards the front door. Signalling Aaron and Cody to come inside, Steve quietly explained the situation of the Africans. Surely they'd heard the commotion made by the torture victims, so Steve told them to join Ali and himself, and they'd take the four at the same time.

Moving up the stairs, the noise of the frightened people who had removed their gags by now, drifted up to the second level. Movement inside the room could be heard, so without another word, the four unit members hit the four doors as one, quickly subduing the four startled Africans. After tying them up, Ali considered leaving them, as they weren't connected to the General and more importantly couldn't recognise them. But Sukai appeared from downstairs stone-faced with anger. He told them that two of the survivors who could speak English had told him the Africans had raped the women last night, along with the General. This brought a prompt end to the four men.

Moving back towards the boat as fast as possible with the captives, Ali pondered what to do with the prisoners they had liberated. Common sense told him to set them free, but he knew that when the authorities arrived, they would be the first to get the chop. He figured that they had been through enough already, the problem was, what to do with them? Arriving back at the river, Ali called the old man across to them for a talk.

"What did you do before you were taken?" Ali asked softly, to the still traumatised man in English.

"He was a Captain in the South Vietnamese Army," answered the girl, they'd rescued from the General's bedroom.

"I'm sorry for not answering you straight away, but we've been in a prison camp since the end of the war! Getting rescued was the last thing I imagined!" the old man told them.

"Do you think you can operate a boat?" Ali asked, thinking at last of a solution.

"Yes, I was attached to a Marine amphibious unit for several years. Navigation would be difficult, but it's better than staying here!" the old man smiled, revealing broken teeth. Ali decided to leave Aaron at the boat in the hope, that he could quickly instruct the Vietnamese on how to navigate the boat. While Aaron did that, the rest of the unit left to meet the second team at the Airfield, which they still had to secure.

Steve led the unit at a faster pace than normal, because of the time restrictions. As they approached the boundary of the field, he resumed a more cautious pace, as they closed in on the airfield guards. As Ali had described there were four guards, and they were playing cards in the hangar, instead of patrolling. There were also two Africans, and by their uniforms, they were the pilots of the Dakota, which filled the hangar. Taking up positions at the hanger doors Steve wondered how the four of them were going to take out six men around a table in a light-filled hanger.

He was just about to query Ali about it when the two Africans headed over to the aeroplane and started checking the engine on the left-hand side. Ali turned to Steve and the others and told them quietly to hold positions until he killed the power, then he moved off towards a noisy generator at the rear of the building. Locating fuel tank, Ali punctured it with his knife, letting the fuel drain out, before heading back. Several minutes passed without a sign of the generator stopping. Ali started thinking that maybe the leak had stopped, but a sudden flicker of lights as the generator coughed indicated it was about to fail.

An argument broke out between the guards as darkness engulfed the hangar. As they stood in the dark shifting blame, four shadows closed in and silenced the room, leaving the African pilots frozen in the dark. While Cody and Steve covered the pilots, Ali went back to the generator and shoved a stick in the hole he'd made. Refilling the device, he restarted it, before returning. Cody had dragged the four soldiers bodies into a corner of the hanger, before returning to the table where the two scared Africans now sat bound and gagged.

"Do they get the same as their friends?" Sukai asked, watching the Africans closely.

"Not yet, let's wait till the others arrive!" Ali suggested as he reached for his radio to signal the 'Okay to land' message.

MERSING AIRFIELD MALAYSIA

Group Two sat at the Airport waiting to go. Having arrived in Singapore a week earlier, they had been unable to secure a plane for their purpose. The group had been forced to travel north into Malaysia, in search of a plane. There they had located a small flying school near a port city called Mersing on the northeast coast of Malaysia. After handing over enough money to buy two planes, the instructor had agreed to take the group on a secret trip to Thailand.

Using the guise of buying drugs, the group hoped to conceal the real destination for as long as possible. Travelling back to Singapore they had gone to the warehouse, found the key, and defused the booby trap. They then loaded up with what they needed and drove back to Mersing. Here they'd waited for the signal, pretending to be tourists. On the departure night, the group made their way cautiously to the airport for their flight, arriving earlier than necessary to check for any problems.

The plane was an old twin-engine Beachcomber, which would only just hold both teams. The instructor, who was going to fly them out, had been in the process of moving the plane when he'd been overpowered and tied up in his office. Sorensen, the Swede as his unit called him, was not only a good Group Leader, he was also a pilot. This was why Steve's group had got the job of going by sea, while the other team flew. At a prearranged time Sorenson sent the second 'harmless weather report' notifying Ali that they were ready. Upon receiving a 'Go' message in return, the Swede gunned the engines and headed down the runway, for their four hour trip to Ali's units position.

Flying at a height just above the wave tips was exhausting, but Sorenson knew he had to keep below the Vietnamese radar to avoid detection. The night was perfect for flying, and the sea below them was relatively flat, making low level flying that much easier. Leaving nothing to chance, at the halfway point, Sorenson went over his gauges checking for any problems. Tapping the fuel gauges which showed full, he became alarmed. After flying for several hours, there should have been a slight drop in the amount of fuel on the dial, they must be faulty he reasoned. Unbeknown to him, when his men had disabled the instructor he had been on his way to fill the plane up, not to get it ready to taxi as the team had first thought. The gauge was indeed faulty and had been for some time.

Since the instructor was the only one who flew the plane, it had never been a problem, until now. Putting the plane on autopilot, Sorenson told one of his men to watch the control, while he went to the rear and checked the fuel level. He did this, by tapping the tanks, an old but practical method. As he made his way towards the back of the plane, the engines suddenly coughed as fuel stopped flowing. Sorensen didn't even get time to yell before the aircraft dived straight into the sea at full speed.

BACK AT THE AIRFIELD

"Where the hell are they?" Ali asked angrily, to no one in particular.

"Maybe they aborted?" Steve said nervously, realising the second team was two hours late.

"They'd have radioed if they'd done that. No, I think whatever has happened is far worse, and they're not coming!" Ali replied sadly, his gut feeling telling him he was right.

"What do we do now? Abort and take the boat?" Cody asked softly, looking along the airfield as if he expected an armoured column to appear. For ten minutes Ali stood there silently, trying to sort out a plan of action, in the end, he put it to the others.

"Anyone got a plan? If not, I suggest we abort and take the boat!" Ali suggested neutrally.

"I've got an idea, but it's risky," Steve answered seriously, getting a smile from the others as they took in their present position.

"Let's hear it!" Ali asked, amazed at Steve's ability to think outside of the box. It took ten minutes for him to outline a plan, with the others contributing as he went. Agreeing it was worth a try, Ali pointed out the only stumbling block, who would fly the plane? Steve's plan was for Sukai and Aaron to take the boat, with the Vietnamese people and sail for Malaysia at full speed. When they left, Ali, Cody and Steve would fly the old Dakota to Thailand. This Steve believed would draw the enemies' attention away from the sea. A straightforward plan, except none of them, knew how to fly a plane. Ali confessed he'd had some flying lessons but didn't feel confident.

"The Africans can!" Cody exclaimed as the team members glanced over at the two tied up men in the hanger.

"I'm sure we can convince them to do it," Steve replied with an evil smile.

"Okay, we'll go with your plan, Steve. Sukai, head back to the boat and tell Aaron what we're doing, and take off as quickly as possible!" Ali ordered as Sukai said his goodbyes, then turned and ran off towards the boat's position. "One more thing before we leave Steve! Take what explosives we have left and see how much damage you can do at the dump. We'll wait three hours for you. That's an hour to spare." Ali smiled, knowing the danger that Steve would face with this little excursion.

"Okay, but I'm not sure how much damage it'll do!" Steve replied, sounding unsure about his excursion. Gathering what explosives and grenades the others were carrying, Steve sprinted off, trying to gain a little time.

The Ammo dump wasn't a great distance from the airfield, and in under an hour, Steve found himself near the perimeter fence which surrounded the position. While silently crawling under the barbwire fence, Steve heard the distant sound of a boat's engine going to full power, before fading away in the distance.

'Well at least Aaron and Sukai are away' he thought, as he crawled slowly towards the first storehouse. Unlike the other targets tonight, the guards here took their job seriously. They vigilantly patrolled around the odd collection of well lit warehouses, making Steve's job difficult. Approaching the door of the first warehouse, he was just about to open it, when he noticed the wire at the bottom of the door. It was stretched across the opening, ending up in a tin can. Looking inside the can, Steve found a grenade with the pin already pulled, waiting for someone to open the door and release it. Using his knife, he quickly cut the wire and opened the door slowly, finding an area full of equipment but nothing that would go "boom". Suddenly an idea came to him, moving to another warehouse he found the same wire and can set up. Moving to the next one, he saw no wire. Carefully he opened the door to find a large area filled to the top with artillery shells, along with mortar rounds and rocket-propelled grenades.

Opening his pack, he quickly removed one of his two timers plus two of his three blocks of C4 explosive. It was two-thirds of his explosives, but he figured that he mightn't find another target as good as this one. Moving carefully down the row of warehouses Steve knew how to avoid the booby-trapped ones. Whoever had laid them, knew better than to booby-trap the warehouses with explosive inside, making Steve's job easier. Turning a corner, Steve spied a large bunker half buried in the hill, surrounded by large mounds of dirt, with two guards at the front. 'Bingo' he thought, as he silently moved around to the rear.

There was no entrance at the rear, but there was a ventilation shaft opening, to help cool the inside of the bunker. Not knowing what was inside Steve grabbed his second timer and the remaining block of C4, and with the help of some string lowered it down into the bunker. Out of explosives, Steve retraced his steps as swiftly as he could, knowing he had little time left. Once through the fence, Steve jogged most of the way back to the airfield and was nearly shot in the process

"Why the hurry Steve, I nearly clipped you!" Cody whispered heatedly, showing how close he'd come to shooting him.

"In half an hour you'll know why!" Steve answered as they both ran to the hanger. Ali already had the two scared pilots at the controls, so when Cody and Steve arrived, they were ready to go.

Opening the hangar doors as wide as they'd go, Cody and Steve hurried to the plane, boarding quickly and knocking away the temporary stairs.

"How'd you go?" Ali asked Steve. Steve told him about the first dump with the artillery shells and mortars, and the second bunker with the guards. Ali swiftly decided it might be better to be in the air when that lot went up. The pilot, who understood English, had heard the conversation and needed no encouragement to get moving. As the two engines burst into life, they quickly turned the plane around in the hangar, headed out onto the runway. Checking his watch as they taxied to the end of the runway, Steve looked over at Ali. He didn't have to say anything, to indicate that time had just about run out.

"Go now, as fast as you can!" Ali yelled at the pilot, who gunned the plane to full throttle. The old workhorse gathered herself and accelerated forward trying to take off, in the smallest space possible, lifting slowly into the air.

"We made it!" Cody yelled excitedly, as Steve looked back towards the munitions dump.

The first explosion lit the surrounding area for several kilometres. Moments later, the shock wave hit the plane sending it sidewards and nearly over on its wing. Luckily the pilot knew his business, righting her, just as they reached enough speed to allow them to retract the wheels. Steve looked down to see secondary explosions erupting around the ammo dump, as mortar rounds and artillery shells rained down onto the surrounding area exploding on impact. A second massive explosion lit the night sky again, as the other bunker complex roared into the air, raining debris down for twenty kilometres.

A sizable piece even hit the rear of their plane causing the pilot to fight for control, as shockwaves battered the aircraft. Time slowed, and silence descended, as everyone hoped the old plane would keep flying. Cody more worried than the rest of them, went white-faced to the rear of the plane, to check on damage. In a short time, Cody reappeared smiling and relieved. He'd found a large hole in the rear of the plane, near the door, but nothing fatal. Relaxing, everyone settled down as the pilot pointed the plane towards the Thai border.

Out to sea Sukai and Aaron saw the two explosions light the sky behind them. Smiling to each other, they entered a rain squall, hoping the others took off before the blast. At full speed they headed for international waters, glad to be at sea. They were not the only ones out there. Further to the north, a Vietnamese frigate was just about to go after the fast-moving patrol boat when it also observed the massive explosions inland. The small ship was quickly forgotten as the frigate sent the location of the explosion and the direction and speed of an unidentified aircraft leaving the area, to their base. When they finally turned back for the fast-moving small craft, it had disappeared into the storm, heading out into open waters.

Unaware that they had already been spotted, the Dakota flew slowly westward towards the border, as Ali checked his map, for a suitable place to land in Thailand. Finding a disused airstrip further to the north just across the border, he told the pilot to turn northwest slightly, altering their course towards the landing field and inadvertently saving their lives. Two Mig fighters which had been scrambled to intercept them, headed south, on the course the frigate had given. Searching the area and finding nothing, the Vietnamese fighters split up. One went south along the border, the other north.

After sweeping the area ahead with his onboard radar, the pilot heading north spotted the Dakota closing on the border. At his maximum range, the Mig pilot launched his two missiles, hoping to destroy the Dakota before it crossed the border. On board, the plane Ali, who was watching the pilots, while the other two slept, was just coming back to ask one of them to relieve him when an explosion knocked him onto the floor. Steve staggering to his feet ran forward. Jumping over the prone figure of Ali, racing into the cockpit, he left Cody to look after Ali. Inside was like walking into a hurricane, all the glass was gone as well as the co-pilot leaving a severely injured pilot at the controls.

"Take that seat and help me steer!" the pilot yelled against the wind, as the plane dropped to the right. Jumping into the co-pilots seat, Steve held the control stick over to the left to compensate for the lean to the right. Steve, doing as he was told, looked out to the left wing of the plane; he was shocked to find the engine was gone completely.

When the MIG fighter had fired his two heat-seeking missiles, they had both converged on the main heat signature being the left engine as it was the closest. As the missiles homed in, they collided with each other before impact, causing one to fail and fall away. The other hit the engine destroying it, sending the deadly shrapnel into the cockpit, achieving its objective. The plane was going down. The fighter seeing the plane hit but still flying, closed in eagerly hoping to finish it off. In range, the pilot fired a quick volley of his machineguns into the plane as he sped by. He was just about to go round again when his threat sensors on his control panel warned him he was in Thai airspace. Reluctantly he turned back towards Vietnamese airspace informing his superiors that the plane was badly hit and going down.

Onboard Steve sat frozen, waiting for the end to come as the plane belched flames from the one remaining engine. One minute he had been getting advice from the pilot on how to keep the plane flying, the next the pilot's head had exploded. The machine-gun rounds seemed to hit everything in the cockpit, except Steve, who sat there petrified. Cody came forward, took one look, and went white with fear.

"Do you know what you're doing?" Cody yelled above the wind.

"Not really, do you?" Steve yelled back, smiling at the stupidity of his situation. Cody at first just stood there open-mouthed, and then broke into uncontrollable laughter, before disappearing back into the cabin. Steve left alone, kept the plane flying, at least straight as it slowly descended. Moments later Cody reappeared, dragging the dead pilot from his seat, replacing him with Ali. Looking confused, Ali tried to make sense of what was going on. He had at least had some flight training, but not enough to fly a plane on his own. Leaning forward he feathered the remaining engine which put out the fire. Steve noticed that the controls seemed more responsive, not trying to pull him to the left anymore, making steering easier. Unfortunately, it didn't improve their situation, as now they were nothing more than a fat glider as they headed towards a mountainous landscape.

Checking the area, and spotting a small valley with a river winding through it, Ali pointed Steve in that direction. He then lowered the flaps and then the landing gear to slow the plane down and maybe cushion the crash. Unfortunately when the flaps and wheels extended Steve nearly lost control of the aircraft, as it tried to turn upside down. This sudden roll tossed Cody back into the cabin, knocking him out. Ali, seeing Steve was losing control, grabbed the wheel helping Steve to get it back on an even keel as the ground rushed up to meet them at a frightening speed.

Buckling their seatbelts seemed a futile gesture, but Steve did it anyway, as the plane hit the creek bed hard. Lifting back into the air, minus one wheel, the plane crashed down again, this time ripping off the other wheel and the rear tail assembly. Turning on its nose, the aircraft dived deeply into a waterhole section of the creek, before it was catapulted into a clearing beside the water's edge. No one knew how long it took for them to realise they weren't dead.

As Steve came to and looked out of what was left of the window he felt it was the best day of his life, next to meeting Michelle. Shaken badly, the three men dragged themselves out of the wreck, where the full extent of the damage could be seen. The trail of debris was strewn for two hundred metres behind the aircraft. All that was left in one piece was the exoskeleton of the cabin and the shattered cockpit. Steve, who was in the best shape, buried the pilot. He then searched around for their gear and made something for them to eat. Tossing security to the wind, they lay down where they were and slept.

Waking up early the next day at about seven, Steve found Ali already up and going through the plane. No one before takeoff had really worried about what was on the plane. Now supplies could be the difference between life and death. On the ground near the aircraft was a pile of things Ali had already sorted, including several AK47 assault rifles and a couple of their own pistols. It was no arsenal, but better than nothing. Food was minimal with the only find being two three day ration packs, which looked just edible. Ali suggested Steve check the cargo section of the plane that had broken off with the tail, while Ali looked at Cody's head.

Arriving and climbing in through where the cabin section used to be, Steve found twenty sealed boxes. Intrigued he broke the seals on one, finding to his surprise that they contained American dollars, hundreds of thousands by the looks. Moving on, realising they couldn't eat money; he located several boxes of canned food. Grabbing one box, he carried it back. Cody, getting the all clear on his head wound, was up and had a fire going. Steve passed him several cans of stew to cook.

"Anything else worth salvaging?" Ali asked Steve after they'd eaten.

"Just a couple of million in American dollars," Steve replied dismissively, looking at the faces of the two men.

"You're joking aren't you?" Cody asked, puzzled.

"The plane is full of money. It must have been to buy the guns." Steve informed them, watching as the other two men rose and walked to the tail section. Curious to see their reaction Steve followed after he buried their leftovers. After twenty minutes of manhandling the containers, they had them lined up next to the tail section.

"Two and a half million, they must have been buying a shit load of weapons!" Cody exclaimed smiling,

"The question is what are we going to do with it?" Ali asked seriously.

"Spend it, of course, a five-way split between the unit members," Cody replied laughing.

"I don't think it would be wise to suddenly start flashing money around. One the people who owned it might come looking for it. Secondly, our American employers might think it belongs to them." Ali explained, being cautious.

"We can't carry it anyway, so best we take just enough to get some transport, and come back," Steve suggested, getting an agreement. As they packed up their gear and headed out, Steve walked along thinking how close this mixed unit had become. There were only three members of the unit here, but Cody had automatically divided the money between the five and Ali hadn't questioned it. It made Steve more comfortable to know the men who had his back were trustworthy.

It took four days to walk out and another three to organise a chopper, returning for the cases, then they headed for Bangkok. With Ali's help, they opened five accounts in a Swiss bank that had a branch in Thailand. They then contacted the Colonel.

"What did he say?" Cody asked Ali, as he put down the phone.

"Over the moon by the sounds," Ali replied his mind miles away.

"What's the problem then?" Steve asked seeing Ali's expression.

"I asked what happened to the other team. He said it wasn't to be discussed till we got back." Ali answered suspiciously.

"Doesn't sound good?" Steve said sadly.

"No it doesn't." Ali answered.

DEBRIEFING FORT BRAGG

They'd been gone over two months when they finally returned to Fort Bragg. It was another three weeks before Sukai and Aaron arrived and told their story. After they had entered a tropical storm, they had sailed straight south for Malaysia, but the Vietnamese refugees became worried about being returned to Vietnam. After what the prisoners had been through, Sukai and Aaron had taken a big chance and decided to slip back into Singapore at night.

There, they had the boat secretly refuelled and supplied using funds left over from the mission. After a brief farewell, the Vietnamese under the command of the old man, headed back to sea, to try for Australia. There they hoped to get refugee status. The Colonel was none too happy about this. He would have preferred they'd been left behind. That aside, he was happy with the mission, it had been a success, and the Vietnamese Government had said nothing of the raid. Obviously too embarrassed by what had happened to protest at the UN, and with no proof, it would be futile anyway.

The only bad news was the loss of the second group, who had perished without a trace. Steve noticed that the Colonel wasn't too upset by the news, something to consider in the future he thought. Sergeant Decker went over the mission reports and was more than impressed by the raid's results. One serious bad guy was gone, and more importantly, a major supply of illegal weapons had been vaporised. Satellite photos of the area showed massive damage over a ten-kilometre radius from the dump.

The Vietnamese Government had released a news report that an old munitions storage facility had been blown up deliberately, to dispose of a dangerous ordinance. A way of saving face Decker concluded. What was a surprise to him was that all this was done by five men, who had adopted a whole new plan on the ground, while engaged with the enemy?

He doubted any other Special Forces unit could have done it as professionally, let alone pulled it off. That evening, Decker went to the Colonel's office to go over the mission and discuss a new training system he had devised, from lessons, learned training these Special Forces soldiers. Decker marched into the office giving the Colonel a salute, which as usual was barely returned. 'Had this guy ever been in the Army?' Decker again wondered as he waited for the Colonel to speak.

"I've been looking over the mission report Sergeant. You and your training staff have done a wonderful job. The training phase of this operation is now over. I want you to reassign all the instructors and yourself back to Army training programs and destroy all paperwork immediately. Is that understood Sergeant?" the Colonel said showing no emotion.

"But Sir, a lot of the training methods used here were new and found to have been very effective. I was going to write a paper on it for Army training in the future!"

"No, I'm afraid not Sergeant. Maybe at your next command, you can try the training there, but not this one. Burn everything. That's an order!" the Colonel insisted, before going back to his paperwork. Decker was furious, and for the first time in his career, he didn't bother to salute, as he left the Colonel's office. When the Sergeant had left, Colonel Dobson picked up his phone and dialled CIA headquarters at Langley.

"Hello, Dobson here. Training is finished, and the unit is ready. Inform the other Section Chiefs would you." He said merrily, before packing his gear up and walking out of the office for the last time.

The next two weeks for Steve at the camp were filled with forms and cleaning up, which was the usual routine in any of the armed forces. They'd all been told that after helping clean up, they could return to their regular units and await orders. The orders would be sent through the mail system, in a small carton. Other than that, they were to resume their normal lives back home. He'd been given the rank of Sergeant being second in command of the unit and Ali was made a Lieutenant which surprised him, along with a pay rise. The pay was a strange affair. He was paid by the Australian Army, as well as the American. He also received travel expenses for each overseas mission, which was nearly a thousand dollars a day. By the look of his bank account, it had already started. This, plus the Swiss account that Ali had set up in Thailand, was more money than he'd ever save in a lifetime.

Steve decided it would be wise not to touch the money for a while, rather invest it, until this relationship with the Americans was over. He could still remember the look on Sukai's and Aaron's faces when

Ali had told them of the money on the plane. He could see how much trust they now put in the others. It made them more than just mercenaries because money wasn't the first thing they worried about. It also meant that at any time they could turn the Americans down and walk away if the mission didn't feel right.

Walking over to the Administration Building Steve spotted Sergeant Decker. He was watching, as two instructors shredded office files near the rear of the building, before burning them, and he didn't look happy.

"Is there a problem Staff Sergeant?" Steve asked as he got closer. In the last couple of days, he'd come to like Decker. He was a tough son of a bitch, but honest, and Steve valued that.

"No. That's the last of the records here, even though the Main Headquarters at Fort Bragg will retain some records that we were here. Unfortunately, what we did here will disappear, and we learned a lot about training."

"Well, I suppose the Colonel has his reasons." Steve put forward.

"That's if he's really is a Colonel?"

"What else could he be Staff? Surely with the power he wields here, he must hold rank in the Army."

"I think he's a spook out of Langley, Steve. He knows diddly squat about the Army procedure and discipline. I'm guessing CIA. So watch your back!" Decker warned him before shaking Steve's hand goodbye. Climbing into a jeep with his gear, Decker gave Steve a rare smile, as he disappeared through the gate.

Going back to the barracks where the rest of the unit was just about to leave, Steve told them of his conversation with Decker.

"They're still the Americans we're working for!" Cody answered wondering how this changed their employment.

"Yes, but I suggest we all watch our backs anyway. Everybody write down the box number the Americans gave you for receiving orders. We can stay in contact that way." Ali suggested.

"I've got a number in Edinburgh; you can all ring there and leave a number, to contact you on, in an emergency!" Cody volunteered, knowing he was breaking security. "And remember you ring four times then hang up and ring again, or it won't be answered." He told them before they shook hands and headed off to their own countries and homes.

After catching a domestic flight from Fort Braggs to Los Angeles, Steve, who didn't want to have a run in with customs again, decided to try something different. Purchasing a business class ticket to Australia, Steve then put on his suit, bought for the trip to Singapore. Ali had discussed this with the team while they were in Singapore. He'd found, that customs looked differently at people wearing a suit and travelling business class. He thought they should remember that when flying to missions from now on. Steve found Ali was right; he received better treatment at customs. Except for the brief check of his belongings, he was passed straight through into the business lounge before boarding, with a minimum of fuss.

Lounging in his seat on the plane Steve thought the only thing missing was Michelle. She'd been continuously in his thoughts lately. He'd even rung her on and off from Fort Bragg, mostly getting a girl called Julie who shared a unit with her near Mascot Airport in Sydney. Several times he'd managed to talk to her, and the magic he had felt on the plane to America had returned. He desperately wanted to see her again, remembering that brief kiss in front of the MPs. It felt a million years since then, and he wanted to be with her badly.

Before reporting back to the SAS in Perth, Steve had wrangled two weeks leave in Sydney. He had decided to visit his sister and if possible, try and see Michelle at the same time. Before leaving America, he had phoned his sister to arrange to stay and get picked up from the airport. Getting a little bored, Steve picked up a copy of a Financial Review, which someone had left behind in the magazine section of his seat. Reading through the magazine, he saw various ads for partnerships in different types of businesses in Australia.

Thumbing through these ads, Steve thought this would be a good way to invest his money. It was also a great way to cover his travelling overseas on missions. After going over an extensive collection of different professions, Steve came to one about a small stock brokerage firm which was looking for a silent partner. With the extra capital, they hoped to expand their business. What struck Steve was the honest way it was written. It didn't guarantee to make you wealthy, only to be part of a respectable firm building a future through investments.

Tearing the ad section from the paper, Steve turned it over in his head. He knew very little about share trading and four hundred thousand was the asking price for the partnership. That would take nearly all of the money he had from the plane. On the other hand, it could be a future for him after the army he thought. It was also in Sydney, which meant his sister might be able to check out the firm through her contacts in the bank, where she worked. It was worth a try he decided as he settled back and thought again of Michelle.

SYDNEY NOVEMBER 1983

Arriving at Sydney Airport Steve realised, he'd been gone over a year, as he strolled down the walkway towards Customs. After a quick once-over of his passport, Steve started to amble for the baggage collection area, when two plainclothes police officers approached him.

"If you could follow us, Sir," One of the officers ordered, as they led Steve into an examination room, where they started to put on gloves.

"If you could take off your clothing Sir, we'll get this search over and done with as quickly as possible," the same Officer asked sternly, flexing his fingers in his tight-fitting rubber gloves.

"Shit mate there's got to be a mistake!" Steve exclaimed, not believing this was happening again. After Steve's plea, the room went quiet, until suddenly both officers broke into laughter, leaving Steve standing there shocked. Looking around Steve found his brother-in-law standing at the door smiling.

"Got yah," Edward barked, chuckling at Steve's discomfort.

"You bastard, you scared the crap out of me!" Steve yelled, joining the others laughing. While Steve had been away, Edward had been accepted into the Federal Police and was stationed at William Street, in the city. He had arranged the special treat with a couple of his friends stationed at the airport. It was a common joke to pull on friends coming back from holidays. Or for people they didn't like, those searches didn't stop so easily. Seated at the bar later with Edward, waiting for his sister to arrive for their lift home, Steve pondered on the fact that Edward was the one who had straightened him out and encourage him to join the Army. He'd been seventeen at the time, it was just after his Mum and Dad had been killed in a car crash. With Louise his only close relation, Steve had turned to drink for support, nearly becoming an alcoholic. His sister had met Edward who'd just come arrived from Ireland and had been out with her on several dates.

One night, upset with her brother, Louise had explained what had happened to him and asked Edward, if he could talk to Steve. He assured her he'd only give him a talking to, which entailed belting the crap out of him and locking him in a room till he'd sobered up. After two days Edward let him out and rang a friend in the Army, who arranged for Steve to be recruited - if he liked it or not. The rest, as they say, is history.

"I never thanked you for straightening me out Edward, thanks for that."

"The only way I'd get your sister to marry me was getting rid of you!" Edward replied smiling, but he grabbed Steve and gave him a hug anyway. Looking Steve over, Edward realised that belting him now was out of the question. He was no longer a scared boy. With a lean athletic build, and the way he regularly watched the room for trouble, showed that he'd had some serious training somewhere. There was something else different about him, Edward thought, he just couldn't put his finger on it, something dangerous. 'Maybe I'm just too much of a cop!' Edward thought to himself as Louise ran towards them out of the crowd.

Running to Steve, she grabbed him fiercely from behind, hugging him. Edward, at the time, was watching Steve and saw the momentary flash of a wild animal in Steve's eyes, at being grabbed unaware. Upon recognizing his attacker Steve instantly relaxed, hugging his sister back, and kissing her at the same time. Edward sat there frozen for a second, realising how close Steve had come to reacting and realisation dawned on him. Steve had been in action somewhere, and it had been bloody. That was the difference he'd spotted in Steve, he had killed. Edward knew that feeling all too well, for he'd been through it in Ireland when in the army there. He'd been attacked and had been forced to kill a man. It had changed him forever as Steve was now. Edward joined in hugging Steve with his wife, shrugging off his worries as his wife welcomed her brother home.

Driving home Edward watched as brother and sister swapped life stories, his wife would have made a good interrogator as she quizzed Steve about his stay in America and if he had met anyone. Steve evaded every question about his training as his eyes always went to Edward's; both knew the other was a danger somehow, though Louise was utterly in the dark about the situation. Arriving at their home, Steve was surprised to find it a two-story home with a three-bedroom unit upstairs and a two bedroom unit downstairs. They told Steve that they had bought it with the intention of renting out downstairs, but since they both had good jobs, they were only letting friends stay here on and off during the year. It meant that he could use downstairs, and come and go as he liked as long as he wanted to.

After he'd had a shower and unpacked, Steve headed upstairs for a coffee with his sister, settling in for the night. Discussions centred on what each had been up to in the years they had been separated and what their plans for the future were. The conversation finally got around to him thinking of becoming a partner in a stockbroking firm, and Steve asked if she could check out the firm he liked. His sister was pleased and impressed by the way he had matured and was looking to the future. She told him she'd check with her boss tomorrow before everyone headed off to bed.

"I can't get over the change in my little brother!" Louise said to Edward later that night as they lay in bed. "He's become so mature you must be proud you talked him into joining the Army." Louise continued merrily.

"Yes, he's certainly changed," Edward replied neutrally, as he thought about Steve's eyes. 'Where have you been? And what did you do?' were the burning questions Edward asked himself, as he settled into an uneasy sleep.

Seven hundred hours in the morning, with sweat streaming down his back, Steve ran heavily through a dry section of sand. He was on his first-morning run, along Cronulla beach, north towards the sand dunes. He'd slept in; he couldn't believe it. If it hadn't been for his sister leaving for work at six, he'd still be asleep. Michelle had talked about getting jetlag from travelling on planes, but he'd thought she'd been kidding. But he felt stuffed, and he shouldn't be in his present shape, so maybe she'd been right.

Finished showering and having breakfast, Steve sat staring at the phone. Seeing it was after eight, he decided to ring Michelle. The phone rang five times before a sleepy voice answered with a tired-sounding hello.

"Hi it's Steve, is that you Michelle?" He asked excitedly.

"No it's Julie, and I've only just got here myself lover boy. She's here tomorrow, and if you don't ring again, I'll give her your phone number, okay!" Julie said sleepily. Steve gave her the number twice, making her say it back before she hung up on him to return to sleep. Steve sat smiling at the prospect of a first date with Michelle. His happy mood started to wane when he realised he really hadn't anything to wear. Except for the suit he'd bought for travelling to Singapore, which had started to fray already, the only other clothes he had were, to say the least, old. Knowing he had to look presentable, Steve put on his only jeans and an old tee shirt and hurried downtown to Cronulla shopping centre.

Strolling aimlessly along, he came to a walkway which led from the railway station down to the ocean. Passing several food shops and a Dive shop, he finally came to a small tailors shop. Strolling in, he casually looked around at the various shirts and suits that hung on racks, seeing if anything looked right for him.

"You haven't got the faintest idea, have you?" said an old man, from behind the counter with a smile. At first, Steve was going to try and bluff it through, pretending he was just looking, but the guy was spot on.

"You're dead right!" he answered honestly, as the old man chuckled. Introducing himself,Isaac, the owner of the storemeasured Steve.He told Steve he had been here for thirty years, even though he admitted trade these days was slow. Steve, in turn, told him how he wanted to be a partner in a stock broking firm after he left the Army. He was also hoping to take out a beautiful girl, confessing he'd bought a suit in America but it wasn't terrific.

"Was the suit made for you Steve?"

"No, I just tried it on and bought it," Steve answered as if admitting he'd stolen a car.

"You get what you pay for Steve. I can dress you so you can go anywhere, and be accepted. Remember in business, a good suit is a passport, and it can open many doors!" Isaac said in a fatherly tone. Thinking back, Steve realised this was exactly what Ali had suggested, about how to blend in, to disappear into a crowd.

"Okay Isaac, do your magic, turn me into a businessman."

"No Steve, I can't do that. But I can make you look like one!" Isaac pointed out, with a smile.

Steve sat at the counter looking at the clock, realising he'd been in this shop for over four hours. Isaac had gone off to buy them both some lunch, leaving Steve in charge of the shop, which luckily, remained quiet. Looking behind the counter, he noticed three photos, one of a soldier, a British paratrooper by the looks from the Second World War. Another was a shot of Isaac and an old woman, most probably his wife. And the third photo was Isaac, his wife and a pretty young girl and a young man in an Australian Army uniform with paratrooper wings on his shoulder.

"That's my family" Isaac sighed, interrupting Steve's thoughts as he stared at the photos. "My son Lindsay wanted to be like his dad, a paratrooper, got killed in Vietnam. My wife took it badly, she died a year later. Kristen my daughter, funnily enough, married an Army buddy of my son. They live in Townsville, he's an Officer now. God, I miss them all!" Isaac exclaimed, pain in his voice.

"I'm sorry Isaac," Steve sadly replied, feeling for the man. Turning away to hide his tears, Isaac quietly lay their lunch out on a small table. Shrugging off the bad memories, Isaac chatted about Steve's girl and their coming date. He wanted to know what Steve's plans were for the future. Late that afternoon, laden with clothing, Steve made ready to go home. He knew he'd have to come back tomorrow to pick up his two tailor-made suits. Saying goodbye to Isaac, he was going out the door when Isaac brought Steve up short.

"You know Steve. I haven't said anything about my son for years. Then just yesterday in the paper, I read that the man who was believed to have tortured my son when he was a POW, died in an explosion. I hope he died in pain Steve, after all these years I still can't forgive him." Isaac said sounding bitter.

"I can assure you the General did!" Steve answered without thinking. Realising his mistake, and getting an unreadable look from Isaac, he said goodbye, walking quickly away. 'You bloody fool,' Steve chastised himself. He was mortified that he'd just told a complete stranger about a mission. Dropping off his purchases, Steve restless, walked down to the rocky headlands. Sitting quietly with his eyes closed, letting the sound of the ocean waves crashing on the rocks, flow over him. It somehow relaxed him, as if the water was washing away his transgression, calming him.

That evening around six, Steve heard a car pull up in the driveway. It was Louise and Edward home from work. Steve happily greeted them, realising how much he needed the company. After dinner, they sat around discussing the day's events. Steve told them about finding the tailor and getting some suits made, as well as buying other casual clothes.

"Steve you should have told me, instead of getting them made!

You could have got them where all the cops get theirs!" Edward suggested, thinking Steve crazy for spending so much money.

"He won't be wrestling crooks in his suit; he'll need a good one," Louise explained, knowing the clothes were for more than just business.

"There's nothing wrong with my suit!" Edward mumbled loudly, as Steve and Louise shared a smile, at Edward's embarrassment, before Louise changed the subject.

"Anyway, Steve I talked to my boss about that firm. He said he'd thought about buying in himself but lacked the funds. Are you sure you can afford it?" Louise said a bit suspicious about the money. That automatically made Edward suspicious too.

"Yes I've got most of it, but I might have to get a small loan as well," Steve explained defensively.

"Well as long as you know what you're doing," Louise replied, before changing the subject again. "What's the girl's name, Steve?" Louise asked quickly, taking Steve by surprise.

"What girl sis?" Steve stuttered, giving himself away.

"I knew it! The race to get new clothing, no man does that for work!" Louise exclaimed confidently, amazing Edward with her interrogation techniques.

"I did meet a girl on the flight to America. I've phoned her a few times, and I'm waiting to see if she rings back." Steve confessed, telling Louise and Edward about Michelle.

Lying in bed that night, Edward asked Louise, if she knew how much money Steve needed for the partnership.

"I'm not sure, but I'd say it's a lot," Louise whispered, tired and wanting to sleep.

"When your parents died did Steve receive the same as you?" Edward asked. He knew she'd received fifty thousand dollars. He wondered how much Steve would have got.

"He received the same Edward, why are you asking?" Louise answered coming fully awake.

"Then where's the money coming from?"

"Well, I'm afraid I don't know detective! Why don't you go rubber hose him instead of bothering me!" Louise exploded angrily, making Edward back off, realising he'd gone too far.

"I'm sorry it's just unusual that's all."

"Go to sleep Edward." was Louise's last words on the subject, as Edward took the hint and rolled over.

The next day Steve phoned the brokerage firm arranging an interview to meet with the Senior Partner, Owen Elliot. He then walked downtown to Isaac's shop, to pick up his remaining clothing, before having lunch with this wise old man. After handing over the rather significant amount of money for his clothing, which Steve would have found criminal a year ago, Isaac made a cup of tea.

"Steve last night I talked to my daughter and her husband. Jeffery, my son-in-law, was surprised that I knew my son's torturer was a General. He'd only just heard himself, and he's in the Intelligence Section there!" Isaac informed him, sipping his tea giving nothing away, as Steve sat there quietly.

"Look Isaac I might have said something…" was all Steve got out before Isaac stopped him.

"I don't want to know Steve, just thank you that's all," Isaac replied, before moving off to serve a customer.

When Isaac returned, they'd both moved onto talking about Steve's upcoming meeting, and his girlfriend, burying Steve's mistake forever. Arriving home, Steve entered to hear the phone ringing. Racing inside, he picked it up hopefully.

"Who is it?" Steve answered, catching his breath.

"Hello, Steve, its Michelle," her voice full of joy at the sound of Steve's voice.

"I can't believe it's you, Michelle, since the other day when I called, I've been scared to leave the phone for fear of missing your call!" Steve blurted out breathlessly, making Michelle giggle on the other end of the phone.

"Well, I'm here now Steve." Michelle laughed merrily, her voice singing in Steve's ears as he laughed too.

"When can I see you?"

"Unfortunately not today or tomorrow Steve I've just arrived from an overseas flight. I'll have to rest tonight and tomorrow, or I'll look a wreck." Michelle answered giggling.

"You never look anything other than beautiful to me!" Steve answered emotionally, meaning every word. Michelle stopped her giggling, knowing he meant it.

"Give me your address, I've got a car. I'll come to where you're staying, the day after tomorrow." Michelle informed him, before hanging up and heading for the shower.

Steve made dinner that night singing merrily in the kitchen, as Louise and Edward waited at the table having both guessed the reason for his happiness.

"Anyone ring today Steve?" Edward asked, getting a smile from Louise.

"No one for you, but I got a call. I'm judging you figured that out!" Steve replied chuckling.

"Meeting her tomorrow?" Louise asked suspiciously.

"Not tomorrow, I've got an appointment with a Mr Elliot from Elliot and Fox. I'll be getting a lift with you in the morning if that's okay. I'll see Michelle the next day." Steve replied honestly, leaving them both thinking. Louise thinking about Michelle, Edward about Steve's business plans.

That night in bed Edward again voiced his suspicions.

"I know you don't want to hear it, but something is going on with that brother of yours!"

"He's falling for that girl. It's all over his face." Louise sighed, hoping she was right for him.

"No, I mean about the money Louise! I was thinking of running a check on him tomorrow!" Louise's eyes focus on Edward.

"You'd better be kidding, or the next time you come home you'll be in the spare room!" Louise barked, secretly scared Edward might find something.

"You sense it too Louise! There's something he's not telling us about his overseas trip!"

"He's my brother that's the end of it!" Louise replied sorrowfully, before rolling over and going to sleep.

The next morning, Steve impressive in his new suit, hopped into the back of Edward's car, and almost immediately, felt the chill there. Louise and Edward sat quietly in the car giving a faint hello before Edward gunned the car out into the morning traffic. The car became as quiet as a tomb as they travelled towards the city, everyone looking miserable.

"If there's a problem that I've caused by staying, I'm sorry." Steve softly apologised, knowing somehow he was the problem.

"It's nothing, Steve! It's just Sherlock Holmes here thinks you're up to no good," Louise replied angrily.

"It's just that you've changed Steve and where is the money coming from? I was about to do a check on you at work, I'm so worried." Edward added guiltily, getting angry looks from his wife.

"I wouldn't do that Edward; the people I work for could react badly!" Steve exclaimed nervously, before falling silent. Staring out the window, he wondered what he should say.

"Right, first, I can afford quite a bit now, as I work for both the Australian Army and the Americans, and they pay me incredibly well for my help. Secondly just telling you could put us all in danger, as the work I do for them is top secret. That's why I'm sure they wouldn't like you checking on me." Steve explained, trying to convey the danger of knowing what he did.

"I'm pretty sure that's illegal Steve! You can't serve in two different Armies at the same time, let alone the conflict of interest!"

"Our government allowed it in exchange for favours. Most probably Intel I'd say!" answered Steve, leaving the other two to ponder this information.

"I appreciate you telling me Steve, I feel an idiot for putting you on the spot. But I've been in action, and I know that look you've got if you get what I mean."

"Yeah you're right, I've been on one mission already, and it got bloody. That's all I'll say, no more questions." Steve begged, getting nods from both of them as the car settled into an enforced silence. At the car park, they all got out and hugged each other without speaking. Steve headed for his appointment while Edward walked Louise to her bank, as they tried to make sense of Steve's job.

"Do you suppose he's like Maxwell Smart a secret agent or something?" Louise asked seriously, making Edward chuckle. Kissing her goodbye, he walked to his office. Sitting at his desk, the smile left Edwards face as he thought about Steve's employment with the Americans. There was only one function they'd use Special Forces for, and it wasn't for spying or deskwork.

Steve had several hours to kill before his meeting, so he wandered around Martin Place doing some window-shopping, before making his way over to the Cenotaph, which honoured the Anzac Soldiers of World War One. Arriving opposite Mr Elliot's building in Pitt Street and still early, he noticed a club in the Hilton Hotel building opposite. Hoping to get a coffee, he wandered towards it. He was surprised when the doorman hurried out, opening the door for him, with a 'good morning Sir'. Asking the doorman where he might get a coffee, he was directed to the refreshment area.

Here he was quickly and professionally served by a young gentleman, who asked questions about how the market was going and did he have any tips. It suddenly dawned on him that his suit conveyed an air of professionalism, which he didn't have. As the lounge area around him filled up with businessmen, the air became charged with energy, as people discussed the goings on in their firms and the market's direction. The most prominent news was the proposed move of the Stock Market, to a new location in the basement of a building in Martin Place. Someone suggested it had been done to stop traders jumping from the windows, which caused an outbreak of laughter.

Steve settled in, mixing with traders and bankers. Until ten minutes before his meeting, he listened to the goings on in the business world around him. He realised how different it was to his own world, and how important it was for him to be able to merge with this group of men. Excusing himself, he quickly hurried across the road and into the building housing the offices of Elliot and Fox. Steve piled into a crowded lift mostly filled with office girls, who took an interest in a young man in an expensive suit. As the door opened on the seventh floor, Steve walked confidently out, followed by giggles from the girls behind him.

This put him in a good mood, slightly covering his nervousness. Walking down a corridor, passing identical office facades, he, at last, came to the office of Elliot & Fox. The office was made up of four rooms, all leading off the reception area. Sitting behind the front desk, was a beautiful young woman dressed in a low and revealing top and an extremely short mini skirt. Steve was puzzled by the woman's dress, as it didn't really fit the image of a stockbroking firm.

"Good morning, I've an appointment with Mr Elliot," Steve announced, aware of the woman's eyes on him.

"Well aren't you a pretty one?" The girl replied, making Steve go red, leaving him speechless.

"Mary, behave yourself!" came an angry voice, from the office behind her, as a man in his late forties appeared at the door.

"Oh Daddy you're no fun!" The receptionist smiled at Steve's embarrassment.

"Hello Steve, I'm Owen. I'll just finish this call and meet you in the boardroom," Owen explained, shaking Steve's hand. He turned and gave Mary a cranky look before walking back into his office.

"Follow me, Mr Roberts." Mary purred, as she led the way into an adjoining room. Steve judged this was used as a lunchroom, as well as a boardroom. Mary could really walk in that short skirt, he admitted to himself, hypnotised by her swaying hips. Slowly, she pulled a chair out for him, smiling at the impact she had on him.

"Where do you live Mr Roberts? Somewhere close by?"

"No, I live in Perth at the moment."

"I'll have to come and visit one day, any room at your place?"

"Not really I share a room with three other men." Steve was referring to his barracks room.

"My father should be here soon, I've got to get back to work," Mary explained dismissing him, walking out. After she'd left, another door opened opposite the one Steve had entered. In walked a solidly built young man in his early thirties. Seeing Steve, he came forward to introduce himself.

"Steve, I'm Warren Fox, the other partner. Owen told me you would be coming in today. You've met Mary, his daughter?" Warren said shaking Steve's hand and smiling.

"Yes, she's quite impressive!" Steve replied as both men shared a grin.

"Our usual secretary is away sick; Owen's daughter is filling in. I've got to admit she certainly adds colour to the office!" Warren said happily.

"Yes but not a great receptionist," Owen added grumbling, as he entered. After introductions, the three men sat down and discussed the silent partnership with Steve. They outlined how they wanted to go global with their business, by joining with stockbrokers in the United States and Great Britain. This way, using the latest computer systems, it would enable them to give their customers more options when investing. Steve took in most of it, however, when Warren started to get excited about the technical side of the computers, he started to flounder.

"How about lunch?" Owen asked, seeing Steve struggling. Lunch was at the same club that Steve had wandered into earlier. The doorman nodded to Steve before greeting Warren and Owen with a friendly hello, leading them to a small corner booth.

"We have lunch here up to three times a week if we have time. It's the best place for picking up the odd bit of information about the goings-on in the financial market!" Owen said looking around the room for anyone with a story to tell.

"The foods also superb and as this is a business lunch, we can claim it," Warren added with a smile.

"Do you ever bring your daughter?" Steve asked seeing how miserable she looked when the three of them had left.

"Sometimes but she has a habit of turning men into boys. Not good for business." Owen replied sternly, but breaking into a smile.

"Yes, poor Mary, she isn't the best secretary, but she'll get heaps of interviews!" Warren replied, smiling at Owen's discomfit.

"What do you do for a living Steve?" Owen asked, changing the subject.

"I'm in the Army, based in Perth. Though for the last year I've been on an assignment in America, training." Steve answered giving the minimum of information, as their meals arrived.

Returning to the office, Warren excused himself as he had another appointment, leaving Owen and Steve to go over the details.

"I'm not going to tell you, that you'll be instantly rich by investing in this firm Steve, all business ventures have risk attached. In the long run, I'm confident that you'll be well looked after by joining this business. I've two questions though, can you afford this? And why?" Owen asked, wondering where a soldier got four hundred thousand from.

"The money is not a problem even though it will take nearly every cent I have. My parents left me quite a bit when they died in a car accident, and since then I saved some. The reason why is, I will need a career outside of the Army some day. I thought by then the business may have grown big enough to get a job here." Steve explained, skirting as close to the truth as he could. For several seconds Owen sat there looking at Steve. He knew not all he'd been told was the truth, but that could just be the line of work Steve was in he thought.

"Welcome aboard then Steve, the contracts here to be signed. If someday you want to work here, you're going to have to study this business from top to bottom." Owen replied offering his hand, which

Steve shook feeling jubilant.

"How did you know I'd sign the contracts?" Steve asked as they shared a coffee.

"When your sister's boss rang me to ask about the business, I asked about you, Steve. In this town information is everything!" Owen explained, smiling.

That afternoon, after Steve had left, Owen sat with Warren and Mary discussing their new partner.

"He seems very mature for his age, I gather he's only about twenty," Mary said thinking about the way he acted.

Looking at Mary, Warren for the first time realised she wasn't just beautiful, she was also clever, for he was just about to say the same thing.

"Yes, his line of work has a habit of ageing you!" Owen replied distantly, thinking about Steve.

"What? He's only a private in the army, how would that age him?" Warren replied not understanding.

"Didn't you hear him say he was overseas and based in Perth!" Owen answered and seeing the bewildered looks on their faces. "He's in the Special Forces. The SAS is based in Perth, and ordinary soldiers don't go overseas!" Owen told them wondering just what Steve did over there.

"I actually thought he was gay when I asked where he lived, he said he lived with three men," Mary answered feeling silly, making the others laugh.

"Well if he gives us any trouble I'll give him what's for, he wasn't that big." Warren joked showing Mary his muscles and getting a small smile from her.

"Don't even joke about that Warren!" Owen warned him, before continuing. "In all dealings with Steve, remember he's no fool and don't ever cross him. As a partner, he will be totally loyal to us, but I wouldn't like to have him as an enemy." Owen added falling quiet.

"Then why take him as a partner?" Mary said feeling slightly excited by this mysterious soldier and Warren's interest in her.

"Did you notice the way he moves and talks? He isn't a big guy, but power radiates from him. When Warren and I went to lunch with him at the club, the doorman acknowledged him before both of us, and we're fairly well known there. No there's something about him that makes me think despite the risk, the man will be good for business." Owen admitted.

Steve's first stop after leaving Owen was the Commercial Bank, where he transferred his funds from his offshore Swiss account to a local account. He then instructed the bank to send a cheque to Elliot and Fox for four hundred thousand dollars. When the money had been cleared, Steve was amazed that his hands weren't shaking. Checking his balance, he found not only was there the remaining one hundred thousand from Thailand, but the Americans had deposited thirty thousand dollars for the mission in Vietnam. So with interest, he still had about one hundred and forty thousand dollars, 'not bad for a private' he thought. Signing the money over Steve found himself invited to have a coffee with the bank General Manager.

Finding Steve had bought a partnership in a local Stock broking firm, and still held a sizable account at his bank; the Manager thought he'd pump Steve for any information on the stock market while he was there. Steve told him, what some of the people at the club had named as good buys. He then threw in the joke about the Stock market moving to the basement, which made the Manager chuckle. Leaving the Manager's office, as if they were best of friends, Steve thought that if he could get through the bullshit, this business could be great fun.

It was just after three in the afternoon when Steve boarded a train at Town Hall railway station. From there he would travel south to Cronulla station and home. It wasn't crowded as the train rattled its way south towards his destination and Steve found himself nodding off. Several stations along and a sudden jolt woke Steve up, as an old drunk boarded the train and shuffled groggily down the aisle of the train. Falling clumsily into an empty seat, near the far end of the carriage, he proceeded to drink what was left of his bottle before he completely collapsed.

The unmistakeable smash of broken glass woke Steve for the second time, startling him. He stared around suddenly alert, wondering when he had dozed off again. He found four young men bent over the drunk threatening him, with the now smashed bottle. All four men were dressed in black shirts with dirty, worn blue jeans. Their footwear was also matching, unpolished army boots, giving them all an untidy militia look. The clothing was bad enough, but to top it off, each wore a desert coloured cap with a swastika at the front.

"You drunken bum! What are you doing on a train with decent people?" The young man holding the broken bottle yelled at the drunk. The poor man's only defence was to roll into a ball on the seat, to try to ward off anymore blows. Looking around at the other travellers on the train, Steve saw no reaction at all. In fact, everyone had turned away, trying to ignore the confrontation.

"Toss the bastard off the train!" another would be stormtrooper shouted out; revealing that they'd all had a few drinks as well. Dragging the drunk towards the exit doors, they tried unsuccessfully, to pull one of the doors open.

"Wait till the station. When the doors open, we'll toss him out!" The holder of the broken bottle laughed, as the helpless drunk struggled half-heartedly.

"I don't think so Adolf!" A voice sounded from behind them, as the first would-be Nazi with the bottle, crashed to the floor with a broken jaw. Looking like a tough guy doesn't make you one Steve thought, as he swiftly dealt with the other tough guys. Stacking the four bodies into the first empty seat available, Steve sat the drunk back down to see if he was okay. Blood flowed from a wound on his head, which Steve stopped by using his handkerchief. While doing this, Steve noticed the dog tags around the drunk's neck.

"You were a soldier?"

"Yeah, conscripted and sent to Nam. Came home to find my girl went off with someone else and all my friends acted like I had the plague!" The drunk replied, letting the sadness roll over Steve. "Anyway, thanks for your help brother, though your handy work won't go unnoticed for much longer." The drunk admitted with a grin.

"Any suggestions?"

"We're coming into Hurstville, it's a big station. Let's say our goodbyes, and I'll take off." He suggested, offering his hand, which Steve took.

"What did you mean by calling me, brother?"

"Sharing combat makes you a brother." The drunk smiled, guessing Steve was a soldier. Wishing him luck, Steve walked to a coffee shop down the other end of the platform, where he waited patiently for the next train. It took longer than expected, as the train he'd left didn't leave, someone had reported the fight.

Steve sipping his coffee watched several ambulance paramedics', and four police officers hurried down the platform towards the train. This was followed moments later by the four young men being carried out to the waiting ambulances. Steve drinking his coffee looked up to see two Police Officers enter the shop and order drinks.

"What do you think Sergeant? Sounds like a rival gang to me!" the young Constable put forward, waiting to hear what his Sergeant thought.

"I'm not sure, one witness said it was a man in a suit helped the drunk!" the Sergeant said seriously. Both chuckled as their coffees arrived.

"Excuse me, Officers, do you know how long the train will be?" Steve asked after listening to their conversation.

"I'm sure any minute now Sir," the Sergeant said politely, before turning to the door and walking out.

"Shit do I look like a bloody railway worker!" the Sergeant growled, at Steve asking him about the train.

"Bet he'd shit himself if someone belted him on the train!" the Constable answered smiling.

"Yeah most probably ring us to get his suit dry-cleaned. These executive types really piss me off!" the Sergeant heatedly replied, as they walked back to the train.

Arriving home without any more problems, Steve realised how close he'd come to getting into serious trouble with the law. Weighing up the situation, he had to admit, he would have done everything exactly the same way. Sometimes you couldn't avoid trouble, but in the future, he'd have to be more careful in the way he handled it, maybe. The night passed quietly with no further questions about his business affairs from Louise or Edward. He told them he had taken a silent partnership in Elliot and Fox, in the hope of one day taking a position there. Louise was more than happy about her brother securing his future, and Edward also thought Steve was right to plan ahead.

"Changing the subject, when are we going to meet this girl?" Edward asked grinning, as Louise pounced on her brother for more information.

"We'd like to meet her Steve!" asked Louise, her tone left no room for debate.

"Well, I'll see how tomorrow goes first before I start introducing her as my wife," Steve said jokingly.

"How serious is it?" Louise exploded, as Edward laughed at Steve's dilemma.

"I think I'll call it a night." Steve sighed, beating a retreat downstairs to his room followed by Edward's hysterical laughter. Lying in bed, Steve thought about his date tomorrow with Michelle and his talking about her as a wife to his sister. He knew it sounded silly, but something felt right about it he concluded, as he tried to get some sleep.

Next morning, Steve ran unsteadily along the beach past the sand dunes at the northern end of Cronulla. He tried to stay focused on his training, but Michelle's image kept intruding into his thoughts. This made him lose concentration and run faster than he should. In the end, his lungs burning, Steve ground to a halt. "Control yourself!" He shouted, startling seagulls at the water's edge, forcing them to take flight.

Sitting down, breathing deeply, Steve smiled at his lack of control. 'She's all I can think off' he admitted happily, as standing up, he started jogging back towards home. Jumping first into a cold shower, Steve swiftly dressed, watching the clock. As the minutes ticked by, he became nervous wondering where she was and if she was coming at all. Racing upstairs to Louise's kitchen Steve grabbed the phone and dialled her number. Getting no answer he replaced the phone, realising she was only ten minutes late.

"You idiot!" he mumbled, before going back down to his unit, to find Michelle getting out of her car. He stood there, soaking in her presence as she too stopped and looked directly into his eyes. She was dressed in a pair of jeans and a simple white blouse. To Steve, she was like an exotic creature that if startled, would take flight and leave him forever alone.

"Hi Steve," Michelle said softly, getting slightly embarrassed and at the same time, aroused by Steve staring at her.

"I'd forgotten just how beautiful you are!"

"I bet you use that line all the time."

"No, I've never done that!" Steve exclaimed, before realising she was teasing him.

"So where are you taking me?"

"For a walk along my favourite beach!" he replied, as coming forward, he took her arm in his, heading for a walk along the beach.

After giving Michelle a guided tour of Cronulla, Steve took her to lunch at a small restaurant at the southern end of the beach. Both sat quietly at first, waiting for the other to begin. In the end, Steve started, telling of his childhood, growing up in a small northern NSW town. He told her about his sister and how they'd been inseparable after the death of their parents in a car accident. Coming clean, he told her of his binge drinking and with Edward's help joining the Army. He also confessed that he hadn't really been out with many girls.

Michelle then told her story. She had lived near Wollongong, south of Sydney. Her parents were both teachers, but her mum had stayed at home when the children came along. She had a younger sister and three older brothers. Two had been conscripted, and sent to Vietnam, though they didn't talk about it. She'd had lots of boyfriends but only one serious, which had been over a year ago. He had been a pilot, and she'd found out through a friend he'd been cheating on her. Since then she'd moved to Sydney near the airport where she'd shared a unit with another flight attendant named Julie.

Lunch finished, they strolled back to the house where he made her a cup of tea, and they continued to learn more about each other's lives. At 3, Michelle told Steve she'd have to be leaving soon, as she had to return to the Airport to pick up her roster. As they both stood to leave, they closed the distance between each other. Silence then settled over them as Steve leaned forward and kissed her. Holding her to him, Steve hungrily kissed her, as his heart started doing overtime in his chest.

Feeling Michelle was holding back, that he was moving too fast, he started to back off and release her. When he went to pull away, he felt Michelle's restraint shatter as she hungrily pulled him closer. Their kissing became more passionate as if both their lives become infused. Surrendering to the moment, their bodies pressed firmly against each other as each became aware of the other's arousal. Breaking reluctantly apart, they smiled guiltily, knowing neither had wanted to stop.

"What do we do now Steve?" Michelle whispered, short of breath, her body covered with a slight shimmering of sweat.

"I don't know Michelle? I've got to go back to Perth in ten days."

"No I meant do you want to go out with me tomorrow?" She giggled. "I thought I'd take you south, to where I grew up," Michelle suggested.

"That would be great!" Steve answered gazing at her.

Michelle knew she'd have to leave right now, or she wouldn't. Hand in hand, they walked to Michelle's car. There Steve kissed her again through the driver's window before she drove away. As Michelle turned onto the road, she thought of that kiss. She'd been kissed hundreds of times before, but never had she felt so alive. What was happening to her? After her last boyfriend she had sworn never to get too serious with a man again, but here she was shaking like a leaf.

Arriving back at her flat, Julie her flatmate pounced on her, wanting to know all about the date. Michelle gave her a complete rundown up on the part where they'd kissed. At which time she confessed how she lost control and wanted to stay with him.

"Oh my God, you're in love with him, I don't believe it!" Julie screamed.

"I can't be. We've only just had our first date."

"It doesn't work that way, Michelle. You've been talking about him since you met him on the plane, you've fallen for him!" Julie sniggered, before bursting into laughter.

Steve in the meantime, tried to defend himself all night, against Louise's questions, as Edward looked on smiling.

"Friday night is two nights away, how about we all go out, my shout!" Steve suggested softly, giving in.

"That would be lovely," Louise replied smiling, wanting to meet this girl who had so captivated him.

"Since you're paying I'll book us into the local Yacht Club. I hear the foods great, and there's dancing!" Edward chuckled happily.

"Then it's a date, I'll ask her tomorrow," Steve answered, before realising his mistake.

"You're going out again tomorrow, where too?" Louise exploded, as Edward again started chuckling at Steve's blunder.

The following morning, Steve had just returned from his run and had a shower, when a knock came at the door. Wrapping a towel around himself, he opened the door to find Michelle standing there looking towards the beach with her back towards him.

"I told you I'd be early!" Michelle said merrily, before turning and looking at Steve wearing just a towel freezing.

"I'll just put something on."

"Okay, I'll meet you at the car," Michelle answered, retreating to her car. Minutes later, Steve appeared dressed and quickly jumped in, as Michelle drove south. Turning off the highway, halfway to Wollongong, Michelle drove down to the old coast road, which followed the cliffs along the coast from Stanwell Tops to Austinmer. This was Michelle's favourite area. When she was young, her parents had taken them too many spots along this rough coastal road. Now she excitedly pointed out different places to Steve as they drove along. Looking across, Michelle noticed that after she would point something out of interest, Steve's invariably returned to gaze at her.

"Steve you're missing all the beauty here!"

"No, I'm looking at the most beautiful thing here!" Steve answered. Pulling over at a lookout car park, Michelle leaned across and kissed him. The kiss went on and on, as both frantically pulled each other all over the vehicle in their battle to satisfy their longing to get closer. They only stopped, when they each realized they weren't alone. Three other cars were parked at the lookout, two with older couples in them. The third was a middle-aged couple, with three young children. Those children now stood beside their car, spellbound by what was going on. Luckily the windows of Michelle's car had fogged up, as looking down Steve realised he had only his pants on, his shirt was gone.

Next, to him, Michelle was down to her underwear, which at this moment, Steve didn't dare look at. Knowing things had gone too far, they both quickly dressed, as the three other vehicles departed, with the beeping of horns. This left them free to get out and walk around, enjoying the sights, shyly grinning at each other at what had just happened.

Driving further south, Michelle indicated a small pub near Austinmer, where they could stop and have lunch. Sitting there quietly eating lunch, they watched the locals, playing rugby on the field opposite. Steve decided to broach the subject of the lookout.

"I'm sorry if I went too far back there," Steve whispered.

"No it was just as much my fault Steve, I never felt like this with anyone else. I don't know what's happening." Michelle answered honestly, as Steve reached across the table holding her hand.

"Michelle what are you doing here?" a voice shouted from across the road, startling them both.

"Oh my god, it's my brothers!" Michelle exclaimed softly. Crossing the road, she hugged three monsters, which Steve guessed were her brothers. Following her across the road, Michelle introduced him to her three brothers. All three put an awful lot of strength into their handshakes, as they sized Steve up. Joe was Michelle's oldest brother, followed by Tony, and Brian, all were over six feet tall and solidly built.

Years of working in the local steel mills, and weekends of rugby, had made them extremely fit. Joe and his brothers were here for a local game, while Michelle told them how she'd brought Steve down to show him where she lived. After introductions, the brother walked back across the road talking to the other players before returning.

"Hey Steve since you're here, we were wondering if you could help us out. Joe's hurt his leg, and we're short. Do you mind playing for us?" Brian asked grinning.

"I'd love to, but I've haven't got a uniform," Steve replied also smiling, sensing a setup.

"No problem Steve, you can wear mine!" Joe put in grinning.

"Are you sure Steve? Can you even play rugby?" Michelle was worried by her brother's sudden interest in Steve playing.

"It's no problem, Michelle. I've played rugby before. I'll be all right." Steve answered sensing satisfaction from the brothers at his decision to play. Steve was quickly introduced to the other players on the team and given a rough outline of their game plan. He then moved into position on the wing. The other side moved into position opposite, Steve coming face to face with a huge guy.

"Who's this little runt?" Steve's opposite number yelled at Tony.

"It's Michelle's new boyfriend Greg, he's taking Joe's place," Tony answered chuckling, as Greg glared at Steve.

"What's your problem friend?" Steve asked Greg.

"Greg was Michelle's boyfriend before she dumped him and moved to Sydney!" Tony interrupted, laughing at the situation, as Steve now realised the purpose of him playing.

"Well I guess she had her reasons, shall we get on with the game," Steve suggested, wanting to avoid trouble, as the whistle sounded and the game began.

"Who's the new guy sis?" Joe asked Michelle, as he watched the two teams get into position.

"I met him on a flight to America over a year ago, we just clicked. He's rung me every so often since then." Michelle answered, watching the game.

"Didn't you learn anything from the last pilot you went out with?" Joe grumbled.

"He isn't a pilot Joe; he was a passenger on the plane. And don't tell me who I can go out with big brother!" Michelle answered, putting Joe in his place.

"What's so special about this one that you'd bring him down here?" Joe said watching Steve take a nasty hit from his opposite out on the field,

"I think I'm in love with him Joe," Michelle whispered, smiling happily, knowing it was true. Joe looked at her closely, taken aback by her confession. He started to feel sorry for setting Steve up opposite Greg. Brian after meeting Steve had suggested Joe let Steve play in his place; see what he was made of. Now Joe had his doubts. Looking out on the field he saw a free for all start between the two teams. Michelle, seeing his attention shift to the game turned and caught sight of Greg on the other team, throwing punches at Steve.

"Joe, what's going on? What's Greg doing here?" Michelle asked angrily seeing her brother flinch at her question.

"I've no idea! He must play for the other team," he answered lamely. "Looks like there's trouble out there I'd better go out and stop it!" Hoping Steve hadn't been too badly hurt. He'd gotten halfway out onto the field when he ran into Brian. He was carrying, part dragging a dazed Tony from the field, assisted by Steve, who had a nasty cut on the head.

"What happened?" Joe asked as he looked out on the field to see a paramedic giving first aid to at least five downed players, from the other team.

"No time for answers Joe. We'd better get Tony to the hospital he's badly concussed!" Brian answered shakily, as Joe helped Tony into his car. Michelle, running up to them, was horrified at the blood running down Steve's face. Grabbing one of her brother's towels, she held it to his head, tears streaming down her face.

"If this was some sort of prank Joe, I'll never forgive you!" Michelle threatened. Joe felt guilty for causing the fight.

"That can wait, sis, Tony and Steve need to go to the hospital. Can you drive Steve?" Joe asked sorrowfully. Seeing her nod and turn away, he started his own car, speeding off. As the brothers drove towards the hospital, Joe finally had a chance to ask about the game.

"What happened out there Brian, it was supposed to be just a joke!" Joe accused his brother angrily.

"It was that shit Greg, he knocked Steve flying in a tackle, then put the boot into his head. Tony tried to intervene when one of Greg's friend's king hit him from behind." Brian said shakily.

"Well, you guys taught them a lesson!" Joe smiled.

"We didn't do anything, Joe. That boyfriend of Michelle's took them all down. I can tell you it was scary!" Brian admitted, obviously upset by what had happened. Seeing Joe's shocked expression, Brian told him about it. When the game started, it became clear that Greg held a lot more resentment than we gave him credit for. After a couple of dangerous tackles on Steve, Tony told Greg angrily to just play the game. Greg then crashes tackled Steve even though he didn't have the ball. He followed it up with a vicious kick to the head.

Seeing things had gone too far Tony rushed at Greg, only to be hit by one of Greg's friends from the side, knocking him out. A brawl then started between both teams. I was on the other wing, and ran across to help, only to see Steve explode from the ground and chop Greg's friend across the neck, flattening him. Greg then said something to Steve. He went straight up to him and knocked him down with a series of punches to the ribs. I tell you, I heard his ribs crack twenty metres away. Greg's teammates seeing their friends cop it, all turned towards Steve.

Instead of running he just stood there watching them come. Then one by one he took them apart until they backed off. That's why we have to take Steve and Tony to the hospital, the paramedic couldn't handle anyone else.

Joe sat silently, taking in this information, wondering, about who his sister was in love with.

Michelle in the meantime followed closely behind her brother's car. She was having trouble concentrating on driving, while continually watching Steve at the same time.

"I'm sorry for hurting those guys Michelle, but one of them said terrible things about you, and I lost my temper," Steve mumbled groggily, as his thoughts dipped in and out of clarity, concentrating on Michelle's face.

"Those thugs could have killed you!" Michelle replied, thinking Steve's statement was caused by his head wound.

"I love you, Michelle!" Steve whispered, before drifting off into unconsciousness. Looking across at him, tears running down her face, Michelle pulled into the hospital emergency car park.

Joe sat with Brian, in the waiting room in the Emergency Department, wondering if the day could get any worse. Michelle quietly sat opposite him, as they all waited.

"I'm sorry Michelle. I never dreamed it would lead to this!" Joe softly pleaded, hoping his sister would forgive him.

"I know you meant it as a joke, but he's not big like you guys, he could have been killed," Michelle answered, seeing her brother was truly sorry for what had happened.

"Are you kidding sis! He could have flattened us all! I've never seen anyone fight like that before!" Brian burst out making Michelle hesitate and think about Steve's ramblings.

"I have," Joe replied, thinking back to his Army days. "What does Steve do for a job?" Joe continued, knowing the answer.

"He's a soldier; he's been overseas in America that's how I met him. He's in the SAS." Michelle replied, seeing Joe nod, his thoughts elsewhere.

"Bloody hell a Super Soldier, that explains a lot!" Brian replied smiling.

"Shut up Brian. Michelle, how do you know he's in the SAS? And what was he doing overseas?" Joe asked suspiciously. Michelle was about to answer when a voice called from across the room.

"Michelle what are you doing here?" a mature man of about fifty asked, as they all got to their feet as he approached.

"Holy shit," Brian whispered a little too loudly, causing the man to give him a stern look.

"Dad, what are you doing here?" Michelle asked.

"I think I asked that question first. Bruiser, one of Joe's teammates, informed me that Tony and Michelle's boyfriend had been hurt playing rugby. So here I am, so what are you doing here?"

George, her father, asked again.

"Well, I brought Steve for a drive down to Austinmer to show him where I grew up and we ran into the boys. They invited Steve to play in their team. Unfortunately, it got a bit rough." She replied, skirting close to the truth. Silence settled over the group as George's eyes read their faces knowing not all the truth had been told. He was just about to speak when the surgery door opened and out walked Steve. Changed back into his own clothes, from Joe's borrowed uniform, he looked unhurt except for the small bandage on his forehead.

Michelle instantly ran towards him, hugging him fiercely. Kissing him, she asked him if he was okay, as her father and brothers looked on. She then turned and shyly introduced her father to Steve.

"Glad to meet you, Steve; though I would have wished for better circumstances," George replied happily, as he gripped Steve's hand and looked him straight in the eye. 'He's here for the long run.' George thought to himself, as he looked this young man over. At that moment Brian emerged from the same door, sitting in a wheelchair smiling and talking to a pretty nurse. His smile disappeared when he saw his father.

"Dad, what are you doing here?" Tony croaked out, wondering what he'd been told.

"Just here to see if you're okay and get you home," George answered, before turning back to Michelle.

"Your mother misses you, Michelle, how about you bring Steve around this Sunday for lunch so she can meet him?" George asked, putting Michelle on the spot.

"I'd love to meet your mother Michelle if it's okay with you," Steve replied, giving her back the option to go if she wanted to.

"Okay, we'll come Sunday," Michelle replied, happy Steve wanted to go visit her family following the afternoon's events.

As Tony drove home with his father and Brian, George managed to get the whole story out of them.

"He's not a big man, but he must have been well trained to take on those guys," George suggested.

"The funny thing is if Tony hadn't been hit, or Greg hadn't made some comment about Michelle, I think he would have done nothing, just taken the beating. I wonder why?" Brian replied, thinking about the fight.

"Just because you know you can beat someone, doesn't mean

you should. He sounds like he has a strong sense of discipline." Tony replied getting a nod from his father.

Sitting there in silence, George thought long and hard, about this new man in his daughter's life.

Michelle drove quietly thinking about the day's events and the coming Sunday with her family.

"A penny for your thoughts," Steve said as he watched her drive.

"You said you loved me on the way to the hospital!"

"I meant it, Michelle, I love you. I know it should take longer, but the first time I saw you on the plane I knew I couldn't live without you." Steve replied as silence settled over the car. Michelle pulled over.

"I love you too Steve. It scares me, but I know it's true," she said as she moved closer and they kissed. Finding they were again going too far, Steve broke away only because his head had begun to ache. Seeing the pain Steve was in, Michelle returned to driving.

"One of these times we're not going to stop!" Steve grinned as if reading her mind, making her laugh.

"Well remember what you missed out on, next time you run off playing rugby." Michelle laughed.

"Can you pull over again Michelle there's something I must tell you."

"What's wrong? There isn't a wife out there somewhere is there?"

"Michelle I'm not just in the SAS, I also work for the Americans as well. I belong to a special unit that takes care of situations that crop up around the world. I won't kid you by saying its safe; I could cop it on any mission. But I love you and want to be with you, for no matter how long I've got. I just thought I'd tell you the truth." Steve explained, waiting for a reply.

"We could get out of this car now and be knocked down by a passing truck. I'll take the chance, Steve. But thanks for being honest with me, it's one of the things I love about you," Michelle answered, kissing him passionately, before pulling back onto the road.

Arriving home, Steve kissed her goodnight and reminded her of the night out with his sister the following evening. Promising to meet him at the club at 7 she drove off, thinking all the way home about meeting Steve's sister. Meanwhile, Steve staggered into the lounge room, his head splitting.

"Bloody hell! What happened to you?" Edward said seeing the bandage and Steve's colour. His sister quickly headed out into the kitchen, returning with a small First Aid kit. She handed him some painkillers, along with a glass of cold water she'd brought with her. Settling down, Steve told them of his day out, punctuated by laughter from Edward who thought Steve's every problem was a reason for merriment.

"So you're going to meet her parents? You must like her a lot to do that little brother?" Louise put forward.

"I love her sis; I think she's the one!" Steve answered his eyes shining, taking the smile off Edwards' face.

"Have you told her what you do?" Edward asked seriously.

"Yes I told her on the way home tonight, she seemed okay with it," Steve replied knowing he'd done the right thing.

"Well, we'd best all turn in. Edward and I have got a day of work tomorrow before we meet your girl. And you brother, have got a day to get over your head wound." Louise informed him, before giving him a big hug and heading off to bed.

Steve awoke at six as usual, but with a brain pounding headache, he wasn't going anywhere. Staggering upstairs Steve found the painkillers that his sister had thoughtfully left out for him. Downing two tablets and thanking his sister silently, he headed back to bed. Waking at ten, Steve was relieved that his head had stopped pounding. Decided to go for a walk instead of a run, he quickly changed, heading downtown, to visit Isaac.

After telling Isaac about his time spent with Michelle, and then his confrontation on the rugby field with her brothers, he told him about his night out with his sister and Sunday with her family. Isaac smiled a smile of true happiness, before bursting into laughter, something he hadn't done for quite some time.

"Steve you lift my spirit and make me feel twenty years younger, by just listening to your escapades." Isaac laughed, as tears streamed from his eyes.

"How would you handle my situation, Isaac?" Steve asked, happy to make this old man laugh.

"Well have you bought her a gift or something for tonight?" Isaac asked. Seeing Steve's blank look, he continued. "It used to be customary to give a girl at least flowers on a special night like tonight.

There's also your sister; it's a big night for her too. And of course, there is Michelle's mother on Sunday, better not forget her, she'll be watching you closely."

"I hadn't even thought of flowers. You sound like you were good at this Isaac!" Steve smiled.

"I did okay" Isaac replied smiling. "Remember Steve a way to a girl's heart is always through her mother. Win her over, and you're halfway there." Isaac continued, with a faraway look, remembering past times.

Leaving Isaac's shop, Steve went looking for the florist, Isaac had recommended, not having the faintest idea what to get. Once in the shop, Steve approached the front counter, where he was served by two ladies one aged about forty, the other younger than Steve, maybe eighteen. After explaining what he wanted, he left it up to the two women to work out what was best. For Michelle, they suggested some beautiful orchids, for his sister a bunch of roses and for Michelle's mum, a large bunch of Australian wildflowers. Steve couldn't have been happier with their choices and paid the ladies giving them a good sized tip, before hurrying home to put his purchases in a cool place.

"Why don't you go out with a guy like that? One who buys his girlfriend's mother flowers?" The lady who'd served Steve asked her daughter.

"Because if they come in here, they're already taken!" her daughter replied smiling, but she had to admit he was cute.

Across town, Michelle sat down to breakfast feeling sick in the stomach.

"Crikey what's wrong with you?" Julie asked wandering in for breakfast. Michelle then unloaded about her day out and her coming night out with Steve's family, before Sunday at her Mums.

"Bloody hell Michelle this is a major deal!"

"I don't think it's that big a deal, it's only his sister and brother-in-law."

"Are you kidding? He's got no parents, and the only one close relation is his sister. Her approval would be everything to him, you get on the wrong side of her, and you're out!" Julie pointed out, watching Michelle's eyes mist up.

"She'll like me I'm sure," Michelle answered defensively looking for support.

"By the time I'm finished, you'll be a shoe-in," Julie assured her.

"Thanks, Julie." Michelle smiled.

"You do have a dress don't you?" Julie asked as Michelle started to mist up again.

BIG NIGHT

"Six O'clock!" Steve moaned to himself as he adjusted his tie for the tenth time, "Oh stuff it!" he bellowed, giving up on the tie, as he grabbed his sports jacket and the flowers for Louise and Michelle and headed upstairs.

"I got you this sis, thanks for making me feel welcome," Steve said giving his sister the flowers and a kiss.

"You're always welcome here Steve, as well as your girl," Louise mumbled, trying not to cry, as she hugged her brother, marvelling at how grown up he looked in his suit.

"Boy oh boy roses and orchids, you're going to have to watch your money Steve, or you'll end up broke," Edward sniggered as he came into the room.

"Maybe he's hoping to get lucky?" Louise replied as she went in to pick up her purse.

"Bugger, what have I said now?" Edward asked his smile gone, as he looked to Steve for advice.

The drive to the club was quiet as each person thought about tonight. Steve hoped Michelle would like his sister and vice versa. While Louise wondered what type of girl, her brother was attracted to. Edward, on the other hand, started to realise how he had been taking Louise for granted lately. It hadn't even occurred to him to buy flowers, and Steve's suit made his look shabby. He would have to make an effort to lift his game before it was too late.

Arriving at the club, Edward stopped to let Louise and Steve out at the front door. Running around, he then opened Louise's door, which made her smile, as he drove off to find a parking spot.

"Lately Edward's been so preoccupied with his new job, I was starting to wonder if the spark was gone."

"He loves you, sis, a blind man can see that," Steve replied.

"I know, but sometimes a girl just likes to be told or shown, like opening the door." She explained, feeling good about the evening. Edward arrived shortly afterwards, and as they waited in the foyer, Louise leaned across, giving him a kiss on the cheek. Edward, at that moment, felt like the luckiest man in the world.

As they stood waiting, Edward told them about his week at work. He had a new team member assigned to his team. His name was Steiner; though he was better known by his nickname 'Stun Gun'. He'd been transferred from Canberra after pulling his gun on a kid with a bow and arrow. Edward didn't know what to do with him, so he'd given him the job on a stakeout as a lookout. His job was to ring the Swat group when all units were ready to enter a drug dealer's house.

Unfortunately, when he'd been given the signal, he'd wrung the drug dealers' phone number by mistake, then hung up, pretending he had the wrong number. This nearly ruined the whole raid. Edward explained that because of seniority, Stun Gun was now being moved to head up a department in Brisbane. His rank was now above Edward's, making Steve and Louise burst into laughter.

"Tell me this is your girlfriend!" Edward exclaimed, stopping the conversation, as Steve and Louise turned, to see Michelle entering the front door. There were about ten men in the foyer, and every one of them looked towards the front door hypnotized by her entry. Gliding towards Steve, Michelle was unaware of the stares of the other men, her eyes only on Steve. She'd worn a long black dress that fitted her incredible body like a glove. Her blonde hair was curled and flowed down over her shoulders captivating Steve, who looked at her face, mesmerized by her eyes. Michelle impressed, stared at Steve, having never seen him in a suit before. Standing there in the foyer he seemed to dominate the room. He had a confident way of standing, making him look older and more mature, it made her want him. Introducing Louise and Edward, Steve then gave Michelle the orchids.

"They're beautiful Steve, thank you," Michelle replied, her eyes sparkling.

"Well let's go find our table," Louise suggested as she grabbed Michelle's hand and led her off towards the dining room, leaving Steve and Edward to follow.

"You've got my permission to marry her," Edward whispered to Steve, as they sat down around the table.

"I heard that Edward." Michelle smiled, as Edward went bright red. All the while, she stared at Steve with those beautiful eyes.

"Okay, you two love birds stop staring at each other," Louise suggested. This succeeded in bringing Steve and Michelle back to earth, as they ordered dinner.

The night was filled with conversation and dancing as Louise asked Michelle about her family and what she wanted out of life. Edward finally stopped Louise by grabbing his wife and taking her out onto the dance floor. Steve hardly noticed the exchange between the women so besotted was he with Michelle. Following Edwards lead, he took Michelle's hand and joined the others on the dance floor.

"Give it up my darling, he's head over heels!" Edward whispered into Louise's ear, as they held each other tightly and danced slowly around the room.

"You're right, he's crazy for her and I've got to admit I like her too," Louise replied enjoying the way Edward held her. In the end, Louise knew there would be no dissuading him, he was in love, and Louise had to admit Michelle was quite a catch.

After several hours of dancing, they all decided to head back to Louise and Edward's for coffee.

"I couldn't believe you could be more beautiful, till I saw you tonight!" Steve confessed lovingly, as he stared at Michelle while she drove along. Michelle turning sideways looked at Steve as he gazed hungrily at her. Pulling to the side of the road, she frantically kissed him, as they wrestled for a position in the front of the car which gave them complete access to each other.

"I think Michelle's got a car problem, she just pulled over!" Edward told Louise, watching his rearview mirror.

"Take the next left and circle back," Louise suggested as she looked back. Edward quickly drove around the block coming up behind them with their lights on high beam, giving them a good idea of what was going on inside.

"I don't think they need a hand!" Edward chuckled, smiling at Louise.

"No I think they'll be okay, but the coffee is off I'd say?" Louise laughed, as they drove past.

Coming up for breath Steve wiped his window and looked outside.

"I know we've only known each other for a short time, but I love you, I want you with me, come to Perth." Steve asked, his voice trembling. Michelle at first didn't answer, having her doubts that it was too soon. Looking into his eyes, she capitulated.

"I love you too Steve. I'll get a transfer, but it might take a little while." Michelle replied, knowing she'd give the job up if that's what it took.

The dry sand crunched rhythmically beneath Steve's feet as he ran effortlessly through the dunes towards the point. Steve felt incredibly powerful this morning, very different from the way he'd dragged himself out of bed the day before. The thought of being with Michelle drove him onwards, his passion flowing through his body pushing him forward through the crusty sand covering the top of the dunes.

Showering and dressing Steve quietly made breakfast, letting Louise and Edward enjoy their Saturday morning sleep in, while he went downtown. His high this morning was quickly disappearing replaced by the reality of leaving Michelle.

Like usual, Steve headed for Isaac's shop. Steve felt that Isaac, through their conversation, had become a defacto father to him. After telling Isaac about the night out and what a hit the flowers had been, he then told him about his dilemma over Michelle, not coming with him straight away.

"Well, there's only one thing for it Steve!" as he led Steve to the front door and closed his shop behind him.

"Where are we going, Isaac? You can't afford to just close your shop!"

"Saturday mornings are always slow, no one will miss me for a while." Isaac smiled, as they walked through the shopping centre, coming to a stop outside a jewellery store, making Steve hesitate.

"Steve you love her, but you can't be with her. This is a sign to her that you're in it for the long run, no matter where she is." Isaac smiled, as they both entered the shop. An hour later after squabbling over the price, Steve left the shop several thousand dollars lighter than when he entered.

"You've done the right thing, my boy," Isaac assured him, as they walked back to his shop. Talking until lunchtime, Steve finally departed, promising to call.

Walking home, Steve tried to work out what he'd say to Michelle before giving her a ring. She was calling in for a quick meal with Louise and Edward tonight, before turning in early, to prepare for tomorrow with her parents. He didn't want to do it the following day, and Michelle was returning to work the next day, so tonight was he guessed the best time.

Helping Louise prepare dinner Steve mulled over what to say wanting it perfect. Louise watched him wondering what was going on as he stood there, deep in thought.

"What's wrong Steve?"

"I'm practising what I'll say to Michelle when I give her this," Steve showed her the ring.

The noise of breaking plates woke Edward from his afternoon snooze. Arriving at the kitchen, he found brother and sister standing over a pile of broken plates.

"What's going on?" Edward asked, looking at his dinner on the floor.

"Steve's going to ask Michelle to marry him; he's giving her a ring tonight!"

"That's great news I'll just go get a bottle of champagne and put it on ice!" Edward grinned, shaking Steve's hand, leaving Louise on the spot.

"Are you happy for me sis?"

"Of course I am. It's just a shock that's all." Louise whispered, hugging her brother, doubts forgotten in an instant.

"I don't want to complain, but shall I order takeaway?" Edward smiled, as they all started to clean up the mess.

When Michelle arrived, Louise and Edward charged for the door, with the excuse of picking up dinner, leaving a suspicious Michelle alone with Steve.

"What's going on Steve? You still want to go tomorrow don't you?" Michelle asked wondering if Steve was getting cold feet.

"Michelle I want you to be my wife. This is something to remember me by until we are together." Steve stammered out, before producing the small box. Michelle without a word took the box, opened it and gazed at the engagement ring. "If you don't like it I can get another one!" Steve continued, hoping she was happy with his choice.

"It's perfect Steve. And yes I want to be your wife." She whispered, rushing into his arms.

While Steve prepared some drinks in the kitchen, Michelle admired her ring. The diamond was reasonably large compared to some of her friend's rings she had seen, she wondered if Steve could afford it.

"It's beautiful Steve, but I hope you didn't spend too much?"

"It was a bit pricey. Though Isaac, my friend I told you about, helped me get a good deal."

"Someday I'll have to meet this friend of yours!" Michelle laughed, as footsteps sounded from the front door.

"Hello inside. Anything happen while we were gone?" Edward shouted from the door. Louise gave him a dig in the ribs playfully, as they hurried in to congratulate them both and see the ring. When dinner was finished, Michelle reluctantly left, as Louise gave Steve advice on how to behave with Michelle's parents. Turning in for the night, Steve hoped tomorrow would go smoothly, better than the last time he met them.

Walking into her flat, Michelle was greeted by Julie, who wanted to find out how her night had gone. Looking down she saw Michelle's hand.

"Oh my God!" Julie exploded, grabbing Michelle's hand. "It's huge. What have you been doing to earn that?" Julie laughed.

Michelle described the night and how Steve's sister and brother-in-law had disappeared, leaving Steve to propose.

"He's lucky to be getting you." Julie sniffed, trying not to cry, hugging her friend. "Oh my God I just had a thought, what are your parents going to say? God, I wish I could be there!" Julie smiled, as Michelle's happy mood evaporated.

The next morning, a very nervous Michelle picked up Steve and headed south towards her parents place.

"Do you think I should take the ring off?"

"It's up to you Michelle."

"No, I'll leave it on. I'll tell mum after you've been introduced to the rest family." Michelle suggested, wanting them to see it.

"Don't worry I'll be right there with you." Steve replied smiling, as the rest of the journey continued in silence.

Pulling up opposite Michelle's parent's place, Steve was

impressed by the house. It was a two story brick home with an old willow tree, which dominated the whole yard. Being on the side of the escarpment above Wollongong, gave the rear of the house an uninterrupted view of the city and the ocean beyond. It was breathtaking. Walking hand in hand towards the front door, their progress was stopped when a younger version of Michelle ran screaming out of the house and into Michelle's arms.

"Steve, this is my little sister Leonie." Michelle giggled, as her younger sister gave Steve a kiss on the cheek.

"Boy, I wonder what your mother looks like to have such beautiful daughters," Steve asked, making Leonie blush. Looking around at the cars in the street, Michelle asked her sister suspiciously who else was here today.

"Just about everyone sis!" Leonie beamed seeing her sister's reaction.

"Well let's get it over with," Michelle mumbled, as Leonie grabbed her hand and looked down.

"You're wearing an engagement ring!" Leonie screamed, as Michelle tried to calm her down and convince her to be quiet.

"Michelle, come on in and introduce Steve," her father's voice sounded from the front door, as Michelle and Steve walked in the front door, into a room full of noise. The first person Steve met was Michelle's mother Emily who gave him a peck on the cheek. He was then passed down the line to the other relations who were there for a barbeque until he completely lost track of who was who.

"So what do you do for a job?" One of the many uncles asked as the room grew quiet for his response.

"I'm in the Army and stationed in Perth" Steve replied honestly getting the nod of approval.

"Have you seen any action?" another uncle asked, getting a cranky look from the women.

"We're not at war with anyone at the moment. I don't think he would have done any fighting yet!" Michelle's father answered.

"If we include rugby, he's seen heaps!" Brian laughed, getting the look of death from his brothers.

"Look at her hand!" Leonie screamed, unable to hold it back any longer, as everyone in the room focused on Michelle's hand, as her face went white. The room went as quiet as a tomb as Emily came forward and lifted Michelle's hand for a better look.

"If you could all excuse us for a minute, Emily and I would like to talk to these two outside alone!" Michelle's father barked sternly, making everyone look anywhere else, rather than at Michelle and Steve, as they were led outside.

"I'm sorry about this George, you and Emily should have been the first to know," was all Steve got out, as George signalled him to stop. He turned to Michelle for an explanation.

"Steve surprised me with the ring last night. He is based in Perth, and I want to be with him. I'm sorry it took you by surprise." Michelle apologised, as her mum came up and hugged her.

"Oh Michelle you always were impatient, but the wedding will have to be here, all your family lives here," Emily said kissing her daughter.

"Wait a minute!" George said gruffly. "We know nothing about this guy? How do we know he can look after her?" George grumbled.

"Michelle will always be my priority, I love her," Steve answered honestly, standing his ground. Looking at his wife and his daughter and seeing the looks they were giving him, George surrendered knowing the battle was over. Walking toward Steve, he shook his hand.

"Welcome to the family," George smiled. Looking Steve straight in the eye he whispered: "you better treat her right". Emily kissed Steve welcoming him, before taking her husband's hand.

"You in the house, you may as well come out, since you've been listening anyway!" George shouted, followed by laughter from inside, as Michelle's family poured out into the backyard to join in the celebrations.

Leonie sat watching Michelle show her ring to the three girls her brothers had brought to the party. The girls looked at the ring to them smiling, making Leonie smile at her brothers discomfit. Michelle's boyfriend Steve intrigued her, as he talked to her father and some other men. Michelle over the years had brought many boys home, better looking than Steve, but there was something different about him. The way he moved that made him seem dangerous somehow. She realised it turned her on. As the day turned to night, the merriment slowly came to a close, Steve and Michelle said their goodbyes and departed, leaving the family to talk freely.

"He seems a pretty decent bloke to me!" Joe admitted as he sat with his father and brothers.

"Yes, he's a nice fellow all right," George answered, thinking about Steve.

"Well, I can tell you one thing I won't be the one who throws him out if you people don't like him!" Brian said remembering the game, which made the others all laugh. The conversation then changed to football, as George sat there quietly remembering when his brother had asked if Steve had seen any action. He'd been watching Michelle at the time, and in her eyes, he had seen fear. Steve's job in the Army, whatever it was, included a lot of danger and that worried him.

Driving Michelle's car home, Steve too thought about the incident with the uncle. He was going to have to learn to lie better. He was sure Michelle's father had spotted his hesitation in answering a straightforward question, something he'd have to watch in the future.

"Steve, are you in a hurry to get home?" Michelle whispered, running her hand around his neck and shoulders massaging them,

"No, I'm not speeding!" Steve replied, before looking across at Michelle and seeing her smiling. He instantly pulled over. Their passion was more controlled this time, but after an hour they were gasping for breath.

"I leave on a flight tomorrow Steve, so this is our last time together. That's until I can arrange a transfer or a flight to Perth." Michelle sighed sadly, not wanting to go.

"The time will pass quickly, and anyway you've got a wedding to plan with your mother, that should keep you busy," Steve said laughing, as Michelle tried to hit him before they kissed again.

Two days after Michelle left, Steve prepared to leave. Saying a quick goodbye to Isaac, promising to stay in touch, Steve left for the airport. After lots of hugs and kisses from his emotional sister, Steve hurried down the boarding ramp and onto his flight. There he was met by a very attractive air hostess who seemed bent on making Steve squeeze past her well-proportioned body, to get onto the plane. Onboard the hostess personally escorted Steve to his seat and following her was quite an experience. She came to a stop at a seat in Business class. This was a surprise, as the Army had booked him in economy.

"I'm sorry miss, but are you sure this is my seat?" Steve stammered out, as the hostess turned and pressed up against him in the passageway.

"Nothing's too good for our soldier boys!" the Hostess replied, putting on a terrific Marilyn Monroe voice, much to the amusement of the other passengers. How does she know I'm a soldier Steve asked himself and the penny dropped?

"You're Julie aren't you?" Steve asked as the hostess burst into laughter.

"Welcome aboard soldier boy, after stealing my roomy, I should put you down near the toilet!" Julie replied cheekily, as she walked away with that award-winning sway, before turning around. "What are you looking at soldier boy? Remember you're getting married!" Julie chastised him, before disappearing down the passageway, leaving the other passengers, chuckling at Steve's embarrassment.

The whole flight continued like this, with the whole crew being in on the act, taking turns in flirting with Steve, both the women and the men. When it finally came time to land, Steve threatened to tell Michelle about Julie's flirting, which made the whole crew laugh. When he'd left, Julie thought maybe she had gone too far, but she had to admit there was something about Steve that made trying fun. Michelle was luckier than she knew Julie thought to herself smiling.

RETURN TO
CAMPBELL BARRACKS, WA

After catching a taxi to Campbell Barracks, Steve went to the Regiments Headquarters. Here he hoped to find out where he'd be billeted. Walking into the office in his new suit, with an extensive collection of luggage he made quite a sight.

"Look someone has come to buy the Regiment!" laughed a Corporal, making the office staff laugh.

"Do you find something funny with the Sergeant's dress Corporal?" the Regiment Sergeant Major roared from the door, freezing every man.

"No Sir," replied the Corporal, sweat running down his face.

"I'll be watching you all more carefully from now on!" the RSM spat out with a vicious smile, which definitely meant trouble. "Sergeant you follow me and leave your bags for the Corporal if you please." The RSM ordered, looking around once more before following Steve out. As they walked along outside as if they were on parade, Steve felt more at home than anywhere.

"Excuse me Sir, but did you say, Sergeant?"

"Yes I did Steve, and you can call me John when the men aren't around, okay,"

"I wasn't sure if my rank overseas stays on here, John," Steve replied, uncomfortable with calling him by his first name.

"You must have done something they liked Sergeant. It didn't have anything to do with the guys who copped it in Malaysia, did it?" John asked softly, as Steve missed a step. "You're going to have to learn to lie better than that Steve!" John chuckled, at how easy Steve slipped up.

"How did you know about that operation?"

"I didn't. The CO's brother-in-law was a Paratrooper in France. His sister met him when he was training here a couple of years ago. He was on the flight. We just didn't buy the story that they were running drugs. Do you know what happened?" John asked softly, knowing he was crossing the line. Steve looked sideways at John before answering. In the end, he decided that if he couldn't trust him, he couldn't trust anyone. He then told him briefly of the mission and how the backup plane had been faulty.

"It was just bad luck," Steve confessed, knowing good men had died and been branded drug runners.

"Thanks, Steve. The information will make the CO and his sister sleep better, but that's as far as it will go." John replied gratefully, looking slightly embarrassed as they continued walking. "Oh, by the way, I hate to agree with the Corporal, but why the suit?"

"In this, I can travel anywhere without being obvious, its part of my cover," Steve replied arriving at his barracks.

"Yes, I suppose your right. It would make you fit in out there. I've been here too long to think of it. Anyway, there's a briefing in one hour at Headquarters. Make sure those stripes are on Sergeant!" John said formally with a slight smile, before marching off. Moments later a sheepish Corporal turned up with his bags.

"Sorry for the trouble before Sergeant, I didn't know."

"It's no problem. I should've known better than to turn up in a suit Corporal. Don't worry I'll fix it up with the RSM. But I need a favour. Do you know how I find out about living off base?"

"Don't worry Sergeant I'll find out for you!" the Corporal replied, happy to help, and hopefully get the RSM off his back.

The meeting started promptly. Steve just made it in, standing at the back and trying to take everything in after being away for so long. The room came to attention, as the CO walked in and told everyone to sit.

"Gentlemen it appears things are hotting up to our North. From now on two battle groups will go on instant readiness with the third in reserve. Any questions?" the CO asked.

"Sir who will be in charge of training the third group, since Lieutenant Baker was transferred?" asked a Captain at the far side to Steve.

"For now Sergeant Roberts will take over training of that group." the CO answered, as grumbling came from several of the men in the room.

"Is there a problem here!" the RSM shouted bringing silence to the room.

"Begging your pardon Sir, but Sergeant Roberts hasn't been here for over a year, and the third group should be led by a man with field experience!" a tall Officer suggested.

"Sergeant Roberts has more battle experience than most men in this room, so that's the end of it, no more questions!" the CO explained heatedly, moving on to another matter. There wasn't a man in that room who didn't glance at Steve, wondering where he'd been.

Several weeks went by, and Steve busied himself with training the third reserve group which numbered about forty men. Of these only eight men at one time be on a mission, the rest were backups in case they got into trouble or to supply logistical support. Regiments usually had strengths of a thousand men, but the Australian Army had been cut back drastically after Vietnam. The SAS was no exception, mustering only about 120 men plus some support staff. These were made up mostly of older unit members, who had earned their positions.

Steve in his spare time, tried to contact Michelle, as well as searching for somewhere for them to live. With Michelle, he'd only had a brief phone conversation. It was better than nothing, but he missed her. With his other task to find a home, he'd finally got lucky. He'd found a three bedroom cabin, down by the ocean, on a secluded road with a great view of the water. It was only a forty minute trip from the city and ten from the base, making it perfect. He'd been out there twice with the agent and had fallen in love with it, so much so that he'd put a deposit on it instantly in the hope of securing a loan.

As he filled in the loan application, Steve knew he had the full amount in his account already. This house he wanted to pay for this himself, so he told the bank he had the deposit but needed to borrow the rest. At first, the manager looked over the application with a bored expression, noting Steve had the money already. He was about to approve it when he noticed that Steve had used Elliot and Fox for a reference.

"You know Owen Elliot do you?" the Manager smiled, thinking Steve was having him on.

"Yes I own a third of the company, I'm a silent partner," Steve explained to a surprised Manager, who quickly ordered Steve a coffee. He then showed him a copy of the Financial Review, a paper published all over Australia. This week it had an article on Owen Elliot. Steve looked at the paper and saw underneath what people at the paper thought the company would be worth in the next year. He was impressed. After being granted the loan plus anything else he wanted, Steve left feeling he'd gained some security for the future. It gave him a lot to think about as he headed out for a quick look at his new home.

The next day at the base, the CO went over the training results for the Regiment over the last month, especially studying the third group.

"Is this true John?"

"Yes Sir, I was rather surprised too." replied the RSM.

"A thirty percent increase in unarmed combat, and a twenty-five percent increase in stealth approach to a target. That's unbelievable!" Paul the CO said in disbelief. "Can the Americans be that much better at training than we are?"

"I don't think so, Sir. I think they used their best instructors to train Roberts in this type of warfare. But I think they had a bloody terrific soldier before they started, they just refined him."

"Well, I'm impressed. I want Roberts to put together a manual for training all our Army units. And I want members of the third group to train with the other groups. That will bring them up to speed straight away!" Paul ordered, sounding pleased. This type of training was just the boost that the Armed Forces needs, Paul thought.

Steve returned to his barracks at about four in the afternoon to find the RSM waiting to give him the news about the training manual.

"I'm not sure I'm up to writing a manual."

"I can help you there. I've helped out on other manuals. For an equal credit, I'll help you write it." John smiled, knowing this was not about money. The only recognition came from having your name on it.

"That's great! When do you want to start?"

"How about, when you move into your new home?" John smiled at Steve's reaction.

"I know being RSM gives you God-like powers but how did you know that?"

"Well God gave me eyes and I've seen you there at the house near the point twice. I'm your neighbour Steve. You have to drive past my house to reach yours."

"How long have you been there?"

"About three years now. My wife Joan actually liked your house better, but Jim the guy who owned it, didn't want to sell it back then. We bought the house down the road instead. Small world isn't it."

"It'll make writing the manual easier!"

"Yes, it certainly will. By the way, the other reason why I came here is that a young lady phoned headquarters looking for you. Said to tell you she's flying in on Friday night for three days. Is it something to do with the house?" John smiled.

"A great deal," Steve answered happily.

The days before Michelle's arrival passed quickly, as Steve madly tried to arrange somewhere for Michelle to stay. Settlement of property usually took up to six weeks in this state, so staying there was not possible. In the end, John had come to the rescue. He managed to get permission from the owner of the home Steve was buying, to use it for a few days. This meant Steve also didn't have to find furniture, as John's friend still hadn't moved his furniture out.

Standing at the airport, Steve tried to be calm as he waited for Michelle to emerge from the arrival gate. All the passengers had already departed and most of the crew, but still no sign of Michelle. Steve started to wonder if there'd been a problem with her arriving on this flight. Worried, he was just about to go to the Qantas counter, when she suddenly appeared, walking with two other flight attendants, before saying goodbye to them and heading over to Steve.

"Miss me?" she asked, her eyes sparkling as she smiled up at him. Without answering he grabbed her firmly, kissing her.

"Well, I suppose that answers that question. Did you manage to find somewhere for me to stay?" She asked smiling.

"Yes, it's a place not far from the base on the ocean, with three bedrooms!" Steve added.

"Sometimes Steve you amaze me," Michelle giggled before they walked out to the car that Steve had borrowed from John.

Driving along Steve couldn't help but steal glances at Michelle, as he headed for the coast. In her crew uniform, she looked absolutely fabulous, giving Steve a great view of her long well-shaped legs.

It was dark by the time they arrived at the cabin. Steve quickly carried Michelle's bags inside, placing them in the second bedroom before showing her around the house.

"It's beautiful Steve; I can't wait to see the view from the deck in the morning. But now if you don't mind, I'll have a quick clean up." she smiled before disappearing into the bathroom. In the meantime, Steve put two steaks on the barbeque and got a prepared salad out of the fridge. Ten minutes later Michelle came walking out wearing a thin long dressing gown over an incredibly small pair of silk pyjamas. The outfit didn't leave much to the imagination, and Steve's was doing overtime. Seeing the direction of Steve's looks, Michelle adjusted her dressing gown a little tighter, which covered her legs more, but emphasised her incredible body beneath it, leaving Steve spellbound.

Turning back to the steaks, Steve managed to concentrate on them enough to stop them burning completely. He then set the meal down on a table on the front deck, accompanied by a bottle of wine. The meal passed quietly with Steve trying not to stare at Michelle's body, while she smiled, loving the way he looked at her. After dinner, they sat on the front porch seat catching up on what had happened in each other's lives while they'd been apart.

The talking quickly turned to kissing, at first slowly then more urgently as their hunger rose. Gasping, Steve looked down to see Michelle's dressing gown gone along with his shorts and shirt. He was about to say something when Michelle put her hands to his lips to silence him.

"I don't want to wait anymore, Steve. No matter what the danger you may face I want to be with you from now on!" Standing up, she walked towards the main bedroom, shedding the rest of her clothing as she did.

It was eight thirty the next morning when Michelle awoke to feel both happy and exhausted from her night with Steve. Turning over she found the bed empty, and a note telling her he'd gone for a run and would be back to make breakfast, next to her pillow.

"Where does he get the strength?" Stretching and throwing back the blankets she decided to see where her man had gone. Walking out on the front deck naked she looked south and realised on this side there was another home. Moving back inside, she found Steve coming out of the second bedroom's shower, dressed only in a towel. Droplets of water were running down his chest, as Steve froze his eyes drawn to Michelle standing in the doorway naked. At first, they both just looked at each other smiling, marvelling at each other's beauty. The spell was broken as Steve came towards her, and there was no hiding that he wanted to make love to her again. Picking her up effortlessly, kissing her, Steve carried her back into the bedroom.

The morning became night, as the two lovers lay exhausted. Agreeing to make an effort the next day to at least go out and see the sights, they both ate some leftovers before falling asleep. As morning broke on their second day, they quietly had breakfast on the front deck. Looking at the waves crashing onto the point, Michelle thought to herself how close this was too perfect.

"God Steve I love this place, I wish we could spend the rest of our lives here, it's so beautiful!"

"Yes, it's beautiful!" His eyes taking in Michelle's outline as she gazed longingly at the view.

"You're doing it again Steve." she giggled.

"How would you like to live here when we're married?"

"Do you think we could afford to rent it?" Michelle replied excitedly, wondering if they could afford it.

"Well, I hope so I bought it two weeks ago. I wasn't sure if you'd mind me going ahead with buying it, without asking you. But it just seemed like fate when it came on the market."

"Oh Steve it's beautiful, but are you sure we can afford it? I mightn't get a job over here for a while!"

Her excitement bubbled to the surface as she took a more serious interest in the furniture and fixtures.

"That's another thing. The furniture belongs to the previous owner, but I've allowed a little money for that and transport, we'll need that when you're here." Not knowing what he had unleashed.

"My god we'll have to go look for furniture immediately. Luckily I've got a fair bit of my own money!" Michelle suggested excitedly. She left Steve to clean up and dress, while she changed and produced a pen and paper. Writing down what she needed, she went room to room, working out what each room required. Steve sensing things were out of his control now, got out of the way, while Michelle whirled around the house like a tornado until a knock on the front door interrupted her.

"Hello, is anyone home? It's the neighbours!" Michelle reluctantly stopped writing to go to the door and meet John and his wife Joan, who'd made a small cake for morning tea. After Michelle told her how Steve had just informed her about buying this house unfurnished, Joan joined her in making notes.

"Better eat quickly Steve, we're going to town!" John laughed before he noticed Steve's uncomprehending look. "You haven't the faintest have you? Take it from a married man; you've made a mistake by not getting furniture. Just pretend interest, and they'll dump us at the pub if we're lucky!" John chuckled at Steve's naivety.

Moments later the women reappeared, herding them out to John's car and headed towards town. As they drove along Joan outlined to Michelle several shops worth looking at once they got there, before John nudged Steve.

"What type of colours are you going with in the lounge Michelle I've always liked brown?" Steve suggested, getting unreadable looks from the girls.

"Why don't you men relax and have a drink while I show Michelle around the stores. It'll be very boring for you two, and you both have been working hard lately." Joan suggested as John gave Steve a knowing look. Pulling up, the men were practically thrown from the car, as the girls drove off.

"Well done Steve, you're learning!" John snorted smiling, as they settled in for a long wait at the pub.

"Do you think I should include Steve in the decisions?" Michelle asked Joan, as they entered the first store, making her laugh.

"Steve's question about colour in the car was made up by John I bet. It was a polite way of getting out of shopping." Joan laughed before continuing. "When you get home tonight I'm sure you'll think of something to stop him worrying!" Joan whispered, making Michelle grin.

"When's the big day?" Joan asked still smiling.

"In about six months, if he's still interested in me buying the furniture," Michelle replied.

"You're kidding aren't you? He's mad about you. It's written all over him!" Joan assured her, as they headed for the cutlery section.

Late that afternoon, the girls picked up two incredibly relaxed men before heading home.

"How'd it go?" Steve asked from the back seat of the car where he and John had been placed.

"We got some amazing deals," Joan answered smiling, which John had warned Steve meant that you really don't want to know.

"That sounds great!" Steve replied smiling which made everyone happy for different reasons.

Getting out of the car Steve saw on the front steps, a message from the base. It informed him that there was a parcel for him, at his post office box. He could pick it up Monday.

Only the Americans knew he had a post box, Steve realised as he squashed the note into his hand.

"Bad news?" John asked softly, seeing Steve's look.

"No, it just means I'm going somewhere, but not until Monday. So I won't worry till then."

"Joan said to come over for dinner tonight around seven. She and your girl have really hit it off!"

"Yeah, that sounds great, I'll see you there," Steve replied as John drove off.

As Michelle went through her shopping list, Steve decided to grab a quick shower. Standing under the warm water, Steve forgot about the message as Michelle entered the bathroom and stripped.

"Is there room in there for two?" She asked seductively, before moving in beside him, causing him to laugh.

"What's so funny?"

"John said if you came into the shower naked I was in for a big bill. But to tell you the truth at this moment I don't care." Steve laughed as Michelle joined in, realising John was more knowing than Joan realised.

Arriving at John's house, Steve found Colonel Stevenson had called in with his wife unexpectedly and were also staying for dinner. John introduced Michelle and Steve, to Elaine and Paul, who seemed glad they'd crashed the party. It turned into a great night after Steve got used to calling his commanding officer Paul, instead of Sir. The girls, of course, had no problems; Elaine even seemed a bit miffed at missing out on their shopping excursion that day.

"It's a big place, there'll be other days!" Joan admitted, giving Elaine a quick rundown on what they'd purchased so far and getting tips on other shops to go to from Elaine. After a great dinner, the men moved out to the front porch house, while the women continued their discussion in the kitchen.

"Thanks for telling John about the Malaysia thing Steve, it helped my sister a lot," Paul said suddenly, upset by the whole affair.

"The truth needed to be told," Steve replied honestly.

"Anyway, I'm glad you did. I ballsed up though, by mentioning you had battle experience." Paul replied, embarrassed by his lack of professionalism.

"While we're on the subject it seems Steve will be leaving again," John revealed, seeing the CO's eyes go wide.

"I thought they said once a year?"

"Well, it is a new year if not twelve months. Must be something important Paul or they wouldn't have contacted me!" Steve answered.

"We'll put you down as helping out with training in Sydney, which should stop any inquiries for a while," John suggested ending the discussion before it soured the night. Talk settled down to local issues and Steve's wife to be.

"She's quite a catch Steve, is she short-sighted or something?" Paul said chuckling.

"It must have been the uniform!" John put in.

"What, you don't think it was my stunning good looks?"

"No!" Both John and Paul yelled at the same time, causing them all to start laughing.

"So what have you shown Michelle while she's been here?" Paul asked innocently, watching Steve hesitate as laughter started again.

"Having a good time boys?" Joan asked suspiciously from the doorway, causing the laughter to subside. The woman took control of the conversation, wanted to know how Michelle and Steve had met. Michelle told of the trip on the plane and Steve giving her a hard time. She also told how he was embarrassed at the airport by being searched by no less than four police officers. This stopped only when a plainclothes officer and some MPs intervened on Steve's behalf by dropping Steve's SAS uniform in front of everyone. This caused laughter from the women, and nervous laughs from the men. They knew this was a breach of security by the Americans.

The women luckily thought it all romantic and moved on asking about their future plans. After spending the rest of the evening talking, Michelle and Steve walked back home.

"That was a wonderful night Steve. I hope we have more of them when I'm here for good." Michelle said, hugging Steve tightly as they walked down the road.

"Yes it was a good time, but it was strange sitting with the CO and calling him Paul."

Arriving at their front door, Steve was suddenly reminded of something. Reaching across he grabbed Michelle and lifted her up into his arms, then awkwardly opened the door and carried her over the threshold and into the house.

"I should have done that the first night!" Steve whispered in Michelle's ear, kicking the door closed he carried her towards the bedroom.

"Do you think you deserve a special reward?" Michelle giggled, as Steve turned off the light.

The next day passed quickly as they both tried to make it last forever. Finally, the time came and] Michelle left hoping to arrange another stopover.

"I'll miss you Mrs Roberts" Steve yelled, grinning, as she walked to her flight.

"And I'll miss you too hubby" she yelled back smiling, making several people turn and look at Steve smiling.

Once she disappeared behind the barrier Steve's smile disappeared, as he headed to his local Post Office. Retrieving the parcel, he quickly drove home, where he cleared off the table and opened it. Examining the contents, he read swiftly through the broad description of the mission and then at the mission timetable.

"Shit!" he said aloud.

He had only two more days to arrive at Karachi International Hotel in Pakistan to meet up with the others. They had been given other assignments and would be there waiting. Leaving the mission details, Steve raced to the phone and quickly dialled the Airport, only to discover that the phone didn't work. Because he was selling the place, Steve figured, the previous owner must have cancelled the line.

"6 pm? It's not that late!" Steve mumbled to himself, as he ran to John's house and banged on the door. John was still up working on the manual and quickly opened the door, as Steve explained the situation.

"Okay Steve, calm down. The phone's on the hallway table, and the phonebook is underneath it. I'll make coffee for us." John said, leaving Steve to make his call.

A male staff member informed him the booking office was closed, as Steve feigning grief, told him it was an emergency, telling him to hold the line. After waiting for several seconds, a female voice asked him what he wanted. Explaining how he needed to get to Pakistan immediately for a funeral of a close family friend, she informed him the only seat available was first class, the following day at 7pm. Taking it and thanking her for her trouble, Steve hung up. Lying was getting easier he told himself, as he joined John for a coffee.

"Everything okay?"

"Yeah it is now," Steve answered telling him he was heading to Pakistan, then over the border into Afghanistan.

"You know there's a major war going on there?"

"I'm sure we'll be in and out John. But just in case, if Michelle rings, say I'm on a training exercise, okay."

"No problem Steve and I'll run you to the Airport tomorrow night if you want."

"That will be great," Steve answered gratefully, before walking home.

At the airport the following night John gave Steve a firm handshake, then got into his car and drove away. He didn't have to say anything; it was in his eyes, 'be careful.'

This trip, like the one before, required no military gear. Nothing but civilian clothing was to be carried, as this was purely a business trip. Even the mission notes had to be destroyed before he left. Settling into his first class seat, the mission kept rolling around in his head. It entailed just walking across a third of Afghanistan and taking out the head of the KGB there, then walking back. Simple he thought, as his stomach churned.

'Anyway, it's Ali's job to plan it, let's see what he's come up with' Steve thought, as he settled down, thinking of his last three days.

KARACHI INTERNATIONAL HOTEL
APRIL 1984

Arriving at the hotel, bathed in sweat from the humidity, Steve headed to his room for a shower, before looking for the others. He had just entered the Hotel, when Aaron intercepted him, crossing the foyer, and pointed to a side door. The door led to a series of meeting rooms for conventions and inside one of these Steve was greeted by the other unit members and by Colonel Dobson.

"You're late Roberts! Luckily you weren't needed! Sit down, and Ali will bring you up to speed" the Colonel barked as if scolding a small child,

Before starting his mission briefing, Ali gave Steve a welcome smile, before gesturing to Cody to check the door. Receiving a nod from Cody he started. Though the mission was as outlined in the parcel, Ali had done a lot of research since then. Steve suspected he'd been in the country a long time.

The mission was to eliminate General Makial Sokolof, head of the KGB and chief intelligence operation officer in Afghanistan.

In other words the head torturer and bad guy in the area. He had been successful in pushing back the rebel groups to the borders, and he wasn't too worried how his units accomplished it. Ali plan was to fly in at low altitude, avoiding radar detection. They'd then parachute in twenty kilometres north of Kabul. They would then approach on foot, along a route Ali had worked out, arriving near the KGB's Headquarters in the Taj Beg Palace, formerly the home of the deposed King. Here they would eliminate their objective, before rendezvousing with a group of Afghan tribesmen who would assist them in getting out of the country.

"Do the tribesmen know what we're doing?" Sukai asked not fully trusting these men.

"No, they don't know the target. But they are being given a large supply of weapons for helping us. These will be delivered when we reach their village safely." Ali answered, happy with the setup.

"Is the Palace well guarded?" Steve asked hating to state the obvious.

"Yes. It's surrounded by at least one hundred soldiers, mostly paratroopers. They are well dug in, with prearranged patrols to avoid the mines that are laid heavily around the palace. Also, the only road in is protected by several armoured vehicles and a couple of tanks." Ali replied smiling, leaving everyone a little taken aback.

"I judge you've got a plan to get inside?" Steve asked.

"Yes I have, but for now that will be my secret." Ali smiled.

"Well, it sounds good to me. Good luck men!" the Colonel exclaimed, before leaving.

"That guy worries me. In the whole time I've been here with him, he hasn't contributed anything in the way of strategies. He's not military that's for sure!" Ali confessed, staring at the door.

"Sounds like everything's arranged without me. I may as well go home!" Steve suggested jokingly.

"I did the planning based on you and Sukai entering the Palace. Let's face it you two are the best at approaching a target" Ali confessed, grinning, as all besides Steve and Sukai broke into laughter.

After going over the mission who knows how many times, Steve headed up for a shower, then met with Ali for dinner.

"The reason for dinner Steve is so we could talk alone about the palace," Ali admitted as they sat down in the hotel restaurant.

It would appear the late King had a mistress in town. To avoid trouble with his people, who are mostly Muslim and a bit touchy about sex outside of marriage, he wanted a way to visit her unseen. To get around this, the King had a secret tunnel built so he could come and go unnoticed. The Americans, who back then had friendly relations with the King, had some army engineer's carry out the work for him.

It was secretly completed while building the sewer system for the palace and the surrounding area at the same time. Luckily it had remained a secret. The only problem was that the King hasn't been at the palace for over ten years, so the condition of the tunnel isn't known."

"Why can't the others know?"

"Our Colonel doesn't want too many knowing, in case we don't make it that far. Someone else in the future could then, try again." Ali answered.

"What do you think of our chances?"

"Pretty good, I've been working on it here for over two weeks. If I didn't think you could do it, I'd have warned you not to come. I've also got a surprise for you that should make a difference on this raid and other missions!" Ali replied smiling. After dinner, they went to Ali's room.

"I'm going to test your ability in the dark Steve. Turn off the lights and see if you can grab me, as I come for you!" Ali laughed from the bedroom. Steve turned the lights off and in the now pitch dark room, he moved carefully to the side wall waiting for Ali. He knew that Ali was not at his best in the dark, so he remained motionless and waited. Several seconds passed as Steve sensed movement, but saw nothing until a tap on his shoulder indicated Ali was right beside him.

"How the hell did you manage to do that?" Turning on the light, Steve saw that Ali was wearing a pair of weird looking glasses.

"They're infrared goggles Steve, and except for a red tinge you can see as good as in daylight!" Ali passed them to Steve and turned off the lights. Steve turned the unit on and at first, had a little trouble adjusting to them. The advantages far outweighed any inconvenience he felt, as silently he moved around the room.

"They're magic!" Steve exclaimed, impressed as he turned on the light switch and was nearly blinded.

"Oh, one thing I forgot to tell you. Never turn them on in daylight." Ali said apologetically. "They're similar to the Starlight scopes the army has used for the last ten years, but a hundred times better, and you don't have to hold it." Steve was impressed.

"Yes, we'll need this if Sukai and I are going in through a tunnel!" Steve admitted.

"We can use them on this mission as long as they don't fall into the enemies hands. The yanks are the only ones who have them, so under no circumstance can we let the Russians get hold of them." Ali warned him, seeing Steve nod his acceptance.

"When do we leave?"

"Tomorrow, now you're here point man!" Ali chuckled, knowing Steve was still disorientated by his flight and lack of sleep.

"That's a bit soon isn't it?"

"Don't worry, tomorrow it will look better!" Ali smiled, as Steve trudged off to his room, for some much-needed sleep.

Waking late the next day, and feeling he had a hangover, Steve quickly showered. Grabbing his gear, he hurried downstairs, hailing a cab. Giving the taxi driver a piece of paper, which outlined where to take him, Steve hung on, hoped he'd get there. Rattling along goat tracks at breakneck speeds, dodging pedestrians and yelling abuse, the taxi driver seemed angry at everyone. Steve sitting mutely prayed that he'd make it.

Arriving at what looked like a disused airstrip, Steve gratefully got out of the cab. Paying the smiling driver, Steve cautiously looked around, as the taxi disappeared. Apparently, he didn't like this spot either. Walking towards the only structure which was a corrugated iron shed, Steve spotted the other members of the unit, loading an old Dakota transport plane with supplies.

"Glad you could make it Steve!" Cody yelled sweating profusely, before throwing a box into the plane doorway, which Aaron then dragged out of sight, inside the plane.

"It's not his fault, I let him sleep in!" Ali answered as he walked out of the hanger with a guy who looked about eighty. The old guy waved to Steve, before limping towards the plane checking its engines.

"Who's the old guy?" Steve asked, fearing the answer.

"He's the pilot, but he's been flying around here for thirty years," Ali answered smiling, as he moved back into the hanger, Steve following. "Leave everything you brought with you here, including your underwear. Nothing goes on the plane, except what we purchase here!" Ali ordered. Steve looked at the hanger, seeing large quantities of munitions and weapons, as well as a pile of Russian uniforms neatly pressed. "Grab what you need Steve for personal use, but you'll have to put together your own killer suit. There are some hessian bags at the rear of the hanger; you can make it on the plane." Ali suggested as Steve gathered up what he'd need.

Tearing pieces of hessian and sewing them roughly onto his camouflaged gear, Steve realised his biggest problem would be adding colours. Sitting on the plane occasionally looking out the window, Steve knew he couldn't add colour until he saw the country he'd be travelling through. The flight so far had been without incident after a pretty smooth takeoff. The old guy really knew his stuff Steve thought as he continued to work on his outfit.

"Could be a waste of time anyway, since we're travelling mostly at night," Sukai admitted, watching Steve work.

"How long have you been here?"

"About a week, Ali was here already. Cody and Aaron arrived after me, after going to Singapore to organise the weapons and ammo." Sukai smiled, remembering the night at the warehouse.

"No problems with Lou?"

"No, Aaron said he couldn't do enough for them!" Sukai replied as Steve laughed.

A change in the engines rhythm signalled their approach to a landing site. Here they would top up their fuel tanks, before crossing the border into Afghanistan that night. They would also meet with the chieftain of the tribe that would escort them out to safety, after the raid. The landing field turned out to be a straight stretch of dirt road, and even though Steve had his misgivings, the old guy landed without a problem.

When the door was opened, and their reception party came into view, Steve wasn't the only one to reach for his weapon. They were the roughest, ugliest bunch of men he'd ever seen. Four years of fighting and running had reduced these tough people to a pitiful existence, and most showed some injury from the fighting. From an ugly scare to a missing limb, they all had a reminder of the Russian invasion. Ali, unarmed, walked forward into the ring of tribesmen and laid a blanket on the ground. Without a care in the world, he sat down waiting to see the reaction from these hostile looking people.

"I admire your courage Arab!" a bearded tribesman laughed, coming forward and sitting opposite Ali.

"It's been done like this for hundreds of years in my country, I was hoping the Afghans still respected it," Ali answered formally.

"Even in war, being welcomed at a man's table is still honoured, Arab. Only my son and I speak English so I will talk, while my son Omar translates for the others," the tribesman replied, impressed with Ali's greeting.

"My name is hard to pronounce, so you and your men can call me Abdul, it is a name of respect." The tribe's chieftain smiled, as Omar translated.

While this formal introduction ceremony was going on, Steve and the others spread out, giving themselves open fields of fire. Steve on the far left noticed he was getting some very unfriendly looks from a very large man with bad teeth. The giant for some unknown reason came forward towards Steve, making a move to slap him. Not wanting to shoot the man, Steve instead put the butt of his weapon into the man's gut winding him. The giant then started yelling at the chief and produced a knife. After much yelling between the tribesman and the chief, Omar the son translated it into English.

"He says you look like a Russian and he doesn't trust you," Omar explained with a slight smile.

"Well that's his bad luck, I can't help my looks," Steve answered, not taking his eyes off the giant. Omar translated what Steve said, which caused a bigger commotion making him wonder about its accuracy. Several minutes passed as a private debate went on between Ali and the chief until they both rose and Ali came over.

"Slight problem Steve, it appears the big ugly is trying to get the tribe to follow him. This is his way of embarrassing the chief. So the chief can't help us unless you put the gorilla in his place." Ali told him with a slight smirk on his face.

"So, I got to fight that ape!" Steve answered, watching the 'would be' chief.

"Yeah, that's about it. Oh, and they use knives here!"

"Any good news?"

"Yeah no matter what happens, after the fight they'll help us." Ali smiled, as Steve stood there thinking.

"Just one thing," Steve asked dropping all his weapons except his combat knife. "If he kills me, have one of the others do him in!" Steve whispered, getting a nod from Ali.

The big tribesman circled Steve, grinning confidently. Using his size and reach of his arms, he kept Steve on the defensive, as his fellow tribesman yelled encouragement. Watching his opponents every move, time slowed down for Steve as he concentrated on his enemy's movement looking for a weakness. The guy, unfortunately, was an experienced knife fighter, but he had only one fault, overconfidence. He thought the westerner would be easy meat. Smiling and jabbing at Steve's face with his long curved knife, the tribesman forgot caution and rushed in.

He hoped to finish Steve off quickly and impress his fellow tribesman, which was the break Steve had been waiting for. As the tribesman lunged confidently forward, all he hit was air. Grounding to a halt, he gasped for breath, as a sharp stabbing pain started in his chest. He collapsed face first into the dry sand. Rolling over and looking up, the tribesman saw the westerner's knife hovering above his left eye and knew his life was over. The realisation of his failure hit him hard, making him inadvertently sob, at which point the westerner walked away sheafing his knife.

Abdul sat dumbfounded; he couldn't believe his eyes. When Belut had rushed in, Abdul had thought it was all over for the soldier named Steve. He knew he could then accuse Belut of stopping the tribe from getting the weapons from the westerners, which would have shamed him. To everyone's disbelief, Belut himself had been hit viciously with the butt of his opponent's knife, paralysing him, leaving him defenceless on the ground.

"Why doesn't he finish him?" Abdul asked Ali, who hadn't even blinked during the fight.

"Steve, the Chief wants to know why you didn't kill big ugly!" Ali yelled grinning. He knew Steve hadn't been in any real danger, being an expert with a knife.

"I'm here to fight the Russians, not the Afghan people!" Steve yelled back, short of breath, as Omar translated again, embellishing the story slightly. As one, the tribesmen rushed forward, raising Steve above their heads, cheering wildly. Word spread of what Steve had said, plus that he had Afghan grandparents. After the noise had died down, Steve walked over and extended his hand to Belut, who in shame hadn't risen from the ground, causing all present to stand in silence watching what was happening.

"Omar tell this man we need everyone to fight the Russians. Tell him we'll need him out there to meet us when we return from Kabul!" Steve told him, which up until now had been a secret. Omar excitedly translated the news that these men were about to attack Kabul, a place no one had dared go for nearly three years. The tribesmen at first were silent thinking that the westerner was just giving a speech, to get Belut up on his feet.

Abdul then informed them that it was the truth, as they all fell to their knees and prayed. Taking Steve's hand, Belut came to his feet and hugged him, saying something at the same time.

"He says that his name is Belut and that you are his brother. He promises that he will never let you down." Omar translated tears in his eyes at Belut's emotional commitment.

"You only told them the target city, not the actual target," Ali asked a little upset.

"If we can't trust them to guide us back, what's the point?" Steve answered, getting nods of agreement from the other team members.

"I may as well give them their presents!" Cody suggested, going to the plane and grabbing a box pulling it out and laying it on the ground. Coming forward, Abdul reached into the box and pulled out a brand new AK47. It was the weapon of choice of their enemy and a fine assault rifle.

Raising it above his head showing the tribesmen, he let out a battle cry, which was taken up by the whole tribe.

"Hey Steve give your knife buddy this, he's big enough to carry it!" Cody yelled, pushing a long thin crate out of the plane. Waving Belut and Omar over, Steve explained the purpose of this weapon and how to use it, which he had only just learned. Abdul, seeing Omar and Belut smiling excitedly came over, looking at the long tube weapon.

"What is it for? I have never seen anything like it. What can it kill?" Abdul asked puzzled.

"Anything that can fly Abdul and I mean anything!" Steve answered cheerfully.

The tribesmen after receiving some brief training on the use of their new weapons swiftly moved towards the border. Every minute counted to these tribesmen, who started their journey into Afghanistan, not knowing what dangers they would encounter. With luck, they would meet them at the halfway point between here and Kabul if any of them made it at all. Just before takeoff, the old pilot wished them luck, before downing several swigs of what he called cough syrup.

The unit all sat watching him, as he swayed forward into the cockpit. Despite his drinking, he took off expertly, much to everyone's relief.

"He's a crazy old bastard isn't he?" Cody laughed, as the unit sat watching their pilot, as he continued to drink.

"He'll get us there don't worry, I just hope he took his heart medicine!" Ali said seriously, as the others, silently took in this information. "I'm only joking!" Ali grinned. The returned looks told him his joke hadn't been well received.

Skimming through the mountain valleys, barely clearing the cliffs at the ends, the whole unit sat quietly, knowing if they hit one, they'd never know it. The old pilot's skill was extraordinary, Steve had a feeling that this wasn't the first time he'd flown people through this area. A green light flashing near the rear cabin warned them to get ready, as Cody pulled open the cabin's rear exit door in preparation. The light changing from green to red meant to jump, and as one the team members rushed out of the door, into the freezing air.

Descending into the pitch-black night, Steve realised that the only light visible came from Kabul to the south. Falling at over 160kph and not being able to see the ground, Steve tried to gauge the right height to pull his chute. Ali, in the end, yelled out, and released his, alerting the others to do the same. The ground to the north of Kabul was the most secure sector the Russian's had. It was also a barren rocky desert area, devoid of life. This is why Ali picked it as their drop zone.

It was also the only part of his plan that was left in God's hands. Ali knew that casualties here when landing, even a sprained ankle, could be fatal to the whole mission. Praying silently, he quietly waited until everyone had landed safely, before breathing a sigh of relief. Quickly hiding their parachutes, the unit removed their coveralls, revealing their Russian paratrooper's uniforms. After checking their gear, they started their approach to Kabul, silently moving through the pitch dark countryside.

An uneventful night walking and dawn fast approaching, the unit members, looked for a position to hole up in, until the following night. Reaching the crest of a ridge, Steve caught a glimpse of the city below. Finding an old abandoned structure, which at one stage must have been an army observation post, the unit set up camp. This gave them a good view of the valley below, and the main road going north to south, which seemed unusually busy. Ali and Steve watched puzzled, at the sheer volume of military equipment streaming down the road, heading south past Kabul.

"Do you think it's a deployment of some kind?" Steve whispered, studying the units rolling by.

"This isn't just a deployment Steve, its way too big. I'd say it's an attack along the Pakistani border!" Ali answered softly, sounding worried.

"Isn't that the direction we've got to go after our mission?" Steve asked.

"For a short time, but then we're going more south-east. Still, we've got to cross the border, and that's where they're heading." Ali replied wondering if the mission should be scrapped.

"Well there's so many of them, they won't notice a few more troops will they?" Steve replied jokingly, as Ali's smiled, a plan coming to mind.

The following night was black again, but with the infrared goggles, the team moved swiftly through the red-tinged countryside. Reaching the highway and trying to avoid being seen, they climbed under the road through a drainage pipe. Cody had discovered it a little south of their route while scouting, making their crossing easy. Approaching the city, the lights of the Kabul grew brighter forcing the group to drop the use of the goggles. Entering the city, they began crossing it, by using numerous alleyways and open trenched sewers that crisscrossed the city.

Stopping continually to get their bearings, and backtracking when it was needed, they, at last, reached the base of the Taj-Beg Palace. It was an impressive defensive position, though Ali had brought the back door key, the secret passageway. Steve for the first time, started to become optimistic that they might yet pull it off, as he led them closer.

Following another open sewage trench, they arrived at an old pumping station. This station controlled the underground sewer system for the richer part of the city, including the Palace. The stench here was overpowering, but it did mean no one came near the area. Going inside Ali soon located the hidden entrance. It was hidden behind some rusted old machinery, purposely discarded to hide the doorway.

"It's up to you and Sukai now!" Ali whispered to Steve, wishing them good luck, as he moved off with Cody and Aaron to await their return. Steve climbed into the tunnel, putting on his night goggles, followed by Sukai. Despite its age, the tunnel was in good condition and could easily have accommodated them both walking next to each other. Hurrying silently along the tunnel, climbing uphill at a leisurely rate, they made good time. Only once was their path blocked by a cave in, which they'd cleared after several minutes of digging.

They'd been travelling for well over an hour, when muffled voices could be heard coming from up ahead, where the tunnel came to an abrupt end. Moving forward carefully, Steve examined the end wall finding it to be a steel door. In it was a peephole, Steve carefully opened it, to see what was going on in. The room he looked into was large in size and gathered there was a large group of Military Officers, attending some type of briefing. Moving back Steve let Sukai take his place, as he knew a spattering of Russian and might get an idea of what was going on.

Twenty minutes of standing there watching and listening passed by, before Sukai signalled Steve to move back down the tunnel. Sitting down, Sukai indicated for Steve to do the same, as he explained what he'd heard.

"They're planning to cross the border into Pakistan and hit the rebel camps there. They then plan to retreat back across the border, saying to Pakistan that it was a provoked response from the rebel raids into Afghanistan." Sukai explained quietly.

"It could work too, it's not like the Pakistanis are going to declare war or anything."

"The briefings nearly finished, so they should move out soon," Sukai whispered, as they settled down to wait. Twenty minutes passed before the movement of chairs and the sharp increase in talking confirmed the meeting was indeed breaking up. Steve and Sukai quietly moved back to the door.

Waiting ten minutes, after the last man in the room had left Steve tried to open the door. Although the lock appeared to work, the door didn't budge. Both putting their shoulders to it, brought the noise of things dropping, as the door opened into the room. The problem was that someone had placed a bookcase in front of the concealed door.

When Steve had a look through the peephole, he'd been looking through the gap in the books between shelves. Not knowing this, when they had opened the door the bookcase toppled over. Both entered the room quickly, closing the concealed door without locking it, and putting the bookshelf back in place, before restacking it. The noise of the doorknob twisting as someone outside tried the door, alerted them that someone had heard. This was followed by voices before footsteps could be heard moving off.

"We're in trouble, Steve!" Sukai whispered nervously, before continuing. "They must have left two guards outside. One just asked was anyone still in here, before the other went to get an Officer with the key!" Reaching for their pistols, they quickly fitted their silencers, before Steve outlined his plan.

The Duty Officer was none too happy about being awoken from his sleep, as he followed the guards to the conference room.

"Are you sure everyone had left?" the Officer grumbled angrily at guards who stood outside the door.

"Yes Sir, I saw the KGB Officer lock it himself!" the guard replied neutrally

"Very well then private, but you'd better be right!" the Officer threatened, knowing there was no other entrance to the room, and he would have to write a report about opening the conference room without permission. As the Officer and the two soldiers entered the room, the first thing they all saw was Sukai dress as a Russian paratrooper, putting slides up on the projector screen. Turning around at the noise Sukai pretended surprise.

"What are you doing in here Captain, this information is Top Secret!" Sukai barked in his best Russian.

"I'm sorry for the disturbance" was all the Officer got out when he stopped abruptly. The paratrooper had called him Captain, he was a Lieutenant, and any Russian soldier would know that.

"Arrest him!" the Officer managed to say before he and the two soldiers were shot by Steve from behind the now open door. For twenty seconds after the shooting Sukai and Steve stood frozen, weapons pointed at the doorway waiting for a response from outside, nothing happened. Taking several deep breaths, Steve looked at Sukai smiling amazed they'd gotten away with it. Brushing their uniforms as best they could, they prepared to leave, to find their target.

THE TARGET

Closing the doors to the conference room behind them, they proceeded cautiously down the corridor to where the King's bedrooms used to be. Except for a few Afghani servants who didn't give them a second look, they encountered no other soldiers, until they reached the King's sleeping quarters. Here two KGB guards called for them to state their business, as they walked casually towards them. "Chug, Chug" was all that was heard, as Sukai and Steve opened fired on the two guards taking them completely by surprise. Dragging their bodies into a hallway closet and hoping the stains on the carpet wouldn't be noticed, they continued on to the main bedroom, where it was understood that their target slept.

Opening the door silently, they both slipped into the room where the voices of a group of men could be heard coming from an adjoining room. Slowly they separated coming into the room about three metres apart, through a wide-open doorway. Before the group could react, they both opened fire, spraying the men with well-aimed shots. It was over in seconds. Except for the thuds of bodies hitting the ground and several glasses breaking, the only noise was the distant bark of a dog outside. After waiting several seconds for a response, Steve advanced and checked the bodies, seeing if Sokolof was amongst the dead, as Sukai watched the door.

He'd turned over two of the four before he found Sokolof and was just about to leave when he saw the face of the fourth man. Steve stared at him for several seconds, before walking towards the door, apprehension showing on his face

"What's wrong Steve?" Sukai whispered, looking back in the room for the source of Steve's anxiety.

"One of the other guys we shot in there I recognise him." Steve softly replied, his voice sounding unsure, as he watched the corridor before continuing. "It's the Russian Defence Minister!" Steve quietly told Sukai, watching his eyes grow wide with surprise.

"Holy shit, what was he doing here?" Sukai asked loudly, as Steve shrugged his shoulders and signalled him to be quiet, as they left the room, locking the door behind them. Hurrying down the corridor, Steve had just turned the corner near the checkpoint had been, when he collided with a young Officer no more than seventeen.

"Sorry I didn't see you." the young Officer smiled, before spotting the silencer on Steve's gun. He was just about to yell, when Sukai's gun came down on the back of his head, knocking him to the ground. Sukai took aim at the young man's head when Steve stopped him.

"There's been too much killing already," Steve whispered as they hurried to the conference room. Locking the door behind them, they went to their backpacks, taking out two blocks of C4. Sukai took the C4, and laid a booby trap on the inside of the door, while Steve gathered up what documents and maps he could find.

Having achieved their objectives, Steve and Sukai entered the secret passage, slamming the door behind them. As an afterthought, they smashed the doors opening device, on the tunnel side. This they hoped, would effectively lock the door to the tunnel, as they put on their goggles, and started running.

Thirty minutes later they both exploded out of the tunnel, startling the others.

"What the fucks going on Steve? We nearly shot you!" Ali said softly, surprised by Steve's lack of caution.

"There's no time to talk, we've got to get away from here!" Steve answered. Ali told the others to load up, knowing something had gone wrong.

Having come into the city from the north, they continued to head south following the main streets of Kabul. Pretending to be one of the many Russian patrols as Steve had suggested to Ali the day before, they walked in the open, making good progress. As they passed a group of empty Russian vehicles, Ali motioned to Cody to hotwire one.

"If we're going to act like their soldiers we may as well drive!"

"And it's also quicker!" Steve added as Ali raised his hand to stop.

"What's wrong Steve? Did you get Sokolof or not?" Ali wanted to know what was bugging Steve.

"Yeah we got him alright, but he wasn't alone. We had to shoot three other men who were with him. One of them was the Russian Defence Minister!" Steve watched Ali's and the others freeze in reaction to his news.

Cody drove south, his eyes glued to the rear vision mirror. Just above the local speed limit, they made good progress through the deserted streets and were even waved through several checkpoints along the way, returning the gesture with a good-natured smile. Coming to the entry and exit checkpoint, on the south side of the city, they thought their luck had run out. The vehicles in front of them slowly ground to a stop at the checkpoint. Everyone's papers were being checked. With no papers, the unit members moved their weapons casually to the ready, expecting the worst. The checkpoint guards slowly made their way down the line, searching the trucks in front of them, as a muffled explosion sounded from the city behind them.

A shroud of silence settled over the checkpoint guards as they stopped searching. Several looked back towards where the palace stood. A nervous guard at the front of the queue quickly waved through the five military trucks in front of them. The other guards, seeing the trucks moving, and thinking that Ali's group was their escort, signalled for them to move as well. Waving to the checkpoint guards, the unit members breathed a sigh of relief, as they cleared the city. They then joined the long line of vehicles heading south along the highway to the border.

Waving to passing soldiers, and secretively checking their maps, for the turn-off, they drove along in the never-ending convoy, praying. It was a cold night, as Steve sat in the jeep sweating, as he stared at the line of armoured troop carriers in front of them and the tanks behind. 'Where's that bloody turn off' Steve asked himself, as he waited for this friendly military convoy to become a vengeful enemy. Twenty kilometres, further along, they spotted it. Pulling to the side of the road, they pretended to be guarding the road junction, to allay suspicion of the passing troops.

When a break in the traffic occurred, they swiftly loaded up, driving up the side road, away from the main highway. Driving for another two hours, when Ali instructed Cody to pull over so he could recheck the map. This allowed everyone to stretch their legs. As Cody turned off the engine and lights, Ali pulled a blanket over his head to check the map by torchlight.

An eerie silence descended on the group as they stood or sat silently, the quiet broken by the distant thud of helicopters.

"The jeeps about half empty, I think it wise that we go as far as possible in it, as time is against us. We'll cover the distance to our rendezvous with the tribe in less time, cutting maybe three days off walking. That gives us a choice then, of being able to hide and wait, instead of walking every night. Is everyone okay with that?" Ali asked, knowing there was a danger of being spotted in a vehicle, though speed at the moment was more important. Nodding their silent agreement, they started immediately.

Four hours and with the sun coming up over the mountains, they abandoned the vehicle, rolling it into a deep ravine. Hoping it wouldn't be spotted, they swiftly walked up into the mountains, to conceal themselves until the next night.

TAJ BEG PALACE

Twenty bodies lay on the parade ground below the palace. Twelve servants, six guards and two KGB Captains, all had been on duty that night. Each had been shot in the back of the head. The soldiers had been shot for dereliction of duty, the servants for knowing too much. General Ogarkov paced back and forwards across the destroyed conference room, while a team of specialist, combed the mess for clues.

"Have you found anything comrades?" the General demanded. Most kept their heads down.

"Several things General!" One brave Sergeant replied.

"Out with it!"

"It would appear that even though there has been a lot of damage, some of the secret maps and documents have been removed." The Sergeant informed him.

"What type of explosive was used?" The General liked this soldier for having the guts to speak up.

"Probably C4 Sir, though I didn't think the tribesmen used sophisticated explosives." The Sergeant was puzzled.

"They don't, but the Americans do." A voice said from the door, as Sergio Andropov entered the room.

"I told you to stay in bed Sergio!" The General reminded him, as Sergio slowly walked into the room taking in the damage. Sergio was the Defence Minister's son, and his uncle was Yuri Andropov the Chairman of the Soviet Union. The Chairman was mad as hell that his brother had been killed in a supposedly secure location. Sergio had just passed his exams as a Cadet Officer and as a reward had come with his father to oversee the border incursion of Pakistan. When hurrying back from a trip to the city, he'd run into the paratrooper with the silencer and had been knocked unconscious.

"Have you found how they got in yet general?" Sergio asked.

"I was told the door was the only entry!" the General grumbled.

"After I regained consciousness, the guards reported finding no soldiers guarding the conference room door, but it was locked. A soldier with a key went and tried the door, reporting that the key was on the inside. I told them to kick it in. It was moments later that the explosion occurred. So the enemy soldiers are either dead in here, or there's another way in!" Sergio explained, getting a nod of approval from the Sergeant.

"There's something like a safe over there behind the furniture Sir. We weren't going to worry about it till later, as we were told they came in through the main door." The Sergeant was sticking up for his men.

"Rip that open and find out where it goes!" the General commanded. Two men with crowbars swiftly pried open the door. Once open, four heavily armed soldiers with torches, rushed into the passageway.

"Good work Sergio, do you remember anything else?" the General asked seeing that the men looked at Sergio with respect, for finding the tunnel.

"I'm sure the paratrooper who hit me was European, and his companion was Asian, most probably Japanese. They both spoke English because when the Asian hit me, the other said. 'No there's been enough killing', that's all I remember." Sergio answered softly.

"You're a lucky man Sergio, that soldier should have killed you, to cover his tracks." the General smiled coldly. He would have.

"General if I might have a moment." interrupted the Sergeant, waiting for a nod to continue. "This was too well planned to be the Afghan's Sir. I believe this raid was about targeting personnel here, maybe General Sokolof. Because of where the tunnel came out, they stumbled onto the operation and killed the Defence Minister by mistake!"

"How long have you been in the Investigation Section?" The General asked the Sergeant.

"About five year's Sir." the Sergeant replied suspiciously.

"Well both you and Sergio are now Captains. You two are going to find these bastards for me understand. No matter how long it takes!" The General ordered. Seeing everything here was under control, the General with his two new captains returned to his Headquarters.

RUNNING

Over 200kms to the south, the sun was going down, as Ali and Steve went over the mission and the route they would take tonight.

"I've got to admit Steve when they send you to do a job, you don't let anything like a nuclear war get in the way." Ali chuckled.

"I'm glad you can smile about it Ali, I've never been so scared in my life. I can't believe we shot an innocent bystander."

"He was no innocent Steve, he was overseeing the operation. Which I'd say will be put on hold now that they think the Pakistanis may have knowledge of the targets of the raid. Remember, they don't know, that we don't have a radio do they?" Ali smiled. Steve realised they'd saved thousands of Afghani lives along the border, by this mission. Their conversation was cut short, by the vibration of a large helicopter that could be heard coming along the valley even before they saw it. The chopper cruised effortlessly along, searching the ground below, only to be followed by another, and then a third, as the search for the men who raided Kabul got into full swing.

Using their goggles to move at night, the unit made good time even though the countryside was rugged and would only get worse the closer they got to the border. Stopping for one of their rare breaks, everyone took off their goggles, as all eyes watched the flares dropping several kilometres to the west and north of their position.

"They must know we turned off to the south-east but not how far, by the way, they're behind us and towards the southern highway!" Ali murmured softly, watching the flares. "Make sure no one looks directly at them with your goggles on. We can't afford anyone going blind even if it is temporary" Ali cautioned.

Steve checked their direction on the map by putting his killer suit over his head and using a small torch and a compass and then checking it against the route they had planned back in the cavern. Moving silently forward Steve had found the easiest way of travelling at night was to follow the terrain. Tonight they had crossed into another valley through a ravine. They were now travelling roughly south, and so as long as they stayed in it, they wouldn't get lost, something that was easy to do in the dark.

It was a long hard slog with few breaks. Even so, no one wanted to stop, knowing the danger which every hour grew closer. When darkness started to turn to pre-dawn, the unit spread out to find a spot to hole up for the day. By luck more than anything, Cody found a small cave. It opened into a box canyon, giving them perfect cover and something they hadn't counted on, water. They all carried enough for three days in their canteens. In this hostile, roughed country, water was life.

Refilling their canteens, they quickly stripped and while Sukai kept guard, they all washed, they then ate, before finding a shaded spot to sleep. Taking his turn on watch, Steve settled down for his shift at the entrance of the cave, wearing his killer suit for protection.

A movement to the south of the valley caught his eye. Using his binoculars; he caught sight of a helicopter landing and dropping off a patrol of Russian soldiers in heavily camouflaged uniforms, as well as two other soldiers who to Steve looked to be Afghans. They probably knew the area, and it dawned on Steve that not all Afghans were against the Russians. As quickly as it had landed, the chopper roared back into the sky, as the patrol moved to the south and away from the cave. This was both good and bad Steve thought. If they had landed further north, they would surely have spotted the units footprints in the sandy areas, which dotted this valley. That was his good news.

The bad news was they were now ahead of them, which meant they were either moving south looking for them or waiting somewhere to block off this valley. Either way, they had a problem. Waking Ali and the others as the sun started to dip behind the hills; Steve explained the situation of the enemy patrol, as they made dinner and prepared to leave.

"We could take them out!" Aaron whispered as the others thought of options.

"They'd be in radio contact with their base. Even if we got them all, they would know we were here, when they didn't report in." Ali replied, having already considered it.

"We could stay here another day, we have plenty of time to reach the rendezvous point, and more importantly we have water," Cody suggested as he cleaned his weapon.

"We could, but that patrol could come back this way and box us in here," Ali answered.

"I think another option is for me to go ahead and scout for the Russians, while you guys follow at a safe distance. That way we've got less chance of being seen. Then we can easily turn back if we can't get past." Steve explained, knowing he was the best to try it.

"Okay we'll give it a try; once it's dark, we'll give Steve an hour start, and then follow in the same direction," Ali stated, as the others packed up their remaining gear and buried their rubbish in a hole.

At General Ogarkov's Headquarters, the General and his Staff Officers studied the map of Southern Afghanistan that covered an entire wall off the room, trying to locate the enemy soldiers. All that day helicopters had dropped patrols over a wide area trying to pick up any sign of these men, but so far nothing. Looking out the window, Sergio could see the light starting to fade, knowing the men who killed his father would now move further away under cover of darkness.

"General we have something!" A young soldier shouted from the communications room.

"What is it, soldier?"

"A patrol to the east of our search area has found an abandoned vehicle fitting the description of one stolen from Kabul last night," the Soldier replied, putting the position up on the wall map for all to see. At least ten more soldiers faced the firing squad for letting the vehicle through checkpoints without stopping them.

Fear was a great incentive to get men to work hard the General knew, as he looked around the room at his staff.

"Move all the search teams south of that position immediately. Are there any patrols in that area?" the General ordered his Senior Staff Officer who quickly went to the radio to issue orders.

"General we have one patrol to the south of that position covering the exit from a valley running due south about twenty kilometres from there," a Colonel replied, from a table used for coordinating troop positioning.

"Good! Tell them to stay there, while we drop patrols in every valley in a hundred kilometre radius from that abandoned vehicle, mostly to the south." the General commanded.

Steve was just getting started down the valley when the first of ten helicopters flew over, some heading north others south, and there were flares to the north maybe fifteen kilometres directly behind them.

"They must have found the jeep!" Ali whispered, watching for movement.

"Yeah, it's no good hiding here. They'll drop patrols all over, trying to block our escape routes and hope to get a sighting." Steve softly replied as the others came up.

"We've got to get out of this valley as fast as possible!" Ali said as he scanned the surrounding area.

With a nod of agreement, Steve fitted his goggles and headed south, followed closely by the others. They had covered about two kilometres when Steve signalled the others, to slow down, as he moved forward more carefully. The valley here formed a pass, the width narrowing no more than a few hundred metres from each side. 'This is where I'd be if I were them' Steve thought to himself as he silently glided forward placing each footstep with extreme care to minimise noise, as the others followed slowly behind him.

Captain Demetrie was not happy as he lay in the pass, not more than a hundred metres from where Steve stood. His men were positioned across the valley and were well camouflaged facing north down the valley. They were here in case the enemy soldiers who attacked Kabul, came south down the valley. What they had attacked in Kabul, no one knew for sure. The only thing he knew was someone wanted them badly. The Captain also had another problem. His two Afghani scouts had gone south to patrol, several hours ago and hadn't returned.

He was just about to radio for help, when the two scouts rushed out of the darkness, babbling in their own language, which Demetrie didn't understand.

"Sergeant Popov what are they saying?" the Captain asked angrily. The Sergeant was the only member of the patrol, who could speak their language.

"They say a large group of rebels maybe thirty or more are headed this way from the south!" the Sergeant replied, excited at seeing his first combat.

"Bring the men in closer to the centre Sergeant, we'll need to concentrate our fire." the Captain ordered. As his men came in and started digging new positions facing south. Demetrie in the meantime radioed for air support.

Steve was not more than twenty paces away when two soldiers rose from the ground in front of him. After they had a quick conversation, they packed up and headed for the middle of the valley. Steve waved Ali forward, telling him what had happened.

"I don't know what's going on, but keep leading us forward Steve." Steve nodded moving forward, hugging the side of the valley. Slowly they continued on for an hour, entering another wide valley, thankful for the miracle that had let them through the trap. Steve was the first to hear movement coming from up ahead and out in the middle of the valley. Quickly moving back to the others, Steve signalled for all of them to hit the dirt, as a large group of men passed them.

With hardly any discipline, the group shuffled along, some even talking. Steve stared in amazement wondering who they were. Once the group had passed, Ali signalled to Steve to get going, as quickly as he could. He was hoping to be away before the mysterious group met the Russian patrol.

Practically running, they covered about three kilometres, when the sounds of automatic fire echoed all around them. This was followed by the unmistakable sound of helicopters as the unit went to ground. Looking back down the valley, Steve could see where flares marked the Russian position, as the choppers came in for the kill. The choppers hammered the area south of the flares, giving the Russian troops on the ground much needed support, as the troops in their prepared positions fired into the surprised tribesmen.

Knowing the place soon would be crawling with enemy patrols Steve led the unit away from the battle as quickly as possible while hugging the valley wall. This gave them some protection from the circling choppers to the north. Two hours of crawling slowly forward forced Ali to abandon the plan of following this valley. Instead, he told Steve to cross over into a valley to the west. This valley ran in a southwest direction into a mountainous area and slightly away from their rendezvous.

Wasting no time, Steve quickly checked his map and signalled the unit to follow him as they climbed up a steep ravine. At some stages of the ascent, Aaron, who had experience in climbing, was called upon to go ahead and throw down a rope for the others to climb up. This slowed them down to a crawl, as they desperately climbed, trying to clear the area. With the fast approaching dawn, the unit had stopped climbing to find shelter in the ravine. This forced Steve, the only one with a killer suit to be the tail end Charlie, keeping watch back down the ravine, while the others hid in whatever cover they could find.

Back at the pass Captain Demetrie checked over the enemy dead wondering if losing Sergeant Popov and two other men of his ten man patrol had been worth it. Thirty-four dead enemy soldiers lay in the pass, and several blood trails indicated that a few had got away. As the sun rose overhead, Demetrie watched as helicopters and two fresh patrols swept the valley, trying to find the enemy survivors. A deep thumping noise from the north announced the approach of large infantry transport chopper. Swooping down into the pass, it landed in a cloud of dust near Demetrie. Several men jumped out and headed across towards him. As they got closer, the Captain recognised General Ogarkov. Demetrie, along with his men, came to attention.

"Relax Captain you and your men have done a fine job!" The General smiled, before heading off to the bodies. "See if they're here Sergio!" He yelled to a young Officer with him, as Demetrie's men protected them. After checking every enemy soldier carefully, the young Officer walked back to the General.

"They're not here Sir, neither one of them!"

"Never mind they can't be far, even if this isn't their group, they've got to be around here somewhere!" the General answered, as he scanned the hills.

"General!" a soldier shouted, running from the helicopter towards the general before continuing. "They've caught the others Sir!" the Soldier exclaimed before the General, and his men ran to the chopper and departed. This left Captain Demetrie standing there wondering what the hell was going on.

Steve, several kilometres away, watched as the last two tribesmen were chased down by the pursuing soldiers as each one fought to the last. Hearing the approach of a helicopter, Steve remained frozen in the shadows as the chopper passed nearly directly overhead as it dived down into the valley below. Looking through his binoculars, Steve saw what looked like a General and a young Officer walk over to the bodies before the young Officer checked them. Steve stared closely at the young man, there was no doubt in his mind it was the one they'd knocked unconscious.

"Shit, they know it's not us now, maybe I should have let Sukai kill him!" Steve raged to himself, as he continued to watch.

In the pass, another group of Russian soldiers had landed. These were replacements for Captain Demetrie's patrol. It also included a sniffer dog. After the raid at the palace, several dogs had been allowed to sniff around at the pump station, and one had successfully followed the scent to where the jeep had been stolen. That dog had been brought here. After going back and forwards across the pass, the dog had picked up the scent leading north. The scent going in the southern direction had been wiped out by explosives and the smell of blood. Following it for several hours, the patrol found the cave the unit had slept in the night before. Returning to his headquarters, General Ogarkov sat at his desk with his staff pondering that question.

"They could have backtracked and climbed out of the valley?" a Staff Officer put forward.

"Then why go near the pass?" Sergio asked, from the side of the room.

"No, I think what happened is they must have slipped through the pass earlier, and these tribesmen just blundered into the patrol later." the General replied, feeling confident he was close to the truth.

"Another thing General, a search of the cave where they rested indicated there were five of them. The Afghani's don't usually travel in such small groups, which suggests they're outsiders!" A Colonel in the KGB pointed out.

"The Americans are behind this I can smell them!" The General exploded, as all present stood there in silence. "You were right all along Sergio. They're a group of Allied soldier's, maybe they're American Special Forces. We need more proof gentlemen, so go find them, or I'll have you all shot!" the General shouted.

"There's one other thing, Sir," Sergio offered. "Captain Demetrie is a good field commander, and his troops are first class. How then did the enemy troops get by him and the tribesmen, who would have certainly fired on anyone in the dark?" Sergio asked. The General stood staring at Sergio for several seconds, contemplating what he'd said.

"In the Vietnam War the Americans used a device called a Starlight scope, to see in the dark, but it was usually used in fixed positions. Maybe they have something better?" the General mused, lost in thought.

"I'll mention it to the KGB Intelligence Officer on my way out," Sergio replied, wondering what had got into the General, as he turned to leave. The General stood staring at the door after Sergio had gone. Sergio was the key for him not ending up in front of a firing squad. Already he talked to him as an equal and going off to tell the KGB Colonel about the night vision, shit who was brave enough to go near the KGB at any time. Sergio hadn't been worried in the least.

Even when he had made his speech about shooting them all, Sergio hadn't been scared like the other staff members, why would he be. His uncle, The Chairman, wanted heads to roll over his brother's death, which had already been reported to the nation as a plane crash in Southern Georgia along with General Sokolof and at least twenty other soldiers. General Ogarkov was glad he wasn't on that plane and knew unless he found these enemy soldiers he could soon have his own accident, something he'd rather avoid if possible.

THE TUNNEL

Steve stood watching until relieved by Ali. He told him what he'd seen in the valley.

"How dangerous is it if we start out now?"

"A lot more than at night, that's for sure. Why?"

"We're getting boxed in, if we don't break out, I don't think we'll make it!"

"Well it will be slow, but we can give it a go." Steve smiled, as he silently moved past the sleeping unit members, as Ali woke them. Moving slowly, the unit crept down the reverse side of the ravine using the shadows to mask their movements, until at last, they entered the next valley. Keeping to the shadows, they headed southwest at a steady pace. By late afternoon they had covered close to ten kilometres and in that time had been forced to hide four times from the ever-present helicopters.

As the valley widened, and it began getting dark, the unit picked up speed. Bone weary, Steve signalled for the others to settle down in a bunch of rocks under an overhang for a break, while Ali checked their position on the map.

"How far," was all Steve managed to whisper, when Ali signalled for everyone to freeze. Looking down the valley, Steve saw several figures moving, silhouetted by torchlight, coming in their direction. Moving as close to the valley wall as possible, Steve watched a Russian patrol pass not twenty metres from where they were hiding. Luckily this patrol was not as well trained as the one at the pass or Steve realised, he would have walked right into them. After ten minutes had passed, Ali walked over, to check with Steve.

"Are you all right Steve? I know you're tired, but that was close!" He knew Steve hadn't slept and being on point stretched a man's nerves and stamina.

"I think I'll be all right, but how about giving Sukai a turn on point, I'm pretty spent."

"Okay I'd say that's the only patrol for a while, and he's nearly as good as you." Ali smiled, patting Steve on the back. Passing on instructions to Sukai, he immediately moved out ahead taking the point. Ali followed Sukai along the valley, and he had to admit that he moved well. Though every now and then, he heard a small noise from him as he moved. The same as he heard from himself and all the others except Steve. What amazed him was that they were the best of the best, but even when Steve was tired as he was now, he still moved silently. No wonder his Aussie mates had nicknamed him the 'Ghost' Ali smiled.

The rest of the night was spent creeping along avoiding the considerable amount of flares being dropped. Moving further away from the pass, the flares became more distant, allowing a faster pace. Examining the map, Ali guessed they'd covered about twenty kilometres. As light started to appear, he pushed the near exhausted unit further south, till the sun was fully overhead. Spotting a large cave the whole unit shuffled in, collapsing in a circle about ten metres from the entrance, leaving Ali to take first watch.

'Ali wake up!" came a voice from a long way off, as Ali came out of a deep sleep. Looking around it appeared to be late afternoon.

"God did I fall asleep on watch!" Ali mumbled trying to clear his mind.

"We all did, don't knock yourself out about it." Steve chuckled, as he handed Ali something to eat.

"Any sign of movement?"

"No, but I've got something to show you!" Steve replied excitedly, pointing to the rear of the cave. Gulping down his food, Ali followed Steve.

Walking deeper into the cave, Ali saw with the aid of his goggles, what appeared to be steps carved into the rock leading back into a cavern.

"Where's it go?" Ali asked Steve in amazement.

"I'm not sure but I followed it for over twenty minutes, it's definitely heading south and up. I thought with the goggles we could try it. Worst scenario we'd have to backtrack." Steve left it up to Ali to decide. Back at his pack Ali went over the map trying to work out where it might come out. He noticed the cave position backed up against two blind canyons to the south.

"I think it's worth a try. We'll give it 12hrs, then if we don't find an exit we can turn back and still make the rendezvous." Ali suggested.

The going in the cave was slow, as in several places the steps were gone or in bad shape. 'At least no one could see them' Ali thought as Steve led them deeper into the cave system. Coming to a cave-in, Steve carefully cleared a tunnel through the rubble, signalling back to Ali that beyond the cave-in looked clear.

"This could be why no one uses this tunnel," Ali said out loud startling the others, as no one had talked since entering the cave. Continuing on and checking his compass frequently, Steve judged they were still basically heading south, as the path twisted and turned so much, sometimes it was hard to tell. Several times the air had become stale worrying Ali. Stopping he placed his hands over a small crack in the overhead rocks detected a breeze. This meant air was getting through, if not everywhere. After travelling for over twelve hours, Ali called a halt to discuss what to do. While stopped, Cody decided to make them all a mug of tea.

"Steve if we don't find an exit soon we'll have to turn back," Ali told him, losing faith with the shortcut.

"We'll give it another two hours," Steve replied.

"Shit Cody that smells revolting!" Aaron barked angrily, dead tired from walking, as he sat across from Cody.

"I haven't started to heat the water yet!" Cody replied

He too was tired from walking. Jumping to his feet, Ali signalled everyone to be quiet, as he too caught a whiff of the smell. Steve getting a signal from Ali, advanced along the trail cautiously, as the smell became more apparent with every step. After ten minutes Steve rounded a corner, to discover the origin of the smell. Entering a large well lit cavern Steve edged silently around a rock face, coming face to face with a large camel. Getting over his shock, he looked past ten more camels, to see the entrance to the cavern. Outside the cave in the sunlight, he could see the shapes of a small group of huts.

"Well, that explains the smell!" Cody whispered, as the group set up camp back from the cave entrance, where they'd stopped for the break earlier.

"The problem is we don't know if they're friends or foes. So it's best if we hide in here for the day, and wait for night, then we'll sneak past the villagers." Ali suggested as the unit members settled down for the rest of the day.

Cody had drawn the third shift, and while watching the cave entrance, he was startled by the unmistakable sound of gunfire. The ceiling shook as rockets roared into the small camp outside followed by the screams of women and children. Cody instantly prepared his weapon starting forward to help, when a hand clamped over his mouth, stopping him. Ali had been approaching Cody to relieve him when the shooting started. He now slowly removed his hand.

"Someone's plastering the village, we've got to help!" Cody explained as the whole unit arrived.

"There's nothing we can do my friend. Stand down!" Ali ordered, pulling Cody back. Without warning, Afghan men, women and children came rushing into the cave mouth, hiding amongst the camels corralled there, forcing Ali and Cody to hit the dirt. Four Russian troops followed them in, spraying the defenceless Afghans and camels with automatic fire until nothing moved in the cavern below them.

Cody looked on helplessly, before moving back into the tunnel with Ali. Silence settled over the cave, punctuated by single shots as the surviving villagers were finished off. The last sound the unit heard was the thud of helicopters leaving. Twenty minutes passed before the unit cautiously emerged, to find the burnt out remains of a once happy village. Humiliated that they had done nothing to help them, they all stood silently feeling ashamed.

"We could have done something!" Cody shouted.

"There was nothing we could have done Cody, other than died with them," Ali replied as the unit moved out gathering the dead. Laying them in the cavern, Sukai planted charges blowing the entrance, sealing them in their grave. Cody said a few words before putting a cross made of wood in the ground next to the cave.

"Do you think it's wise to do this? They'll know someone's been here" Steve pointed out, as they prepared to leave.

"No, it's not. Though the chances of the Russians coming back here aren't high, considering, they wiped the place out." Ali admitted.

Leaving, the unit continued south with only this nights walk to the rendezvous. Looking around at his friendst, Steve knew that this little village would always haunt them.

GENERAL OGARKOV'S HEADQUARTERS

The General stared at the map. 'Where are they?' he asked himself. All day thousands of men had patrolled the mountains, and choppers had wasted thousands of gallons of fuel searching the same mountains, finding nothing.

"What about that shooting that was heard by a patrol in the southern area Colonel?" the General said to the KGB Intelligence Officer, who looked up from his map, giving the General a superior look.

"A raid by my men on a suspected rebel village Sir," the Colonel answered.

"Was the village searched?" Sergio asked, getting an unreadable look from the Colonel.

"No, it was in a box canyon only opening to the south, there's no chance they went that way!" the Colonel answered, staring at Sergio, wishing he could give him a flogging for his impertinence.

"Get them back there immediately, and see if there were any survivors who can be questioned." the General ordered, happy to see Sergio taking some of the starch out of the Colonel knowing there'd be no survivors.

"Unfortunately because of the valley,s steep sides the choppers cannot land until first light tomorrow Sir," the Colonel replied smugly, before leaving in a foul mood.

THE RENDEZVOUS

The rest of the night passed quickly and silently as the unit continued the journey south, finally approaching the agreed meeting point, only to find Omar the chief's son there alone.

"Where are the others?" Steve asked softly, coming up behind Omar, who grabed his weapon in surprise.

"You surprised me!" Omar replied, looking like he'd lost a year from fright. Lowering his weapon, Omar was shocked that a westerner could move so quietly.

"How are you Omar, I suppose the others are around here somewhere aren't they? "Ali asked casually.

"Yes they're up in the mountains to the south; there are too many

Russians for us all to come to this place," Omar informed them, looking at the strange goggles they all wore.

Waving for them to follow, Omar led them up an old goat track. With the sun starting to light up the surrounding mountains, they entered a narrow ravine.

At times the ravine became so constricted that they could only squeeze through sideways with their backpacks in their hands. After 3hrs of travelling, the ravine emptied into a large cavern, where the other tribesmen were gathered waiting nervously.

"I judge your raid was successful?" Abdul smiled, commenting on the increased Russian activities.

"Yes, it exceeded our own expectations!" Ali smiled.

"Since the raid part is finished can we know the target?" Abdul asked politely, obviously wanting to know if risking his men was worth it.

"I suppose it doesn't matter now Abdul, the target was General Sokolof and the Russian Defence Minister," Ali replied as if he was talking about a walk in the park. Omar with wide eyes translated to the others. At first, fear could be seen in the tribesmen's eyes at the thought of what the Russians would do. It passed quickly when the size of the blow they had delivered to their enemy made the tribesmen go crazy, shouting at the tops of their voices. Abdul waving his hands wildly reminded them where they were. Belut rushed through the now silent crowd, to grab Steve in a hug, tears in his eyes, as he spoke emotionally.

"He says he owes you a great debt!" Omar explained translating, his eyes misty as well, as he continued. "His whole family were tortured and killed by Sokolof's soldiers. He thinks you were sent by God to help us!" Omar said with a look that told them he thought it too.

"We are just men doing God's work," Steve replied as Omar translated, getting approval from the tribesmen.

"Enough talk we must keep moving, let's go!" Abdul ordered, a smile on his face, as the whole group grabbed their belongings and started for the border.

The General sat in his office sweating, and it had nothing to do with the heat. On his desk was another message from Chairman Andropov. It simply read 'Where are the men responsible?' But the General knew it had a double meaning for him if he failed. Looking up, the General saw the KGB Colonel walk in confidently before handing Sergio a report from the village.

"It's all there General, a full report, there were no survivors as I suspected!" the Colonel said arrogantly as he turned to leave.

"Excuse me Colonel, but it says here all the villagers were bodies were buried by blowing up a cave." Sergio pointed out.

"So what's your point?" The Colonel answered angrily.

"It means Colonel that the villagers were buried by a group who had powerful lightweight explosive, like C4, like the group which attack here. No doubt the enemy we are looking for was probably there during the attack, or just after it. I suggest you send your men back immediately, to find out where they went!" the General ordered, as the Colonel all his bravado gone, hurriedly left the room.

"Good work Sergio!" the General smiled after the Colonel had left, turning to his staff.

"Gentlemen, the KGB have dropped the ball on this one. Concentrate all troops along the border south of this village, somehow these murderers have found a way through the mountains to this blind canyon. After we catch these men, I want that valley searched. But for now get those men!" the General shouted, realising that even if they didn't catch them, the KGB would now take the fall for the failure.

THE BORDER

For the next four hours, the tribesmen led the unit through a maze of ravines and canyons hidden from observation from the air until at last, they came to an open valley. It was roughly ten kilometres across, and on the other side was the mountain range of the border. Stopping just before the exit, Abdul told them that no one could cross till dark, so settling down they waited for night to come. Staring across, Steve knew that once through this valley they were home, and he couldn't wait. He thought they'd been here too long and even though he felt for these people, it wasn't his war.

Steve had just closed his eyes when the thunder of engines echoed off the walls of the canyon as a flight of Russian planes flew down the valley dropping canisters along the valley below them. Rocketing down, they burst open about fifty metres above the ground showering the area with small objects.

"What's going on?" Steve asked Ali who lay motionless beside him scanning the valley through his binoculars.

"I've never seen it done before, but I say they're laying mines through this area of the valley!" Ali answered softly, his mind far away, as he pulled out his map as if to seek guidance. Abdul drawn by the noise sat down beside them.

"This is not good my friends, the Russian must know we are close to have done this," Abdul stated, looking around as if expecting them to appear at any second.

"If they knew we were this close Abdul, they would have dropped something a lot worse!" Ali replied still studying the ground in the valley.

"How tired are you Steve?" Ali asked a smile on his lips.

"Not too bad for a guy who walked most of the night. Why?"

"These mines have been dropped randomly along this side of the valley. The reason for this, is on the other side of the valley is one of their main roads; we just can't see it from here. The mines out there are visible at the moment, but by tonight they could be buried. Someone is going to have to go out there now, and without being seen, mark a way through the minefield to the road." Ali pointed out, looking hard at Steve.

"And I'm the only one with a killer suit!" Steve answered flatly opening his pack and pulling out his suit with a bad premonition about this task.

"Everyone loves a volunteer," Ali chuckled as Steve made to move off.

"Stuff you!" Steve said quietly as he lay down, and slid forward into the valley. Ali and Abdul both chuckling quietly, moved back into the shadows.

Crawling forward through the thick tufts of grass which covered the valley floor, Steve gazed back at the ravine which he had emerged from. From out here on the valley floor, the ravine was nothing more than a crack in the face of the steep valley side, perfectly hidden. The mines Steve discovered, had fallen in clumps, leaving the surrounding areas thinly covered. This made marking them with upright sticks and a section of string easier.

Ali had given Steve two balls of string that he'd brought with him for this very purpose. To anyone looking at them they were a flat green colour, but through their infra goggles, the string glowed making it easy to see. On each side of the trail, Steve was making he placed a piece of string one twice as long as the other to indicate right and left, roughly thirty metres apart. Coming to a high spot on the valley floor Steve looked cautiously down onto the road, which divided the valley into two sections. He found himself staring right down the barrel of a Russian tank that sat silently beside the road.

Steve in his worn out state, hadn't bothered to scan the area ahead of him. Yet here he sat 30 metres from an armoured column, which quietly waited on the edge of the road, for someone stupid enough to walk into them. The continuous thump, thump behind him, sounded the approach of a helicopter, Steve lay frozen looking down on the tank, hoping his killer suit hid him from the approaching danger. Too scared even to blink, Steve watched, as the Russian soldiers emerged from their vehicles on the road to watch the chopper, as it dived down to the road barely clearing the ground where he lay motionless.

Sergio was the first out of the chopper followed by the General and his personal guard, as the armoured columns men surged forward to greet their General.

"Any sign of the enemy?" The General asked the Captain in charge who jumped to attention, not saluting, as out here, that could get someone killed.

"No Sir, with the mines out there, I don't think we'll see anyone General," the Captain replied a small grin on his face.

Too scared to breathe, Steve couldn't believe the young Officer from the castle was here again. 'I definitely should have killed him,' Steve cursed to himself, as the group moved off. The young Officer and the General, with their guards, boarded the chopper taking off, moving west along the valley floor. Backing down the blind side Steve, crawled back along his corridor. He'd made it roughly halfway back to the ravine when he came upon a herd of goats. Seeing a great lump of vegetation heading towards them, the goats panicked running into a group of mines scattered near them. Steve, seeing this, hit the ground.

The explosions continued for about twenty seconds, but to Steve, they went on for hours, as parts of goats sailed everywhere. In the distance, Steve again heard the approach of the chopper.

When the explosion occurred, the Captain at the road immediately picked up his radio, as his men climbed aboard and manned their vehicles, expecting the worst. The Generals helicopter turned around and returned at full speed, straight at the cloud of debris rising from the ground. For the second time that day Steve lay frozen as the chopper rapidly closed in on his position, circling around guns swinging right and left looking for anything to shoot at.

"There's the problem General!" the Pilot smiled, as the others looked down on the remains of the herd of goats that had wandered into the minefield.

"Damn I thought we might have had them!" the General growled, looking at Sergio who looked down, disappointment on his face.

"Don't worry Sergio we'll get them no matter how long it takes," the General said patting Sergio on the shoulder, as the pilot radioed the armoured column telling them what had happened.

On the ground, Steve lay exhausted by the whole experience. Resting for 20 minutes feeling better he carefully moved towards the canyon. Arriving two hours later, he was surprised to find the area deserted. Too tired to worry where everyone had gone Steve fell to the ground falling fast asleep.

Waking up and finding everyone back and night coming on, Steve got to his feet, as Ali and Abdul approached.

"Sorry about leaving Steve, but we thought you'd bought it. So we decided to move further back up the ravine, just in case." Ali explained.

"I sent a man back here to see if the Russian's were looking for us. Instead, he found you sleeping like a baby!" Abdul grinned, impressed with Steve's nerve at sleeping.

Steve then explained about running into the armoured tank and the poor goats, getting smiles and a few sniggers from the men at Steve's predicament.

"Well, you're rested now, do you mind leading?" Ali smiled, at the look on Steve's face. The tribesmen's respect for Steve was becoming close to hero worship, as Omar translated his tale of clearing the mine and tangling with the Russians. Then, when they heard he'd come back there and slept while they ran, made a few men slightly ashamed of not waiting longer for him.

Steve moved forward silently along his path, using his goggles, as the tribesmen followed silently. They couldn't see anything and were in awe of Steve's bravery as he seemed to glide forward afraid of nothing. Upon reaching the road, he led them behind the armoured column that sat motionless in the dark, before again leading at a faster pace, towards the safety of the border. They had only a few hundred metres to go to a ravine that was their exit from this valley when a helicopter approached from the west. Everyone hit the dirt, except two young tribesmen who panicked and opened fired on the chopper as it passed out of range to the north.

"Spread out, run for cover!" Ali yelled as Abdul told his men to do the same. Most made it into the rocks before the chopper pilot worked out what was going on and opened fire. When the tanks on the road joined in, the whole group became pinned down in the open or on the rocky outcrops that lined the border side of the valley. The thud of more approaching helicopters could be heard now, over the scream and impact of shells, as Ali tried to bring some calm into the tribesmen, which would allow them to get away. In the end, Belut solved the problem for them. Forgotten in a rush to safety, Belut who was still carrying the special weapon had been left behind.

Lying out in a shell hole in the open wondering what to do, he calmly unpacked his weapon, turning on the sensors as Steve had told him. Pointing the weapon at the approaching helicopter, Belut got an instant growl of approval from the weapon and made ready to fire. On board the helicopter the pilot looked at his instruments in disbelief.

"Must be a fault, the tribesmen don't have missiles!" the co-pilot pointed out, sounding unsure. The pilot taking no chances, hastily manoeuvred out of range, radioing the other choppers, telling them what had happened. In the second group of choppers that were just arriving, KGB Colonel Bolshou, the KGB Colonel from General Ogarkov Headquarters looked out the window, as the other helicopter retreated away from the border range.

"What is going on Captain Hess?" He asked his pilot.

"The first helicopter reported getting locked on by a missile system," Hess replied.

"Is he crazy it must be a fault? Get in there Captain, I want those rebels!"

"It might be prudent to wait Colonel."

"I gave you an order Captain!"

"Yes, Sir," Hess replied, radioing his escort helicopter to follow him in, for a pass on the rebel position.

On the ground, Belut looked at the weapon wondering why it had stopped growling. Not realising that the helicopter had turned and was out of range. He was just wondering what to do when two other choppers started their run in. Belut, pointing the weapon at them heard the growl returned, making him pull the trigger in case it stopped again. On board the Colonel's chopper and the escort chopper, the threat alert light flashed.

"Sir, I just saw a missile launch from the ground!" screamed the co-pilot as Captain Hess, yelled a warning to the other chopper, before he swiftly turned away from the rising missile. The other chopper turned as well, unfortunately under the first chopper making itself the main target, as the missile slammed into its engine compartment turning the entire helicopter into a fireball. The Colonel's chopper didn't escape either, as parts of the escort chopper smashed into its underbelly with a sickening crunch.

Hess, white with fear, used every trick he knew to control the chopper. It had become a wild beast as it bucked and jumped all over the sky finally coming to ground only metres away from a shocked armoured column. The first helicopter having seen what happened to the other two choppers retreated across the valley. It then sent a salvo of rockets into the area where the missile had come from. The rockets exploded on impact, sending a massive cloud of debris into the air, also ending Belut's life. He'd just stood there, staring proudly at the downed helicopters.

As sand and debris drifted with the wind, an unnatural silence descended, as the blinded Russian gunners stopped firing at the rebels.

"Get everyone moving!" Ali yelled pointing to a small ravine which led away from the valley, as an eerie stillness settled over the valley. Omar quickly translated, and as one the tribesmen and the unit left their shelter, racing into the small ravine, all hoping to get away from the carnage. Carrying anyone who they thought might make it and leaving the rest behind, Abdul yelled to his men to keep moving, as the dust and debris began to clear. The shelling returned in earnest though not as heavy as before. Most of the Russians armoured force was busy trying to rescue the helicopter crew. Only three got out, Captain Hess, his Co-pilot and the KGB Colonel.

"You fool Bolshou! I'll see you court marshalled for this!" Hess shouted, holding his co-pilots leg, trying to stem the bleeding, as a medic wrapped a bandage tightly around his wound. Looking around the Colonel Bolshou, still dazed from the crash, took in the devastation caused by the crash of the two choppers. Standing unsteadily, he pulled out his pistol, pointing it at Hess. To the Colonel's amazement, several soldiers raised their rifles, telling him to drop his pistol.

Knowing with this disaster his career was over and unwilling to be dragged before a firing squad, Colonel Bolshou placed his pistol in his mouth a pulled the trigger.

Crossing the border after losing ten men including Belut, and with eight wounded, the tribesmen hurried towards their camp, to be greeted as conquering heroes. Word had already spread about the raid on Kabul, even though what had happened there was unknown. The fact that a raid had taken place was a major victory to these tribesmen. Abdul gave a moving speech in which he praised Belut for downing two enemy helicopters, a feat never achieved before, which had allowed everyone else to escape. Steve kept seeing Belut standing in the open. He must have known he had little chance of living once he fired the weapon, but he'd done it anyway.

The party continued for two days until the old Dakota with its ancient pilot landed again on the small road. He was not only here to pick them up, but he'd also brought the weapons the tribesmen had been promised for their help on the raid.

"We will not forget what you have done!" Abdul exclaimed as the unit prepared to board their plane.

"Thank you, Abdul, may God protect your people," Ali replied, shaking his hand.

"If you want to protect us, send some more missiles!" Abdul said seriously, before grinning.

"We'll see what we can do." Ali smiled, as he boarded the plane.

Closing the rear door, Ali hoped Abdul's people would be safe. They certainly deserved it he thought, as the plane rolled forward, launching itself into the sky.

Back in Karachi, Colonel Dobson was overjoyed with the raid's success which took the unit by surprise. They were expecting a dressing down for accidentally killing the Russian Defence Minister.

"This is just what the doctor ordered!" Dobson said smiling before continuing. "When the news was released about the plane crash with the Defence Minister and General Sokolof on board, we thought a plane really had crashed and that the General was just added to the death toll. But here you are with the real truth of the situation. Plus evidence of a coming attack that the Russians were about to launch, that has now been cancelled. I can't wait to pass this on to my superiors!" Dobson grinned, struggling to keep his excitement under control.

"Sir what about the tribesmen, they really need those missiles!" Ali asked while the Colonel was happy.

"Yes sounds like those stingers really did a job on those choppers. I'll make sure they get plenty more, to give our Russian friends a hard time." Dobson replied enthusiastically, before leaving with the mission reports and a quick thank you to the team for a job well done.

"What do you make of that guy?" Cody asked after the Colonel had departed.

"I'm not sure, but he definitely isn't military!" Ali grumbled, watching the door

"Do you think he's a problem?" Steve asked seriously.

"No! Not as long as we do our bit." Ali replied, but his face showed mixed emotions as he sat there thinking about the Colonel. Steve decided to change the subject.

"Anyway, now the missions finished I thought I'd tell you I'm getting married. The weddings in about six months time and I'd like you all to be there if you can. You're the closest friends I have!" Steve confessed. The unit members, momentarily just stood there knowing that Steve was talking from his heart, and as one they came forward, congratulated him.

"You know that going would be against the rules of this unit for keeping secrecy and not getting too close to each other," Ali informed him, although his face showed his pleasure in being asked.

"I'd like to go to see what woman would have him!" Sukai said smiling.

"Does she have bad teeth or warts? I'm not going if she's ugly!" Aaron grinned as the others starting laughing.

"She's absolutely beautiful, and seriously if you can't come, I'll understand," Steve added, getting nods from all present as they settled down to talk about their individual lives and what they hoped for in the future.

In the afternoon, they travelled to the airstrip, to pack up and dispose of any evidence that would link them to this operation. Any leftover military hardware was sent out to the tribesmen, where it would be put to good use.

"Look after yourselves." the old pilot barked with a smile, as he loaded up his plane for another trip to the border.

"We'll miss you pop!" Cody yelled smiling, getting the finger for his remark about his age, as the others laughed.

Travelling to the airport, Steve sat in the back of the beat up airport bus and looked around at the members of the unit thinking how lucky they'd been to make it. On this mission, they had become a close-knit group, and Steve hoped that their luck held until the time they all decided to call it quits.

PERTH AIRPORT
JUNE 1984

Passing through customs without any trouble, Steve in his business suit had become invisible, blending in. Hailing a cab, Steve headed for the cottage where he quickly changed before going for a run along the beach. Upon returning he noticed a figure sitting on his front deck, and when he jogged closer, he recognised John sitting there drinking a beer.

"Made yourself comfortable I see!" Steve smiled, shaking John's hand before getting a beer from the fridge himself and sitting down on a seat sweating profusely from the run.

"You know a beer always tastes better when it's from another man's fridge," John replied laughing at his own joke.

"Fridge?" Steve responded, going back into the kitchen. The old fridge was gone. Looking around, Steve noticed all the second-hand furniture had been changed to new, and he hadn't even noticed.

"Yeah, your girl has been busy!"

"Michelle's been here?"

"Last week she was here for most of the week. She knew you were working so she kept herself busy with your bank account I'd say." John grinned. John told Steve how she'd called in several times for dinner, and had even given John and Joan an invitation to the wedding as well as Paul and his wife.

"God I miss her," Steve moaned, wishing he'd been here.

"How'd you go, if you don't mind me asking?"

"Afghanistan was ugly. We dropped in on a few bad guys, and then had to leave in a big hurry!" Steve answered vaguely, leaving it at that.

"The locals could use a break there. The Russians have sure been pounding them for years." John replied, before moving on. "We've had a few problems here too. Captain Lenton's about to drop into New Guinea near the border to discourage some people from crossing it."

It appeared the Indonesians were getting tired of rebels crossing over the border into Irian Jaya. They had warned the Australian Defence Minister, that they might have to invade, and what would Australia do about it. To everyone's shock, he'd told them that he'd bomb the shit out of them. Fearing an all-out war, he ordered the SAS to watch the border and if the Indonesian's tried anything to let them have it. So the CO had ordered Captain Lenton, to take two teams of eight men and keep watch with the help of the local natives.

"The problem is Steve we're up against it in the night. It's hard to move silently in that jungle."

"Bloody hell John, I've got just the thing!" Steve grinned, running to his pack, and returning with the goggles. At the end of the mission, the Colonel had given Steve the five sets of goggles begrudgingly, supposedly for the SAS to evaluate. The real reason was at the time the US was negotiating for a base near Pine Gap. His superior suggested technology and intelligence exchange might be a way of getting the base. So it was suggested that it wouldn't hurt to hand them over and bait the hook a bit so to speak. John at first wondered what they were for and then looking at Steve he guessed.

"They're infra aren't they?"

"Yes, and except for a red tinge, it's like walking in daylight. I was going to take them to the barracks tomorrow for evaluation."

"We've got to go right now!" John grabbed Steve and headed for the door.

"What's the hurry John?" as jumping into John's car, John flattened it up the road past his surprised wife.

"They're flying out tonight, which means they must be leaving soon, it's almost four. Shit, I hope we make it!" John grimaced, gunning his old car down the road.

Arriving at the base dressed in their shorts and tee-shirts, in a car doing close to a hundred kilometres an hour, they were nearly arrested by the guards on duty before being escorted to the CO.

"What the hell's going on Sergeant Major?" Paul yelled angrily, at seeing one of his Sergeants and his Regimental Sergeant Major turning up escorted by guards and without their uniforms.

"Have the men left yet Sir?" John asked excitedly.

"No they haven't, and if you two are drunk, I'll break you both to privates!" Paul warned.

"We have to see you inside immediately Sir and alone," John asked softly, getting a nod from the CO, as he waved off the guards and pointed to his office. Steve with his small bag followed them.

"Shit, they're both dead for this!" A private laughed in the office, as ten minutes went by and the CO still hadn't appeared.

"God did you see what they were wearing!" Smiled one of the guards, hoping the RSM got a demotion for this.

"Private! Go get Captain Lenton up here straight away!" the CO bellowed through his door, unnerving everyone in the office with its suddenness.

Shortly afterwards, an out of breath Captain Lenton arrived at the office. He'd heard the tale of two drunken Sergeants going berserk at the front gates. Knocking on the door and entering the CO's office, Captain Lenton was confronted by John, Steve and Paul sitting in the dark, wearing strange looking goggles on their heads. He thought the rumours for once were true.

"Is everything okay here?" Captain Lenton asked softly. The three men look at each other than at Captain Lenton, before bursting into laughter.

That night, John, Paul and Steve sat on Steve's front deck having chicken and chips for dinner, going over the day's events, including the ruckus they had caused.

"Look, we're all good friends, but a warning gentleman, don't ever turn up without uniforms again okay. Next time you'll be cleaning the urinals and saluting privates." Paul informed them, trying to be firm.

"There just wasn't time Paul. I couldn't let Lenton go without giving him every advantage." John replied slightly ashamed by his lack of discipline at the base.

"I know John. It's just the military code we live by." Paul decided to change the subject. "Hey did you see the look on Col's face when he entered the office. Shit, he thought we'd all lost it!" Paul grinned, as they all started laughing. As the night wore on, the conversation turned to Steve's excursion overseas.

"Heard you went after some more bad guys?" Paul asked wondering if Steve had picked up any more information for the Regiments benefit.

"Yeah, I'll say one thing for the yanks they have good Intel," Steve replied knowing he could trust these guys.

"If you don't mind me asking, did you see anything we could use, other than the goggles?" Paul asked sheepishly.

"Yeah, the yanks have a new weapon. It's a surface to air missile called a stinger. It's a shoulder-fired weapon, and it leaves everything else for dead I can tell you." Steve exclaimed, impressed by the weapon.

"You didn't have anything to do with shooting down the Defence Ministers plane, did you?" John asked suspiciously.

"He couldn't have, that plane went down in Georgia or someplace didn't it?" Paul replied defensively.

"No, we shot down a chopper with it. The Defence Minister copped it in Kabul along with General Sokolov." Steve softly replied as Paul's glass smashed on the floor. It took twenty minutes for Steve to explain the whole mission. Two very quiet men pondered the outcome of such a mission.

"Whoever is running your operations Steve, likes to flirt with death. Not for him but your units!" Paul was impressed they'd pulled it off.

"Yeah, Ali, my units CO, said the same thing."

"Someday I'll have to meet him. He sounds like a formidable soldier." John smiled, getting agreement from Paul.

"Maybe you will sooner than you think. I asked him to the wedding. He mustn't know I've told you about the mission." Steve replied.

"Nothing goes beyond this room, Steve. But your Colonel worries me. I'd watch my back if I were you!" Paul advised him, as they dropped the subject and went back to discussing the Regiments activities.

A month passed, and Steve continued to train the Regiments men as they rotated from active service back to the base for training and rest. Captain Lenton's mission had not been as boring as they first thought. The Indonesians, maybe to test Australia's resolve, had sent several patrols across the border, terrorising the local population. This went on, until one night an enemy patrol numbering about forty, ran smack bang into Captain Lenton's two eight-man units.

They were setting up camp in the early hours of the morning, when the scouts wearing the infrared goggles spotted the approaching patrol. The scouts quickly informed Captain Lenton. In the firefight that followed, the whole enemy patrol had been wiped out. The SAS unit's suffered only two casualties, both not serious. Unfortunately, it also left the two exhausted groups to bury forty enemy soldiers. This was the policy of the SAS. Never let the enemy know what had happened to their men, an impressive fear tactic.

The Australian Government, upon getting wind of what the SAS had done, promptly withdrew them fearing they might have gone too far. However, the Indonesians never crossed the border again. At one of the fortnightly briefings, Captain Lenton had praised John and Steve for giving his men the goggles. Admitting without them his men might have suffered more casualties. He also hoped if they went out drinking again he wanted to go.

This brought a roar of laughter from everyone there, who knew about how they had arrived that day. Paul suggested it would be best that this story be put to rest. Or at least not told outside the Regiment, pointing out that some peoples reputations might be damaged if the story leaked out. After the meeting, Captain Lenton approached Steve and shook his hand.

"I owe you one!" Lenton said with a smile, before moving off with his unit. 'I hope I never have to collect,' Steve thought to himself, as a private ran up to him.

"Sergeant, the Post Office just rung, they've got another parcel for you."

"Thanks, private." Was all Steve could say, as he stood staring at the package? Steve waited till after work to check out its contents at home. Going over the mission, Steve looked carefully at the time frame, before a tap came from his front door. Looking through the window, Steve saw a small car parked in the driveway.

As a precaution, he grabbed a knife from the kitchen and slid it into the rear of his pants. Upon opening the front door, he was surprised to find Ali standing there holding a suitcase.

"Hello, Steve. Which rooms mine?" Ali asked with a smile, as Steve pointed towards the second bedroom, taking the knife out of his pants.

"About time you started taking precautions!" Ali exclaimed, looking at the knife. "If you keep reading your instructions, you'll get to the part concerning me," Ali explained, disappearing into the second bedroom, as Steve read his orders. Towards the end, they informed Steve that, to cut the time down in the field, Ali would contact Steve and arrange a place to meet in Perth.

"Well, obviously he doesn't know that we are in contact with each other!" Steve chuckled, going to the fridge and getting himself a beer and Ali a coke.

"And let's keep it that way, Steve. For all intents and purposes, I've booked two rooms at the Hilton in Perth, where we are meeting." Ali pointed out, as Steve passed him his drink.

"I don't get it. I thought there'd be only one mission a year unless there's an emergency."

"Well the Vietnam mission was last year, while Afghanistan has been the only one this year until this emergency came up, and it has a tight time restraint on it!" Ali replied academically. "This one's straight in and straight out, no more than a week on the ground plus preparation, I'd say no more than a month. Plenty of time before the big day Steve," Ali replied, sensing the reason for Steve's jumpiness.

"How do you do it, Ali? My Regiments going to have a fit when I tell them I'm going again!"

"That parts easy Steve. I'm no longer in the Army!" Ali replied. Ali had been in the Special Forces of the Iranian Army, but with growing discontent in the ranks and the death of his parents by extremists, Ali had left Iran and now lived on the outskirts of Zurich. "This is my only job now, and I spend a lot of my time planning these missions," Ali explained, knowing it made him reliant on the Americans for everything.

"How long for?"

"At the most, another four years. By then I'll have enough of my own money to kiss them goodbye." Ali replied smiling, hoping it was true.

"Okay you get set up, I'll cook tea," Steve suggested, as Ali went to his bedroom and brought out a large folder, spreading the contents all over the dining table. Over a couple of pieces of fish and some chips, which was about as flashy as Steve got, they both poured over the maps and aerial photographs of the target and the surrounding area.

"It's got to be South Africa Steve, it's the only country that we can travel to and remain undetectable. Also, it has several weapon smugglers who can get us into the Congo," Ali explained objectively, as he studied the maps of the target. Steve was just about to answer, when a knock came at the door, causing Ali to quickly throw the tablecloth that he had removed from the table earlier, over the mission notes and plans they had on the table. Walking to the door, Steve found John standing there.

"Hello, John," Steve answered as Ali joined him. "This is Ali, we work together overseas," Steve explained, watching the two men appraise each other.

"Good to meet you, Ali. Any friend of Steve's a friend of mine." John said honestly, putting out his hand and shaking Ali's firmly.

"You must be Steve's superior at the base!" Ali asked, gauging the man who stood in front of him.

"I'm the RSM, we're not too superior. Anyway, my wife thought that Steve's girl may have returned and might want to go out shopping tomorrow. I'll leave you two alone." John suggested not wanting to intrude.

"You may as well stay for coffee John. Obviously, Steve trusts you," Ali replied smiling, as John played dumb. "You didn't even blink when Steve mentioned my name John, and you know I work with Steve," Ali replied stating the obvious.

"He's one of my Sergeant's Ali, and my friend, we don't have too many secrets," John replied honestly.

"That's good enough for me!" Ali smiled, as the three men walked through the house and sat down on the deck and relaxed. Like, true soldiers, the three men sat down and discussed army life and tactics. Ali even managed to do a few scenarios on the coming mission to get John's slant on them. Steve's wedding even came up with John raising an eyebrow at Steve's unit being asked.

"See Steve even John can see a problem with your overseas friends attending!" Ali smiled.

"No, I think if you can it would be great. It's just, don't the yanks want your involvement kept, let's say low key." John replied diplomatically.

"Exactly what I told him, but he'll still send the invitations anyway," Ali said happily to have been invited in spite of everything.

"Well, it's up to individual members to work out if they want to risk it," Steve answered, hoping they would come.

"By the way, what's Michelle look like, the others would like to know what girl would marry Steve?" Ali asked smiling.

"You can judge for yourself!" came a female voice from the front door of the house making the three men spin round and up onto their feet.

In the doorway stood two Air hostesses with small carry bags, one was Michelle the other her roommate, Julie.

"Well, that's quite a welcome lover boy, leaving the front door open! If you're planning to take over the country, you better improve your security!" Julie giggled, smiling at Steve's discomfort.

"It appears my wife was right." John smiled, going forward to welcome Michelle, as Steve and Ali quickly cleaned everything off the table before they too greeted the women. After John had left and Julie had moved into the third bedroom, they all settled down. Michelle explained what had happened. The flight they were both on from London to Sydney had landed in Perth, to pick up some passengers. Michelle had arranged for Julie and herself to have a stopover for three days so Julie could see the house.

"Well I'm glad you did Michelle, now I can tell my friends that Steve is incredibly blessed!" Ali told her, making her smile.

"I thought all you Arab boys just pinched girl's bottoms, not gave out compliments." Julie smiled teasingly at Ali.

"If I pitch your bottom Julie, it will be because you want me too," Ali replied softly, looking Julie in the eyes and making her go crimson. This caused Steve and Michelle turn away and hide their grins. Julie was ready with a witty reply, but when her eyes locked onto his, she was lost for words. This surprised Michelle, who smiled at her girlfriend's confusion. After the girls had gone into the kitchen, Steve asked Ali about planning the mission.

"Most I've already worked out, and the rest can wait till Monday when the girls depart," Ali replied.

"She's a beautiful woman that Julie!" Steve smiled, watching Ali.

"Yes, she is," Ali said quietly, before turning to Steve, knowing his stares had been noticed.

"Maybe you could take her for a drive tomorrow downtown for lunch or something?" Steve suggested secretively.

"What and leave you and Michelle here alone, what would you talk about?" Ali replied at Steve's attempt to get Michelle alone. That night Steve and Michelle made love trying to keep the noise to a minimum for the benefit of their visitors. It was still fantastic, although trying to keep quiet, killed the passion slightly.

The next morning at six, as usual, Steve ran along the beach accompanied this time by Ali. For twenty minutes they pushed themselves, before turning and jogging back.

"I forgot how crazy you Aussie SAS soldiers are on runningng. How long have you been doing that distance?"

"I've done it since I've been here. It's like waking up to me." Steve answered, thinking about it.

"If I had a beautiful woman like you've got back there, the last thing I'd be doing was leaving my bed." Ali grinned, as he ground to a halt out of breath, letting Steve run on chuckling.

As the four sat around having breakfast, Julie finally got around to asking how Steve knew Ali.

"We do a little business on the side swapping tips on stocks. We met in America when we were both doing some training with the Americans" Ali answered smoothly to Julie, as Michelle gave him an unreadable look.

"So you're a soldier too?" Julie replied watching Ali closely.

"No. Not any longer. Iran, my homeland is in turmoil, so I now live near Zurich on a small estate my parents used to own, and I do a lot of contracting work for the Americans," Ali truthfully answered.

"Why we fly to Switzerland, we'll have to call in and visit," Julie suggested, a small smile playing across her lips.

"I will look forward to that day when you can visit my home," Ali replied studying Julie, making her go quietly.

"Well, since Ali and Steve have business to discuss, I thought I'd take Julie shopping, as there isn't much to eat here," Michelle suggested.

"If its okay I thought I'd take Julie and look around the countryside while you and Steve have some time to talk about your coming wedding. We can shop on the way back?" Ali suggested, getting smiles from everyone there.

"That sounds great Ali, Julie hasn't seen much of this area, and I do have to go over a few things with Steve," Michelle replied merrily before they all wandered off to change. Waving goodbye to Ali and Julie, Steve grabbed Michelle, kissing her.

"Actually, we have to discuss the wedding plans!" Michelle reminded him, as Steve pulled her inside and kissed her again. "We'll go over the plans later." Michelle giggled, as Steve steered her towards the bedroom.

In the meantime, Ali drove the car at a leisurely pace along the coast road taking in the sites as well as Julie.

"That was nice of you to let them have time together," Julie said softly, feeling like a school girl out on her first date.

"What makes you think it wasn't to get you alone," Ali answered smiling, as Julie looked him in the eye and scoffed.

"I knew you were trouble when I first saw you!" Julie replied laughing.

"I knew you were the one for me as soon as I saw you!" Ali confessed, as he pulled to the side of the road and pulled the stunned Julie towards him, kissing her full on the lips, taking her breath away.

Michelle lay covered with sweat from the lovemaking that had filled their whole morning. Walking naked out to the kitchen she found Steve there also naked hastily making sandwiches for them both

"I hope they don't come back early!" Steve chuckled, as he grabbed two plates and placed them on the table. Michelle slowly chewed her food, letting her eyes wander over Steve. She wondered if he would mention what Ali was doing here.

"That was good of Ali to let us have some time together." Steve smiled, as his gaze never left Michelle's face.

"I think he also wanted to be alone with Julie. I've never seen her so smitten with a man before." Michelle giggled, thinking of her friend, who had always been so in control with men, till now.

"I never thanked you for all the furniture. It must have taken you ages." Steve said looking around the house.

"Yeah, I got a little carried away with Joan and Elaine. I hope you didn't mind me putting some of it on your account, I used up nearly all of my money first." Michelle replied defensively.

"I don't mind at all, and I have something for you," Steve replied handing her a chequebook. "You know why Ali's here, it's another mission. He came here to plan it with me, so we'll be, in country, for a shorter time. I thought it best that I made my account for both of us. This way you can purchase things for the wedding or for us, if I'm not here for a while" Steve continued, watching her reaction.

"I thought the story of stock trading was good for Julie but was the other about living near Zurich true?" Michelle asked mostly for her friend.

"Yes, it was. It shocked me that he really told the truth to her about where he lived. Maybe he is attracted to her." Steve said smiling.

"How long?" Michelle asked sadly.

"Not more than a month, I'll be back with plenty of time to spare,"

Steve answered smiling reassuringly. Standing up, she grabbed his hand, before walking silently back to the bedroom. It was four in the afternoon before Ali's rental car appeared at the front of the house. Loaded with groceries Ali and Julie carried them into the kitchen, before going to their rooms to freshen up. Steve and Michelle sat on the front deck while the other two showered.

"Looks like they'd been swimming?" Michelle smiled suspiciously.

"That doesn't mean anything happened. It was just a good day for it that's all." Steve replied wondering what she was getting at.

"They didn't take bathers, what did they swim in?" Michelle giggled, at which point Steve laughed.

"What's so funny?" Ali asked happily as he came out onto the veranda with Julie, holding his hand, something not lost on Michelle.

"You know Michelle. She's a little suspicious of how you went swimming without bathers." Steve smiled, as both Ali and Julie went quiet, making Michelle and Steve both burst into laughter again.

The night went quickly with Julie doing the cooking, helped by Ali who made a traditional dish from his homeland. It usually was made with goat, but chicken became a substitute much to everyone's delight. In bed that night Michelle was worried that their lovemaking might be heard by the other two in the house. The noise from Ali's room reassured them that they didn't seem to mind making a noise, so with a bit of quiet laughter, they got back to being together with renewed passion.

The next morning Steve jogged along the beach minus his friend who was sleeping in, not feeling himself he had said when Steve knocked on his door.

'That was pretty clear' Steve thought, smiling.

Running along the beach, taking in how magical the world was today for him, Steve thought about how long he'd stay with the unit. Turning around and heading back he saw Michelle walking towards him wearing his dressing gown.

"What are you doing up so early?" he asked as he came up to her.

"Thought I'd find out what swimming naked is all about!" She laughed, as she dropped the dressing gown to the sand, running naked screaming into the surf. Watching mesmerised Steve stripped and followed her. Pulling her towards him, he lifted her into his arms, kissing her, enjoying being with her.

Sitting at breakfast Steve and Michelle watched as Julie came walking out of her room, and Ali emerged from his. Everyone pretended they hadn't heard anything last night.

"Sleep well, Ali?" Steve asked, a small smile playing on his lips.

"Yes, it truly has been a lovely experience staying here Steve, I will miss it!" Ali replied meaning every word, his eyes locked on Julie's. Sadness settled over the group as they all realised it was their last day together, as the girl's flight left that afternoon, giving them only the morning together.

"I thought we could spend the time looking around Perth, have a late lunch and see the girls off if that's okay with you?" Steve suggested. After they all agreed to Steve's plan, they finished their breakfast and wandered off, the girls to get ready and the men to think about their future with the women and their mission.

The ride back from the Airport that afternoon was spent in silent contemplation, as each man thought about what being in love would mean to their lives. Steve couldn't wait to be married to Michelle, so this disjointed lifestyle could end, and they could be together. He had decided only to continue with the Americans for maybe two more years. He thought by then he would have earned his release from the unit. He also worried how long Michelle would put up with it.

Ali, on the other hand, wondered if Julie could handle his coming and going on missions. Unlike Steve, he spent a great deal of extra time making these missions work, maybe three times more than he had told Steve. He was well paid, but it wasn't a life for a wife. Another problem Ali faced was his religion. Though he was only a moderate Muslim, his religion was important to him, and he knew how hard it was for a western woman to understand it. The hard part was he knew he loved her and that's what made it difficult.

Arriving back at the house around seven, Ali cooked some leftovers as Steve put the mission documents and maps back on the table. Sometimes working was the best cure to keep your mind off other things. Things you could do nothing about.

THE CONGO MISSION

By twelve that night they had a pretty tight plan for achieving the mission. The target was twofold. The Congo at the moment was divided into two zones. One zone was the coastal section of the country controlled by the Russian backed President Jamal Robessa. The other region, mostly the inland jungle was controlled by a drug lord named General Mogar. Both men were vicious killers, and each had the blood of thousands of innocent people on their hands.

The President had the most extensive military forces, with two armour brigades and a significant amount of artillery. This was backed up by over thirty Mig fighters, flown by Russian advisers. Up until now, the Americans had shown no interest in interfering in the Congo until through sources in Moscow, they got wind of what the Russians planned. It appeared the Russians were arranging peace talks between the two warring sides. Peace though was not their objective, the use of ports and airfields in the country were. With naval and air support, the Russians planned to turn the South Atlantic into a Russian bastion, threatening American trade and security.

The mission was to sabotage the peace talks and destroy the Russian attempt at getting bases there, without the Russians finding out. The plan was to pose as gunrunners visiting General Mogar who was still arming his militias even though he hoped for a peace deal. He didn't mind peace, for it would allow him to export his drugs and other contraband without fighting, for a far more significant profit. Ali had already gone over the groundwork and had procured the necessary equipment and transport. The specialised equipment for this mission was coming from their old friend Mr Lou, who, as always, proved dependable.

"We meet in Johannesburg in seven days, at exactly eight in the morning. There is no room for being late on this one Steve." Ali told him.

"Is the Colonel going to be there?" Steve asked still not happy with him.

"No, he'll meet us later on in London." Ali was also worried by this man.

"Well, we'd better hit the sack. I have to be at the base at six!" Steve pointed out offering his hand knowing Ali would most probably get up later for his midday flight.

"Thanks for letting me stay Steve it has been quite a visit." Ali smiled.

"I'm glad you enjoyed it Ali, but tonight can you keep the noise down. Last night you moaned a lot in your sleep." Steve chuckled, leaving Ali lost for words.

"You should talk! I had my fingers in my ears from the creaking of your bed, even though it didn't last long." Ali finally answered grinning, as they both went off to their rooms.

The next morning, Steve quickly dressed. Hurrying out to the car he found Ali dressed and waiting.

"You're not the only one who can get up early!" Ali smiled, as they both departed.

Steve arrived at the base to find John had already been preparing his travel orders. His cover story, this time, was a training exercise in New Zealand.

"You really get around Sergeant!" The Corporal in charge of transport commented.

"Yeah, another boring training stint with the Kiwis!" Steve replied as the RSM shoved him into the CO office, Paul looking less than pleased.

"I thought the deal was only one trip a year?" Paul exploded from behind his desk. Pointing to the seat, Paul told the two of them to sit down.

"It was a shock to me too Sir. I judge this one has only a small window of opportunity." Steve replied apologetically.

"It's just Steve it's hard to use you here when the yanks have first call on you all the time!" Paul informed him.

"Well at least the manuals finished now, we'll see what the brass thinks of it while you're gone," John replied, throwing Steve a way out.

"I know it's not your fault Steve, but we'll have to look into your position here when you return. Until then good luck my friend." Paul said shaking Steve's hand, as Steve sadly left the office. When Steve had left, John sat with Paul pondering Steve's fate.

"I'm worried John, these missions he's doing are high risk, they'll burn his unit out at this rate!" Paul put forward.

"No, I don't think that's the problem. I met his team leader Ali, the other night. I was impressed by how good they are at planning their operations. No, I think the problem is what happens to them if their cover gets blown?" John replied, getting a nod from Paul, as they both contemplated Steve's position.

The next day after packing his suitcase Steve tried again to contact Michelle before leaving. Still, the only answer was the answering machine. After leaving a message explaining that he would be overseas on business for a month, knowing she'd understand, he drove to the airport. Leaving the Ford he'd purchased recently in the long-term car park, he walked into the departure lounge and checked in. Travelling Business Class, which Steve found helpful at customs, he quickly boarded the plane and settled in for his flight to London. From there he'd catch a different flight to South Africa.

"Well lookie here its soldier boy!" Julie exclaimed loudly, which drew attention from the other passengers.

"God, what are you doing here?"

"I'm an air hostess with Qantas Steve. What do you think I'm doing here?" Julie replied, taken aback by his reaction, as she looked after the other passengers boarding.

Once the flight had got underway, and the passengers were settled, Julie went to economy class and found Michelle preparing drinks in the galley.

"There's a surprise for you in Business Class!" Julie whispered secretively.

"Okay, Julie what is it?"

"Soldier boys up there, he's dressed in a nice business suit," Julie replied smiled. Her smile soon faded with the crestfallen look on Michelle.

"What's wrong, I thought you'd be overjoyed?"

"He's on a mission Julie, the Army doesn't send him overseas for fun!" Michelle answered a little fear in her eyes, as Julie stood there, her mind racing.

"Ali wasn't there at the house for business, was he? He's part of this isn't he?" She now knew why Ali had not wanted to get too involved. This was his life, he was trying to shield her from it.

"Yes, he's Steve's CO while he's overseas. I can't tell you anymore Julie." Michelle replied close to tears.

"I'm sorry Michelle I never knew there was danger in Steve's job, I thought they just did training," Julie confessed hugging her friend.

"I'll go up and see him in a minute, but don't let on I'm scared. It would worry him." Michelle replied, pulling herself together.

"There's one other thing I called him soldier boy in front of the passengers. I suppose that doesn't matter does it?"

"I don't think so. It's not like the planes full of spies." Michelle laughed as they both went back to work.

"Surprise!" Michelle whispered, giving him a quick kiss.

"I'll say, after seeing Julie I should've known," Steve replied his eyes saying everything she wanted to know.

"You know First Class is empty on this flight. For an extra couple of hundred dollars, I think I could move you up there. You'll be all by yourself. Do you think your bosses would pay for that?" Michelle asked.

"I'll pay myself!" Steve smiled, as she led him through the mostly sleeping passengers into the deserted First Class section, securing the door behind her.

"Are you sure this is okay?" Steve asked nervously, as Michelle started to unbutton her uniform.

"Julie will cover for me for the next six hours, it's the dead shift as we call it. At this time of the night, most passengers are asleep. I can go if you don't want me to stay." Michelle said seductively.

"No. To tell you the truth I don't care if you do get fired, then you'll be at home with me all the time." Steve replied honestly, as they made themselves comfortable.

When the plane landed at Heathrow, unlike most flights where the First class passengers are first off, Steve held off leaving to get a special goodbye kiss from Michelle.

"Hope you enjoyed your flight, Sir!" Julie asked, smiling.

"Yes, I'll have to recommend it to Ali!" Steve replied as Julie stopped him.

"If you see him, tell him to ring me," Julie asked, trying to sound uncaring, her voice saying otherwise.

"I'll tell him," Steve answered, waving to them both, as he joined the crowd of departing passengers.

Standing near the carousel waiting for his bags, Steve didn't notice a small man standing in the corner watching him. Brad Connor worked for the Defence Department in Canberra. He was in charge of overseeing the movement of Defence personnel overseas, and while on the flight, he'd heard the stewardess call him soldier boy. The young man had boarded at Perth, and despite the suit, he looked every inch a soldier and had travelled with these stewardesses before.

'What's he up to?' Brad asked himself as he watched this mystery man grab his bag and head for the departure lounge. Taking a bit of a risk, Brad followed the soldier until he stopped at the South African Airlines check-in counter. Looking around, Brad realised he might be tagged by the Airport security cameras for following the soldier, so he moved away, retrieving his bag, before leaving the Airport to meet his contact. Brad didn't just work for the Australians, he also worked for the Russians who were always interested in bits of information like this, he thought, as he hurried off, to meet his handler.

The flight to Johannesburg was uneventful after his flight from Perth, Steve thought, smiling to himself remembering. The only thing that had worried him was that Michelle seemed nervous. He knew she didn't like the missions overseas and it dawned on him that he might have to stop them earlier than he thought. But could he? The Americans mightn't like it, he realised, as the plane touched down with a jarring crunch. With one day to spare Steve met the others at the hotel before showering and going to bed early.

Boarding an old minibus at seven the next morning the unit members sat in silence as the bus driver weaved his way through the downtown traffic. Driving out of the city, they finally stopped at a rundown airstrip in the outer suburbs. After handing over a sizable tip, the driver warned them it was a dangerous area, before driving off in search of another fare, his passengers forgotten. Approaching the airport front gate, Steve couldn't help but notice the three-metre electric fence topped with razor wire, running around the airstrip.

At the only entrance gate, stood two guards, armed with assault rifles, adding significantly to the already tight security. With a slight glance at their tickets for a flight, the guards passed them through, directing them to hanger five down from the gate. Opening the door to the office, the group were surprised to find it was air-conditioned, a welcomed relief from the heat outside.

"Good morning gentlemen!" A young man shouted from a doorway.

"This is Brent, our pilot. Our friends have brought him in from the States to fly for us." Ali informed them.

"Why all the security?" Aaron asked suspiciously.

"This is South Africa my friend, security like you see outside is normal here, I can assure you," Brent answered smiling, before showing them into the hangar. Stacked neatly against one wall was a selection of weapons, including several killer suits. 'At least I won't have to make one this mission' Steve thought as he browsed through the array of equipment noticing the gold-handled pair of forty-five automatic pistols.

"They're a present for the general!" Ali explained to Steve, as he ushered the unit into a room to the side of the hanger, set up for the briefing. Ali started by briefing everyone on their individual assignments.

Brent, the pilot, was amazed by the unconcerned faces of the unit members, as the plan was explained in detail. It revealed the major effort each one of them was expected to perform during the mission as if it was a walk in the park. Next, to their jobs, his was straightforward. All he had to do was fly there and stay with the plane. Of course, he also had to be ready for a fast getaway if things went south.

He wondered while sitting there if any of them would actually make it back to the plane.

"Ah, Brent, do you have your flight maps with you?" Ali asked as he discussed the approach.

"No they're on the plane, I'll get them," Brent replied turning and leaving the room. As he departed to retrieve the maps from the plane, Ali stared after him, until he was out of sight.

"Remember he's not one of us, he works for the Colonel!" Ali stated seriously, as they all took in his meaning.

"Do you think he's a problem?" Cody asked smiling, knowing how to take care of problems.

"No, not as long as everything goes okay, but watch him anyway," Ali replied as Brent rejoined them and the briefing continued.

The next day, after sleeping in the hangar and going over the mission for the tenth time, the unit loaded onto the plane. It was another Dakota, though it was in a lot better condition than the one in Afghanistan. Steve wondered where all these old aircraft had come from, as he settled in next to Aaron, for the four-hour flight.

One hour out from their destination, Sukai, Aaron and Steve walked to the rear cargo door. Putting on their parachutes, they opened the rear door. Ali sat studying the ground and comparing it to his map, as the wind gusted into the plane forcing everyone to hold on for fear of being sucked out.

"Go!" Ali yelled above the wind, as Sukai and Aaron followed closely by Steve exited the plane. Once the three had jumped, Ali and Cody manhandled a container full of their gear to the door, tossing it out after them, its chute opening automatically as it left the plane. Dropping towards the jungle below, travelling at over a hundred kilometres an hour, Steve hoped this mission went according to plan. They were a long way from home if they were discovered early, and he had the feeling the Colonel wouldn't cry too many tears if they didn't make it.

Looking down, Steve saw the ground coming up toward him at a frightening rate. Gauging the distance to the ground, he reached for his release handle. As his chute came to life above him, his decent suddenly halted, stretching his tense body. Drifting down towards the ground, he looked for a safe landing place, spotting a small clearing to his right, steering towards it. Checking for Sukai and Aaron, Steve looked skywards, spotting the supply chute instead, as it descended nearly directly above him. This made finding it a lot easier, but also increased the chances of it hitting him, as he landed.

Touching down smoothly on the eastern side of the small clearing, Steve had just taken his chute off, when the cargo container crashed to the ground about twenty metres from him. 'Well at least it didn't hit me,' Steve smiled, as he took in his surroundings. Gathering in his chute, he was just about to walk across the clearing to the supply chute, when Aaron yelled for him to freeze. Looking for something he'd missed, he saw Sukai walk up next to Aaron, who instantly put his hand out to stop him going further. For Steve's benefit, he pointed at a sign lying on the ground in front of him. It had two words on it "Warning Mines" and a skull and crossed bones painted across it.

A shiver ran through Steve as pulling out his combat knife. Bending down, he worked his blade through the grass and dirt in front of him clearing a space. He then got down on his hands and knees to be more comfortable. Working slowly and carefully he made his way towards the supply container. His friends, copying Steve, headed towards his position. It took an hour to cover the twenty metres between him and the supply chute. Looking back, he saw Sukai and Aaron had reached Steve's trail. They both rose from the ground and walked along Steve's track meeting him at the container, before carefully getting their gear out. Retracing their steps, back along the safe paths, they reached Aaron's starting point, breathing a sigh of relief.

"Thanks for the help, though I didn't prod one mine all the way across," Steve whispered breathlessly, as they all seated themselves and divided up the gear from the container.

"They did," Aaron replied, pointing to Steve's right, where two bodies could be seen lying behind some bushes that hid them from Steve's sight.

"How do we know we're clear then?" Sukai asked Aaron, looking at the ground.

"The clearing was once a farm. The Army mined the cleared areas to stop anyone coming back and trying to start again." Aaron explained.

"Were you ever here with the French army?" Sukai asked.

"No not here, but for a while, France controlled this country. Who do you think planted these mines?" Aaron answered, before moving forward and loading his pack.

Gathering up their individual gear, the three started off at a fast pace to make up for the time lost in the minefield. Stopping only to check their compass, they hurried through the thick undergrowth making the minimum of noise. Closing onto the suspected enemy positions, they halted and put on their killer suits, applying camouflage paint to their faces. The three then proceeded slowly through the scrub, nearly invisible to anyone watching.

Covering the last kilometre at a much slower pace, they reached a large river, which was their first objective. Pulling out a small inflatable boat from Sukai's pack, Aaron attached a small cylinder of compressed air and swiftly inflated the craft. The original plan had Sukai and Aaron wade across the river. The presence of crocodiles put a stop to that idea. Even in this raft, the two knew there were dangers, as they pulled out their pistols just in case.

"Good luck and don't fall out!" Steve whispered smiling. After getting a few finger gestures in return for his remark, he pushed the craft out into the fast flowing current. The two then paddled furiously against the river to the other side while he covered them. Once they'd made it, Steve started up river to his final objective, hoping Ali and Cody were alright.

On the plane, Cody and Ali closed the rear plane door, after the others had jumped. They then busied themselves making sure nothing remained of their departed friends before preparing to land. With the help of a known gunrunner to General Mogar, who owed the Americans a favour, Ali had set up a meeting with the General to try to sell him some equipment. Landing at a small airstrip that had at one time been owned by a rich landowner, they were greeted by a friendly welcoming committee of about twenty soldiers. Surrounding the plane, and supported by a fifty calibre machine gun, mounted on an old jeep, they were ordered to come out.

"Well here goes nothing!" Ali said to Cody and Brent as he opened the planes rear door and jumped down to the ground waving a greeting to the men waiting.

"Hello, does anyone speak English?"

"I do." Answered a tall black soldier who by his shoulder epaulettes showed he was some sort of officer, in this sloppy looking militia.

"I'm here to see the General. I've brought him some special presents," Ali smiled as Cody came forward carrying a small briefcase-sized box.

"I will take everything to the General, you can wait here!" said the Officer ordered.

"You could try, but one of us might push one of these buttons, and everything, including the plane, will go sky high. I don't think your General would be too happy." Ali said, pulling a small transmitter from his pocket. The Officer stood his ground for a few seconds more, before caving in and signalling his men to bring up several jeeps.

"You'll get along with the General, you think like he does. I didn't get your name?" the Officer asked as if they were best friends now.

"Ali, just Ali," Signalling for Brent to stay with the plane, Ali boarded the jeep, as Cody came forward carrying two long cases climb in as well. This was all watched by the Officer, who made no move to stop the pilot from staying, or Cody coming along. After ten minutes of being thrown around on a bumpy road, while being glared at by their escort, they finally arrived at the Generals base. At one time it must have been a prosperous town, but after years of war, anything worth taking was long since gone. Only the shells of the former buildings remained, which now held the Generals militia.

Not all the units here were as sloppy as the ones at the airport Cody observed. Hidden in some of the buildings, were some wicked looking surfaces to air missile. Even though they weren't the latest models, they'd certainly give the Mig fighters a run for their money. The soldiers who maintained these batteries looked first class too, meaning the General had some serious money to have these professional soldiers or mercenaries, working for him.

The Officer from the airfield showed them to a hut where they could remain until the General saw fit to see them. He warned them not to wander around, as he marched off, leaving a guard outside their door.

"Not the Ritz, but I've been in worse!" Cody said as he searched the room for bugs, and found both types.

"It doesn't matter Cody, we need these sales, or we'll be broke remember that!" Ali replied grinning, as he continued to talk for the entertainment of the listeners. Cody meanwhile, opened the cases and prepared the equipment for the Generals inspection. At the old church which had become the Generals Headquarters, the General and his staff discussed the gunrunners.

"The men who are listening to the receiver in their hut report that the two men are in a lot of debt and need this sale General!" a short Officer with glasses reported.

"Well that is most useful, it can be a great advantage knowing another man's hand when playing cards." the General said laughing, which on cue was joined in by his men. All except one Officer the General noticed.

"Jamison why aren't you laughing?" the General asked making all the others stop. Jamison was one of the Generals best Officers. Born in England, he'd even served in the English Army as a Sergeant, until a run in over stolen property had made him leave England and join the General.

"I don't like the look of them, they're ex-military for sure, and there's something else, something deadly about them," Jamison warned.

"Well, in that case, we'll see what they've got, and after the meeting, they can disappear along with their plane. I've always wanted my own plane!" the General laughed. This time Jamison joined in the laughter as well.

That evening, Ali and Cody were invited to dine with the General and his Officers, who laughed a lot Ali noticed, especially at him.

"Well gentlemen what have you got!" the General asked merrily, getting smiles from all there.

"Just these General," Ali replied, pulling open a bag to reveal the latest in communication equipment. Putting on the small headset, Ali demonstrated how this type of gear was used. He also pointed out that it was the type used by American Special Forces. An officer in charge of the General's communications came forward and went over the equipment, pleased with what he saw.

"General these will be indispensable at the coming meeting. All the men with you can be monitored from our headquarters instantly." The Officer explained excitedly, getting a wave from the general to calm down.

"That appears to have impressed my com officer" the General replied smiling, getting nods from his men. "What else do you have?"

"A surprise General!" Ali said, signalling for Cody to open the second case and assemble a Stinger Missile.

"My God!" yelled one of the three white Officers in the Generals Army, as he hurried from his seat to look at the weapon. The two others followed him, causing confusion, from the other soldiers present.

"Silence!" the General yelled at the sudden disturbance, which slowly subsided. "Captain Rosewood, please explain to me what's got you so excited?"

"General nothing can fly or be driven that can't be destroyed by this weapon Sir, it's infrared and radar guided. I had heard the Americans were working on one, but I never thought I'd see one!" Rosewood said excitedly.

"Would the Russians be impressed by this weapon?" the General asked his excitement building.

"They'll shit themselves if they think we've got them. They definitely won't fly near us that's for sure." Rosewood explained as the General sat silently contemplating the new opportunities opening before him.

"I also have a personal present for the General," Ali said softly, holding out the briefcase-sized box to him, which he opened. A huge smile lit the General's face, as he showed his men the two gold-plated matching forty-five calibre automatic pistols.

"I've got to say, what's your name? Yes, Ali. I'm impressed by this gift and by the equipment. What are you asking?"

"Well, twenty sets of the com gear are about fifty thousand dollars American. The stingers are half a million each!" Ali replied poker faced.

"Are you crazy, why would I pay that much?"

"You don't trust the Russians. These weapons give you leverage." Ali answered, watching the General.

"You knew we'd bugged your room didn't you?"

"I would have done the same," Ali answered, not knowing how the General might react.

"And how did you come by this equipment?" Jamison asked from the side of the room.

"We stole it from the testing grounds in Arizona" Ali replied, watching Jamison, as the General burst into laughter, followed by his men on cue, all except Jamison.

After Ali and Cody left, the General met with his Officers, to discuss the weapons and their new weapon suppliers.

"General, these weapons and the older system we already have, put us on an equal footing with the President's forces. His air power is useless if we have a good supply of these missiles," Captain Rosewood said smiling getting nods of approval from his fellow officers.

"They have only a small supply of these missiles, and I do not trust them!" Jamison replied getting angry looks from the other Officers.

"They have another nineteen missiles, that's twenty with this one. That's more than enough to put fear into the Russians I can assure you!" Rosewood argued, getting a little sick of Jamison being so negative.

"Look, Jamison, even without the missiles, the radio gear is years ahead of the enemies. It will make us look a more professional force when we meet the President and his Russian friends." the

Communication officer added getting a nod from the General.

"I trust your opinion Captain Jamison, but we need those missiles, especially if things don't go well tomorrow at the meeting. I'll pay them the seven hundred thousand plus a quarter of the cost of purchase as a deposit for the other missiles. But Jamison's right, I too don't trust them either. So when the other missiles arrive, Ali and his friend can be taken care of, but not until then. Am I understood?" the General asked, getting agreement from all. "I expect you all to go over the new equipment before the meeting tomorrow. We cannot afford to look amateurish, so good night gentlemen," the General said, before departing leaving his men to sort out the equipment.

Cody and Ali had a busy night instructing the Officers on how to work the equipment mostly the communication system. Rosewoods men already had the basics of preparing a missile for launch, which made instructing them easy. All the time they worked with the General's men, Jamison sat in the background watching.

"Have you got a problem friend?" Ali asked suddenly to Jamison putting him on the defensive

"I don't trust you. And you are not my friend," Jamison replied, reaching for his gun, as one of Rosewoods men pointed a rifle at him.

"Don't do it, Jamison, the General ordered us to look after these men, and they are helping us!" Rosewood said as the room went quiet.

"Maybe he's working for the Russians?" Cody added smiling, getting support from some of the men there, as everyone watched Jamison.

"I am loyal to the General!" Jamison loudly replied as sweat rolled down his face. Suddenly turning he pushed through the crowd, walking towards his camp.

"He's a strange one, but he is loyal I think?" Rosewood said watching the departing figure, unsure about his fellow Officer, as the men went back to training.

THE MEETING

The following morning, the camp emptied of soldiers, as the great majority of the Generals men, moved forward to take up positions. The meeting place was in the middle of an old bridge, built in better times. It was a four-lane concrete structure, the only crossing point on the river for twenty kilometres in either direction. The Russians, to make sure nothing went wrong, had supplied fifty elite paratroopers to oversee the cease-fire and protect the President. They did this by patrolling both the approaches to the bridge, as well as the meeting place right in the centre.

Through his binoculars Major Brascos scanned the rebel side of the border, seeing the rebels moving into prearranged positions. He was not alarmed by this, as he'd watched them prepare several days before. He was confident they were only there for the General's protection.

The sound of approaching vehicles signalled the arrival of the General, who impressed the Major by walking straight out to the meeting spot as if he owned the place. Major Brasco came forward and gave the General a formal salute getting a smile and salute in return.

"Welcome General, it's an honour to ....." the Major said stopping, as he caught sight of the communication devices the Generals men were wearing.

"Where did you get those from?" the Major asked pointing to one of the officer's headsets.

"I have a new supplier. He supplied those and that." The General smiled, pointing to a soldier who was carrying the stinger missile. Shocked, the Russian major forgot his mission of guarding the bridge and with two of his officers headed over to the soldier with the missile launcher, looking it over unable to believe what he was seeing. The Major realised he was the first Russian soldier to see this advanced piece of equipment, and peace talks or not he knew he must get it back to Russia at all costs. Walking back to the amused General and his officers, the Major was speechless.

"How did you get it, General? My superiors will pay anything to see one of these!" the Major asked excitedly, first in Russian, then realising his mistake in English, which made the General roar with laughter.

"You may have it, Major, we have plenty more." the General added casually, as the Major again looked up at the rebel position above him, suddenly a little worried.

"Don't worry Major, I'm here to talk." the General smiled, seeing where the Major had looked, knowing he now had the advantage over these men.

Moments later a convoy of armoured vehicles arrived at the Governments side of the bridge, and the President got out. Surrounded by his security, he made his way out to the middle. Unlike the Major, the President was not impressed by his enemy rearming with more advanced equipment, and as the two seated themselves to discuss the peace treaty, the President brought this point up.

"I do not like the escalation your new weaponry bring to this table!" the President snarled.

"I too wasn't happy either, to see Russian planes flying over this country my friend, what did you think I would do?" the General replied calmly knowing he had the upper hand. The President was about to launch into a stinging rebuke when a shot rang out from the hills followed by shocked silence, as the President catapulted out of his chair.

Up above on the hill where the Rebel forces were positioned, Steve cleaned his knife. He'd just taken care of the three men who manned a gun position located there. Only one had been at his post the other two sleeping when Steve had come over the sandbagged wall on the opposite side of the river killing the guard first and the other two as they slept. Settling down with only the dead for company, Steve watched the arrival of the General followed twenty minutes later by the President, which triggered the final phase of the mission.

Preparing his sniper rifle, which up until then had been secured on his back, Steve trained the weapon on the conference table, locating the President, who sat facing him. Reaching into his pocket, he brought out a small transmitter, placing it next to his rifle. When Ali had worked out this plan, baiting it with the advanced communications equipment and the Stinger Missiles, the Colonel had exploded angrily. He pointed out that both systems were secret and should not fall into the enemies hands. It was then that Ali and Steve had explained to him the twist, all the equipment had been altered allowing a small amount of explosive to be added to each device. The headsets and their battery packs worn on the soldier's belts, both had been crammed with plastic explosive, along with a much more significant charge in the stinger missile near the propellant section of the rocket.

The final two pieces of plastic explosive were in the butts of the Generals new pistols, which he was proudly wearing today. Connected to each piece of explosive was a detonator that in turn was connected to a receiver, they waited silently for Steve to press his transmitter that would cause the explosions of all the devices. Grabbing his small radio, Steve contacted the others.

"One ready!" Steve said quickly waiting for two answers.

"Two ready!" Sukai replied as he and Aaron removed the bodies of the four Mortar crewmen, they had despatched earlier, to prepare the mortar for firing. Sukai and Aaron, after leaving the river had made their way behind the President's forces until they found one of his mortar positions. The President taking no chances had prepared firing positions for his artillery and mortars in case things went wrong at the meeting. Of course, no one had thought about anyone crossing the river, so except for a few patrols, these positions were only defended by their four-man crews, a big mistake.

Aaron seeing Sukai give Steve the ready signal broke open two boxes of mortar rounds, containing two each. He then adjusted the explosive bags on each mortar round for the distance to the bridge, before holding one round near the opening of the tube, waiting for Steve's final signal.

"Three ready!" Ali signalled from the General's base, as he and Cody prepared for what was coming. Opening the secret compartment at the bottom of the two large cases Cody removed the two pistols. They then sat down and waited for the party to start. Steve after getting the two "Okays" lifted the rifle and zeroed it in again on the President's head, pulling the trigger, seeing him catapult backwards from the impact. Still watching through the scope, Steve saw the shocked look on the General and the Russian Majors faces as he then pressed the transmitter button.

On the bridge, the President lay dead on the ground, as Major Brasco's fought through his shock.

"Prepare for attack!" he yelled, as his men reacted, instantly, aiming their weapons at the General's confused escort. For a split second, calm descended, as the General clearly frightened, was just about to speak, when he and his men exploded, bursting into flames before the Russians eyes.

Aaron hearing the explosions, in quick succession, dropped the four rounds, one after the other, into the tube. Not even waiting for impact, he and Sukai grabbed their gear and raced towards the river, their mission completed. On the bridge, Major Brasco slightly wounded, looked around at the carnage. The General and most of his entourage were either dead or severely hurt. 'What is going on?' he asked himself, as the four mortar rounds came crashing down on him and his men.

In the gun position above the bridge, Steve saw the mortar rounds hit straddling the bridge, knowing there was one thing left to do. Dropping his rifle, he swung the heavy machine gun around. Firing onto the bridge in a long thundering burst, Steve swept the entire length, dropping anyone still on their feet to the ground. Finished, he grabbed his rifle and hurried towards the airstrip. Behind him, he heard both the Rebel forces and the Presidents forces heavy weapons open up on each other, as both sides responded to the treachery.

"What's going on Captain?" Ali asked Captain Rosewood, who headed up the headquarters command staff while the General was absent.

"We don't know, there's no answer from the General!" Rosewood answered looking a little scared.

"They've ambushed the General! You've got to save him!" Ali replied angrily, but still, no one reacted. "You've got to order your men to open fire, or the General will be furious!" This time he got a reaction, as the whole staff ordered every man forward and all weapons to open fire.

"Can you give me a driver? We have more weapons back on the plane?" Ali declared, getting a nod from Rosewood, who told two men to go with them. On the way to the airstrip, Cody and Ali took care of the guards, before turning parallel to the river. Here they waited at a prearranged position for Sukai and Aaron to turn up. One hour past the agreed time, a nervous Ali relaxed, as a wet Sukai and Aaron thankfully appeared. They were lucky to have made it.

"What happened?" Cody asked equally worried, as Sukai and Aaron climb into the back of the jeep. Sukai explained as Ali drove. They had been crossing the river when a stray mortar round had hit the bank they had just left, missing them but not the raft. Nearly across and losing air, they had come to the attention of a four-metre crocodile. Sukai had been forced to shoot it several times at point-blank range. Forced then to abandon the raft, they'd swam the last ten metres, losing all their gear, but thankfully had not being eaten.

"Is that all?" Cody grinned, knowing both men had been shaken up by the experience.

On the other side of the rebel position, Steve hurried as fast as he could away from the developing war zone. He stopped occasionally to find cover, as the General's troops, at times reluctantly, headed towards the river and the fighting. Stopping to check his bearing, Steve decided to forget a zigzag approach and make straight for the airstrip. Time was more important at the moment than being spotted.

Even so several times, he was forced to hit the ground, as shells screamed overhead dropping with a mighty crunch sending shock waves out, shaking the jungle in every direction. This gave Steve a real close up impression, of what war was really like. Not knowing the others had been delayed, and not wanting to break radio silence, Steve stripped off his pack and threw away all his gear. The only thing he kept was his rifle and killer suit which he still wore. Moving as fast he could go through the jungle, which began to thin, he arrived at the outskirts of the airstrip. He saw that the others still hadn't arrived which surprised him, considering they had planned to grab a jeep while he was on foot. Looking closely at the plane, through his scope, Steve spotted Jamison and ten of his men waiting on the blind side of the plane. They had Brent the pilot tied up on the ground near the front wheel.

When Jamison had first heard the fighting, he knew it was the end of the General, which surprisingly didn't bother him at all. After the trouble last night with Ali the gunrunner and the General, he had been assigned the task of delivering the General's money to the plane as punishment. In doing so, he had missed out on meeting the President. Now hearing the impact of Artillery and mortars, Jamison knew it was all over, and he had the money and a plane. All that remained was to take care of the two bastards, who he realised were behind this whole betrayal.

He wasn't sure how, but he knew somehow Ali and Cody had set them up. Steve knowing it was a trap was just about to signal Ali, when their jeep appeared from the tree line and came to a halt near the plane as Jamison's men surged out from behind the plane surrounding them. Ali had no time to do anything but freeze as Jamison, a smile on his face approached the jeep. Cody next to Ali carefully reached for his weapon.

"Put your hands where I can see them, or we start shooting!" Jamison ordered, knowing he had the upper hand.

"What's going on Jamison? The General sent us to get help, he's been wounded!" Ali shouted.

"So he sent you two for help, with two other men, wearing camouflage suits did he?" Jamison laughed, looking at Sukai and Aaron who hadn't changed yet.

"They're spies we caught them on the way here. See they have no weapons."

"Well, you won't mind me shooting them then!" Jamison smiled, raising his pistol. He never got to pull the trigger, as he heard the crack of a rifle shot. A sharp pain in his chest was the last thing Jamison felt, as he stumbled backwards, blood and bone spraying over his men. Jamison's soldiers stood momentarily paralysed by shock, as two more men were shot down. Their Sergeant getting over it, ordered all his men behind the jeep and out of the line of fire, while he thought of what to do.

"We could shoot the four spies and run for it!" One of the soldiers shouted.

"I think the only reason the sniper is not shooting, is that we have them captive." The Sergeant replied, trying to locate the sniper. As the soldiers looked around the area trying to spot the sniper, an eerie silence settled over the airfield. Steve in the meantime was circling around trying to get a better shot at the remaining men. He was just about to fire when the noise of an approaching jeep filled the air. The Sergeant and his men cheered, as Captain Rosewood and four other men pulled up next to the jeep they were sheltering behind.

"Get down Sir, there's a sniper!" the Sergeant warned, relieved by Rosewoods appearance.

"No, we saw him run off as we approached!" Rosewood shouted, to all there including Steve who was only fifteen metres away.

"We have captured these men, Sir. How is the General?" the Sergeant asked.

"He's alive, but badly wounded, we're all moving to the south. Load up your men and head towards our main base, the General will need all his brave men. We'll take care of these gentlemen after we question them." Rosewood assured them, as his men tied up the four men in the jeep. After the Sergeant and his men had loaded up and left, Rosewood quickly untied Ali and the others and sent one of his men to check on Brent.

"You can tell your sniper to come in now; I hope we have proved we're friends!" Rosewood shouted.

"There's no need to yell Captain," Steve said as he appeared right behind him, looking like something out of a nightmare, scaring Rosewood half to death.

"Have any of your men medical training, one of my friends is hit!" Rosewood asked.

"Aaron, go have a look at him," Ali ordered as he saw Brent wave from the plane, that he was okay.

"Now Captain what's your story," Ali asked seriously, pulling out a hidden pistol.

"It's a long story, but we've got some time," Rosewood confessed, as he leaned back against the jeep and unburdened himself. Three years ago Rosewood and the men around him had come to fight for the General to free the Congo from a dictator. It had all gone well until the General had decided to fund his war with drug money. At first, they had been shocked, but they needed weapons, so they'd gone along with it. This helped the General fight back against the enemy, who grew stronger with Russian help.

It was only when one of their friends had complained about the local populations suffering and been shot for it, that they knew they were trapped here.

"When you came into the headquarters and told us to send all the men forward, we realised this was our chance, so we took it," Rosewood explained

"What's in the boxes in the jeep?" Ali asked.

"Our superannuation" Rosewood answered, with a small grin on his face. In the panic at the camp from the shelling, Rosewood had ordered all the army units to retreat southwards towards their permanent base, after radioing that the General was okay. In confusion he and his men had loaded up a fair amount of the Generals money and drove here, hoping the plane had not left yet.

"The problem is our unit's kind of secret Rosewood. What if you or your men talk?" Ali asked.

"My friend, I can only give you my word and that of my men, that if you give us a lift, we'll disappear forever," Rosewood promised his hand still on his weapon.

"That's good enough for me!" Cody smiled, before walking off towards the plane.

"Those soldiers had us cold. Even if Steve had got them all, we'd still be dead!" Sukai added getting agreement from Ali.

"Get your stuff aboard Captain," Ali grinned, as they all walked to the plane.

"Hey Ali, can we split the money over there like they are?" Brent yelled out, aware that Jamison's men had brought the money for the weapons as well.

"Of course!" Ali replied, amazed at their luck, knowing he'd moved closer to retiring, as the unit and Brent loaded the money.

The split up of money, once they were airborne, was nearly a quarter of a million each. Brent received an equal share, who of course wouldn't tell the Colonel, making them all feel a lot safer. Steve sat there with the others trying not to think of how many people had died in agony from the drugs sold to obtain this money. Opposite him, Rosewood sat quietly. His relief at being finally out of it was plain to see. In the distant future, Steve would think back wondering if Rosewood and his men had found peace after all that death, he hoped they had.

At the airfield in South Africa, the unit members said goodbye to Rosewood and his friends as they hailed down a passing truck, vanishing with their large cases.

"I hope they're okay and their friend sees a doctor," Aaron warned, after checking Rosewood's friend, who had been shot in the leg. It didn't look good, Aaron had suggested seeing a doctor as soon as possible, he hoped he did.

"They'll be okay. Did you notice they didn't even blink when we shared out our money? Makes you wonder how much was in those cases doesn't it!" Sukai smiled.

"I'll say my goodbyes too, I've got a bank to find," Brent chuckled. He was about to turn away when he turned back to them becoming serious. "By the way, the Colonel ordered me to leave you if there was any trouble, I just thought I'd let you know," Brent confessed, before disappearing into a cab.

"That was good of him to warn us," Cody admitted, watching the pilot leave.

"It was good of him to wait when Jamison turned up. He might have got away and not risked getting shot by staying!" Sukai admitted, knowing this unknown pilot was one of them now.

"Anyway, we'll meet in London for our debriefing with the Colonel. Cody has to stay behind and clean up the plane and the equipment before leaving. So I suggest we all give him the money, with your Swiss bank details we opened in Thailand. He can arrange to deposit it for us all, while we meet the Colonel." Ali suggested, getting nods from everyone, as they all boarded a taxi bus and drove back to the hotel.

Getting to London was a bit of an anti-climax as the Colonel, so excited by the success of the operation, had already left for Washington to receive his accolades. They were met by a junior member of the Colonel's staff, named Don Brooks who told them how proud he was of the unit, even if his boss wasn't. This made him at least a bit more acceptable.

Promising to get all the paperwork done, he let them go, after only keeping them there for one day. This impressed them all, especially Steve, who had a wedding fast approaching. That night they went out for a well-deserved drink, minus Cody who was still in Africa. Ali was the designated driver as usual.

"What's Steve wife look like anyway Ali, you've seen her?" Aaron asked as he downed a glass of scotch

"Her looks are okay, but she must weight twice as much as Steve."

"I'm going to tell her that Ali, or maybe I should tell Julie," Steve said as Ali uncharacteristically went quiet. This made the others ask who Julie was, much to Ali embarrassment, deflecting the attention from Steve. It was a good night, only saddened when Sukai who'd had quite a few drinks, brought up the point that we'd just caused the deaths of hundreds, maybe thousands of soldiers and civilians. Even Ali who was sober admitted the mission had done nothing for the population, which left everyone depressed.

Saying their goodbyes to each other, they started to leave. Steve quickly reminded them of the wedding, getting a subdued "we'll try" in return, which didn't inspire him that they would attend. As Steve and Ali walked to their hotel, Steve asked how many of the team members did he think would be coming to the wedding?

"It's hard to say, Steve. We all want to come, but no one wants to get caught breaking security."

"I suppose I'm asking a lot," Steve admitted.

"Don't worry, at least they'll send good presents after this mission!" Ali chuckled.

The flight home the next day was quieter and lonelier than the last one. Steve settled into Business class, thinking of his trip in First class with Michelle last time. He missed her badly, wondering if these missions achieved anything. And if they did for whom, as he drifted off into a deeply troubled sleep.

LUBYANKA MOSCOW

Two Captains in the KGB Headquarters in Moscow stared at the pile of maps and information from around the world, which lay strewn on the desk in front of them.

"Where are you hiding?" said a furious Captain Sergio Andropov.

"We'll get them, my friend, it's only a matter of time," replied Captain Josef Yakof, formerly a Sergeant in the forensic team in Kabul, until General Ogarkov had made him a Captain. Together they had been assigned to track down the enemy team that had killed Sergio's father and created so much destruction in Afghanistan.

"I know on this table or in our files is a clue to these men, but I can't put my finger on it," Sergio yelled, frustrated with tracking down dead-end leads. A knock at the door made both the Captains jump, as a soldier appeared carrying a new file.

"What's this?" Sergio asked sharply, looking at the private.

"You asked the department to forward anything similar to Afghanistan. This one from the Congo just came in!" the Soldier replied, not caring one way or the other as he laid it on top of the other files and left.

Reading the file, written by a badly wounded Major, it described how the rebels had been set up by two gunrunners. One was believed to be an Arab, the other a Scotsman by the accent. They had rigged explosives into radio equipment and a stinger missile the rebels carried, to sabotage the truce. It continued on to say that captured rebels, after interrogation, had revealed that the same two men were later captured along with an Asian soldier and another soldier dressed in camouflaged suits.

"What are the chances of the Asian soldier being involved with a stinger twice? Remember, they still haven't been released to the American army yet?" Josef pointed out, having read the report.

"It's good, but do we have anything else?" Sergio answered, knowing it could be just a coincidence. After pouring over all the information they had, the only other thing that had happened at the same time was a report on an Australian soldier, possible SAS, travelling to South Africa. This was just before the problem in the Congo started.

"It's pretty thin Josef. Even I have trouble believing there's a link, especially when no Americans are present." Sergio replied, studying the information looking for something.

"You've got it, Sergio!" Josef barked suddenly, as Josef, grabbed at the table and looked again at the facts. "They're all foreigners, no Americans, it's the perfect unit. There's no link to the Americans at all, so if something goes wrong, it doesn't touch them." Josef continued excitedly, as Sergio smiled for the first time in days.

"But how do we catch them? We don't know anything about them?"

"We wait for the next sighting of this unit, and this time we follow them home. They're specially trained soldiers and the Australian SAS regiment isn't that big." Josef smiled gleefully.

PERTH

Arriving back in Australia, Steve felt like kissing the ground as the Pope did on his last visit. He was so glad to be home. Grabbing his car from the long-term parking, he drove home, hoping maybe Michelle might be there. Unfortunately, the house was in darkness, as he drove down the road, and parked. Checking the mailbox, Steve found an extensive collection of junk mail and bills. There was nothing from Michelle, leaving him a bit disappointed as he carried his bags into the front foyer. Looking at the small table inside the door, where he usually left his keys, Steve spotted an envelope with a simple "I love you" written on the front. It made his day.

The note was from Michelle, told how she'd been here only two days earlier. She'd been out with Joan and Elaine who were looking forward to the wedding. It was now only a month away she reminded him.

"God I miss you!" Steve said out loud smiling.

"And I missed you too!" came a male voice from the doorway behind him, making him spin around.

"John you scared the crap out of me!" Steve chuckled, hugging his friend.

"You know you might be a formidable soldier, but closing a door behind you, mightn't be a bad idea!" John grinned, welcoming him home.

"I'd offer you something, but I've just walked in."

"That's why I'm here. Joan said to get you to come over for dinner, Captain!" John said seriously, smiling at Steve confused look. "You must have impressed someone over there. You've been given a field commission, and I can tell you that's rare."

Shaking Steve's hand John waited for him to change, before they walked to John's house, for a meal and a few celebratory drinks. At dinner Steve settling back into the lifestyle, he liked best, as John chatted on about the everyday goings on at the base and operations running at the moment.

"Oh, another thing, I finished the manual and two weeks ago sent it off to Canberra, for the desk chair warriors to look over," John explained proudly as if he was announcing winning the lottery.

"Do you think they'll like it," Steve replied, hoping that the Army would go with it.

"Hard to tell, but I know the training base at Holsworthy in Sydney wanted a few copies of their training. It appears our new training here has been talked about by the men."

"I'd have thought the harder training program, wouldn't be something they'd brag about!"

"Yeah, you're right, it is harder, but in an exercise with the Third Parachute Regiment a couple of weeks ago, our men were all over them. It was embarrassing for the Para's, and our men came away pretty pumped up. I'd say that's why a few other units want the manual." John was proud of his men.

Joan getting bored with the Army talk steered the conversation back to the wedding, telling Steve how lucky he was and how excited she and Elaine were to be getting another friend to go out with. She didn't have to tell Steve he was lucky, as he sat there with his friends. The thought that in a few weeks she'd would be his wife made him over the moon, as he totally relaxed.

Monday morning at six, Steve walked into the Headquarters office. In his freshly starched and ironed uniform, compliments of John's wife, he proudly received his first salute from the Privates and NCOs on duty. It was a moment that would always stay with him. Knocking on the COs door, Steve entered to find Paul, John and Captain Lenton in a meeting.

"Here he is, our newest Captain!" Paul exclaimed, coming forward to shake Steve's hand, followed by the others.

"Bloody hell, Sergeant to Captain, who'd you have to kill to get that promotion," Cole asked jokingly, causing an embarrassing silence and an angry look from his CO.

"I'm sorry Steve. That was thoughtless of me, I was only joking." Cole said feeling stupid for saying it, even though everyone there knew it was a joke.

"It's okay Captain, I mean Cole, and it was a shock to me as well," Steve said smiling breaking the ice.

"Gentlemen, now you're here we can start," Paul said before continuing. "The Americans are, in a week's time, carrying out some field exercises near Darwin and have asked us to be the enemy. In the exercise they will defend an area of about twenty square kilometres; our job is to capture their Command Post. For this exercise, they'll be observing how their new Marine Ready Response unit, including their Seal unit's fares against our men." Paul explained, watching their reactions and handing the meeting over to them for questions.

"Their Seals are pretty good aren't they?" Steve asked.

"Yeah, they're the Navy's Special Forces, and they'll be no pushover!" John admitted, watching Steve studying the maps.

"The exercise area is on the gulf, surrounded by desert. Where were you planning to hit them?" Steve asked.

"We thought we'd use two teams and come in from the sea in rubber dinghies. Then penetrate their position from two separate directions." Cole answered showing Steve the directions and landing positions

"Will the yanks have armour patrolling?" Steve asked his mind racing.

"Yes, they will. As well as fixed positions, they'll have mobile patrols all over the area. Why do you ask?" Paul said wondering what

Steve was thinking.

"Oh it's just Ali, my unit leader overseas, noticed something about their patrols, which might come in handy." Steve smiled, before explaining.

THE EXERCISE

Major Chuck Granger met Paul and John at the entrance to his Command Bunker, with a hearty slap on the back, he welcomed them to his Command.

"Good of you to come and be observers, even though I don't think your men have got a chance in hell of getting this far!" he chuckled, as the whole Command Centre staff broke into laughter.

"Well, they might surprise you!" Paul said smiling, wanting to belt this smartarse in the mouth.

"There are more than four hundred Marines dug in out there plus patrols, and this Command Centre is surrounded by Navy Seals. You wouldn't like to wager a bet would ya?" the Major replied confidently to Paul.

"How about whoever loses flies the other unit's flag over their home base for a month!" John suggested smiling cheekily.

"Hey, I like the way your Sergeant thinks," the Major grinned, sealing the bet with a handshake, feeling the strength the Sergeant Major put into it. Letting go, the Major glared at John, giving him the, 'I'll get you look', before excusing himself, leaving the two Australians to observe. While they were looking around, another American walked over.

"The Major can be a pain in the arse, but he knows his stuff!" A voice behind them barked, as both Paul and John turned, and recognised his rank as a General before saluting him.

"Forget that I'm only here to observe as well." General Mosley replied looking the two men over, and what he saw impressed him, as he told them to follow him for coffee. Sitting down, the General introduced himself and talked about the military life and world affairs, before he suddenly switched back to the exercise.

"You're confident they're going to take this base aren't you?" he smiled.

"Yes sir, we think so," Paul answered, like this man.

"Is the Ghost out there?" the General asked making John spill his coffee and Paul looked stunned. The General at their reaction, roared with laughter before he explained. On his travels around Australia, he was visiting Sydney when he was introduced to several SAS soldiers passing through on their way back to Perth. He'd asked them candidly had anyone ever got the drop on them. It was then that one of them told the story of Steve getting through to the headquarters on his entry trial.

"So is he out there or not?" the General asked Paul.

"Yes, he's leading one of our teams," Paul answered, thinking it funny sitting here talking to an American General about Steve.

"He was a Private, wasn't he? What's he doing leading a team?" the General asked, knowing how hard it was to rise up the ranks in a small Army.

"He's a Captain now partly due to his service in your Army Sir," Paul replied hesitantly, wondering if he was allowed to say anything more. Seeing the sideways looks on the two Australian faces at the other soldiers in the room around them, the General suddenly stood up.

"Anyone not Australian, out of this room now!" The General shouted as the men around them stampeded out the door.

"What's going on Colonel, what's one of your soldiers doing in my countries Army!" the General asked, as John looked at Paul, realising maybe he shouldn't have mentioned it.

"It was a deal done between our top brass and yours Sir. I don't know if I'm allowed to tell you anymore." Paul confessed, knowing how a Private would feel, being grilled by John.

"Next year I take a seat on the General Staff, Colonel, it doesn't get any higher. I can assure you, gentlemen, it's safe with me." the General promised, looking them both in the eye.

"Colonel I think you should tell him, more has happened than you know!" John blurted out, looking at his friend knowing more had happened, since Vietnam and Afghanistan. Paul started first telling the General about Colonel Dobson turning up at their base, then about the hit on the Vietnamese General and the ammo dump before stopping and telling the General that John knew the rest better.

"I heard rumours that someone got Tran Vin, but I thought it was a just a rumour." the General whispered, mostly to himself, as he stared at the Australians before speaking again.

"Okay Sergeant, what do you know?" the General said seeing the sweat on the Sergeant, knowing he wasn't going to like it. John started with the mission to Afghanistan and the shooting of General Sokolof, and the accidental killing of the Defence Minister at which point even the General started to sweat. He then told the General about Steve's latest mission, which although Steve hadn't said much about it, indicated it had something to do with the renewed fighting in the Congo. After this download, the General told him to stop.

"Holy Shit Colonel if you two are putting me on, I'll bust you both to privates!" the General exploded, knowing they were telling the truth, before reaching into his jacket pocket and pulling out a flask. Having a large swig of its contents, he offered it to Paul and John.

"No thanks Sir, but it is the truth," Paul said shakily.

"Yeah I know it's just hard to believe that's all. Especially when I know zip about it." the General replied dismayed.

"If it's any help, Sir, I doubt Colonel Dobson was Army, he didn't return salutes, unless it was unavoidable," John added.

"I think you're right Sergeant, it stinks like CIA to me!" he growled angrily, knowing whoever was running this was pushing the envelope to the edge.

"I want to meet this Ghost. Can that be arranged?" the General asked quietly.

"He'll be here soon General, I can assure you!" Paul answered confidently, as they all went back to observe the exercise.

COMING IN DUMB

Steve spat the dirt out of his mouth as he quickly gathered in his parachute, and ran to rendezvous with the other men. The run in had been rough, as the four men had jumped from a small scout aircraft. This type of aircraft was not usually used for jumping from, but at low altitude, it was almost impossible to spot on radar. Checking his jump helmet, Steve found a crack in the front where his head had clipped the rear tail rudder on the plane, as he exited. It had temporarily disorientated him, costing him vital seconds to pull his chute.

"You must have a hard head Captain; I thought you were a goner." Tim, his Sergeant, said, a little worried as the other two men ran up and quickly looked at his head.

"I'm okay; the helmet took most of the impact. Change into your killer suits and paint your faces, we've got some friends to meet." Steve grinned before he too applied the camouflage paint to his face.

On the other side of the American position two rubber rafts glided silently onto the beach roughly a mile apart, one to the north and one to the south of the yanks command post. Instead of hiding the craft, they left them on the beach and ran swiftly inland. Twenty minutes later an armoured patrol spotted one of the landing craft.

"Sir, a mobile patrol on the southern beach has found a rubber dingy!" the Radio operator in the American command bunker excitedly shouted to the Major Granger.

"What's their position?" the Major asked, as the radio operator pointed to the map next to him.

"That boat holds eight at the most, there's got to be more. Tell him to keep going along the beach north, he might spot more of them!" the Major ordered confidently, as he looked with a smile towards the two Aussies. Ten minutes passed before the same patrol radioed in again confirming the spotting of another dingy. The Command post instantly went to red alert, as all their positions were told to expect company.

"Sir two positions haven't answered!" The radio operator in charge of the fixed positions reported.

"Let's see where they are." the Major asked calmly, as the operator indicated two positions about a kilometre inland from the beaches.

"They're trying to break through from two separate waves!" the Major voiced to his subordinates.

"It could be fake Sir, the SAS isn't dumb!" a Captain from the Seals Teams said, studying the map.

"Maybe, or they've got too cocky. But we'll leave our forces where they are and just use the mobile units from the beach for now." the Major conceded, thinking the Captain could be right. An hour passed without any sightings, so the Major asked for a radio check. This time another position to the north, failed to report.

"Send units between that position and this base immediately. Contact the position to the south and tell them to be on watch for an immediate attack." the Major commanded, sweat appearing on his face. In the southern position which consisted of a command post of three men and two gun positions manned by four men each, the radio operator turned to warn his Sergeant.

The words caught in his throat, as a piece of vegetation hurtled through the door, weapon firing.

"Major!" the radio operated yelled loudly.

"Settle down soldier. What is it?" the Major asked, calmly, trying to bring the nervousness of his staff under control.

"I had just finished talking to the position to the south Sir when I heard gunfire. Now I can't raise them!" the Radio Operator stammered out, more in control this time.

"Get a patrol straight there!" the Major ordered another operator, as he looked at the map and saw the SAS had pushed nearly halfway through the positions.

"Send all the mobile patrols on the desert side of the position, towards the enemies' last positions!" the Major ordered, as all the four radio operators started moving men from the desert side towards the ocean.

"Sir, mobile unit seven reports he's low on fuel, he's coming back to refuel." an Operator in charge of mobile units reported sheepishly, waiting for the explosion.

"That incompetent fool, doesn't he read the standard patrol instructions about keeping the tanks full!" the Major shouted to no one in particular, as he marched up to the Radio Operator and grabbed the radio.

"Mobile unit seven report to the Command post before you go to refuel!" the Major ordered angrily.

"Will do," was the only response from unit seven.

"I'll kick him another arsehole, the sorry excuse for an Officer!" the Major grumbled to his fellow Officers as they turned their attention back to the enemy. All went quiet for a while when several radio operators at once reported contact with the enemy who seemed to be retreating back towards the sea.

"You've got em now!" the Seal team Captain chuckled to the Major, as the whole room sensed victory.

"Looks like you underestimated the defences here!" the Major said to Paul, noticing the Australians remained silent. At that moment an armoured vehicle roared into the compound, stopping right outside the Command Centre. The guards gathered round to see the Major do a number on the Officer in charge.

"Looks like the action here is over!" the Major smiled, as his men cheered.

"Now I'll just go out and chew the arse of this slacker!" the Major grumbled, as he opened the outside door to chaos. Gunfire erupted from the armoured patrol vehicle, as evil looking nightmares, forced their way through the door, firing at point-blank range into the Command centres staff.

The General sat tied on the ground with everyone else, as these piles of vegetation spread out into the compound, taking position after position from the inside. It was over quickly as more camouflaged soldiers, who had come from the beach, linked up and roared off in the captured vehicles. The fixed positions were taken by surprise as units called on their radios, getting false reports from their Command Post, now controlled by these walking nightmares.

By daylight, it was all over, with only mopping up to be done, as the operation was officially judged over and all units headed in, for debriefing. The General who was tied up along with everyone else, including Paul and John, watched astounded from the floor. He was amazed, at how one heavily camouflaged soldier, using their captured radio, single hand-idly moved his units around the terrain, taking out position after position as if it was a chess game. With the exercise over, the impressed General watched as the man they called the Ghost, walked out and congratulated his men, making sure everyone was okay before he relaxed.

"I'll be damned! What I could do with a hundred men like him!" the General whispered, smiling.

Changing out of their killer suits, Steve greeted Captain Lenton, who, with three other men had led the Americans back towards the coast while the others had hurried to meet Steve's men, at the Command Centre.

"Looks like your plan worked out, even though they nearly got me!" Cole grinned as he shook Steve's hand.

"I think you're getting old Cole, but since you're here, I'll let you untie the CO and the RSM, they'll be in a good mood by now." Steve smiled. After checking the men for injuries, and congratulating them, Steve and Cole headed to the Command Centre. Untying the men in the room, Steve was shocked to find a General amongst them.

"I'm sorry Sir; I didn't know you were a General?" Steve stammered out, seeing John and Paul looking on smiling.

"That's okay Captain I've had worse done to me by my wife!" the General replied as most men there burst into laughter, easing the anger that some of the American Officers felt.

"So you're the Ghost?" the General asked. The SAS soldiers there look towards Steve surprised, wondering how the General knew his nickname.

"We didn't tell him, Captain," Paul said as Steve looked at him and John.

"We need to have a talk Captain." the General informed him, pointing to a side room and holding up his hand when several Officers including Paul went to follow. "This is private gentlemen." The General closed the door behind them, leaving a whole room wondering what was going on.

"Steve isn't it. You can call me Max, for now, sit down and relax." the General smiled, sitting down opposite Steve and passing him his hip flask.

"I was talking to your CO who let slip you worked for us. Since then I've made a few discreet calls to some friends on the Joint Staff. I can tell you no one knows anything about the unit you work for, so how about you fill me in on what's been going on?" Max asked softly, leaving Steve with no option but to tell him everything.

He started with his training at Fort Bragg. He then went on to tell him of each operation in detail leaving nothing out, as the General sat there dumbfounded.

"Steve if I hadn't seen you at work, I wouldn't have believed it. Even after your CO and Sergeant had told me, I doubted it to be true, but not after tonight. And you say you don't usually do the planning?" Max asked smiling.

"No sir, Ali actually commands the unit and plans the missions, with the help of Intel from the Colonel," Steve answered sure that he could trust this man.

"Look, I'm not sure who's running this Steve, but I can hazard a guess. But until I know if they have Presidential approval, you'll have to trust me to get to the bottom of this."

"I was thinking of quitting Max anyway, I'm getting married in two weeks time."

"Congratulations Steve I wish you good luck, but I'd be careful. Whoever's running this unit mightn't be too happy about you leaving."

"I'm not an easy man to kill General!"

"I don't doubt it, but what about your family Steve? Just be careful till you hear from me." Max suggested. Steve for once, felt afraid. "Don't take me too seriously Steve I might be blowing this all out of proportion, but it's best to be safe. Now go join your friends they most probably think I wanted you to join my marines, so we'll go with that." Max smiled, as they walked out and joined the others.

"You'll regret not coming over to the Marines, Captain" the General barked with a wink to Steve. Boarding his jeep to leave, he turned to Major Granger, suggesting the Major and his Officers try a little harder before his driver gunned the jeep down the road to the airfield.

"How did your conversation go with the General?" Paul asked later as they prepared to head home.

"Good, he's checking into who's running the unit," Steve answered quietly looking around.

"He's a good man you can trust him!" Paul said softly.

"It's not him I'm worried about."

THE MARRIAGE

Two weeks before the marriage, and time was flying, as Steve frantically tried to get himself organised. His jobs were to try and arrange transport, accommodation and suits from the other side of the continent. The two cars were easy, as Edward had a mate in the Feds, who moonlighted as a limo driver. For some extra cash, he arranged the cars. They were to pick up Michelle and the girls from her flat which included Julie and the other bridesmaids, then take them to the church in Wollongong. From the church, they'd drive the bridal party to Michelle's parent's house for a casual reception.

Accommodation proved harder as he didn't have the faintest where she'd want to go. In the end, he rang Michelle's mother and asked her.

"She always loved the coast Steve, especially Stanwell Park maybe you can find something there." Steve could tell she was holding back tears, as she talked to the man who was taking her daughter to live a couple of thousand kilometres away.

"Emily I love her with all my heart I'll always keep her safe. Why don't you and George come for a visit once we get settled?" Steve suggested, reassuring her.

"That would be great Steve, I'd love that. I'll book a room for you two at a place George, and I stayed in at Stanwell Tops. It overlooks Stanwell Park beach and the coast, I'm sure she'll love it." her confidence in Steve growing.

The third problem, the suits, were easy and expensive at the same time, he'd rung Isaac to arrange the suits and spent over two hours on the phone long distance catching up. Only at the end of the actual conversation did they discuss the outfits, which Isaac assured him were no problem, much to Steve's relief.

A week before the big day Steve left Campbell Barracks for the last time as a single man. Driving to the Airport Steve remembered he had one more problem, who was to be best man? He'd given it a lot of thought, and though John was his friend here and Edward his closest friend in his family, there was only one man that Steve had come to depend on. The only problem was he hadn't heard from Ali or the other members of the unit and wasn't sure if they were coming. Sitting on the plane in economy, as he was paying for this one, Steve hoped that at least one member of the team might come. He knew it was risky for them, so he began to plan to use John in case he needed another groomsman.

Arriving in Sydney at ten in the morning, Steve grabbed his bags from the turnstiles and caught a train into town hoping to catch up with Owen and see how the stock brokerage business was going. The lift opened at the seventh floor, this time the whole floor was Elliot and Fox exclusively, and the hallway leading to their small offices was gone replaced by a large reception area with three young ladies working behind separate desks.

"My name is Joanne, how can I help you Sir?" the young girl asked from the desk closest to the lift door.

"Hello, I was just hoping to catch up with Owen for a talk or lunch if possible."

"Mr Elliot is extremely busy, do you have an appointment?"

"Well no, I've just arrived in town from Perth. I'm sorry I should have thought."

"That's okay if you give me your number I'll have him ring soon." Joanne smiled, thinking to herself who would come all this way, without making an appointment first.

"My name is Steve Roberts and" was all Steve got to say, as Joanne's eyes went wide and the other two ladies who had been listening to the exchange came to their feet.

"I'm terribly sorry Mr Roberts, of course, Mr Elliot will see you if you could just wait a moment." Joanne stammered out, as one of the other girls disappeared inside leaving the other two girls standing.

"You can sit down, I won't bite you!" Steve chuckled, as the girls settled back into their chairs making him smile.

"You're not terrifying the staff, are you Steve?" a familiar voice asked from the office door. Turning Steve saw Mary standing there smiling. Gone was the revealing clothing, replaced by an attractive business suit which made her still beautiful, but more professional.

"Hello Mary, like usual you look stunning." Steve smiled, getting a small, dignified kiss on the cheek in return.

"We weren't expecting to see you until the wedding!" Mary smiled, having been invited by Michelle along with Owen, Warren and their partners, being his only business friends outside of the Army.

"Yes, I'm sorry about that. Things have changed in the time I've been away. I thought I'd just call in on Owen and have lunch. I didn't realise the firm's size had increased so much!" Steve answered, embarrassed at causing so much fuss.

"You're a full partner Steve you can call in whenever you like. But ringing first would be a good idea." Mary replied, slightly chastising him for not ringing

"Steve! I thought I recognised that voice!" Owen shouted, as he appeared from an interior office waving him in.

"Good to see you Owen, things have certainly changed here," Steve replied with a smile, as they shook hands.

"Yes, I'd better give you the ten dollar tour!" Owen suggested with a laugh, as he showed Steve around the office introducing him to other staff members. It was quite a tour, as the staff numbered close to thirty now. Most sat at monitors, watching names and numbers flash on their screens.

"These computers are the future Steve! They link us to America and England and save us thousands of working hours." Owen exclaimed proud of his achievement, in this area. As Steve walked around, he was repeatedly asked for his view of the market, and which shares he owned. Although he bluffed his way through with the help of Owen, he realised he needed to know more about this firm he was now a partner in.

"What did you think Steve?" Owen asked once they were back in his office.

"That if someday I want to work here, I'd better find out a lot more about this business!" Steve replied getting a nod of agreement from Owen, who too had seen Steve's weakness.

"We've put together a wedding present that should help." Owen smiled, thinking of the books he'd picked out for Steve.

"I'm glad you can all come, is Warren here?" Steve asked.

"Yes but he's a bit busy at the moment, he and I are travelling to London to open a branch there, finding accommodation is difficult," Owen replied.

"That's great news, Owen. I was there a couple of weeks ago. We stayed in the new Hilton Hotel. It was fabulous, and it's close to the business district." Steve informed him, glad to be able to help, as Owens' face grew serious.

"Steve it's good to help us with information, but think before you speak!" Owen replied, getting a blank look from Steve. "What's a soldier doing at an expensive hotel in London Steve?" Owen asked softly, watching Steve's face show concern at his own stupidity.

"Yes I see what you mean; I'll try to be more careful," Steve replied, knowing this wasn't the first time he'd made this mistake.

"Advice is good, but put it in a way that someone else was there not you," Owen suggested, a little worried by his friend's honesty in his line of work. The matter was quickly forgotten as Warren arrived with Mary. Crossing the road to the same club he'd been to the last time with Owen for lunch, he received the same professional welcome, from a different doorman.

"What happened to the other doorman?" Steve asked.

"He's the Manager here now, it appears he picked up quite a few share tips from customers and with the money he made he bought into the club," Owen answered smiling, as people walking by waved to Warren, Owen and Mary. At one stage during the meal Mary excused herself, and Steve noticed that she kissed Warren on the cheek as she left, making Steve look at her father Owen, who just smiled.

"They're getting engaged Steve, you most probably have noticed the change in her."

"Yes, I did notice the change in a dress!" Steve chuckled, as Warren and Owen burst into laughter. Steve congratulated Warren on taming her.

"I didn't do anything! We just went out one night, and she blossomed before my eyes. Since then we've been inseparable, and she practically runs the business!" Warren smiled lost in thought, deeply enchanted by her.

"Yes, it certainly makes it easy when we both go away, leaving her in charge." Owen chuckled, happy at Mary for choosing Warren. After they had toasted Mary and Warren, Owen asked Steve how long before he came on board and left the Army for a career at the firm.

"Last year I would have said in five to ten years, but lately I've been thinking maybe another two." Steve confided quietly, and Owen sensed the strain in him.

"Just ring Steve when you're ready," Owen replied smiling, wondering what he'd been up to be in London.

Leaving Owen and the others, Steve grabbed his bags and boarded the train, for an uneventful trip to his sister's house at

Cronulla. He thought seriously about the firm and how he'd fit in after his time in the Army life. Arriving in the afternoon, Steve found Michelle waiting for him, and all his fears for the future washed away as he kissed her.

"Easy there soldier! At least wait till we're inside!" Michelle giggled, as they went inside together. Much later Steve broke away from Michelle as they both lay in Steve's bedroom downstairs, their clothes in a pile on the floor.

"Another four days and this will be legal!" Michelle smiled, exhausted from their afternoon together.

"God I'll be glad when I can take you home finally to be with me!" Steve exclaimed emotionally, showing the loneliness he felt without her, making her hold him next to her. The noise of a car in the driveway indicated the arrival of Steve's sister and brother-in-law, causing both Michelle and Steve to hastily leave the bed. Hurrying to the shower, they quickly dressed, before heading upstairs to meet a smiling Edward.

"I see you've both been freshening up down there?" Edward chuckled at Steve's embarrassment.

"All ready for the wedding?" Steve asked Edward, changing the subject.

"Yep, went down to Isaacs shop yesterday, how about you?"

"I'm going there tomorrow, no problems!"

"And the best man?" Michelle added, watching Steve at the same time.

"I'm fairly confident he'll turn up."

"Have you a backup in case your friends from overseas don't make it?" Louise asked from the kitchen door, not too happy with her brother.

"John and Paul are coming with their wives if I get stuck, I'll ask one of them," Steve answered smoothly, feeling cornered.

"I hope so Steve, Julie was looking forward to seeing Ali again. I'd hate to tell her there was no groomsman for her escort!" Michelle added sternly, wondering how serious Steve was taking this wedding.

"Look I can't guarantee they'll turn up, they'll be breaking some pretty strict rules to be here!" Steve replied, getting defensive knowing how difficult it must be for his friends.

"Don't worry Steve I'm sure they'll make it," Edward said

confidently, hugging his brother-in-law, calming him down.

That evening during dinner, Steve sat with Michelle feeling anything but confident; as he looked at Edward who still assured him, they would make it.

"I like your confidence Edward, how come you're so sure?" Steve replied puzzled.

"Let's just say a little bird told me!" Edward smiled, before explaining. Earlier that day, at work, Edward had been called down from his office at the Airport to check on some recent arrivals that had aroused suspicion. Joe Sparrow, or the "little bird" to his workmates, had been watching four men while waiting for Edward to arrive.

"See the four men in row seven talking?" Sparrow said excitedly to Edward

"Yeah, so what, they look normal to me?"

"Two came on this flight; the other two arrived on two separate flights. Even the ones on the same flight boarded in different countries, yet they all appear friends. Why aren't they travelling together?"

"You're right that is unusual, let's go talk to them shall we," Edward replied, his eyes never leaving the four men as he spoke. Arriving at the customs barrier Edward waited for the first of the four men, who appeared to be Middle Eastern, to reach the customs declaration counter. One thing struck Edward as he stood there, was that they all looked military. As the Customs Officer looked over the first man's passport, the Arabs eyes focused on the Federal Police Officers who had taken up position standing behind the barrier. Edward felt his eyes just for a second lock on his before the man looked away.

"What's your reason for visiting this country?" the Customs Officer asked flatly, wondering why the Feds were here.

"I'm here to attend a wedding with my friends," Ali replied indicating the three men behind him. The interview ended there when one of the Federal Police Officers burst into laughter.

After clearing the customs barrier, Ali and the others were escorted to a side room to wait while the Federal Police talked outside the door.

"Everyone remain quiet, I'll do the talking!" Ali suggested, a little rattled as the Fed who had started laughing entered the room.

"So you guys are Steve's army mates from overseas!" Edward smiled, as Ali and the others surprised, look at each other.

"How could you possibly know that?" Aaron replied, forgetting Ali was doing the talking.

"Relax I'm Steve's brother-in-law Edward. I work here at the airport, and your arrival on separate flights was picked up by one of my Officers. Luckily he called me, or you could have been in a little trouble!"

"Why would we be in trouble, we are travelling legitimately?" Sukai asked puzzled.

"You were all talking together after deplaning from separate flights, that's kind of unusual. I'd watch that in future." Edward said, showing them Steve had told them about the unit.

"Thank you, Edward we shouldn't be here at all, the last thing we need is police attention!" Ali answered coming forward and introducing the others to Edward.

"Right then where are you staying?" Edward asked.

"Well, we haven't actually booked. We find it better to pay cash. It's safer!" Sukai answered.

"Not anymore my friend, from now on I'd think about booking ahead. With the latest computers that immigration departments have at our airports, and for that matter, most Western countries, it would raise a red flag against you immediately. I'm not trying to worry you, but you'll stay under the radar if you seem to follow the rules." Edward replied, getting nods from the unit members.

"As you know Edward we're just soldiers, this cloak and dagger stuff is new to us!" Ali replied, wondering how much they could learn from this police officer

"That's another thing, Ali. I spotted you as military straight away. Mind you I was a soldier! You could try letting your hair grow a bit and not stand practically at attention when talking to someone in authority!" Edward suggested with a smile, getting chuckles from them all.

"You are right Edward, but since the age of sixteen the military life is all that I have known, acting like a civilian is hard," Ali replied, wondering how he would look with a beard.

"What are the chances of that?" Steve asked Edward amazed.

"Yeah, it was lucky for them. Once you're in the computer, everyone would be watching them." Edward replied liking Steve's mates, glad he was there to help.

"Where were they staying?" Michelle asked wanting to meet these men that Steve's life seemed to revolve around.

"I'm not sure, probably around here somewhere. On Saturday they are going to follow me to the church from this address. I gave it to them at the airport, along with my home phone number."

"If I know Ali he's already driven past here to check, he's rather thorough."

"Well I hope you find them tomorrow little brother, it's the last day to get a matching suit for this Ali friend of yours," Louise added, not smiling as Michelle and Louise went to the kitchen, to do the dishes and discuss the wedding. The rest of the night passed quickly, and Steve found himself saying goodbye to Michelle for the last time before he saw her at the church.

"I'll see you on Saturday Mrs Robert's" Steve chuckled, as he kissed her through the car window.

"I'll see you there too hubby," Michelle replied giggling, as she drove off for what Steve hoped would be the last time, as he hurried into the house to bed.

Six in the morning and Steve, as usual, found himself running along the beach, heading north towards the sand hills. It was a cool morning, and except for the breaking of the surf on the beach, the only sound was the crunch of sand under his feet. His long strides swiftly ate the distance to the point, where turning he started back. Out the corner of his eye, he caught the movement of several shapes leaving the dune and taking position behind him. It struck him as unusual as this area was pretty remote. Shaking his head and smiling to himself, he reminded himself that he was in Sydney not overseas. Looking at his watch, Steve guessed he had twenty minutes of hard running left when he sensed that the people behind him were gaining swiftly on him.

That was an impressive feat, considering the physical condition he was in and the pace he was setting. Feeling slightly uneasy and not knowing why he was about to turn around and check out his pursuers when he was crashed tackled from behind. Going down heavily, gaining a mouthful of sand in the process, Steve's survival instincts took over. Adrenaline surged through his body, as he came up from the ground spitting out sand and breathing heavily. Preparing to deliver a killer blow if necessary, he was caught off guard, when the sound of laughter washed over him.

"You know Steve it wouldn't hurt to turn around and see who's following you once in a while!" Cody grinned at Steve's confusion.

"I should have known it was you guys when my brother-in-law told me about your run in at customs." Steve chuckled, feeling stupid, as they all shook hands.

Wandering back to Cronulla shops, they decided to have breakfast in a seaside café. Steve found that the unit members had booked a hotel here in Cronulla, hoping to catch him on one of his famous beach runs to the point that he'd told them all about.

"There's one thing I don't get! How did you four manage to catch me on that run to the point and back?"

"We cheated a bit there Steve!" Sukai said before continuing. "When we spotted you heading off towards the point we got a taxi to drop us out near the point. All we had to do was wait for you to turn, leaving you tired and us fresh." Sukai laughed with the others.

"I thought I'd find you all down here somewhere!" Edward said from behind Steve, making him and the others turn round. "Your sister was wondering where you'd got to." Edward continued as he shook hands with the others.

"Yeah I'm sorry about that, we were just catching up," Steve replied.

"She was more worried about the best man!" Edward reminded him, knowing he hadn't actually asked Ali.

"That's right! Ali, I'd forgotten to ask you if you'd be my best man!" Steve asked as a quiet Ali sat there looking at Steve.

"Steve you do me a great honour, but you realise I am a Muslim!" Ali replied watching Steve's reaction.

"You're my closest friend Ali. I trust you and the others here with my life every time we go on a mission together. Anyway, he's the same god that I pray to my friend!" Steve replied seriously, to a quiet table. Ali got up silently and hugged Steve, causing the others to look around quietly, slightly embarrassed by showing their emotions in public. Even Edward an outsider, felt the emotion of this group of men, something he hadn't felt since his Army days.

"So are we going out tonight drinking?" Cody smiled as the others relaxed and finished their breakfast. After eating, Steve led the group down to Isaacs shop and introduced him to his friends, as Ali was measured for his suit. After several hours of talking and measuring, Isaac, as usual, managed to sell everyone something even Edward, who surprisingly had become a good customer of Isaacs.

"After seeing you in that suit at the club with Michelle, I realised I had to lift my game!" Edward admitted, watching Steve interact with his friends, sensing the bond of comradeship between them. Edward knew that he had been accepted as a trusted friend by these men and even though he didn't share the bond they had as a unit, it felt good.

Waving goodbye and saying they'd see him at the wedding; the group left Isaac in peace and hurried off to find a pub, for a drink. Several hours later they trooped into Edwards house. Steve was at first worried that his sister might get a little cranky. Ali, who didn't drink smoothed the way, presenting Louise with a bunch of roses. He also complimented Edward on how lucky he was to find such a beautiful woman, making Louise blush. She told them all to get comfortable while she prepared them something to eat for lunch.

"You're a dangerous man Ali! Is he always this confident with women?" Edward asked

"Let's see how he goes when he meets his partner Julie at the wedding tomorrow," Steve replied, watching Ali nearly choke on his soft drink, causing the others to laugh.

"Tell us, Edward, what does Michelle look like, Ali says she's fat, while Steve says she's beautiful, which is the truth?" Cody whispered with a slur, having enjoyed the afternoon a little more than the others. As they all waited for an answer, Edward sat there with a look that made out he was giving the question some thought, much to Steve's amusement.

"Well to tell you the truth they're both correct, she's not bad looking, but she's twice as big as Louise!" Edward replied with a straight face, leaving all of them in the dark as to whether he was lying. Silence descended on the lounge, until a pillow thrown from Steve hit Edward in the face, knocking him backwards of his chair. As they all laughed at Steve's discomfort, Louise listening in the kitchen wondered, if men ever really grew up. Putting their lunches on a tray, Louise hoped that Michelle knew what she was getting into.

The rest of the afternoon and night was spent at the local pub, where Ali made sure the group behaved themselves up to a point. Around 11, Steve decided that with the big day tomorrow, it might be best to head to bed, while he still had one. Lying in bed that night, Steve contemplated his place in the unit and how much he would miss his friends if he retired. The thought of going on killing for no clear reason steadied his resolve. He knew when the time was right, he'd get out no matter what, his life with Michelle was far more important to him in the long run.

THE WEDDING

"God, how do you get this tie right?" Steve yelled at the mirror, for the fourth time, feeling his hands had five thumbs on each of them.

"It takes practice that's all," Edward replied smugly, as he entered Steve's room, having been sent down by Louise to see what was keeping her brother.

"It's okay for you; in your job, you're always wearing one!" Steve shot back, seeing Edwards tie look perfect making him fumble his again on the fifth attempt.

"Not my fault you Army grunts, don't know how to dress properly!" Edward chuckled at Steve's growing frustration.

"Also the fact I did his for him!" Louise's voice sounded from the door. Taking control of Steve's tie, Louise expertly made a perfect knot much to Steve's delight, before shepherding them out to their car as quickly as possible.

Standing in the driveway as if on parade were all the unit members, quietly waiting for Steve and his family to appear so they could follow them to the church.

"It's never too late to make a run for it!" Cody said mischievously, who like the others, looked out of place, in a suit.

"Don't even think about it!" Louise replied looking at her brother sternly, knowing all the time her brother was madly in love with Michelle, which got them laughing anyway.

"Whatever she looks like Steve she's getting one of the best men I've ever known," Sukai said quietly, causing an embarrassing silence as the other unit members nodded their support.

"Well, we'd better hurry, or we'll not get to see her at all." Aaron laughed as they all piled into the cars and drove south towards Wollongong.

Arriving at the church, Steve was surprised to see a significant crowd waiting.

"Bugger I didn't think there would be this many!" Steve said getting a little nervous.

"Our family might be a little small Steve; Michelle's on the other hand, is rather large. You'd have known that if you'd spent a bit of time looking at the invitations." Louise replied quietly, chastising him for having only a small input into the wedding. Getting out of the cars Louise quickly herded Steve and the others into the church. Checking Ali, Edward and Steve's suits out, making sure everything was perfect; she positioned them at the front of the church. Looking around Steve gave a quick wave or nod to his friends.

Owen with Warren and Mary were three rows back with Isaac, who Michelle had invited especially. Owen was at the moment having a deep discussion with Isaac, which knowing Owen, was on investing. Steve's CO Paul, was with John, talking to Cody, Aaron, and Sukai, while Paul and Johns wives, seeing their men talking shop, had come down to sit with Louise. That took care of Steve's side of the wedding, on the other side sat over a hundred relations and friends of Michelle, who seeing the disparity had drifted across to Steve's side of the church to even things out a bit.

Sitting in the front rows on Michelle's side were her parents and closest family friends. Michelle's brothers stood at the rear of the church waiting for their sister's arrival and keeping away from their three girlfriends who found this wedding a little too romantic for their liking. The rest Steve hadn't seen before, but some of the girls who sat in a group towards the rear must have been from Qantas, by the way, they watched the male members of the church. While Steve looked over the gathering Joe, Tony and Brian, Michelle's brothers discussed the coming wedding.

"What do you think of Steve's friends?" Brian said looking at Steve's army mates and feeling the raw power which radiated from the group.

"I hope she knows what she's doing?" Tony replied wondering if they could all fight like Steve.

"Well, you know at a wedding, how someone from the bride's side, usually drunk, causes trouble with the groom thinking he's not good enough. I'm telling you now it won't be me!" Joe said seriously, getting laughs from his two brothers and sideways looks from the people gathered there.

Steve at the front also looked towards the brothers wondering what they were talking about when he suddenly caught sight of a flower girl near the door to the church. Michelle had arrived.

"Too late to run now," Edward whispered, getting a grin from Ali and a frown from the minister at the same time. Steve didn't even hear, his eyes and total concentration were on that church door waiting nervously.

The small flower girl throwing rose petals slowly walked up the aisle, as the wedding march sounded from the church organ, causing everyone to stand up and face the entrance to the church. The first bridesmaid was Julie who looked stunning, and an intake of breath from Ali to Steve's side told him that Ali had not forgotten her. Next was Leonie who looked beautiful, if not a bit scared, a younger version of her sister.

Next came Michelle with her father, and Steve found his eyes misting up as he stared into those beautiful eyes. A sideways look at Sukai, Cody and Aaron showed they approved of his bride. They all gave Edward and Ali the "liars" look, for saying Michelle was a whale, getting a grin from them both in return. A stern look from Michelle's father took the grins of Edwards, and Ali faces as he approached Steve. He placed Michelle's hand in Steve's, before turning solemnly and sitting with his wife, who tearfully watched her eldest daughter get married.

The service over, Steve took great delight in kissing his wife soundly, before he was pushed to the side, as family and friends crowded forward to congratulate the couple. Through a sea of rice, Steve led his new wife at last, out into the sunshine, then into the waiting limousines. Ali and Julie shared their car, while Edward, Louise, Leonie and the flower girl followed in the second limo. Steve and Michelle couldn't be happier, as Ali sat quietly opposite Julie looking forlorn.

"You look beautiful Julie. I've missed you." Ali sighed softly, making everyone go quiet.

"Then why didn't you ring me?" Julie replied, trying to sound unemotional but failing.

"It's my job and what I am, which made me not ring you," Ali answered sadly.

"That is for me to decide, not you Ali. We'll talk about it later." Julie answered trying not to cry, as Ali nodded his agreement, looking at Steve and Michelle.

"I'm sorry Michelle for bringing sadness to your special day," Ali whispered.

"You are Steve's best friend Ali, and no one could make me sad today!" Michelle smiled, before kissing Ali on the cheek making him blush.

"And that's the last kiss you get from her!" Steve warned him, as they all broke into laughter.

The wedding reception was full of speeches and toasting as various friends and relatives stood up to wish the newlyweds well. Ali delivered a speech from the members of the unit giving nothing away. He made it sound boring, only doing assignments that the army did during peacetime. But he didn't fool everyone, as Isaac and Owen raised an eyebrow at each other during the speech. Isaac was one of the last to get up, giving an emotional speech about how Steve had helped fill the gap left by the death of his son. He described how Michelle had come in person and given him the invitation. It had shown him how special she was and how much Steve meant to her. When he had finished his speech, Steve got up and went across to Isaac and embraced him making the room go silent.

"Thank you, Isaac. Knowing you has changed my life!" Steve said, getting a little choked up, causing the room to remain quiet.

"Will this get us a discount on clothing?" Edward yelled from across the room, trying to restore the happy mood.

"Not in this lifetime young fellow!" Isaac replied smiling, as the room again burst into laughter, but both Isaac and Steve would never forget that moment.

Much later that night as Michelle lay in his arms, Steve thought how incredibly lucky he was, and again the question came to him, how much longer could his luck last, and what would happen when it ran out.

The next month went past in a rush as Michelle, with minor help from Steve, moved over to Perth and put Steve's house in order, something he hadn't really thought about. Up till then he'd mostly eaten at the barracks and only had food in the house when he knew someone was coming. Things like dinner sets or linen hadn't really bothered him until now. Michelle, during this time always seemed to get her way. He found that no matter what decisions he made about not purchasing something, got overturned. This usually occurred at night, when he found he was vulnerable to her persuasion.

Back at the barracks except for training, Steve found that his comings and goings with the Americans had made him unreliable to head up a team. In the meantime, he was happy just to train the Regiments men, while Michelle slowly settled in. That was about to change.

"Captain Roberts there's a parcel here for you!" One of the office staff informed him as Steve entered the Regimental Headquarters, startling him.

"Thank you Private," Steve replied absentmindedly, as he headed into his office. Opening the parcel, Steve found the units next mission, and it was a classic. A knock at the door startled him, and he quickly covered the 'Intel' before telling the person to enter. John entered the room, took one look at the parcel and sat down.

"Going somewhere?"

"Yeah, but at least it's for a good cause this time!" Steve answered, breaking another rule and showing John the mission outline. At first, John hesitated about reading it. Steve trusted his opinion, so he scanned the information.

"Your right Steve this is something to be proud of. I even wish I could go!"

"I hope Michelle feels that way."

"She's a soldiers wife my friend, she'll be okay. I'll arrange for you to disappear again for training." John replied, shaking his friend's hand and forgetting the reason why he'd come here in the first place.

That night Michelle knew something was up, as Steve seemed jumpy and overly helpful with dinner, she'd realised early on cooking wasn't Steve's first love.

"What's up Steve?" Michelle asked when they'd sat down for dinner. Steve at first had hesitated but gave in and told her.

"It's another mission with the unit, but this one is for a good cause."

"Where?" Michelle asked quietly, a little frightened.

"South America, it appears a drug cartel is holding a group of people hostage, we're going in to free them!"

"I know you shouldn't have told me, and there's most probably more to the story, but just promise me you'll be careful," Michelle asked softly.

"There's always risk honey, but we are the best at this, don't worry!" Steve smiled, holding her hand across the table.

The rest of the evening was subdued as Steve poured over the information on the mission, while Michelle busied herself around the house, wondering if now was the time to tell him her exciting news. A knock at the front door startled both of them.

"Anyone home?" John's voice sounded from the front door, as Michelle hurried to the door to let him in. "Hello Michelle, sorry to call so late, but I forgot to tell Steve something at the office today."

"He's in doing some paperwork. I'll get him, and put the jug on." Michelle replied, putting on a brave smile. Steve having heard John came out to meet him.

"Anything wrong?"

"No nothing wrong. At work today when you told me you'd be going off again, I forgot to tell you, you've been reassigned. They're sending you to Holsworthy training camp in Sydney, to try out our manual to see if it works" John replied excitedly.

"What about the Regiment?"

"It's only for a year then you come back!"

"What's this about Sydney?" Michelle yelled from the kitchen obviously listening.

"I'm being transferred there for a year!" Steve answered, with mixed feelings.

"When?" Michelle asked excitedly.

"In about three months, that's of course if he's back from his overseas training," John replied navigating around the truth.

"I thought you liked it here?" Steve asked, surprised by her reaction.

"It's just I miss mum and the family, it will be good to catch up with them," Michelle replied hesitantly, wondering if she should tell him, and getting suspicious looks from John.

As they sat having coffee John kept thinking about Michelle. He'd been surprised that she wanted to move to Sydney after just getting here. Joan, his wife and she were close, why the excitement about being back with her family.

"Good God, you're not pregnant are you?" John blurted out, not thinking, making Steve upend the coffee table.

"Bloody hell John, you scared the shit out of me!" Steve blurted out shakily, before turning to his silent wife expecting her to laugh.

"I only found out today Steve, I was going to tell you, but this mission came up and I thought it best to wait," Michelle answered sheepishly, before Steve closed the distance to her, hugging and kissing her.

"God Michelle I couldn't be happier, knowing this will make me hurry home as fast as I can!"

"It might be best if I got going," John suggested, feeling a bit embarrassed about causing tonight's developments.

"No, don't be silly John how about ringing your wife and asking her to come over and celebrate," Steve replied excitedly, making the other two smile.

"No problems, Joan will be thrilled," John grinned, giving Michelle a hug, before racing out the door to go tell his wife.

Two days passed quickly, and Steve less than happy, waved to a teary Michelle at the Airport and boarded a plane heading for America, his first stop on the way to South America and the mission.

PANAMA

Steve had been in Balboa Panama for ten minutes, and he hated the place. The heat made him sweat constantly and the open drains he passed reminded him of the sewers in Kabul. Once again, the taxi driver swerved onto the wrong side of the road to overtake a car, going about the same speed that he had been doing as if speed would impress his fare.

"I'm just homesick," Steve said to himself sadly, getting a look from the driver at the same time. He had come to the conclusion that this would be his last mission. Being a family man now, he realised how much he had to lose, and they depended on him.

With a screech of brakes, the taxi pulled up at an old steel barrier which barred the way to a disused airfield rusting apart through neglect. After paying the driver more than he deserved, Steve grabbed his bags and walked down the rows of disused rusty corrugated iron hangars still showing old military numbers, from a war long since passed.

"Finally number seven!" Steve said out loud, arriving at his destination where his lift was supposed to be waiting.

"You're a long way from South Africa, my friend." a familiar voice yelled out, from the shade inside the hangar.

"Brent, what the hell are you doing here? I thought with the money you were retiring?" Steve smiled.

"You don't think the Colonel would think that suspicious, me up and retiring?" Brent replied seriously.

"You might be right there. Anyway, what are you doing here?"

"When I heard about this job I figured it would be you guys, so here I am to transport you to your destination," Brent replied bowing, waving Steve forward to an Army camouflaged Iroquois chopper.

"Where to?" Steve asked.

"The end of the world."

PANAMA SPY BASE

When Nam had finished, and the Cold War hotted up, old Uncle Sam had decided it might be best to keep a close watch on their Southern neighbours. So with the right incentives, the Panamanian Government had let the Americans lease some land near the southern border with Colombia. Twenty kilometres inland from Cape Tiburon in the Gulf of Darien sits a dormant Volcano, which in its day must have been quite impressive. The inside crater was roughly a kilometre across, and at the height of 5,000 metres, it dominated the surrounding area. Coming into land Steve thought Brent's description was reasonably correct; it did appear to be the end of the world.

As the chopper landed, six marines appeared from a camouflaged bunker giving the chopper the once over, before escorting the two new arrivals into the heavily camouflaged base headquarters. After being cleared Brent disappeared back to his chopper, while Steve with just one marine continued on to where his unit was housed. After thanking the marine for the escort, Steve turned to go inside when the marine grabbed him.

"No offence Sir, but if you need backup on your mission, recon will be right here if you need us!" the Soldier said, with deadly seriousness.

"You'll be the first I call!" Steve answered, not having the faintest what the marine was talking about. Getting an excited grin from the marine, Steve hurried inside. Steve was greeted by Ali and the others who were going over aerial photos of what appeared to be a small inlet on the coast.

"Keeping busy?" Steve asked smiling.

"Not as busy as you'll be!" Cody replied grinning, as he threw Steve a can of coke.

"Thanks, Cody, what gives with the marines? One just tried to invite his unit along with us!" Steve asked.

"They're all bored shitless down here protecting this installation. They'd do anything for some action and the words out that we're here for some." Sukai replied worried about security.

"Since we've been here even the camp commander asked if he could come!" Ali smiled, as he filled Steve in on the base. The base was as secure as you could get, there were no roads, and everything had to be flown in, making guarding the complex rather boring. There were two hundred marines from the First Battalion's recon company, and they were bored at looking after just fifty Air Force technicians who worked here, all men.

"Even the technicians wanted to come!" Aaron laughed.

"So how's married life?" Ali asked smiling.

"Great, I'm going to be a dad!" Steve replied happily, bringing a shocked silence, as unreadable looks passed across the unit members faces. As one they came forward and wished him well. Later as Ali showed him to his bunk, he asked him why they had all hesitated.

"They all know you'll leave the unit, Steve, we'll all miss you."

"Yeah, I thought this could be the last one." Steve sadly replied knowing he'd miss his friends and the comradeship they shared.

"Well, I'm sure that at least I'll keep in touch and visit!"

"Keep in touch with me or Michelle's girlfriend?"

"Maybe a bit of both," Ali replied laughing, as they headed back to join the others, to start familiarizing Steve with the mission.

THE MISSION

To the South of Panama just over the border in Colombia was a small speck of a town called De Cusa. It was totally isolated with the only sizable town being Turbo, a hundred kilometres to the east. It had been an old pirate base over a hundred years ago, but the Spaniards had conquered the area and built a fort there. This was to make sure that the pirates didn't return, as well as the French who at the time were at war with them, and held Panama to the north. Unlike Panama, the Colombians had for self-defence, built an old road along the coast to this small forgotten seaport, which had brought it to the attention of a drug cartel. They had taken control of this area and swiftly established a base at the small port.

The villagers were now nothing better than slaves, used mostly by the cartel to grow the poppies that produced their heroin. They then processed and refined it in the village, before being sent by sea north to their customers in America. The mission was straightforward. Stop shipments, and free the villagers, making sure the cartel knew not to return. When the mission was first proposed it seemed simple enough, go in kill the bad guys and free the poor people. Aerial shots showed it quite different. The old fort, which was a mile from the actual village, was used as a prison to hold the villagers each night.

They were allowed to leave only to work in the fields and return the next night. Their children were never allowed to leave the fort at all, a guarantee that no one would escape. There were over one thousand villagers held in the fort including women and children, and they were heavily guarded. The village itself was also heavily defended including several anti-aircraft guns and a small flotilla of patrol boats which were moored in the harbour or secured to the docks.

Estimated size of the enemy troops was around four hundred, and, even though they were mostly militia, there were still a lot of them. Ali planned to chopper in about ten kilometres inland, and then make their way to the coast at nightfall, hitting both the fort and the village at the same time. At the fort, the militia troops were billeted in two large barrack structures outside the walls, with only about ten men guarding the only gate to the fort. With the use of explosives, it was hoped to take out nearly all the militia while they slept, leaving only the guards at the gate to be neutralised. At the village, they hoped to use explosives, to mine all heavy weapon positions, plus lay magnetic limpet mines to any vessels in the harbour.

"That's a fair bit for five guys!" Steve said breaking the silence as everyone sat there studying the plan.

"That's where you come in Steve!" Ali replied as the others chuckled before he continued. "My plan is for you and Sukai to take the village, while Cody, Aaron and I take the fort. Of course, with a little help from a few marines. Which you will help train. That's why you're the last man on the ground here." Ali smiled as the others sniggered at the look on Steve's face.

The next day, Steve like usual, got up at six for his early morning run to be greeted by nearly one hundred marines, who had all decided to go jogging at the same time.

"Atten hutt!" echoed across the camp, as Steve staggered out of his barracks.

"Fine day for a run Sir, my name is Sergeant Baker. Would you today like to lead us on our exercise run, Sir!" asked a tough looking black soldier, followed by laughter from inside Steve's barracks.

"We'll both lead Sergeant, as I don't know the way yet." Steve smiled, knowing now that the rumour was out about the mission. After covering about ten kilometres through pretty rough country, Steve was surprised to find most of the men still with him.

"They're in good shape Sergeant. It's going to be hard to pick who to take!"

"Dammed I can't believe it! There really is a mission!" the Sergeant yelled as the news went back down the column.

"Well, it a black op's Sergeant, there isn't going to be any medals for this one!" Steve replied wondering if he should have said anything.

"Anything special you're looking for?" Baker asked secretively.

"We need your best men in the dark, plus knife work and keeping quiet, okay?" Steve admitted, getting nods from the Sergeant and anyone within hearing distance.

"How are you going to find all that out, Sir?"

"We're going to start tonight!" Steve smiled as he increased speed and headed back.

"Shit Steve, why'd you tell them they could go, before I asked their CO?" Ali exploded, surprised at Steve.

"I thought they knew already, the way they were waiting this morning!" Steve answered, a little confused, as Cody and Sukai sniggered in the background.

"I should have warned you, they do it every morning hoping one of us will spill the beans," Ali replied getting over it.

"And anyway the CO knows!" came a voice from the door, as Steve looked around, and saw a Marine Captain standing there.

"Bob Johnson's the name, you must be Steve!" the Marine Captain asked as he came forward shaking Steve's hand.

"Sorry about talking to your men," Steve said apologetically.

"Don't be stupid. It was me who ordered them to try and find out in the first place. First I like to hear your plan, and then I'll decide if my men will go." Bob said getting serious, before sitting down and waiting, while Ali went over the plan with him. It took an hour to outline the mission, while all the time, Captain Johnson just sat there thinking.

"I've got to tell yah, it's quite a mission. Problem is it's over the border my friend, which makes it very risky!" Bob pointed out, thinking it over.

"We understand if you don't want to commit your men to it," Ali replied knowing they were asking a lot.

"Are you kidding! A chance to strike at the drug cartels and free those people, of course, we're going! It's just not getting caught that's the secret." Bob grinned, as they went over the plan again.

Two gruelling weeks went by, as Steve trimmed the two hundred marines to twenty-five men. Because he was the best in the dark and he'd tipped them off, Ali had put him in charge of selecting the men to go with them, and it had been hard. Steve had been impressed by these marines who had given their all to be selected for this raid, and along the way had gained their respect. He'd started with fitness runs each day which had taken out about fifty, not that they weren't fit, it's just the others were better. He'd then started night skirmishes, putting one group against the other; this finally knocked the number down to what they needed.

During the day Steve gave lessons, to not only the twenty-five but anyone who was interested in hand to hand combat. He trained them the same way, as he did in the Regiment back home and it showed. Captain Johnson had been impressed by the improvement in his men and surprised to know the Australian army had a manual on this kind of training. Finding it was in circulation, he contacted his superiors to see if he could get a copy for his unit.

Seeing Steve was being swamped, Aaron took over the knife fighting training from Steve, and Sukai instructed them on explosives, while Ali and Cody got the weapons and logistics in place for the mission.

Two weeks from the start of training, Sergeant Baker found himself in the dark, lying motionless along with the four other men of his unit. Watching the trial in front of him, he couldn't believe he'd made the final twenty-five for this mission, it had nearly killed him.

Their assignment tonight was to try and catch the Aussie instructor and his team, no one had yet come close, something Baker hoped to change. To narrow the odds they had set up trip wires all around their position, knowing that the Aussie liked to sneak up behind his prey. Looking across the clearing Baker thought he saw movement and he noticed his men go rigid as they too sensed movement in front. It was at that moment he knew he'd been had. Turning around swiftly, rifle ready, Baker knew he'd be too late, as a barrel pressed against his head.

"Good move Sergeant, how did you know?" the Aussie asked softly, as he saw the other four members of his team being held by Ali and the other unit members.

"The noise and the movement, your team wouldn't have made either!" Baker answered angrily. He was cranky that he'd been fooled, though getting a well-done look the Aussie helped make him feel better.

"Good work Baker, your group, did well, remember we had night vision you didn't!" Ali explained, coming up beside them both.

"Well looks like you've got your support group, Steve." Sukai smiled at Baker, as he passed them.

"You poor bastards" Cody chuckled, as he too trudged by, leaving Baker and the other four wondering what he meant.

THE RAID

The sound of the three choppers faded into the night as the thirty men lay in the jungle waiting for any sign that they had been detected. Ten minutes passed, and nothing stirred as Ali signalled the group forward while Steve and Sukai disappeared ahead of them.

"Colombia looks just as shitty as Panama" Jones, one of Bakers group whispered in his ear, getting a nod in return, as they tried to move silently. Travelling through the dense dark jungle was a nightmare, only made a little easier by their night vision. Baker couldn't believe how much he was sweating. The plan was to close in on the fort where the majority of enemy troops were, and then he and his group would travel with Sukai and Steve to the village.

There his group's job was to plant explosives on the heavy weapons pits and set up their M60 machine gun to take care of any problems. While his group did that, Steve and Sukai would take care of the boats in the harbour. Baker had to admit as he walked along with these Black ops guys, that he was a little scared. He'd had the urge to urinate several times since landing, wondering if he was the only one.

After two hours of walking, suddenly the man in front of Baker froze, as he in turn froze and those behind him froze. This informed them that they had arrived at the drop off point near the fort. With a handshake and a wave, the raiding party split into two groups, who silently moved off towards their separate missions, hoping everything went to plan.

Steve leading headed towards the village with Sukai and Bakers group, while Ali took the main group towards the fort circling to the east. Ali's plan included setting up an ambush group on the road to Turbo, to stop any reinforcements and more importantly to prevent anyone escaping. Here they left five Marines who quickly laid a string of mines across the road, before setting up a machine gun to cover both directions. That left Cody, Aaron and Ali plus fifteen marines to take the fort and rescue the villagers.

Steve's group in the meantime had made good progress and had arrived at the village outskirts finding quite a party going on judging by the noise and lights. Finding their night vision was affected by the lights; Steve's group took them off and moved in closer for a better look. Scanning the village with his binoculars, Steve counted at least a hundred armed men, and out in the harbour, there were two coastal freighters plus four patrol boats, a lot more than anticipated.

"What's going on?" Steve asked Sukai softly.

"Looks like a big drug deal is going down," Sukai whispered, as Steve nodding his agreement, worried by the large number of soldiers. Giving the marines a get ready signal, Steve and Sukai headed for the water's edge, while the others spread out. With great care, the marines crawled through the undergrowth, securing their explosives to the gun emplacements and anything else that looked threatening, and they had plenty of explosives. Baker couldn't believe how easy it was compared to the training for it, but then again, the calibre of the soldiers during training, was far superior to this bunch of thugs he thought.

The noise was so great that when the marines met back at their starting point, they found they could even talk quietly to each other without fear of being heard. Even so they still quickly set up the M60 to face down into the killing ground in the front of the village huts, before they settled down to wait for the return of Steve and Sukai.

At the waterfront, Sukai inflated a small rubber boat they'd brought with them, in which Steve carefully placed the limpet mines. The idea was for them both to swim beside the rubber raft out to the ships, but the sight of a dorsal fin whipping through the water ended that idea. In the end, Sukai decided to go alone leaving Steve to watch his back. As Sukai silently paddle out towards the first vessel, his raft was suddenly bumped by an unseen creature, causing him to freeze and hang on. Whatever it was swam on not bothering him again, but it shook him up, and it took several seconds before he could continue. Steve, onshore, watched the collision between Sukai and the shark with apprehension.

'Why were the sharks so aggressive' he wondered. Refitting his night glasses, he scanned the water until he found what had the sharks in a frenzy. It appeared several people for punishment, had been tied to a buoy in the harbour, and although they were long since dead, the sharks, unfortunately, weren't finished with them yet. Luckily Sukai hadn't seen this, or he wouldn't have gone out in a flimsy raft at all. Steve unable to warn him watched him continue on unaware of the danger.

Attaching mine after mine to the unsuspecting vessels, Sukai made sure every craft had at least one, saving any extras for the larger vessels, so that they would do the greatest possible damage. Paddling back towards the shore he was hit again, this time the creature surfaced going for Sukai, forcing him to belt it with his paddle. This saved himself but made a noise in the process. A light stabbed out from the shore, as a vigilant guard tried to locate the noise, on the water. Sukai lying flat in the raft watched the beam swing slowly towards him.

When the light was just about to hit him, for no reason, it disappeared, and darkness returned. Thanking his lucky stars, Sukai paddled rapidly towards the shore, more scared of the sharks, than the soldiers. Pulling up swiftly to the beach, Sukai found Steve cleaning his knife on an unmoving body. That's why the light had stopped probing Sukai realised. Nodding his thanks, they both moved off silently to rendezvous with the marines.

Steve with great care approached the marines, and carefully signalled them with his night vision glasses. Night vision glasses showed up as a flash, only to another person wearing them, so after a return flash they moved in, and took up a position beside the M60.

"How many charges did you use?" Sukai whispered to Baker as they dug shallow pits to lie in.

"All of them!" Baker smiled, as Steve and Sukai looked at each other, decided to dig their pits a bit deeper.

Back at the fort, after dropping off the blocking force on the road, Ali led his group to the fort stopping just short of the barracks buildings that housed the militia. Ten marines left the group here and silently crawled forward to the buildings. Climbing underneath the structures, they planted their charges before moving away to safety to await Ali's signal. He, in the meantime, led the remaining five marines, plus Aaron and Cody towards the fort gates. Their approach was made easy, by the loud music thumping out of an old radio hanging from a nail next to the gate. Coming in close Ali removed his night vision glasses and hand signalled the others to do the same, as the gate area was well lit making them useless.

Spreading out, the eight men approached their ten targets, four of which were rolled up in blankets asleep, near the entrance. This left only six armed men to contend with. It was over quickly, as the group took aim with their silenced pistols, firing repeatedly. Each target received at least three shots in rapid succession, the ones on guard crumbling to the ground silently. Moving forward Cody checked all the downed soldiers and cleared each man of weapons before coming close to Ali.

"Piece of cake," Cody whispered to Ali, before pointing back towards the barracks.

"What about the villagers?" a Marine corporal asked softly, as the group started to move off.

"We'll come back for them after we take care of the barracks troops. They can wait a little while longer." Ali replied, before picking up his radio and saying two words.

"Blow it!" came over the small radio sets worn by each member of this raiding party, and it was the first break in radio silence they had heard since leaving Panama. The ten marines lying prone in their hastily dug pits around the barracks building, ducked down as their group leader fingered the toggle switch, setting off the charges laid under the barrack. Unfortunately, like Bakers team, in their zealousness to do a good job the ten marines had used three times as much explosive as was necessary. The resulting explosion was far more devastating than they had prepared for.

Shockwaves roared out from the barracks, inflicting massive casualties on the militia, as well as wounding several members of the group sent to cover the buildings. Ali and his men were also knocked to the ground by the concussion waves, as debris including body parts, crashed down to earth in all directions. Forced to take cover and wait out the aftermath of the explosion, Ali had no doubt that Steve's group had heard the signal.

At the village, the party mood sobered as the explosion lit the sky towards the fort. Most of the partygoers ran outside to see what was happening, revealing a far more significant number of soldiers than first thought.

"Blow em!" Steve whispered into his headset, which made Sukai press his handheld transmitter, sending a signal to the explosives planted around the camp. Mayhem broke out as explosions rocked the village sending deadly shrapnel through the exposed huts. Steve's group simultaneously opened up on the confused crowd with a lethal burst of automatic fire. They'd killed at least fifty men before the others knew what was happening.

For the first few minutes, Steve's group poured concentrated fire into the hapless militia troops, whose only response was to go to ground or try to run for the boats. Both proved fatal, as ten minutes later the preset limpet mines detonated on the now overcrowded vessels, giving the militia only two choices fight or die. Despite the slaughter, as time went by, the large number of troops still alive became evident. The return fire became more organised and increased in volume to such an extent, that Steve's group was forced to move back.

Leaving their prepared positions to stop attempts to flank them, Steve became worried.

"Hammer, this is Ghost!" Steve yelled into his radio. 'Hammer' being Ali's group's name and 'Ghost' being Steve's group.

"How's it going Ghost we can hear a lot of fire. What's up?" Ali was worried, as he and his group helped finish of any militia left alive at the barracks area.

"Have at least a hundred enemy troops closing in on us; we've already been forced back once!" Steve shouted over the firefight.

"On the way; out!" Ali answered, before giving orders to the others. "Blocking force on the road, move to the barracks area and make sure all the enemy soldiers are dead. The rest of you, to me, Ghost's group is in trouble!" Ali informed them. Quickly forming his group into a skirmish line, he led them towards the village, abandoning radio silence.

Watching tracers fly towards him and hearing the sound like a windscreen breaking, as a round passed close by, was to close for comfit for Steve. Firing into the advancing enemy, Sukai and Steve were covering the marines as they moved back to new position yet again. Coming to the kneeling position, they both tossed their last grenades towards the advancing troops. Ducking back down towards the safety of the ground, Steve glanced sideways at Sukai seeing rounds dug up the dirt around him. The white flash of exploding grenades and the whistle of shrapnel in the air was accompanied by the screams of the dying and injured, as their grenades exploded. Steve was about to tell Sukai to move back, a wasp-like sting struck his shoulder, throwing him back onto the ground.

"Shit! I'm hit!" Steve yelled in pain, as Sukai dragged him behind a tree, as bullets pounded the ground around them.

"You'd better hurry Hammer we're in big trouble!" Sukai shouted into his radio, as he pressed a field dressing to Steve's shoulder, trying to slow the bleeding.

"We're coming in on your right!" Cody answered as a devastating crossfire opened up on the surprised militia troops. This broke their will, as they turned and ran for the false safety of the village. Many tried to surrender, but on this mission, there were to be no prisoners, so the slaughter continued until no enemy soldiers were left on the shore.

Aaron spotting Sukai kneeing on the ground, walked over to see what he was up to when he saw Steve lying next to him. Rushing forward he quickly cut Steve's clothing away, revealing a small entry wound at Steve's collarbone with a much more significant exit wound in his back.

"Bloody hell Steve we leave you for a couple of hours and look what happens!" Aaron smiled reassuringly at Steve, as he expertly applied a dressing to the wound.

"How bad is it?" Steve replied, feeling the pain as the shock wore off.

"Shit, I cut myself worse shaving." Sukai laughed, looking more assured now Aaron was here.

"You'll be right, but I'll give you something for the pain," Aaron replied confidently, sticking a small needle into Steve's arm. This after several seconds cut down the pain. As the shooting died down, screams in the direction of the camp could be heard. Sukai keyed his radio to find out what was happening. After several seconds Ali filled them in.

It appeared with the sinking of the vessels in the harbour, a large number of sharks had moved into the area, finishing off the men, who are still out there.

"They deserve it!" Steve replied angrily telling them all, what he had seen in the harbour that night in the harbour.

It still took another three hours till Ali was sure all the cartel's soldiers had been taken care of and most of their bodies dumped into the ocean. They then grabbed Steve and another wounded marine, hurrying back to rendezvous with the other wounded men at the fort. Making good time by travelling along the road without secrecy, they were greeted by a large number of villagers. In near starving condition, they still cheered and cried, happy beyond belief that they were free from the cartel.

Of the group deployed on the mission, only two were severely wounded, Steve and the marine from the village. The only other casualties were six Marines with various broken bones and hearing problems, from the barracks explosion. They all knew how lucky they'd been, considering the enemy numbers. Aaron, after checking over the villagers reported they were in poor shape and urgently needed food and medical supplies, something they hadn't planned for.

"They'll have to wait for now!" Ali told them, as he ordered the whole group to leave what medical and food supplies they had and head for their pickup site with the choppers. The villagers, unfortunately, would have to look after themselves, until something could be arranged.

Like clockwork, the choppers appeared out of the now lightening skies as daybreak approached. The pilot, seeing they had wounded, called their base telling them to expect casualties. Ferrying the men back to their base in Panama, the choppers, upon landing, were swamped with base personnel, who helped remove the wounded. Ali went straight to the CO office and gave him an update on the mission and the state of the villagers.

He was surprised when Captain Johnson ordered a medical team and several choppers to take supplies back, along with more marines.

"Well, we've gone this far, I can't just let those people starve can I!" Captain Johnson replied smiling, knowing he was putting his career on the line.

"We can go back as well." Ali volunteered his unit, proud to serve with these marines.

"No, you've done a great job, best you keep a low profile and look after your man," Johnson replied giving Ali a firm handshake. Picking up a phone, Johnson called the duty officer to arrange a second relief force.

THE AWAKENING

Steve missed the arrival back. He'd passed out during the flight and awoke later lying in a clean white bed surrounded by six other wounded marines.

"Hey you're back with the living brother!" a Marine across from him yelled before a male nurse told him to settle down.

"He's deaf from the explosion at the barracks, luckily it's only temporarily!" The male nurse explained as he checked Steve's wound.

"Is everyone else okay?"

"Yes only one other was seriously wounded, and he's been sent stateside." the Nurse replied.

"Way to go Ghost you really showed em something!" another soldier exclaimed before realising his mistake.

"Sorry I mean Captain Sir" the soldier added, as the other marines laughed.

"Captain Roberts! What the hell have you done?" sounded an angry voice from the door, as Colonel Dobson stormed in followed by his two aids. One of the aids was Brooks, who Steve remembered from London.

"Sorry, Sir what do you mean?" Steve asked, still not completely focused

"Getting these marines involved! It was supposed to be secret operation you fool, and you take along these dimwits. I should have you all shot!" the Colonel bellowed before he realised what he had said. Looking around at the startled and angry faces on the marines and the nurses in the ward, the Colonel and his aides quickly departed, leaving a silent room behind them.

"That man could have a nasty accident while he's here!" One of the Marines suggested, getting agreement from the others as Steve again drifted off to sleep.

Several hours passed before Steve again woke from a drug-induced sleep and found Ali sitting beside his bed.

"You're getting slack Steve, afternoon and you're still in bed!" Ali smiled, but his face showed concern.

"I could still outrun you." Steve groaned, trying to laugh, but failing.

"Still hurt?" Ali asked softly.

"No just a constant throb."

"Heard you had a visitor this morning?"

"Yeah, it was pretty unpleasant."

"He can be pretty unpleasant our Colonel Dobson if that's his name," Ali whispered, seeing they were getting attention from the other patients.

"Someone should frag that mans arse!" a Marine across from Steve suggested angrily.

"He's a Colonel, soldier remember that!" Ali said seriously, quietening the room. "But I had thought about it." He continued, getting a thunder of laughter in return.

"Where is he anyway?" Steve asked puzzled.

"Well after he left you, he came to our barracks and chewed us all out about using the marines. He then went to leave to find Captain Johnson had commandeered his helicopter, to take supplies to the village. He's over at the Captain's office, throwing a fit at the moment!"

"How's Captain Johnson handling it?"

"Better than I'd thought, considering Dobson's a Colonel," Ali replied going silent, wondering why Johnson didn't seem scared of the Colonel. Steve was just about to ask another question when the sound of an approaching chopper drifted in.

"Sounds like the relief choppers are back?" Steve smiled, thinking how happy those villages must be.

"Seems too soon to me? They only left for the second run an hour ago." Ali explained, starting to rise, to go have a look. He froze, as a group of officers entered the ward, followed by a General. This brought every soldier, who could stand to his feet.

"Relax men just come down to visit my marines on this boring base!" the General chuckled, looking straight at Steve before continuing. "Well, well, well, if it isn't the Ghost!" Leaving Ali and every man and nurse there, staring at Steve.

"Good morning General it's a long way from Australia!" Steve answered grinning, leaving Ali bewildered.

"Yes, it sure is Captain. It's a bit crowded in here can you walk?"

"Yeah, I think I'm okay Sir," Steve answered, as he slowly swung out of bed throwing his pants on.

"You to sunshine!" the General barked, pointing at Ali who followed reluctantly, wondering what Steve had gotten him into. Once away from the crowd, the General dismissed his Officers, sitting down on a bench, pointing Ali and Steve to the seat opposite.

"Who's this?" the General asked, pointing at Ali.

"He's my CO General," Steve said with a bit of pride.

"Jim Mosley," the General said putting out his hand which Ali shook.

"My name is Ali Moustaffer," Ali answered suspiciously, still wondering what was happening.

"Relax Ali, I ran into Captain Roberts during an exercise in Australia. His commander, thinking I knew, informed me that Roberts was working for us, something I didn't know. So since it's your mission suppose you fill me in." the General asked pleasantly. Ali, of course, knew it was an order.

"Well the plan was simple it," was all Ali got out before a shout made him stop.

"Tell that man nothing!" Colonel Dobson yelled, as he rapidly approached, followed by Captain Baker and Dobson's two aides.

"Last time I looked, I had stars on my uniform Colonel!" Mosley exploded.

"These men belong to a special unit, outside of your jurisdiction and with the President's approval!" Dobson replied dismissing the General and signalling Ali and Steve to follow him, who of course didn't move. "I said follow me!" Dobson bellowed at Ali and Steve, who remained seated.

"The problem with you Colonel, if that's your real title, is to know when you're in deep shit. These two men both know it and so do your aids by their colour." Mosley replied signalling Baker forward.

"You are making a grave mistake General, if I have to call the President about this, there will be trouble!" Dobson snarled, trying to stare the General down.

"Funny, when I talked to the President this morning about an operation down here, he knew nothing Colonel, but if you want we'll go over to the office and ring him directly." the General smiled.

"Look General there's no need for that. We can put this behind us." Dobson replied smiling, sweating badly.

"You're under arrest Colonel; I'll talk to you later. Baker, take him away!" Mosley ordered as Baker pulled an automatic from his holster.

"General!" The Colonel stammered, as Baker cut him off. Shoving him from behind, leading him off at gunpoint, followed by his two silent aides.

"Now Ali before we were interrupted, you were saying." The General chuckled, as Ali impressed by what had happened, filled him in on the operation. It took nearly an hour and when Ali was finished the General got up and stretched.

"How many enemy casualties?"

"Six hundred maybe seven, is my estimate Sir, it was quite a big drug operation!" Ali replied, knowing no one would ever know for sure.

"And we suffered ten casualties only two serious?" The General murmured softly, thinking about what a successful operation and outstanding victory it had been.

"Yes Sir," Ali replied proudly.

"It was well planned and executed Ali. You only slipped up in two things. One, the choppers were picked up on our radar, and two your radio chatter though short was also picked up. Mostly because our new radios have a wider range than the old ones." the General smiled, before explaining.

The General had been visiting an American base near the Panama Canal. While there, the Base Commander had called him into the Command centre to ask him if anything was happening down south at the Surveillance Base. When he had told them no, the CO had told him about the chopper flights being picked up going into Colombia. It was after this that brief transmissions clearly indicating combat, began being picked up.

"At first I thought it might be an exercise. But when one of my marines went stateside with battle wounds, I called Captain Johnson. He admitted there'd been a raid by an unknown unit over the border, sanctioned by the White House. When he told me my marines had gone too, I smelt bullshit and headed down here. Especially after hearing that one unit call sign, was Ghost!" the General chuckled.

"Unfortunately this won't stay a secret for long," Steve added.

"Your right there Captain. So I've thought up an alternative plan on the way here. I know a Major in the Colombian Army, commands a battalion of paratroops. With a few calls, I think it can be arranged, that this was a joint operation and the marines only assisted the Colombians on this mission. That way everyone's happy and your unit can go on being invisible." The General explained. Giving Ali and Steve a well done he went to the Base Communication centre to put his plan into reality.

For the next five days, the unit waited at the base, while Mosley wove a cover story over the whole operation. This gave Steve some time to recover from his injuries. The only bad part was that Dobson was allowed to leave unpunished. Talking to his aide, Brooks, who Steve had met before in London, Brooks assured Steve that the Colonel was finished. It was at this meeting that Steve had told him that he was retiring from the unit, mainly because he was becoming a father. Brooks had seemed pleased and wished him well, saying it would be no problem, before heading off to his waiting helicopter.

That afternoon Steve was asked to meet General Mosley in the COs office before he left. Walking in, Steve gave his best salute, before Mosley pointed him to a chair.

"Well, it came off okay Steve. The press ate it up, and the Colombians got all the credit, even managed to get a few medals for my men!" the General smiled. He then sighed looking seriously at Steve. "The problem is Steve, whoever is running this operation now Dobson's gone, will get a lot of credit. This means I can't interfere too much, as the White House sees this as a successful operation!" Mosley admitted.

"So the unit is still in business then?"

"Yes, I'm afraid so."

"I'm out anyway Sir. I tendered my resignation this morning, and they accepted it."

"Why?"

"My wife's pregnant Sir, one army is enough for a married man with children."

"A wise decision Steve, good luck." the General smiled, before shaking Steve's hand and leaving.

The next day the unit said their goodbyes to the marines who lined the landing pad giving them a formal salute as they boarded their chopper, piloted by Brent.

"What no money? I should make you all walk!" Brent laughed, as they rapidly rose into the sky, thundering away from the base, heading home.

MOSCOW

Captain Sergio Andropov sat at his desk, sifting through Intelligence reports, from around the world. He was looking for some clue to his father's killers hiding spot when Captain Josef Yakof crashed through the door.

"We got them, Sergio!"

"Where?"

"South America" Josef replied, as they both raced for the door.

The only place for the marines on the surveillance base in Panama to go for R&R was Balboa. It was hot and sweaty, but it was the only place where female company could be found, and a soldier could let his hair down. Sitting around a table at the marine's local watering hole, Bakers group from the raid into Colombia sat toasting their success. Helping them celebrate, were some wealthy businessmen, down from the states.

"So you actually helped the Colombians beat those druggies. You've done our country proud!" A businessman with a Texas accent exclaimed, before ordering these brave men another round of drinks, as Baker left the table for a leak.

"The Colombians did squat!" a Private answered angrily, upset with the cover-up.

"But the papers said you only observed?" the Texan put in upsetting them further.

"That's bullshit! Twenty-five of us flew in with these five foreign special forces types, and we wasted nearly seven hundred militia soldiers, without taking hardly any casualties!" the Private spat out, getting support from the others. Josef, who was playing the Texan, sat shocked at the amount of killing on this raid. One of their two South American operatives picked up the conversation, watched by Sergio.

"That's hard to believe soldier." the Operative said with a slightly Spanish accent.

"He's not lying, the only serious casualties were a marine from our unit and the Aussie SAS soldier he took one in the shoulder." said another Private.

"An Australian, what was he doing there?" Sergio asked, his accent barely disguising his origin, which lucky for him the drunken marines didn't pick up on.

"He was part of this black op's team, and he was the best!" the first Private answered proudly, getting bangs on the table from the other marines in support.

"That's enough private!" Baker's voice cut through the group, silencing the men at the table, as Baker looked their new friends over. "It's time to go!" Baker ordered, as the Marines got to their feet and reluctantly staggered towards the door.

Once outside Bakers gut feeling told him something was wrong with those businessmen, but what to do he thought. Looking across the street, he spotted a nosy reporter from the local newspaper, who always pestered him and other soldiers for a visit to the base. Hurrying over to him Baker had an idea.

"Hey, Tony how would you like a visit to the base!"

"Who do I have to kill?" Tony smiled back.

"No, not kill, just shoot, with your camera there," Baker replied telling him what he wanted, as the reporter eagerly agreed.

It was two in the morning before the Russian team arrived back in their hotel, the two local agents unimpressed with their two Russian visitors.

"Sergio you might be important back in Moscow, here you keep your mouth shut!" the local Agent warned. "Your accent is easily recognisable."

"My apologies comrade, but at least I got the information," Sergio replied angrily with himself for nearly giving them away.

"So one of these special unit members is an SAS soldier from Australia, and he's injured, he won't be hard to find." Josef pointed out, wondering if Sergio could be counted on to keep his emotions in check.

"So you're both going after him. I'd remember what they said about him being the best. You might need back up?" The other agent warned, glad to be rid of these two fools.

"Don't worry comrades a special team of Paratroopers is at this moment ready to meet us wherever we go!" Sergio answered, his eyes shining with revenge as he drew closer to his father's killer.

THE NEW JOB

Flying into Sydney, Steve's arm still bandaged, he was greeted by Michelle and his sister Louise, who both looked at his arm with fear.

"Hey you two relax its okay," Steve said as he hugged Michelle, who looked close to tears.

"What happened to your arm?" His sister asked coming forward and kissing him on the cheek.

"I got shot, it happens, but I'm okay!" Steve answered sensing he had said the wrong thing, by the looks on their faces.

"My God Steve, how did it happen?" Michelle gasped crying, as Steve stumbled over what to say.

"He's most probably not supposed to tell us!" Edward replied coming to Steve's rescue and shaking his good arm. "Sorry, I'm late Steve had some paperwork to do," Edward explained as he herded his wife and Michelle away from the arrival lounge and out into the car. The trip back to his sister's house was quiet as everyone waited for someone to say something, leaving Steve an opening to make things right.

"I resigned from the unit, this mission was my last!" Steve suddenly blurted out, getting a nod from Edward in the front, but the girls just sat there lost in thought, until Michelle broke the silence.

"I was really scared this time Steve, I thought you weren't coming back!" She stammered out, bursting into tears while Steve hugged her.

"I'm sorry Shell, from now on I'll stick to just training others," Steve replied afraid to let her go.

"I know it's your job Steve, but soon you're going to be a father, you've got to think about that!" his sister added close to tears as well.

"Well I'm staying in Sydney at Holsworthy, training ordinary soldiers, there's not much happening here."

"Hey what's this name 'Shell' you're calling your wife now?" Edward laughed trying to cheer up the women.

"Just she reminds me of the beautiful ocean at our home in WA" Steve answered, hugging Michelle close as they continued south.

Three weeks after landing in Sydney, Steve, at six o'clock on the dot, presented himself to the Base Commander of Holsworthy, Major Brown, getting a warm welcome in return.

"Glad to have you here Captain Roberts, your manual sure has created a storm in the training of recruits, I can tell you!"

"Thank you, Sir, I'm glad it made a difference."

"Are you kidding! This year's exercise against the Kiwis on their South Island was a decisive victory." the Major beamed proudly of his men's achievement.

"Yes being fit and well trained pays dividends, even against an enemy on home ground."

"We heard rumours that two SAS teams, one led by you, showed the yanks near Darwin just how effective fitness and training can be?"

"Yes, we certainly did major. Captain Lenton led the other team and did most of the hard work I can tell you." Steve replied, sensing he'd enjoy working with this man.

WASHINGTON DC

At CIA headquarters at Langley, two of their best counterintelligence analysts poured over the photos of the four men, that 'Tony the reporter' had shot coming out of a bar in Balboa.

"The first two are the local agents for the KGB, they try to grab bits and pieces of what's going on from our soldiers down there, but the other two are new. I haven't seen them before." Bill, one analyst, admitted to his assistant.

"There's something familiar about the guy, at the rear, on the right!" Keith, the other analyst, said staring at the photo.

"Your right I've seen him before somewhere. Keith, can you grab the Moscow shoots of the KGB headquarters thanks." Rummaging through countless photos taken of people coming and going from the KGB headquarters, Bill suddenly got a hit.

"Do you see those two officers talking together by the entrance?" Bill said excitedly as Keith focused on the photo.

"Your right, it's them, what the hell are they doing in Panama? See if we have a name for either of them?" Bill checked the photo against Intel on the people in the photo.

"Shit, we've hit the jackpot!" Bill grinned, handing the sheet to Keith.

"The son of the dead defence minister Sergio Andropov, nephew of the President!" Keith answered quietly, as Bill dialled their new boss.

"Mr Brooks, I think we have something big!"

Sitting behind his new desk, Don Brooks stared at the photos of the two officers.

"Good work, you're right it's him, who's the other?"

"We're not sure? They have been working together since his father was killed." Keith replied all business; he knew Brooks reputation for being tough.

"Do we know what information they got?"

"Mostly about an Australian SAS soldier shot in Colombia, nothing important," Bill added smiling.

"I'll decide what's important here!"

"What's wrong sir?" Keith asked, surprised by his bosses reaction.

"This Australian soldier works for us, and it would be a bit embarrassing if they get him to talk."

"Well the SAS are pretty tough it would take a fair sized force to grab him I would say. I don't think they would be stupid enough to try that would they?" Keith felt confused.

"It's the kid's father he killed, of course, he'll try!" Don said thinking out loud, as the two analysts digested this information. Both speculated how and when the Aussie had killed Sergio's father?

"We could send some of our men," Bill suggested, getting over the shock.

"No, I've a better idea; send these photos and a warning to the SAS in Australia through their Intelligence Services immediately. That way when the shooting starts it won't come back to us!" Brooks ordered, dismissing the men.

Sitting there after the men had left Don thought long and hard about this special unit. He came to the conclusion that maybe it was time for it to disappear like Colonel Dobson.

CAMPBELL BARRACKS WA

The desk clerk sat upright in his chair as his scrambler connected to Army headquarters in Canberra came to life. He'd been working in the office for nearly a year after damaging his leg in a parachute jump. This was the first time he seen the scrambler work since he'd been there. When it had finished the private grabbed the photos and information, practically running to the COs office, banging on the door.

"Come in," Paul shouted, looking up from the paperwork, which he and John were sorting through.

"Sir, a message from Canberra on the scrambler!" The private told them excitedly.

"Thanks, private that will be all."

"What is it, Paul?" John asked seeing his face.

"The Russians are on to Steve I'm afraid," Paul answered sadly, as he arranged a meeting with all his men.

The Regiments soldiers gathered in their main hall, wondering why they'd been summoned. As the CO entered, several men noted how serious he looked, as he walked to the front to address the men.

"Sit down men; I won't mince words, it appears that a Russian military unit may be near this base. Has anyone noticed anyone acting suspiciously or asking questions lately?" Paul asked as complete silence settled on the room. At first, Paul thought maybe the information was wrong when four men to the right raised their hands.

"Okay you four to my office, all the rest of you break into groups, from now on I want plain clothes armed patrols through the streets where our families live. RSM take charge and organise a roster!" Paul ordered, before leaving a bewildered and worried group of men. In his office, Paul sat the four soldiers down and asked what they knew.

"It mightn't be anything, but for the last few nights a few new guys have been hanging around the local pub, and they asked a lot of questions!" a Private Bidwill explained.

"What sort of questions?"

"Nothing important Sir, just who do we think the best Officer is and has anyone been injured in training lately. Just questions in general about army life."

"Is he one of these men in the photos?" Paul asked dreading the answer, as the four privates scanned the shots.

"That's one of them, Sir!"

"What about the others with him?"

"They were pretty quiet, didn't talk much."

"Good work men you might just have saved someone's life!" Paul smiled and was just about to dismiss them when another private spoke up.

"One other thing Sir, the quiet guys looked pretty tough. I'd say they could be soldiers." He mumbled, getting nods from the other three men.

"Well good work again, I'll be in touch," Paul said as John and Captain Lenton appeared at the door.

After the others had left Paul sat them down, his mind racing.

"What did they have to say, Sir?" John asked, hoping nothing.

"They confirmed it RSM, one of the men in the photos is here and by the description some soldiers as well!" Paul answered, never realising that their troubles might someday follow them home.

"What are they here for?" Captain Lenton asked bewildered.

"They're here for Captain Roberts?" John answered.

"Why are they after him?"

"He was involved in the firefight in Colombia with the drug cartels Captain. It was on the news several weeks ago. Unfortunately, he took a hit in the shoulder. They're looking for an injured SAS soldier." Paul replied, getting a nod of understanding from Lenton.

"So the rumours are true, he's been overseas working with the yanks!" Lenton responded.

"Yes he has, and that doesn't leave this room Captain," Paul warned him.

"So what do we do?" John asked.

"We watch them and follow them back to their lair. In the meantime ring Captain Roberts. I want him here pronto!" Paul ordered as the two men left the room.

HOLSWORTHY TRAINING

Steve was sweating heavily as he turned his new group of recruits back towards the base. He had to admit these ones were in good shape, as he increased the pace slightly hearing grumbles behind him.

"Someone back there say something?" Steve bellowed, getting a "No sir" back from the tired recruits.

"I didn't think so," Steve replied, smiling to himself.

In the distance, a jeep could be seen coming towards them at speed. Pulling up swiftly, Major Brown yelled to Steve to get on board. Roaring off in a cloud of dust, they left the men to continue on back to base.

"What's up Sir?" Steve yelled above the noise of the vehicle, as they cannoned down the dirt road, back to the Commanders office

"You're wanted urgently at Campbell Barracks in Perth, something's up Steve!" the Major shouted back. Steve stop asking questions, as he sat there wondering what had happened. Making a quick call to Michelle telling her he had to go back to Perth and promising to ring her. He was then taken to Richmond Airforce base where he boarded a Hercules transport heading to Perth.

Upon landing, Steve was greeted by John, who without a word shoved him into a jeep and headed towards Campbell barracks. Looking across at John, too surprised to say anything, Steve looked his friend over, seeing a bulge near his waist indicating a weapon.

"What the hell's going on John? Why are you carrying a weapon?"

"Your work overseas has followed you home my friend."

Upon reaching the base, Steve couldn't help noticing the slight difference in behaviour of the men there. Everyone was armed, something that he hadn't seen before. He could also sense of feeling of suppressed anger, at having to wait. Walking into the main hall, where a briefing was underway, Steve seated himself near the rear as photos of the visitors were flashed on the projector screen at the front. Most of the faces Steve hadn't seen before, but suddenly a shot of Sergio appeared on the screen and Steve without realising let out a loud 'Shit' making everyone turn around.

"You know this man, Captain?" Paul said formally from the front

"Yes sir, we met in Kabul!" Steve replied, getting shocked looks from the men gathered there.

"Your covers blown Captain you may as well fill these men in with what's been going on. Why are these men after you?"

"I was sent on a mission there to take out the head of the KGB in Afghanistan. Unfortunately we also took out the Defence Minister of

Russia, that's his son!" Steve explained to a room full of surprised soldiers.

"That explains gentlemen why this Russian and twenty of his friends are just outside of town on an old wheat farm at this moment. They're waiting to capture or kill Captain Robert's, along with anyone who gets in the way!" Paul informed them.

"Let the bastards have him!" Captain Lenton yelled, with a grin on his face, as the room burst into laughter, relieving the pressure.

"That's not an option men. Remember, we've all made enemies overseas, this was bound to happen sooner or later. Even though, Captain Roberts sure picks some big ones!" Paul smiled, as laughter erupted again.

"Now what can we do to stop violence coming to our neighbourhood men? Anyone have a suggestion?" John asked seriously.

"Wipe em out in their lair," a Sergeant suggested, getting agreement from the room.

"That might just make them send more. I think I have a better idea to end this!" Steve replied.

CONFRONTATION

Sergio, Josef and Major Drevnov sat around a small table looking over information gathered by their men.

"I should have been able to go out more often!" Sergio pointed out angrily, at being confined to the farm property, instead of going into town with the others.

"Your accent and manner give you away comrade. " Josef replied. He was getting a little fed up with Sergio and his moods.

"And I promised Moscow you wouldn't be put in danger!" Drevnov shut down any further argument.

"So what have we got?" Sergio asked, admitting defeat.

"A great deal comrade, we know this Captain Roberts is called 'the Ghost' for his skills. He was away at the time of the Colombian raid, and more importantly the Afghanistan raid." Josef explained, hating going over this again.

"So where is he?" Sergio repeated loudly.

"Stop worrying Sergio he will soon surface, his wound must have been more severe than first thought." Major Drevnov answered, wanting to punch this spoilt brat. Drevnov had at first been proud that his specially trained unit was given the task of capturing this terrorist, who had caused so much grief in Afghanistan. His twenty man squad had all served in Afghanistan and had performed well there, though no one wanted to go back to that hell hole. This mission, if successful, could elevate them too much better assignments.

"Have the scouts radioed in?" Drevnov yelled down the hallway, where one of his men sat at a window, a radio receiver in his hand.

"Yes Sir, just ten minutes ago." the Radio Operator answered solemnly, bored like the others, as he turned back to watch the road approach to the house. Out two hundred metres in front of the farmhouse, Sergeant Bravner scanned the area with his sniper rifle checking the surrounding wheat fields. 'God I'd love to live here,' the Sergeant thought as he lay motionless in the sunshine, almost invisible in his killer suit. It really was beautiful here, and the people were friendly. He secretly hoped their quarry would never appear and he could stay here longer.

Bravner's dreams suddenly halted, as a barrel of a pistol suddenly touched the back of his head. The mystery intruder swiftly removed his radio and weapons from his hands.

"Do you understand English?"

"Yes." was all Bravner could get out.

"Good, then if you come with me, we can end this without bloodshed." his Captor said as he was led towards the farmhouse. Stopping, his captor dressed in an Australian army officer's uniform, pointed to a wheat field beside the road. Bravner discovered the other three lookouts bound and gagged. With a quick cut of the Aussie's knife all three men were released, and as a group, they walked down the road towards the front door. At his window the radio operator looked in disbelief as the four lookouts accompanied by an Australian army officer, walked casually down the road, heading straight towards him.

"Major we've got trouble!" the Radioman yelled, galvanising all the men in the house, rushing to their battle stations. The Australian stopped near the front door and bid the lookouts go inside. At that moment Major Drevnov opened the door, letting his men in.

"What happened?" Drevnov asked his lookouts in Russian, as they passed.

"He came out of nowhere Sir and got us all. I assure you I wasn't asleep!" Sergeant Bravner answered humiliated.

"It's okay Sergeant, I think we just found the Ghost," Drevnov replied gazing at this Officer, who waited patiently for him outside the door.

"Captain Roberts I presume!" Drevnov asked, smiling at the situation and introducing himself, shaking Steve's hand.

"It's a beautiful day Major. Is Sergio in there we have much to discuss." Steve answered, aware of the weapons pointed at him.

"Sergio can you come out, and comrade don't bring a weapon!" the Major instructed him, scanning the wheat fields for soldiers, his hand resting on his gun.

"They're out there Major, don't be foolish!" Steve said reading the Majors mind, getting an acknowledgement from him.

"It's you, at last, you bastard. You killed my father, kill him, Major!" Sergio yelled, coming through the door, eyes wild with anger.

"Be silent Captain. It's the Australians who will be doing the killing if you don't shut up!" Drevnov ordered, grabbing Sergio and shaking him violently, which brought him back to his senses.

"You're right Sergio, I did kill your father, and I am sorry for the grief it has caused you. If we could just all sit down, I'll explain what happened." Steve replied hoping he would understand.

It seemed strange to the heavily camouflaged SAS soldiers in the fields, and the Russian troops holed up in the house that these three men sat there in the open for over ten minutes just talking. While the soldiers on both sides waited tensely for the killing to begin.

"So it was an accident?"

"Yes, unfortunately, your father went for a weapon one of his aides had dropped, we had no choice I'm afraid," Steve answered flatly.

"Is that why you didn't kill me?"

"There'd been enough killing already. I didn't want more blood on my hands that night." Steve replied, meaning it.

"So what happens now?" Drevnov asked still scanning the tree line.

"You have two choices Major. You either leave or die. Which one do you want?" Steve said simply.

"To live of course, what do you propose?"

"We figure you must have some means of leaving, I will stay here as a hostage with you until you're all gone."

"Okay Captain you have a deal, but if one of my men dies so will you." the Major assured him, as he yelled to his radioman.

Twenty minutes passed when from the west a large helicopter came in over the wheat fields and settled in the front yard. Instantly the Russian assault team poured from the house, watching in all directions as they quickly in twos and threes mounted the chopper. Finally, only Steve, Major Drevnov and Sergio remained.

"I cannot forgive you Captain for killing my father, but I thank you for letting the Majors men go," Sergio said solemnly, before climbing slowly onto the helicopter.

"Yes, I too thank you, Captain, until we meet again," Drevnov added, before shaking Steve's hand again and boarding after Sergio.

The Pilot knowing the situation wasted no time in taking the chopper straight up, before rapidly flying towards the coast. As Drevnov and his men looked down at Steve standing in the yard, they saw at least forty lumps get up in the surrounding fields and join their Officer near the house. All knew they were lucky men to be alive.

"Do you think that's the end of it, Steve?" John asked, walking up to Steve in his killer suit.

"In more ways than one John, it means my identity is known to the Russians, I'm afraid my Army life is at an end," Steve answered sadly, as they both waited in silence for their transport to arrive.

FINAL DAYS HOLSWORTHY

Arriving back from the showers, Steve reluctantly cleaned out his locker and headed for the COs office where he said his goodbyes.

"I'm sorry your career was cut short Steve, but you're a liability in the SAS, and I couldn't see you being a paper pusher. Why not stay here, you're a good instructor?" Major Brown asked, hoping he would.

"I'd love to Sir, but they know me, and someone bound to come looking for me unless I leave. It's best that I find a different career." He answered, hoping that would work, as he shook hands with Major Brown and departed. Arriving back at his sister's house, he found a very pregnant Michelle jubilant that he was out.

"Don't worry Steve when the baby is here you'll be too busy to miss the Army. We'll move back to our house near John, he'll keep you informed on what's happening in the regiment." Michelle assured him, giving him a hug, knowing how much it hurt him leaving.

"Your right, but I'll need something to do to keep me busy. I thought I'd see Owen about working over in Perth." Steve answered happily, knowing his whole life was standing here with him now.

The next day Steve rang Owen, making an appointment for that afternoon, then took Michelle for a walk before driving into Sydney to see Owen. After a couple of hours, Owen consented to open an office in Perth. One condition was that Steve took several key personnel from the Sydney office. With these people, he could set up the office, and hire the appropriate staff for the job there. He would also have to spend, the rest of his time in Sydney learning from himself and Warren, while he waited for the birth of his child. After Steve promised to do as he was told, Owen arranged an office near his and handed Steve a stack of books.

"When you finish these come and see me." Owen smiled, as he turned to leave.

"Thanks for opening the office in Perth Owen; I know you're taking a chance."

"Nonsense Steve, I was already about to open an office. I just needed someone there I could trust."

"Then why didn't you just say that instead of getting me to bargain?"

"Would you have worked or studied as hard if I just gave it to you?"

"Yes, I'm sure I would have."

"I'm sorry Steve. You're right, you would have. You're a rarity, most would not have. That's why I like people to earn what they get, it keeps them honest." Owen pointed out, as he turned and left the office. As Owen sat in his office, he smiled over what Steve had said. 'You're a better man than most, my friend,' Owen admitted to himself grinning, as he worked out the staff Steve would need for this undertaking.

The next three months passed quickly as Steve studied and Michelle grew bigger until leaving for work became riskier. Michelle's mother now stayed with Michelle during the daytime so Steve could work, but he still felt guilty not being there. During this time Ali had called in on the way to a mission, to check on Steve and visit Julie of course. Julie was often at Steve's home, visiting Michelle, or off overseas visiting Ali. The unit missed Steve, but they were all doing well, and this mission was just for training Ali assured Steve.

Days crept by until one morning just before lunch, Owen burst into Steve's office.

"Better move it, boy, Michelle's gone to the hospital!" Owen smiled seeing for the first time Steve panic, as he rushed for the door. "Hey settle down Steve, I'll drive you, or are you forgetting that you come to work by train." Jumping into Owens car, they drove south to Sutherland hospital, the closest hospital to Louise's house where Michelle and Steve were staying. 'God look after my wife and child.' Steve prayed as a million thoughts went through his mind, wanting only to be with her during the birth.

Arriving at the entrance Steve sprang from the car, leaving Owen to park while he ran to the maternity section. Turning a corner, he found Michelle's mum and Isaac in the waiting room.

"Is she okay?"

"She's just gone in Steve. We had car trouble, and I thought of Isaac, and here we are." Michelle's mother answered excitedly, pushing Steve towards the door, as they waited. Walking in, a nurse told Steve to put on an apron and try to keep out of the way.

"And if you're going to faint, fall in a corner!" she added, getting a giggle from the other nurses. Steve kept his distance, making his way around the room until he reached the head of the bed and bent down, kissing his wife.

"I knew you'd make it!" Michelle said, sweating badly as pain showed on her face as the baby again tried to escape its confines and enter the world. After an hour of promising Michelle everything he could think of, to stop her from hurting, their little girl was born, and Steve was a father. Walking out to the waiting room, the proud father informed everyone that it was a girl. Michelle's mother and father, getting the nod from the nurse, were the first in to see her, followed closely by Louise and Edward.

"What's her name, Steve?" Owen asked smiling, still there, caught up in the excitement along with Isaac.

"Lindsey; after Isaac's son," Steve replied. Without a word, Isaac got up and hugged Steve. Breaking away he wiped tears from his eyes.

"Thank you, Steve," was all Isaac got out, leaving suddenly, overcome with grief and joy at the same time.

"That was a kind thing to do Steve." Owen smiled, wishing Michelle and Steve the best as he walked off after Isaac, leaving Steve to wait for another turn with his wife and daughter.

PERTH WESTERN AUSTRALIA
1989

Six in the morning and Steve ran along the beach powering through the sand like he did every morning he could. His daughter Lindsey had celebrated her fourth birthday along with her two-year-old sister Robin. The years since Lindsey's birth had been demanding on Steve. Building the business in Perth to a size where it rivalled their main office in Sydney, in clientele and profit, filled Steve's every day. Michelle helped with the firm, first as a secretary then as an assistant, as her grasp of the business grew. When their second child, Robin arrived, Michelle decided to look after the two girls, wanting them to have a stable family life at home.

This, of course, didn't mean that she was completely uninvolved, as on the occasions when Steve went away on business she would fill in, running the firm. In the time Steve had been there, he'd seen his unit friends a great deal, especially Ali who now lived in Zurich with Julie. They visited quite often, staying at Steve's house on the ocean for several days at a time before heading back home again.

Cody, Aaron and Sukai usually turned up together as being all bachelors they had more freedom and all shared a love of game fishing. They often called in on the way to, or returning from, an adventure along the coast of Australia somewhere. The unit was still doing missions, but Ali made it a rule never to involve Steve in what they were doing, which Michelle appreciated.

John, his neighbour, and Steve's RSM had retired and still lived up the road. He now ran the local Volunteer Fire Brigade in the same way that he'd run the regiment, much to the shock of the firemen. It was a great time to be alive, and as Steve powered along the beach, he thought his world couldn't be more perfect.

The only bad thing to happen that year was Isaac passing away, but Steve knew at least the man had died happy, having moved up to Queensland to live with his daughter, only four months earlier.

After a brisk shower, Steve sat out on the front veranda going over some business reports, when the doorbell sounded. It was a courier from the post office with a parcel, the type Steve hadn't seen for over four years. An hour later at eight am Michelle strolled out and found her husband sitting on the front veranda staring at nothing, the unopened parcel on the table in front of him.

"What's wrong Steve?" Michelle asked, a little scared by his sad facial expression.

"It's one of the parcels I used to get from the yanks before a mission!" Steve answered his eyes still distant.

"That's behind you Steve forget about it, don't open it," Michelle suggested lightly, trying to cover the fear she felt.

"Why send it now?" Steve asked distantly, more to himself than her. Sensing something might be wrong Michelle went to the phone and called their neighbour John to come over. Ten minutes passed when John knocked at the door. Giving the girls a hug as they greeted their adopted uncle, he then walked out to where Steve sat frozen.

"Hey, get a hold of yourself, Steve, you're scaring your family," John said softly awakening Steve out of his trance.

"Why did they send it now?" Steve asked angrily looking at John.

"I suggest you open it and find out instead of worrying about it!" John said calmly, as Michelle took their two girls for a walk on the beach. Carefully opening the parcel, Steve reviewed the information before handing it to John, who studied the mission.

"Shit Steve this is bad. Even if you go, they're most probably dead!" John admitted, after reading the reports.

"They're my friends, what would you do?"

"You know the answer to that already."

"That's why the bastards sent it to me!" Steve growled, knowing he was going.

The unit was missing in Afghanistan. They had gone in to rescue Abdul the tribal leader who had helped them get out of Kabul. It appeared he'd been captured by another tribe called the Taliban, who had grown in strength over the past few years. They had demanded a ransom for his release. Omar, the chieftain's son, had instead contacted the Americans, who had sent Ali and the team to get him back. After parachuting in to rescue him, the unit had disappeared, that was over two weeks ago.

Don Brooks, who was running the unit now, told Steve in the report that the unit had been written off. They'd pay his expenses if he wanted to go look. Otherwise, that was it.

"What a scumbag!" John muttered, reading Brooks letter again.

"Yeah I know, but if I don't go who will?"

"And where are you going?" Michelle whispered, a tremor in her voice, as she stood in the doorway holding their two girls.

"How about I take the girls for ice cream at my house?" John suggested, getting excited screams from the girls. Grabbing one of his hands each, they pulled John towards the door excitedly leaving Steve to explain the situation to Michelle.

"Poor Julie she'll be devastated if Ali's dead!" Michelle dried her tears with a tissue after Steve had finished.

"He could still be alive; Ali's a hard guy to kill."

"Promise me you'll be careful."

"I'll be in and out as fast as possible!"

"I know Ali and the others would go if it was you. It's no good me trying to stop you, but I'm scared Steve." Michelle admitted as the phone started to ring, making them both jump. Picking it up, Steve asked who was calling.

He was surprised to find Julie on the other end, wanting to know if Steve knew anything about Ali.

"Where are you, Julie?" Steve asked loudly for Michelle's benefit, which made her pull herself together and come to the phone.

"I've just landed at Perth Airport. Is it okay if I come over?" Julie replied nervously.

"Of course it is, you're always welcome Julie," Steve answered, glad she was here.

An hour later Julie pulled up at the house in a taxi, carrying a bag and came slowly towards the house. The door opened, and Michelle ran out hugging her as they both burst into tears. This lets Julie know that they knew about Ali.

Once inside Julie told them how Ali had left on a mission two months ago and had promised to ring her over a week ago but she had heard nothing.

"I thought if I came here in person you might help me?"

"I don't know much more than you, Julie, only that they're missing, probably just overdue," Steve reassured her.

"Then what do we do?"

"You stay here with Michelle, and I'll hop on a plane and go find out which bar they're staying in." Steve smiled.

"Thank you, Steve," was all Julie could say, as she held Michelle. While the girls talked, Steve hurried into the main bedroom and dialled the Airport to book a flight.

John, worried for Steve, came back over to drop off the kids and to find out what Steve was going to do about his friend's situation. Steve told him about Julie's arrival and how he'd managed to get a flight tomorrow to Karachi. From there he'd go to where Abdul's tribe was camped and ask Omar, his son for help.

"You're going on your own Steve, is that wise?"

"One or ten John it would be the same plan, it's all I can do."

"I'll run you to the Airport tomorrow that way Julie and Michelle will worry less." Steve agreeing thanked him.

It was an early five am start the next morning, as both Michelle and Julie waved him goodbye, as John drove Steve to the airport. John seemed quiet on the way in, and Steve was surprised when he drove into the car park instead of dropping him off at the departure gate. He was even more surprised when John pulled another bag from the boot as well as Steve's.

"What's going on John?"

"Someone's got to cover your back, my friend," John replied stony-faced as they both walked into the departure lounge.

"John you're a little older than me remember!"

"I'll walk you into the ground, my friend!" John answered, with a stern look on his face and Steve knew it was no use arguing.

"Thanks." was all Steve got out, as they walked towards their flight. John had bought an economy ticket for this flight, Steve changed it to business class so that they would be together much to Johns disgust at paying the extra.

"God Steve we're paying three times the price and arriving at the same time as everybody else!" He fumed. This changed when they'd settled in, and the hostess brought him a drink. John started to appreciate the little extras that made travelling this way more enjoyable.

By the time they had landed, they had nutted out a rough plan for looking for the lost unit. Clearing customs, Steve wasted no time in finding out the location of Abdul's tribe. He then hired a small plane to get them there. The last thing Steve did before leaving was to give Michelle a quick ring, telling her John was with him. He promised to contact her again in under four weeks, getting a 'Gods speed and be careful' from her in return.

Flying towards the border brought back memories of the last time Steve had been here. It was over six years ago and still this useless war ground on. At least now the tribes had the upper hand, meaning flights like this one were a lot safer than before.

Landing beside a huge collection of tents and canvas homes on the Pakistan side of the border, Steve and John were taken straight to the chieftain's tent. Here they were welcomed by Omar. He was no longer the happy young man that Steve remembered and had aged badly looking ten years older than he really was. The main difference in his appearance was a long scar he had on the left side of his face. Seeing Steve's sadness, Omar guessed what he was thinking.

"I got a little close to a gunship just before it exploded!" Omar answered, with a small smile.

"It's been a long time my friend."

"I'm surprised you're here Steve, I thought the others said you had left the unit."

"I had left Omar, but they're friends, I have to try and find them," Steve replied getting a nod of understanding in return. After they had sat down to eat, Steve introduced John to Omar impressing him by telling him John had trained him back in Australia.

"You are most welcome," Omar told John before getting down to business. It appeared that the pullback of Russian forces into safer areas had given the larger Taliban tribes more freedom. They had started to exert pressure on the other tribes to adopt their extreme interpretation of Islam or perish. Even though all the tribes were mostly Muslim, they were fiercely independent and rejected threats made by the Taliban, forcing open conflict between them. Abdul had gone under a white flag to parley with them and had been seized and held as a hostage until Ali's unit had broken him out.

Omar's men, unfortunately, had lost track of them after the breakout. Now because the Taliban were massing to their west, Omar couldn't afford to send too many men to locate them.

"How do you know they're alive?" John asked politely.

"We have seen their troops searching, and our scouts intercepted one of their groups. One survivor, under questioning, admitted they were still looking for them." Omar showed disappointed at not being able to rescue his father.

"We'll do our best to find them," Steve promised, as two men and a young girl entered the tent.

"These are my best scouts they will accompany you on your search," Omar said proudly.

"Isn't the girl a bit young?" John asked quietly.

"If an old goat can go, so can I!" the young girl answered in English, making John go red.

"Who are you calling an old goat?" John stammered out, surprised she could speak English, as the others broke into laughter at John's embarrassment. After they had discussed the best way to travel, Omar excused himself. He had other matters at the moment that were more pressing. Steve and the guides then thrash out a plan for searching, before turning in for the night.

Starting out before dawn the very next day, the small group silently started up into the dark, forbidding mountains that marked the border of Afghanistan. Following a rough trail punctuated by craters from past bombings, the guides told them to not veer from the path, as mines in this area were in abundance.

"Then why come this way?" John asked nervously watching the ground.

"We know the path by experience, our enemies do not." Mary the young girl answered.

Mary was a strange name for a tribesmen's daughter. They found out that Mary's mother's life had been saved by a Catholic priest, here doing missionary work. Mary's father in gratitude to the man had named her Mary after Jesus' mother. Unfortunately, when Mary was twelve, her parents were killed in an air strike, leaving the tribe to look after her.

They walked from sun up till way past sundown, trying to cover as much of the ground as possible, before they reached enemy territory. Once in Taliban controlled land, they would only be able to travel at night, and even then it was still dangerous. Omar had supplied them with M16's assault rifles, which had been given to the tribesmen by the American's, for opposing the Russians. Although they worked efficiently, they were noisy, and noise was the enemy out here. Steve's primary weapon was an old hunting knife one of the tribesmen had given him. He knew that if they ran into anyone, this was the only way they could fight and not be detected.

Towards midnight, exhausted from walking over rocky outcrops, the group piled into a small cave and collapsed. Awaking at daybreak, stiff and sore, they swiftly dug themselves holes in the cave entrance to escape the heat. Only one member at a time kept watch, until darkness fell again, at which time they continued their search. This way of travelling continued for three more nights, moving ever deeper into Afghanistan.

Back at the camp, Mary told them that the Taliban controlled the southern and western areas and their camp was located to the east. This meant the only safe route for Abdul was north, into Russian held territory. She had worked this out, from the information the Taliban prisoner had given them, and she also pointed out, that this was where the Taliban were looking for him. Taking a chance, Steve had decided to go with her intuition and search this area first.

On the fourth night as Steve lead the way, he spotted a large group moving in the same direction just ahead of them. Signalling the group to stay put, Steve closed in on the group ahead to see what was going on. What he found was worrying. Coming back to his group he reported at least two hundred tribesmen, almost certainly Taliban were moving towards the large valley ahead. Steve remembered this valley, as it was where they had shot down the chopper while fighting for their lives to escape from the Russians. He knew it was a long way across, with a road on this side of the valley.

Taking Mary with him this time Steve silently approached the tribesmen. They had stopped on an escarpment that overlooked the valley and were having a heated discussion. After listening for twenty minutes, Mary tugged at Steve's arm pointing back towards their group. Travelling at speed, they hurried back, where Mary then explained what she had heard.

It appeared Abdul and Steve's friends were pinned down in a blind canyon to the west. The Taliban there were waiting for more men to dig them out. The problem was that a Russian mobile patrol was camped on the road across from the Taliban's exit point of this escarpment. They had thought of sneaking past the Russians in the remaining darkness, but then their escape route would be compromised. So they had decided to wait until reinforcements arrived and hit the Russians, just before first light.

As if on cue, movement could be heard coming up behind Steve's group. They quickly hid, letting the second group of Taliban pass them in the darkness. Once the second group had passed, Steve tried to figure out what to do. They couldn't wait here knowing once the Taliban finished with the Russians, they'd go after Abdul. On the other hand, they couldn't sneak past such a large group, which now numbered over four hundred, without being seen. So what should they do to do? John, in the end, came up with an idea.

"Can we get the Russians to do our dirty work by tipping them off?" John suggested softly, getting a look of disgust from Mary.

"They are our enemies!" Mary answered angrily.

"So are the Taliban!" Steve replied just as angrily, as he thought about what John had said, before coming up with a plan.

"I'll sneak down past the Taliban and tip off the Russians. You four, when the shooting starts, will head to where Abdul is trapped, I'll catch up to you there." Steve explained, leaving no room for arguments. Getting reluctant agreement from all present, Steve started to go, when John's hand stopped him.

"Good luck Steve and don't be a hero. I wouldn't like being out here on my own!" John whispered before he moved off with the others. Skirting the Taliban who had started moving again, Steve hurried down the ravine that emptied out onto the valley below.

Moving swiftly he reached the Russians position before the Taliban. Although the Russians were silent, Steve had no problem spotting them by the shapes of armoured vehicles in the moonlight. Creeping ever closer, Steve came upon the first Russian foxhole to find both soldiers sleeping peacefully in it. Smiling to himself, Steve moved along the side of the vehicles, before he heard the telltale sound of a radio transmitter. It was coming from a camouflaged jeep in the centre of the encampment.

Approaching with absolute stealth, Steve was about to set up an explosive and leave, when looking into the command jeep, he couldn't believe his eyes. Moving closer Steve grabbed a pistol lying beside the officer, tapping both men on their shoulders with it. Sergio and another man slowly turned around. Steve recognised the second man from Perth.

"Sergio, what are you doing here?" Steve whispered, seeing the absolute shock on Sergio's face and the officer next to him, by his appearance. A gun being place against the back of Steve's head told him not everyone was asleep.

"It would be best if you do not move!" Major Drevnov said from behind Steve, as Sergio and Josef recovered from the shock.

"Good God, don't tell me you're here too Major?" Steve asked, turning and facing a startled Major, who stood staggered at recognising Steve.

"Give me one reason why I shouldn't shoot you right now!" Sergio demanded, pointing his regained pistol straight at Steve, making him turn back around.

"I can give you four hundred reasons and they're encircling your position right now!"

"You could be lying?" Drevnov suggested from behind him.

"Then pull the trigger and find out. First I'd suggest waking your sentries since they're asleep!" Steve replied studying their faces.

"Sergio and you too Josef go check on the men. Robert's you hand over your weapons." Major Drevnov ordered as Sergio and Josef ran off into the night.

"Are they your friends out there?" Drevnov asked before sitting down, pointing for Steve to do the same.

"No, they'll kill me just as quickly as you."

"Then what the hell are you doing here?"

"The unit I used to belong to is being hunted by the Taliban, I came to try and find them," Steve confessed.

"And you expect me to believe that?"

"I know it's hard to believe, but I could ask what you three are doing here as well."

"We've been here since we failed to bring you home!" Drevnov said angrily, clearly hating being in this country.

"Well now's the time to become heroes and leave." Steve smiled. "Can you call in air support on that radio?" Drevnov not answering, stare at Steve, as footsteps could be heard rapidly approaching.

"Major he was right the men were asleep," Josef said breathing heavily.

"And I think I heard movement out there," Sergio said, fear in his voice, as he came up behind Josef.

Drevnov making a decision, ordered all his men to man there weapon's, before reaching for the radio and calling in an air strike, his eyes never leaving Steve's.

"Anything else you'd like to suggest Roberts?" Drevnov asked sarcastically, as his men manned their positions.

"How about turning up the radio in the last armoured vehicle over there and turn on a small light in it as well," Steve suggested, getting confused looks from the men around him. Drevnov in return laughed, ordering his men to do it, waving Steve towards a dugout position.

Out in the dark, the Taliban fighters closed in on the Russians. Their leader seeing the faint light coming from the vehicle with the radio blaring ordered all their grenade launchers and mortars to concentrate on it. He did this to prevent their enemy from calling for help. Sensing total surprise, the Taliban opened fired and surged forward. They were met by a wall of hot metal which exploded out of the Russian positions.

From from the safety of their trench, Drevnov watched the lit up armoured vehicle exploded into the sky. It had been hit by several rockets and mortars in the first barrage. Drevnov realised how lucky they had been that the opening attack, had landed on an empty target, leaving his men free to return fire.

The Taliban could not believe what had happened, as they found themselves pinned to the ground, unable to move forward. Their leader shocked by the Russian response, was just about to move their mortar fire to the other vehicles when the sound of helicopters filled the air. Knowing it was already too late, he quickly sounded the retreat and prayed for deliverance, as a stray round cut him down.

The pilots of the helicopters couldn't have timed it better, as they came in spotting the enemy positions by their gun flashes. This made it easier to drop their cluster bombs and rockets on the enemy soldiers, scattering them.

Daylight broke as the Russians sent out patrols to track down the survivors. The Russians had lost only four men with ten wounded, and of course, one armoured vehicle, to the nearly three hundred and fifty enemy dead. Knowing his superiors would be more than impressed with this victory, Drevnov accompanied by Sergio and Roberts surveyed the battlefield. Josef, unfortunately, had been hit and although it wasn't fatal, had been airlifted with the other wounded to a mobile hospital.

"Well Captain Roberts again you have saved my life, so what do I do with you?" Drevnov asked .

"I was hoping to slip out last night, but I didn't get the chance," Steve replied half smiling, not looking forward to going to prison in Russia.

"When you came in and warned us, was that your original plan?"

Sergio asked softly.

"I had planned to lay an explosive charge and leave, triggering it later. When I saw you inside, I couldn't let them finish you off."

"Then as far as I'm concerned an undercover Russian soldier warned us of the attack and then disappeared. No one else here will say anything different." Sergio informed him, before turning and walking back towards the camp.

"Being here has turned Sergio into a good man," Drevnov explained softly, watching Sergio walk away.

"I hope he finds peace now," Steve replied truthfully.

"Well I suppose we'll be heroes now, and able to go home after this!" Drevnov grinned, as he too turned and following Sergio leaving Steve standing there alone. Looking around not believing his luck, Steve left, to find his friends.

Reaching the side of the valley where the Taliban had come down through a ravine, Steve found fresh tracks heading west, indicating not all the Taliban had been killed by the Russians. Worried for his friends, Steve travelled in the remaining daylight along the valley wall, hoping the Russian presence would slow the Taliban down. He made slow progress until after attracting the attention of a Russian helicopter; he decided to settle down to wait for nightfall.

When the sun started to set, he started off again, continuing west, until the sound of gunfire came to him. Making for high ground, Steve saw ahead the telltale muzzle flash of weapon fire. Having surrendered his weapons to Drevnov, Steve found himself approaching a firefight, with nothing but the rocks on the ground as a weapon. He also knew that in the darkness, people had a habit of shooting at anything that moved.

Silently moving closer Steve encountered his first combatant, who, luckily for Steve, lay dead on the ground with a large messy wound in his back. Quickly Steve relieved him of his weapons, a rusty AK47 and an old bayonet. Moving forward again Steve came upon several more bodies picking up more ammo and a few grenades, as the noise of gunfire grew louder and more intense. Reaching a small valley entrance, Steve looked down to see a battle going on between two distinct groups, one facing down the valley away from him the other facing towards him, further down the valley.

John, with the three scouts had fought their way to where Abdul and the unit were trapped, only to become trapped themselves.

Steve figured that the Taliban survivors from the Russian camp battle may have arrived after them. With no radio, Steve's only option was to persuade the enemy to abandon their position. Without delay, he crept slowly forward looking for some advantage that would make the Taliban leave.

At the other end of the valley, John lay huddled behind a rocky outcrop wishing he hadn't come to this god-forsaken hole. At first, the rescue had gone to plan. He and the three scouts had come into the valley and opened fired on the ten Taliban soldiers guarding the entrance. Because they were expecting reinforcements, the attack was a total surprise.

In a panic the tribesmen had run past John's group and back the way they had come from the east, losing half their men in the process. John's group had then run forward to see how Abdul and the unit were when a force of thirty tribesmen had turned up. With the five survivors from the surprise attack earlier, they had quickly sealed the valley off again. Since then the tribesmen had continually attacked their position, not trying any longer to wait them out, they wanted blood for their losses.

Steve, in the meantime, crawled up onto a ledge above the Taliban. Looking down, he saw that the Taliban had broken into two groups. The largest group below him was keeping his friends pinned down, while a second group crawled forward further out in the valley, trying to flank Abdul's position. Pulling the pins from the three grenades he had picked up, Steve, in quick succession, hurled them with all his strength at the group crawling forward. Seeing them land amongst the tribesmen, he ducked out of sight and waited for the result.

It wasn't long in coming as the area where the tribesmen were crawling became a sea of sound and shrapnel as each grenade exploded with a brilliant flash. John in his position was nearly as shocked as the Taliban, at how close the enemy had gotten. But unlike the poor bastards out there, he and the others were protected by the rocks. John and the others then poured concentrated fire into the survivors, who staggered to their feet and tried to run for safety, not one made it.

The Taliban soldiers in the covering group were no fools and knew that grenades that had caused this havoc amongst comrades had been thrown from behind them. After a brief meeting, they had broken into two groups, one to search for the culprits, while the others kept Abdul's group pinned down. Making a quick calculation, Steve guessed that about ten tribesmen had been killed in the attack. He knew they couldn't look everywhere, so he slowly left his position and silently moved out, to find the searching tribesmen.

Abdul appeared beside John, giving him a toothy smile.

"The Ghost is out there!" he whispered in broken English into John's ear, as John turned in surprise, wondering how he knew that name.

"Yes, I think it's him. But where did you hear that name?" John asked softly, as Abdul pointed back towards the cave. When they arrived, John had found that both Ali and Aaron had been wounded, Ali seriously. They were now resting in a cave at the back of the position, hoping for a miracle.

"They said he would come. I did not believe them, much to my shame." Abdul said softly to John.

"I didn't think he would either!" John smiled, as Abdul burst into laughter, getting a spray of bullets into the surrounding rock for his outburst. Patting John on the shoulder, he moved off.

"You fight well old man!" Mary whispered from the darkness to the right, having listened to Abdul and John talking.

"Do you think it's Steve out there too?" John asked.

"We will soon know, though who else could it be?" Mary answered honestly, ever searching for movement. Since this journey had begun, John had become close to this young orphan girl who deserved better than this life. He'd found her to be well educated and when they got back if they did, he hoped to help her. She continually asked about Australia wanting to know if it was true that everyone was welcome. John told her that it was a land to get a fresh start, to leave your troubles behind.

He told of his wife and not being able to have children, hoping she'd come with him to maybe become part of his family. She was excited by this offer telling him she'd think about it if they made it back. John hoped she would, this war-torn country was no place for a young girl.

Out at the valley entrance, the group searching had spread out forming a rough skirmish line across the valley. With great care swept the area, looking for their adversary. Coming up behind the first man, Steve grabbed his mouth and stabbed the old bayonet up through his ribs and into his heart, holding him tight as his life flowed away. Moving to the next man Steve repeated the attack. Unfortunately, the bayonet broke in two, with a loud crack, after getting caught in the man's ribs. Turning the man over Steve grabbed his knife, which resembled an old bowie knife and moved on.

The next tribesman, having heard the cracking noise yelled out towards his comrade. Getting no answer, he sent a stream of bullets in Steve's direction, forcing him to hit the ground. At least four tribesmen charged towards Steve's position, weapons blazing. Steve lying flat on the ground cut them down as they charged in blindly. Rising to his feet, checking the area for any survivors and finding none, Steve moved cautiously back towards the valley.

The Taliban blocking force hearing the firing, called out to their men, trying to find out what had happened. Back in his position on the ledge, Steve now looked down on the spooked tribesmen, as two of them argued about what to do. One was clearly indicating that they should stay and guard the valley while the other man, backed by most of the men, wanted to leave. The argument finally finished when a tribesman shot the one who wanted to stay in the back. The rest keeping in a tight group headed to the east at a fast pace.

Waiting a good hour to be safe, Steve climbed down and slowly walked down the valley, passing many dead tribesmen, before halting at Abdul's position.

"It's Steve is it safe to come in?" He yelled from behind a rock.

"What took you so long?" John yelled back, as Steve's friend ran out welcoming him. After hugs from everyone Steve, made his way to the cave, to see how Ali and Aaron were.

Looking Ali over Steve knew he couldn't make a forced march back to Abdul's camp in his present condition. They also couldn't stay here, so using a couple of groundsheets they quickly made a rough stretcher and started east, hoping they wouldn't catch up with the fleeing Taliban.

As daylight broke, John, who was on point with Mary, guessed they had made about five kilometres. It wasn't much, but at least they were out of that dead-end valley. Sheltering in a small cave in the cliff face, John stood watched, while the others bedded down for the day. Steve looked around the group worried about Ali, as Cody came over and sat down.

"Thanks for coming. I'd thought we'd all bought it this time." Cody admitted, looking towards Ali.

"What happened?" Steve asked softly, as Cody went over their mission.

As usual, Ali had planned the mission perfectly. They had parachuted in and grabbed Abdul from the surprised Taliban tribesmen. Moving quickly they had then moved north, where a chopper was supposed to pick them up. It never showed. They had then run into a Taliban patrol, and even though they'd killed them all, another group had heard the exchange and chased them. Having no choice, they had slowly headed further north hoping to lose them. After two weeks they'd been caught in that valley and having nowhere to run they'd been forced to dig in and wait.

"You know Ali always thought you'd come." Cody smiled, looking at Ali as he lay asleep.

"You're just lucky John and I were on a fishing trip near here." Steve grinned, getting a grin from Cody, something he hadn't done for some time. Thanking Steve again, he moved off to relieve John as lookout.

The next night was just the same as they slowly travelled down the valley coming finally opposite where the Russian camp had been. Here they reached the exit point from the valley, which would take them back towards Abdul's camp.

Steve, in a deep sleep, was woken by John at midday.

"Come and have a look at this," John whispered excitedly, as Steve followed him to a spot where they could look out over the valley. Grabbing the binoculars from John, Steve looked out to where the battle had been fought by the Russians. Sitting near the burnt out armoured vehicle, was a large helicopter. To his amazement, he saw several civilians and what looked like a camera crew, filming the area.

"What do you make of that?" John asked as Steve looked towards the chopper hungrily.

"I see a lift home if we're lucky!" Steve whispered hopefully, as he made his way back to the cave to get Cody and Sukai.

It had taken nearly two hours for Cody, Sukai and Steve to close in on the helicopter, fearing at any moment it would take off in a cloud of dust. Approaching from the blind side away from the film crew, Steve couldn't believe the cheek of this bunch of people to be so casual in enemy territory. Inside the helicopter, the pilot and co-pilot sat bored. They were both ex-military and had been supplied by the Russian government so that a good slant could be put on the war here. Neither had been stationed in Afghanistan, and the area was now presumed safe, or so they had been told.

The journalists and television presenters were from several countries friendly to the Soviet Union and had been given permission to film what they liked. So they were making every second count on this field trip. The first sign the pilot knew that something was wrong was when the muzzle of Cody's rifle touched the back of his head as he sat in the cockpit.

"Can either of you speak English?" Cody asked softly, as the co-pilot turned and saw the weapon.

"I can." The pilot answered nervously.

"That's good. Now turn off your radio really slowly and just sit there quietly, understood?" Cody ordered. The pilot nodded and did as he'd was told, silently waiting.

Outside Steve and Sukai rose from the scrub. Heavily camouflaged, they walked towards the group of reporters who were having lunch at a small portable picnic table in the centre of the clearing. So intent were they on their lunch, they only noticed Sukai and Steve when their shadows crossed the table. As one they exploded to their feet, some screaming, the others too scared to make noise. When Steve and Sukai didn't shoot them, they calmed down, as a stunning brunette stepped forward. Looking unafraid, she sternly asked them something in Russian showing more courage than the men present.

"Can you speak English?" Steve asked politely as the group gasped, realising these men weren't Afghanis tribesmen. The importance of finding foreign soldiers here was starting to dawn on them.

"Yes, I do. Why are you here?" replied the brunette, again without fear.

"A couple of my men are hurt, they need medical aid immediately!" Steve answered smiling, trying to calm the others, as woman translated.

"Can we film you surrendering?" The woman asked. Sukai burst into laughter, making the group watch him nervously.

"We're not surrendering lady. We're taking your helicopter!" Steve explained.

"That is impossible we need that helicopter ourselves!" the Brunette replied angrily, hands on hips.

"I'm not asking lady, you either come with us or stay here if you want. The Taliban are likely to be here soon looking for us so I wouldn't advise staying." Steve informed her.

At the mention of Taliban, the media crew fearfully watched the surrounding countryside for movement. All of them knew what would happen if they were caught.

"I thought you foreign devils were backing the Taliban!" the Brunette replied.

"Our friend here Abdul and his tribe had a falling out with their Taliban allies. So we came to help them get out of a tight spot, and the Taliban weren't happy about it." Steve explained, getting some grins from his companions at his summary of the mission.

"Will we be safe?" She asked, looking at Abdul and the Afghan guides.

"You have my word," Steve answered removing his camouflage and herding everyone towards the chopper. As the film crew helped load Ali and Aaron onto the chopper, Cody and Sukai stripped all excess gear, hoping to lighten it.

"We're still too heavy!" the Pilot pointed out, in broken English, as the helicopter tried to rise from the ground and failed.

"Throw everything you can overboard!" Steve ordered the crowd, causing consternation from the film crew as their personnel gear sailed out the door, along with most of the unit's weapons.

"We're still too heavy!" the Pilot repeated his warning, as the three Afghan guides, sensing the problem climbed out of the chopper. Steve and Abdul looked with pride on the two men and Mary knowing the chances of them making it weren't great.

"John can you make sure the Russians are released after you make it!" Steve asked as he too stepped off the chopper.

"I'll come too!" John suggested, knowing he was nearly at his end physically. Steve's hand stopped him.

"No, you can look after her." Steve grinned, as he lifted Mary back into the chopper. Mary furious made to climb out again when Abdul told her to be quiet and sit down.

"No Steve, don't do it!" Ali moaned in pain, having woken up and seen their predicament. Cody and Sukai both started to make for the door, telling Aaron who was also injured, to stay with Ali.

"Get back all of you. You're all in bad shape. We three have the best chance of making it!" Steve yelled, slamming the side door closed in their faces, ending the argument, as the helicopter staggered into the air.

"They're taking quite a chance aren't they?" the Brunette asked, looking down at the three men who gathered up some of the discarded gear and trotted towards the south.

"The ghost will make it!" Sukai announced softly, getting a nod from John, as he stared down at the three men who became smaller, as the chopper rose out of the valley and headed south leaving them far behind.

Looking up at the helicopter as it disappeared over the mountain range to the south, Steve glanced sideways to find the two guides looking at him with respect, at his decision to join them.

"It was too crowded anyway, and those Russians stink!" Steve grinned, as the tribesmen both smiled, not understanding a word of what he was saying. Shouldering their weapons, they moved swiftly towards the valley wall, before climbing up into the surrounding mountains.

On the chopper, the pilot had taken the helicopter up to its maximum height to keep away from the deadly missiles the tribesmen now possessed. He was aware of both the fuel gauge and Cody, who hovered just behind him watching his every move, as they approached the border. After some changes to their course, they arrived over Abdul's tribe's village.

This caused a hive of activity at the appearance of a Russian chopper on this side of the border. Dropping a message attached to a long ribbon the helicopter circled until a large fire belched smoke indicating it was safe to land. Coming in warily the pilot dropped down right in the centre of the village as hundreds of armed men and women surrounded the chopper. A cry of relief and jubilation roared from the tribesmen, as Abdul opened the side door of the chopper and swung down onto the ground. Tears in his eyes, he stood looking at his people, as his son rushed through the crowd to hug him.

Pointing to the helicopter, Abdul told his people of the wounded men on board who had saved his life. Ali and Aaron were then carefully carried to a tent where they were to be cared for until a doctor could be found. All while the Russian film crew stood watching.

"What about the Russians?" Omar asked his father amazed by their presence here.

"The Ghost promised their safety, my son, I must honour it!" Abdul informed him, wondering about his friend Robert's and the two guides.

"Who is the Ghost?" Omar asked, not understanding.

"It is the warrior name for the soldier named Robert's," Abdul told him. "He stayed behind with your two guides so we might escape!" Abdul exclaimed, tears running down his face, showing his respect for Omar's men and the westerner.

"They are brave warrior's father, they'll make it," Omar replied. His eyes told another story.

"Anyway, the Russians will have to stay here as our guests, until we hear news of the Ghost."

"As you wish father," Omar replied, before turning and finding Cody and Sukai standing there.

"Omar could we borrow some men and go," was all Cody got out before Omar stopped him.

"You two are too weak to go out my friends. I forbid it. Don't worry, I will send out all the men I can spare to look for your friend, so go and rest." Omar ordered, getting a supporting nod from his father. Cody and Sukai grumbling turned and sadly walked off to find a bed to rest in for now until their strength returned.

"Watch them, my son!" Abdul suggested smiling, knowing the two westerners would take off after their friend as soon as possible. Omar smiled, nodding his understanding, as they walked to their tent.

It was another five days before Steve, and one guide arrived back at Abdul's village, both wounded. The trip had been mostly without incident until one day out Jamal the lead guide had stepped on a mine. Realising his mistake, the guide had collapsed onto the hidden device shielding Steve and the other guide from the explosion. Even so, some shrapnel had hit both Steve and the remaining guide in the legs, forcing them to slowly limp towards the village. Luckily a patrol sent out by Omar had come across them.

Entering the village to a hero's welcome, Steve was surprised to find the Russians still there. Omar explained the situation. It appeared being true reporters they had taken advantage of their time here to research the Afghan view of the war, making themselves quite at home.

"Now you're back we will let them leave, and maybe they'll tell a story from our perspective." Omar smiled, as the brunette Steve had met earlier, came over to greet him.

"So you made it after all Captain Roberts or should I say Ghost!"

"So how are you enjoying your stay?" Steve asked, wondering how she knew so much about him.

"Natasha" She replied giggling, at his attempt to change the subject.

"Natasha. I hope you've been treated well."

"Don't worry Captain your secret is safe with me. From what I've heard, you've retired anyway, and are only here to help your friends." Natasha replied, the smile still on her lips.

"That would be appreciated, Natasha. This whole situation is rather unorthodox, to put it mildly. And my name's Steve," he answered, finding himself off balance by this attractive young woman.

That night after he had rested, Steve was told that Aaron and Ali were doing well. They'd been transferred to Karachi's main hospital for further treatment. Steve had also been informed that John, Cody and Sukai weren't here at the moment, having snuck out with Mary to look for Steve. They were expected back tomorrow with luck, Omar said amazed they had got past the men watching them. Sitting as a special guest next to Omar and Abdul for dinner, Steve asked what they intended to do about the Taliban.

"We can't do much my friend, they're too many!" Abdul spat out angrily, before continuing. "Our best bet is to move northeast away from Pakistan, that is where the Taliban are consolidating their control." Abdul fumed, none too happy about leaving this area.

"Only through strength can we survive father!" Omar added, like always backing his father's decisions, getting a hug from his father in return. Feeling a bump beside him, Steve look around to find Natasha sitting herself down beside him, as the Russian film crew joined the celebrations.

"I hear we're leaving tomorrow, so I'd like to thank you both for treating us so fairly," Natasha said, addressing Abdul and Omar.

"It would have been quite different if the Ghost hadn't made me promise," Abdul replied smiling.

"No doubt, but I thank you anyway." Natasha smiled, showing no fear, which impressed the tribe's two leaders. Sitting there, Steve could not help but feel how close this young woman was to him. More unsettling was the smell of her perfume that drifted towards him making him dizzy, as the heat of her body radiated into his side warming him.

"Did I tell you I was married?" Steve suddenly blurted out, as Natasha looked him in the eyes and burst into laughter. She then translated what he had said to the other Russians, causing them all of them to burst into laughter as well.

"For a man who shows no fear in battle, it amazes me how easily you are startled by a woman!" Natasha smiled her eyes sparkling, before going back to her meal as if nothing had happened.

When the evening was finally over Steve walked to his tent and was just about to enter, when Natasha called his name. Stopping and turning around, Natasha came towards him, pushing him up against a tree, as she ravenously kissed him, while her lower body thrust against his, arousing him. Stopping she pulled away looking at him.

"Just so you know what you're missing!" Natasha smiled wickedly, before turning and disappearing into the darkness.

"Shit there goes a whole lot of trouble!" Steve said out loud, breathing heavily, knowing how much she had excited him.

"Big night Steve!" a voice said from the dark as John, Cody and Sukai, accompanied by Mary came into view. Running forward Steve hugged them all.

"God I'm glad you're all here I was worried about you."

"You didn't look too worried a moment ago!" Cody commented as the others chuckled.

"Hey, nothing happened!" Steve burst out like a child caught doing the wrong thing.

"We know Steve; we're just pulling your leg." John laughed, grabbing hold of his friend and hugging him again.

The next day the whole village turned out to say goodbye to the Russians. Having helped the tribesmen strip the chopper of all its weapons, they loaded up all the souvenirs the helicopter could carry, before saying goodbye. Natasha being the last on board blew Steve a kiss, making all present burst into laughter.

"Bloody hell does everyone know?" Steve smiled, as the chopper quickly rose and disappeared into the northern sky.

"It amazes me, but I will miss those Russians." Omar grinned, waving to the chopper.

"Who knows someday you might be allies against the Taliban!" John said smiling.

"That my friend would be impossible," Omar replied, touching his scar, showing the hurt went deep for all Afghans.

As the Russian helicopter moved over the border range to the north, vanishing amongst the mountains, their plane appeared from the south, landing beside the village. Saying their goodbyes, they prepared to board the small two-engine plane for their flight back to Karachi.

"You will always be welcome at our table!" Abdul told Steve and his friends, embracing each one of them and bidding them good luck. They sadly realised that the chances were none of them would ever return. Boarding the plane, Steve noticed Mary follow John on board.

"What's going on John?"

"I've adopted her Steve. She's coming back with me to Australia!"

"I thought you two were always fighting?" Cody put in shocked.

"That's what I mean. We're just like father and daughter already!" John chuckled at their confusion.

"What about customs?" Steve asked.

"I'll work it out," John replied confidently, as everyone settled down for the trip back to Karachi.

Once landed, they all caught a minibus to the Hilton Intercontinental hotel, arriving at midnight. Without further discussions, the group booked in, went up to their rooms and collapsed.

BETRAYED

Getting up early feeling refreshed, Steve decided on a morning run. Wondering where he would actually run, he approached the doorman. Seeing Steve's clothes, he informed him that behind the hotel was a large park, with a running track through it. Despite the heat, he found it surprisingly peaceful. It was good to be out on his own again, running for exercise instead of his life, as he jogged slowly through the park. Looking forward to returning to his boring job and his loving family, he relaxed letting his mission tension go. Deep in thought, thinking of going home, he failed to notice two men who took turns following him at a distance.

Back at the hotel after a long shower, Steve met Cody and Sukai, before travelling to the hospital. While the unit members visited Ali and Aaron, John took Mary off to the embassy, to see about a passport for her trip to Australia. Arriving at the hospital they found Aaron, now fully recovered, Ali, on the other hand, was still bedridden. Ali was excited to see his friends, as each of them tried to cheer him. After the jokes had settled down and the nurses had told them to keep it down several times, Ali became serious.

"This was the last mission men. I'm out after this one!"

"You're not serious are you Ali?" Cody asked, thinking he was overreacting.

"It was a setup Cody. I don't think it was an accident that the chopper didn't arrive."

"Why would they do that?" Sukai whispered, still not convinced.

"We've become too well known. It's only a matter of time before someone blows our cover. I think Brooks realises that too."

"Then why would they send for me?" Steve asked hoping he was wrong.

"I don't know Steve, maybe to tie up loose ends. Still, I'm glad you came." Ali smiled, gratefully, as the others added their thanks.

"You'd have done the same for me!"

"Bullshit I would have!" Aaron chuckled, making everyone laugh. When the others had left, Steve sat with Ali filling him in on what had happened.

"So your friend is trying to take Mary home as his daughter, that's great."

"Yes, he's got a good heart. I just hope the embassy has one."

"Have you heard from Brooks?"

"No nothing, not since I left Australia."

"I know you're thinking I'm overreacting, but there's something wrong Steve, I can feel it!"

"Then why get me to rescue you?"

"Maybe you were supposed to die as well. Maybe they thought you might ask questions if we just disappeared." Steve recalled how Julie had turned up just as he was about to leave.

"What is it?" Ali asked seeing Steve's guarded look.

"I wasn't going to worry you, but just before I left, Julie turned up scared that you hadn't contacted her."

"Is she okay?"

"Yes she's fine, but she's worried."

"Then let's get a phone and ring them both!" Ali suggested excitedly, as Steve hurried out to find a nurse and a phone.

The call cost them a small fortune, but it was worth every cent to hear the sound of relief in their voices.

"How long will you be?" Michelle asked, missing him.

"About a week. John's adopted an Afghan girl named Mary. Don't tell his wife until he does." Steve warned, wanting Johns surprise to be complete and giving Ali another week to recover.

"That's great news, Steve. Joan always wanted a child."

It was then Ali's turn to talk, telling Julie he was out for good. Overjoyed she promised him something special when she met him next, before ringing off. 'I better get well real quick!' Ali smiled, still looking at the phone, thinking seriously of proposing to Julie when he got back.

"Anything you need?" Steve asked, after being asked to leave by the head nurse.

"No, just watch your back Steve, I'm worried."

"Well don't be, I'll be here tomorrow," Steve assured him, heading back to the hotel.

Arriving back before John, Steve put on a pair of new runners he had bought in a market outside the hotel and hit the park track. Tired and sweating, he returned two hours later feeling the stress of the last month starting to leave him. Across the lobby, in the restaurant, John sat with Mary having a late afternoon ice cream. Mary had never had ice cream before and had developed quite a liking for it.

Seeing Steve enter the front door he was just about to call to him when he saw a well-built man enter from a side door watching Steve. The man took up position near the front door, signalling to another man who was already in the foyer.

John froze where he was, staring at the men as Mary opposite, picked up on his silence.

"What's wrong John?"

"Probably nothing, but two men seem to be following Steve," John replied, his eyes discreetly following the two men as they walked right by him, talking among themselves.

"A man like Steve must make enemies."

"Yes, you're right Mary, though they looked and sounded like Americans. They're supposed to be our friends." John answered quietly, before paying his bill and leading Mary upstairs to their rooms.

Getting out of a long hot shower Steve was surprised by the loud banging on his door, as swiftly throwing on a dressing gown, he opened the door.

"What's up John?"

"Look it could be nothing, but you're being tailed" John replied, telling Steve what he had seen, as Steve stood there quietly. "So what do you think?"

"How long before you and Mary can be on a plane?" Steve asked softly, as he saw the concern in John's eyes.

"I was going to tell you tonight, but after beating my head against the embassies paper pushers and their bullshit, I was just about to give up and try sneaking her in. As I went to leave, a clerk there told me that five grand in a bag was the going rate for a passport. So I came back here hoping to borrow it from you." John admitted. He was a proud man not usually open to borrowing money, but Mary was important to him.

"I'll have it for you tomorrow morning, now go get all of our flights arranged for the following day, that's two days time," Steve warned.

"Thanks, Steve," John replied as he moved towards the door.

"Another thing, they most probably don't know you're with me John, so keep your distance. I'll meet you at the Airport." Steve told him, before saying goodnight.

Dialling Cody's room, Steve gave him a quick outline of the situation before ringing Sukai and arranging a meeting in his room in an hour. Going to his suitcase, Steve pulled out the hunting knife he'd taken from the dead Taliban tribesman. Placing it in reach, he sat waiting. On time, his unit friends arrived, including Aaron, still a bit groggy on his feet. Steve quickly explained the situation, and even though he told them that it could be nothing, a dead silence fell over the room.

"No, I think Ali's right. They're finished with us, they're just tidying up loose ends." Sukai answered, knowing he would not be meeting with his friends again for a while, if ever.

"Sorry to drag you back into this mess Steve," Cody added getting apologies from the others as well.

"Forget it and remember Brooks got me to come here as well. Obviously, the CIA wanted us all gone."

"So what can we do?" Aaron asked.

"First of all, we have to know what we're up against. Second, we've got to get Ali and Aaron out of here as quickly as possible!" Steve then went over a plan he'd worked out. After two hours they all knew their parts and broke up for the night, all wondering what the Americans were up to and how far along their plans had progressed.

The next day Steve hit the park for his morning run, conscious that a bullet could take his life at any second, as he ran along showing not a care in the world. Arriving back at the hotel Steve entered, not looking right or left, before going up to his room for a shower. Getting out he found Sukai sitting on his bed and his face told him everything.

"So they were there?" Steve asked, putting on his pants as Sukai explained the morning.

"Yes after you left for your run, Cody and I took up our positions, we made sure we weren't tailed. We observed the two men John had described, watching you from different positions around the park. So far they only seemed to be watching you."

"Where's Aaron?" Steve asked.

"At the hospital keeping watch on Ali, who I might say is taking it all fairly calmly." Sukai smiled.

"Yeah, I'm glad it's not me laying there unable to move, waiting for someone unfriendly to drop by."

"Not for long, we've arranged for a private flight on an air ambulance to Switzerland tomorrow at the same time your flight leaves. But I've got to tell you it was expensive!" Sukai smiled, knowing they all could afford it.

"Are you all on that flight?"

"Yes, the four of us will stay at Ali's for a while then go home for a long retirement, if we're lucky," Sukai replied putting a good spin on it. A tap at the door put them both on alert as Cody entered.

"You ever lock your door, Steve?" Cody asked, astounded at Steve's casualness.

"Do you think it would stop them, Cody? And anyway, I was expecting you two, remember?"

"I followed them," Cody said before continuing. "You wouldn't believe it, but they're across the road from the American embassy in a pretty nice hotel, just the two of them." After following Steve back to the hotel, the two men had returned to their hotel. Cody, after giving the hotel clerk a few hundred American dollars, had found out that three other rooms had been booked by these men for three night's time.

"So we've got company coming!" Steve answered, feeling the ground slipping from under them.

"Yeah, they must know Ali's booked in at the hospital for five more days gives them plenty of time," Sukai added.

"It's lucky John spotted them, or we'd all be for it!" Cody pointed out.

"Yes it was, but how do we stop them coming after us when we leave?" Sukai asked.

"Just make sure you're all at the Airport tomorrow, and on that plane, I'll take care of this problem," Steve replied, before getting dressed to visit Ali. As Cody and Sukai left, they both wondered what Steve intended to do.

At the hospital, Steve found Ali to be in a talkative, cautious mood, as his eyes continually went to the door, at each sound of footsteps outside.

"Relax Ali, we know they're waiting for more men, you'll be long gone by then." Steve smiled, as his eyes went to the door as well.

"What's to stop them coming after us Steve?" Ali asked sadly, feeling helpless lying in bed. Steve then told Ali what he planned for tonight. Ali's eyes widened, staring at him.

"Are you sure Steve, even by our standards that's a pretty wild plan?" Ali admitted. He thought how Steve had changed from the young recruit that had worried about killing his first enemy soldier.

"It's the only way to send them a message," Steve told him, wondering if a man like him would ever find peace after this.

"Thanks for everything Steve. I owe you. Though I don't think it's wise for us to see each other for a while." Ali answered sadly, gripping his friend's hand as they both sat quietly.

At precisely eight o'clock that night, Don Brooks crossed the road to attend a briefing with two men from his new unit. He had arrived that morning from the States, here for top-level meetings with the Pakistan Secret Service. The real reason was Ali's troublesome unit. Catching the lift to the third floor, he walked down the small corridor to be greeted by one of his men who was waiting in the hallway.

"Good to see you, Mr Brooks. Did you have a good flight?" the man asked

"Forget the friendly intros, Simons, let's get inside and find out what you two have been up to," Brooks replied.

Inside the two men showed Brooks the location of each of the five targets and their plan for dealing with each.

"I don't have to remind you how dangerous these men are, do I," Brooks asked them, getting nods from both men before continuing. "How they survived in Afghanistan after we left them stranded there amazes me. And how Roberts managed to find them is truly incredible, but they've got to be taken care of before the press finds out about them." Brooks showed no emotion at killing these men.

"There will be two of us for each of them, and two of them are badly hurt sir, I see no problems," Simon replied confidently getting a rare smile from Brooks before he left without a backwards glance.

"He's a cold bastard!" Johnson, the second man, said to Simon, watching the door close behind Brooks.

"Yeah, we're all expendable to him." Simon was beginning to wonder what they'd got themselves into, as he went into the bathroom.

Coming back out, he was just about to talk Johnson into going out on the town, when a knife sailed across the room, burying itself in his chest. Too stunned to yell out, Simon's slid down onto the floor. Looking across the room, he saw Johnson already dead. In Simon's final moments, what Brooks had said, rang in his ears.

"These men are dangerous."

Don Brooks arose the next day at seven o'clock and showered and shaved. He was glad this whole affair, would soon be behind him, as he could move on and up to the position he craved more than anything, Director of the CIA. Putting on his best suit for breakfast with the Ambassador and several of Pakistan's security personnel, his thoughts were interrupted by the scream of sirens on the road outside the embassy. Thinking the building was under attack Brooks ran to the door and opened it to find a heavily armed marine standing there.

"Back in your room Sir, we're in lockdown at the moment." The young marine told him, like a machine.

"Is everything okay?"

"You'll know when I do Sir. Now close the door!" The marine barked. Closing his door, Brook's went back to dressing, a little frightened. Ten minutes later a knock sounded on Brook's door. Opening it, he found a Marine Sergeant standing there.

"Would you accompany me to the Ambassadors Office Sir, we seem to have a problem."

"What is this all about Sergeant?" Brooks asked as the sergeant led him down several hallways.

"You'll see when you get there Sir." was all the Sergeant would say, as they approached the Ambassadors office. The first thing Brooks sensed was the smell of vomit coming from the office. Looking at the Ambassador, he guessed he'd been sick.

"What seems to be the problem, Jack?" Brooks asked the Ambassador.

"Don, when I came into the office this morning, I found these two boxes on my desk addressed to you. I thought I'd have a look." Was all the Ambassador got out, before he was sick again into a waste bin a marine had handed him. Coming forward Brooks looked into one of the boxes to find Simon's head looking back at him, causing him to vomit all over his new suit. Looking out of the corner of his watering eyes, Brooks notice the Marine Sergeant watching him.

"Do you know these men Sir?" the Sergeant asked him.

"No, I've never seen them before," Brooks replied shakily, as looking the Sergeant straight in the eye, he knew the Marine knew he was lying.

"Someone went to a lot of trouble to place these two heads here." the Sergeant informed him, his eyes never leaving Brooks.

"I really don't know anything about what's happened here. But if you want professional help, I'd be glad to assist, once I've changed my suit." Brooks replied, sounding more confident than he felt, as he left for his room, under the watchful eye of a marine.

In the Ambassador's office, the Sergeant continued to talk with the Ambassador about the morning's events.

"What do you make of all this Sergeant Ney?" the Ambassador nervously asked, after the room had emptied of the people.

"I think someone sent Brooks a message Sir."

"Well anyway, whoever it was, didn't hurt anyone here and showed us some weaknesses in our security. I expect that to be fixed Sergeant!" the Ambassador replied, recovering from the shock.

"It will be fixed immediately, Sir"

"Do you think Brooks got the message?" the Ambassador asked quietly, looking towards the door.

"You'd hope so Sir. Anyone good enough to walk in here and deliver those heads undetected isn't someone I'd want after me!" the Sergeant replied, leaving.

Back in his room, away from the marine's surveillance, Brooks again vomited into his toilet, collapsing to the floor, too frightened to stand up. After a good hour, he'd pulled himself together enough to shower and dress again. The realisation came to him that they could have come for him instead of delivering their warning. Forcing down the urge to vomit again, Brooks picked up his phone next to his bed and dialled a number stateside. On the second ring, it was answered.

"Westland's storage." a voice answered politely.

"It's Brooks here, put on your boss."

"Black here what's up?"

"The mission is cancelled. Stand down your men."

"But the team is just about to leave!"

"The situation's changed, Black. I'll fill you in when I get back." Brooks informed him, hanging up. Looking at the phone, Brooks noted that his hands no longer shook, taking it as a sign. As far as he was concerned, Ali's unit could just retire and disappear. He made a mental note to destroy all evidence of the unit, before putting the whole affair behind him, leaving for his meeting.

At the same time as the Ambassador was opening his surprise packages, Ali was being moved from the hospital. Arriving at the airport, he was loaded onto a private jet for his trip with the other team members back to Switzerland. After an awkward and sad farewell to Steve from the unit members, they quickly boarded their hired jet, which immediately closed its doors. As if sensing the urgency, the jet rolled forward, taxi-ing for an immediate takeoff. Accelerating rapidly it roared down the runway, leaving Steve standing alone. He waved a silent goodbye to the fast disappearing jet, before hurrying off to the main airport to meet up with John and Mary.

Boarding their flight back to Perth, Mary chatted excitedly about travelling on such a large plane. She constantly asked John questions about Australia and his wife, her excitement obvious. John with a smile, gladly answered, as Steve sat there locked in his own thoughts. Thinking about what he'd done, wondering would the American's now leave the unit members alone. He'd been shocked at how easily he had cut the two men down and the savagery he had displayed in cutting off their heads and sending them to Brooks. He knew he'd had no choice; it was either them or the unit.

A feeling of impending doom settled over him as if fate had finally caught up with him.

HOME FOR GOOD

John and Mary excitedly collected their language, hurrying to meet Joan. Looking across at Steve, John for the first time, truly saw Steve's depressed appearance. Telling Mary to wait a moment, he grabbed Steve's arm and pulled him to the side of the walkway.

"Steve lighten up man, you can't go out looking like you do!"

"I know John, it's just I crossed the line on this one, and my guts are in a knot."

"Get a hold of yourself man! You've got nothing to feel ashamed of. You saved all your friends lives and mine too. If that murder squad had of turned up, we'd all be dead. Your family's going to be out there, and they're worried enough so for God's sake, cheer up!" John warned, putting his arm around Steve's shoulders at the same time.

"Is this some sort of male custom?" Mary asked from behind John. Breaking apart, the two men broke into laughter at Mary's comment.

Steve pulling himself together, walked out into the arrival area to be greeted by his two daughters and a relieved looking wife.

It took several hours to leave the airport, as Joan greeted her new daughter. Michelle tried to explain to the girls how Mary could become Joan's daughter and not be a baby, but already a teenager. Finally, with the two girls buckled up, Steve settled into the passenger seat, while his wife brought him up to date on what had been happening. Everyone had been told at the office, that he and John had gone fishing. Michelle had continued telling them stories of the ones that got away, keeping them happy. Julie had flown out earlier that day, after Steve had told them that Ali was heading back home, still slightly injured from his so-called business trip.

"I wouldn't be surprised if Ali pops the question," Steve said smiling, before realising they'd all agreed to not contact each other for a year, meaning they couldn't attend their wedding if it happened.

"That would be great, especially now he's quit this dangerous business too," Michelle replied happily, not seeing Steve's face. As Michelle merrily continued on, Steve listened silently, as a dark cloud of depression built up in him. It wasn't until the car came to a halt, that Steve looked up and realised they were home. It was then that his pent-up emotions swamped his self-control, and he began shaking.

Getting out of the car dizziness overwhelmed him as looking out into the dark night; he heard the ocean pounding onto the headland like a giant hammer. Holding his head trying to stop the pounding, Steve fought for his sanity as the feeling of security he felt here, clashed with what he had been doing.

Sinking to the ground, ending up on his knees, he cried out in pain. In the car Michelle sat stunned by her husband's sudden breakdown, too shocked to move, tears filling her eyes as the realisation of what this mission had cost him emotionally.

"Is daddy okay?" a frightened voice asked from the rear seat, breaking the spell that held Michelle. Jumping from the car she ran to Steve, dropping to the ground next to him, hugging him. They stayed there until the yells of their children got them both up off the ground, and back to their lives again.

After that day they never discussed Steve's missions again.

WASHINGTON DC
1992

Don Brooks sat at his desk working diligently on his speech, for when he became Director of the CIA, and hopefully, he thought to himself, it would be soon. It had been a long hard road to the top, sprinkled with successes and luckily only a few failures. He was now finally close to his lifelong objective. Unfortunately, his concentration on his speech was broken as his two assistants entered the room, failing to knock in the process. This caused him to stop what he was doing and look up angrily.

"What do you want?"

"Sorry to interrupt you Sir, but there's a problem." Richard Preston, Brook's senior assistant, answered.

"Out with it!"

"Stuart's been asking questions about some black ops unit you ran back in the eighties." Roger the other assistant answered first.

"Well has he found anything?" Brook's asked, with a slight smile on his lips, giving nothing away.

"We don't think so, but he is digging for something," Richard replied worried.

Since the day the Director of the CIA had announced his retirement, Brooks had been playing cat and mouse with Stuart trying to get something on the other to put them out of the running. So far Brooks was the favourite to be the next Director, as Stuart had made some bad decisions in the past, which Brooks had used to press his case, further cementing his position.

"Tell me if he finds anything interesting," Brooks told his assistants, dismissing them, pretending indifference.

For several minutes after they had left, Brooks sat thinking, and he had to admit, he was a little scared at what this development meant. Somehow his Achilles heel had been discovered. Picking up his private phone, he dialled a number known only to him and waited.

"Westland storage." a voice answered, after three rings.

"We have to meet. Usual place in two hours," Brooks ordered.

Telling his secretary he was having an early lunch, Brooks walked down to the car park and drove out of the CIA headquarters at Langley heading towards downtown Washington. Constantly checking his mirror for tails, Brooks thoroughly checked the surrounding area for anything out of the ordinary, before parking his car in a shopping centre mall. From there he caught a bus to Arlington Cemetery where after checking again for anyone tailing him, he sat down on a bench in the park, pulled out his paper and waited.

Ten minutes had passed, when Brooks noticed two men casually walking towards him. As they came closer, one took up station as a lookout, while the other seated himself next to Don.

"So what's the problem boss?"

"Remember back a few years ago when two of your men had an accident in Karachi," Brooks asked, getting a grunt and nod from his companion. "Well, the man responsible at the time belonged to an elite fighting force consisting of five men. He held something over me at the time, preventing me from taking action." Brooks admitted, in a hushed tone.

"So they threatened to get you did they?" answered Dave Black, the head of Brooks wet unit, a slight smile on his lips.

"Be careful Black!"

"Sorry boss. So he could hurt you physically or professionally, to stop us getting revenge back then." Black answered apologetically.

"At the time because these men were from countries all over the world, the chance of silencing them all at the same time seemed remote. There was also a reference to them getting even with me at the time." Brooks confessed, giving away as little as possible to his employee.

Black looked closely at Brooks and sensed the fear in him. No matter how he pretended, these guys scared him and anyone who could take down two of his men on his own deserved respect.

"So what's changed, why now?" Black asked.

"Nothing changed with them, they're still scattered around the world. What has changed is someone inside the agency may try to locate them to stop my career from advancing. This would indirectly affect your employment, as well as your team of assistants."

"Is it Stuart who's digging?"

"Yes, I believe so,"

"It would be easier to stop him, but you already know that don't you?"

"No matter how you did it, everyone would point the finger at me.

No, I'll take care of him when I've got the top job." Brooks replied, feeling he would enjoy humiliating Stuart more than getting rid of him. Passing Black a dossier on each man and their locations, Brooks gave his employee one more bit of advice.

"These men must never know who's really after them, do you understand!" Brooks commanded, watching Black.

"No problem boss. Looks like they've made a few enemies along the way? We could make it look like one of their targets was out for revenge."

"Sounds good, just don't mess up, or you and your men will all be back where I found you." Brooks threatened. Folding his paper, Brooks stood brushing his pants, before walking to the bus stop, Black forgotten. Watching Brook's depart, Black secretly wanting to put two rounds in the back of his head. A blind man could read his face. Black knew that he too would get the chop after this one, just to tie up loose ends. Signalling to his two men, one who was in plain sight as the lookout, and the other who had remained hidden from their boss during the meeting. Stepping out from behind a garden hedge carrying a video camera the second man hurried to join the others.

"Hey, boss why do you always video these meetings?" The lookout asked as they walked to their vehicle.

"Let's just say its protection for our future," Black answered with a smile. He really was smarter than Brooks thought, and a lot more cautious. But then in his line of work, it was the only way to live to retirement.

That afternoon at the Wet unit's operational headquarters, Black gathered all his men together for a meeting. Unlike Steve's unit, these men's loyalty was to whoever paid the most money. And although they had come from the military, prison was a more familiar home to them all. Looking over the ten hard men, Dave, Black knew he ruled here by fear. Each of these men was supposed to be behind bars for manslaughter or worse. Brooks had somehow wrangled a deal to get them each released on parole to the agency. Everyone knew it could be reversed if anyone stepped out of line immediately.

Black himself had been given the same deal after a run in with a fellow officer in the Army which led to the officer's death, even though Black swore it was an accident.

"Settle down!" Black snarled at the men getting their instant attention. "We have five targets, each with a lot of military training. As a matter of fact, one of these men capped two of my men a few years back, so don't underestimate them." Black barked in a severe tone.

"Do they know we're coming?" piped in one of Blacks men.

"No, and don't interrupt till I'm finished!" Black ordered, getting their full attention. "This is going to be our retirement hit boys, and the pay for this one is in the millions if everyone does as he's told." Black smiled, seeing the confusion on their faces. They were usually paid as Sergeants, that and the added bonus of not being in jail.

"I'll explain. These five men were part of a group which led an attack on a drug cartel in Colombia several years back. Luckily for us, they didn't get all of them, and there's a million dollar reward for information on these men. How much do you think they would pay for killing these men?" Black asked grinning, as his men thinking about it, started to grin as well.

COLOMBIA

Two weeks had passed before Blacks team boarded a small private jet and headed south for a meeting with the leaders of Lardona Cartel. All Blacks men were heavily armed because you never knew what could happen when dealing with drug traffickers.

"Dave, what's the agency going to do if they find out we went to the cartel?" One of Blacks team asked on the plane flight.

"My friend, they already know. I told Brook's we were doing this to point the finger at the cartels and away from the agency. Of course, I didn't mention the money." Black smiled.

Six hours later, Black was awoken from a deep sleep by one of his men. The plane was coming in to land at a disused airstrip about hundred kilometres south of Bogotá, as their hosts had arranged. Shaking himself fully awake, Black and his team stared out the windows at their welcoming committee, which consisted of over a hundred well-dressed men, armed and unhappy. Black's men, feeling the tension fingered their weapons, as their leader continued to look out the window calmly.

"Everyone keeps cool, and no one fires unless I tell you too," Black ordered, as he moved from the window and walked to the door.

"What if they shoot you first?" One of Blacks men asked with a smile.

"Then feel free to fire back, smartarse!" Black replied as everyone laughed, relieving the tension. Throwing caution to the wind, Black opened the door, and trotted down the improvised stairs, walking confidently towards the waiting men. His own men, not as confident as their leader, cautiously fanned out behind him. They watched his back while trying to get a clear field of fire at the enemy. Black seeing three men seated in the centre, who seemed to be in charge walked up to them and waited. Of the three men, only one was old, maybe sixty. The other two were in their early twenties and had a dangerous look about them.

"I'll say one thing for you Mr Black you've got gut's coming here and expecting to leave again. Especially after saying you know who killed our people and want me to reward you" The old man said a cruel smile on his lips.

"Well, how would my men and I kill them for you if you didn't let us leave?" Black answered smiling. The three men seated men, put their heads together, discussing this new information.

"This is more than we hoped for, but you have only ten men. How is it you know so much and how many men are to be taken care of by so few?" One of the young men asked.

"We know where each man is and there were only five well-trained men, who took down your cartel with the assistance of a handful of marines," Black replied seeing the shock the information caused.

"You lie! It was a massive force that killed our fathers!" One of the young men spat out in anger, reaching for his weapon before the older man grabbed his hand.

"I'm sorry for my nephew's lack of respect Mr Black, but this is not what we were told." The old man admitted, clearly surprised.

"I too was astonished by the operation. I have with me a complete copy of the mission which came straight from the CIA, who used to control these men." Black watched the two young men's reactions. They worried him.

"I suggest you and your men accompany us back to my residence Mr Black, where we can go over this information. But first, can you all turn over your weapons!" the Old man asked, iron in his voice. At first, Black and his men tensed, not being armed, meant they would have to trust these men with their lives, which they didn't. After a nod from Black the others reluctantly handed over a surprisingly impressive collection of weapons. It showed the Cartel leaders, just how prepared they had been for this meeting.

"Thank you, Mr Black, that impresses me more than you think." the Old man said happily, before waving to a group of vehicles parked at the end of the runway, which instantly drove over to pick them up. Black walked confidently beside his new business partners, hopping into a limo, where he was formally introduced to his host. The older man introduced himself as Mr Santini, along with his two nephews Toni and Nick. Black knew that he would never address this man by anything else. He knew he would never be Santini's equal, only an employee. But for a large amount of money, he could handle that for a while he thought.

Pulling up at a large building complex that resembled a castle, Black ushered into a large lounge area himself comfortable. While he relaxed, Santini poured over the information that Black had gathered on the unit. Toni and Nick kept him company wanting to find out what he knew about the raid. Both of their fathers and several of their uncles had been killed in the attack. Black found that he was the first person since the raid had taken place to give them a chance to restore their honour.

At about eight thirty that night, Santini gathered his two nephews and ten of his most trusted lieutenants, along with Black and had a meeting.

"I am convinced that what Mr Black has told us about what happened during the attack is the truth!" Santini announced as the table broke into pandemonium, forcing him to raise his hand, getting silence before he continued. "The men, who carried out this deed, were incredibly well trained and ruthless, and going after them will not be easy," Santini concluded, waiting now for questions.

"No matter what the risk these men must die, for our fathers and friends honour!" Toni shouted, tears forming in his eyes, making the room explode into cheering and clapping.

"I agree with my cousin," Nick yelled above the others, in a voice choked with grief.

"Then it is agreed!" Santini shouted, signalling for silence. "What is your plan, Mr Black?" He asked.

"The five targets are spread across the world in five separate countries. The plan is to locate all five and set up surveillance on each. Then at a prearranged time, hit all the targets at the same time.

We know roughly each mans location so this won't be too hard. And because each one is isolated from the others, they should be easy meat." Black informed them, seeing nods and agreement from the others.

"Have you enough men Mr Black?" asked Santini.

"I would think so. Only the Australian will need me, and two assistants. Each of the other targets will have two of my men each, which should be more than enough!" Black felt trouble coming on this point.

"You are wrong Mr Black. Honour is at stake here, so for each target, I will send ten of my best men with each of your groups. They will witness and help in the killing of these monsters." Santini spat out, leaving no room for argument, as cheers broke out from the gathered men. Black looked around the room at the inexperienced men. They were more used to killing defenceless people than taking on trained soldiers and a sense of foreboding settled over him.

'Shit, what have I done?' Black said to himself.

Celebrations broke out throughout Santini's castle, as news of the vendetta raid filtered through to Santini's men. After the celebration had slowed down, Black walked across to where his men were staying. Once inside the barracks type room, Black told the others about the plan.

"Can we trust them Dave?" asked one of Blacks men, as weapons fire came from outside, making his men tense.

"Santini agreed to put five million in each of our bank accounts in Switzerland when we leave here, so I think we can trust them," Black informed them, seeing the disbelief on their faces. Of course, he didn't mention that he was getting twice that.

"It sounds good to me now, but who's in charge?" another man answered with a grin.

"Until the attack starts, they will obey our orders, each target will have a pair of us, and you will each command a team of five of these idiots, except Pete who'll come with Rob and me. You all know the score on their locations. All you do is set up the hit at each targets home, and let the cartel boys do the dirty work. The only rule, is don't move until the time is approved by me, is everyone clear on that." Black asked looking at his men, getting acknowledgement. All clear, he divided them up into twos, nominating their targets. After several hours of planning, Black figured that everyone was up on the mission and decided to turn in.

"Right, anyone got a question?"

"Will we meet up after the operation?" Rob asked.

"Only if you can find the beach and the girl I'm lying on," replied Black smiling, sending the others into hysterical laughter. They were all keen to start the mission and get their blood money.

Back at the house, Mr Santini had another problem; both Nick and Toni wanted to accompany Black on the raid, which he thought was too risky.

"It will be okay uncle neither of us is wanted, and Australia is by far the safest target with Black and his two assistants with us," Toni explained, pleading with his uncle until he unhappily agreed.

"Okay you can go, but I am not overjoyed with you two going with these men!" Santini replied.

"What is the problem with Blacks men?" Nick asked.

"When the monsters are killed, Black and his men must all die as well!" Santini told all present. His two nephews were shocked.

"Why must they die Uncle? They're helping us kill our enemies, and you're paying them!" Toni asked confused.

"The money is nothing! These men cannot be trusted to be quiet. Remember, the men who we are after used to work for the CIA. As do Blacks men now. They work for money, not loyalty, remember that." Santini spat out, making sure his nephews understood the disgust he felt for these men.

The following day Black met again with Santini, where he was told about Nick and Toni coming. He then with his men flew back to America to organise the five missions. They were to meet the cartel's men at different International Airports throughout America in 10 days time. From there they would take separate flights to their targets around the world.

THE HUNT BEGINS

Sitting cramped in economy class, squashed between Pete and Rob surrounded by the other cartel men, Black occasionally spotted Tony and Nick in the first class section through the curtain. They were behaving like schoolboys on their first excursion, and the feeling of dread returned to him. The feeling he had was not only from their attitude on the plane, though it didn't help. No, it had started back at the airport where they had met for the flight.

Black noticed that they couldn't look him in the eye when he talked to them. Also, the cartel men gave him and his subordinates a wide berth only talking to them after getting a nod from Tony or Nick. Something wasn't right, and Black decided that maybe he should keep a close eye on these two upstarts, especially after the mission.

Touching down in Sydney, Black and his two men separated from the others as they went through customs, trying to keep a low profile, prior to boarding a domestic flight to Perth. Tony and Nick, on the other hand, didn't like the way they had to line up with the other passengers.

They became angry at being treated like ordinary people by customs, which started to draw attention from the Federal Police stationed behind the Customs area. To make matters worse, the other cartel men who owed their allegiance to these men started moving towards their bosses. Black intercepted them, quietly ordering them back into their lines. He then walked over and told both the brats to settle down. Threatening to send them back home right now, had the desired effect on them both, as the whole group proceeded through customs without any further trouble.

As Nick and Toni waited to board their flight to Perth, they discussed Black's attitude to them with their men.

"How dare he talk to us like that, we should kill him now slowly?" Nick suggested angrily in Spanish, getting agreement from his men.

"No my cousin, wait till Roberts is taken care off, then we'll teach him some manners," Tony answered, smiling for the benefit of Black and Pete who were watching them from across the room.

"Yes you're right, it will be better that way." Nick chuckled, grinning with his men at Toni's cleverness. Above them unobserved, a hidden video camera watched and listened, recording every word, as they walked to their flight.

AIRPORT CUSTOMS

The Customs officer carefully went through the photos, taken by the hidden camera, at the domestic terminal.

Are they the men from the overseas flight, who had the argument?" John, one of the Federal Police officers stationed at the airport, asked the Customs officer on duty that day.

"Yeah, that's them alright. Looks like they're still arguing too." the Customs officer replied with a grin.

"Where did they come from?"

"South America I think." the Customs officer replied.

"Then it must be Spanish they're speaking. We'll have to get someone in to translate the tape." John suggested, talking more to himself, than the others, as he studied the film. He'd been stationed at the airport for several years and had developed a knack for spotting trouble. Just the way they stood and acted, smelt of the drug trade John thought, as he grabbed a phone and dialled his headquarters.

It wasn't until two days later that someone was brought in and a translation of the tape was made. When it was discovered that someone was going to be taken care off, it was immediately sent to Federal Police Headquarters in Canberra to be dealt with.

"Is that all we've got! That someone named Roberts is going to be taken care off!" the Commissioner looked dubiously at George, thinking the information thin.

"Yes Sir it's not much to go on, but the two men talking have been identified. They're high ranking members of a drug cartel in Colombia" George replied.

"Do we know where they were going?" the Commissioner asked, sensing something big was going on.

"They boarded a plane for Perth, we believe as many as ten men could be travelling with them." George knew this was serious.

"Sounds like a big hit on someone. Contact the Western Australian office and call in the State police as well. We mightn't know the target, but we can try to locate them and stop them from leaving." the Commissioner replied.

"We could put a warning out to all of our offices Sir. See if someone knows this Roberts, it could help." George suggested.

"Yes, see that it's done." the Commissioner replied, hoping they got to these men before they reached their target. It would look good for the Federal Police on the news, he thought.

Two days later Edward sat at his desk in Sydney at nine in the morning working his way through the stacks of paperwork. The pile of paper in front of him was connected to the drug bust he'd organised on the South Coast. It had involved a stakeout of a small fishing port, a combined operation between the State police and the Feds. For a change, it had been a major success. Over twenty people had been arrested, and millions of dollars of drugs had been seized.

Edward smiled at the back-slapping that had gone on by the jubilant police officers involved in the operation just yesterday. And now after the cheering had died away the paperwork had to be done. God, he hated it.

"How's the hero going?" Shane, one of Edward's fellow officers, asked from the doorway.

"Makes you wonder why we catch em! All it does is create more paperwork." Edward replied making Shane smile. It was well known around the office that Edward loved catching bad guys.

"They say the price of heroin doubled after the raid!"

"Yeah but it's still getting in."

"We can't catch em all Edward. At least we're starting to make a difference." Shane pointed out.

"Anything happen while I was gone?" Edward asked changing the subject.

"Not much, the only big news is we're searching for a group of Colombians. They reckon they're here to carry out a hit on someone over in Western Australia," Shane replied thinking it a little over the top.

"I've never heard of much activity in WA before?"

"Who knows what they're up to? It appears they landed in Perth several days ago and haven't been heard of since. Maybe there playing golf?" Shane laughed, as he walked towards the door.

"Who's the target?"

"The only clue they have is someone named Roberts," Shane answered from the doorway.

"Shit No!" Edward shouted gasping, as he frantically rummaged through the desk, till he found his address book.

"What's wrong Edward?"

"They're after my brother-in-law" Edward stuttered, dialling.

"He's a stockbroker isn't he?"

"He was in the SAS. One of his missions with the Americans was to wipe out a cartel in Colombia. I only know about it because he was shot during the operation and told me. Looks like someone else found out!" Edward said on the other end of the phone, Steve's phone rang out.

"I'll ring our people in Perth and get them and the local police out there," Shane replied, copying Steve's home and business address and running for a phone in his office.

"Come on Steve answer that phone!" Edward yelled to an empty room as the phone kept ringing. "Shit" Edward yelled again, realising with the time difference it was only eight in the morning in Perth. Steve would still be at home he thought, as he hung up and dialled Steve's home number instead.

PERTH

The blast of the shotgun was deafening. Pete and the other Colombians turned to see the beautiful woman catapulted across the room reduced to a bloody pile of flesh.

"What the fuck you do that for?" Pete yelled from the veranda, shocked by Nick's stupidity in firing.

"She was going for the phone!" Nick replied, grinning proud of his handy work, taking pleasure in killing.

"The phone has been disconnected!" Pete pointed out, turning back to the beach to check on Roberts.

For three days, Blacks men had watched Robert's house till a solid plan had been worked out, and Black was confident enough to go ahead. They had observed that each morning Roberts wife would drop off their two girls at school then return to the house. Roberts while his wife was gone jogged along the beach, returning and having breakfast with her. He then drove to work.

They planned to pretend to be linesmen working on streets power. The first group would gain access to the house and hold Roberts wife till he returned from his run. The second group would park at the end of the street as a covering force. Black at first wanted a straightforward hit, by just gunning Robert's down on the beach. Nick and Toni wanted a lot more; they wanted him to beg for death.

That's why the plan included having Robert's wife there, especially after seeing how beautiful she was. Toni and Nick intended to use her for their entertainment, while Robert's was forced to watch. Once finished, they'd let their men do what they liked with her before killing her. Then Robert's would be cut to pieces.

Confident his plan would work even with their changes, Black had his men steal two power company vans for the operation. He then obtained weapons, from a contact Brooks had given them in Perth.

The night before the Hit, Black contacted the other four squads. Finding them all in position and ready, he decided to get it over with, instructing them, to hit all of the targets at eight the next morning Perth time. Wishing them good luck and a happy retirement he hung up, giving his team the go-ahead for tomorrow. Nick and Toni also rang their other men telling them in Spanish that after the attacks at 8am they were to finish Black's men. Hanging up the two Nephews didn't realise that they'd changed Black's precise instructions.

When Black's four teams sat down with the Cartel men to explain the plan the attack, they found they were adamant that they should attack at 8 in the morning. Black's teams tried to point out that the attacks should be coordinated with the Perth attack to stop any warning getting out. The Cartel men, not being military, wouldn't budge, saying their orders from their leaders were final. In the end, Blacks men caved in, not really caring anyway, feeling the chances of any problems were minimal. As long as they got their money, they didn't really care.

The next day at eight, just after Roberts wife had left with the children, Blacks group cut the phone and power to the area. Pete, Toni and Nick plus five of his men, drove down to Roberts house, breaking in. Pete and one Cartel member remained in the van, while the others hid inside. All of them eagerly awaited her return. Like the days before, at ten past eight, Robert's wife turned down the road passing Blacks van, before pulling up out front of her home

When Michelle pulled up at the house and saw the van, she wondered why they were there. Getting out of her car she saw the two men also leave their van walking towards her.

"Can I help you?" She asked becoming unnerved by their silence, as one swiftly moved forward, punching her in the stomach. Winded, doubled up in pain, she was unable to breathe or scream out, as the two men dragged her into the house.

Throwing her on the lounge room floor, Michelle trembling with terror, looked around at the circle of men who closed in around her.

"What do you want?" Michelle croaked out as her lungs gulped for air. All the men she noticed appeared to be foreigners, except one, who left the group, walking out onto the veranda. This in itself seemed ominous, as the remaining men continued to stand silently, looking hungrily down at her. The two youngest of the group reached down, grabbing hold of her dress. Smiling, they both ripped the material in two leaving her lying on the floor in her bra and undies.

Screaming, Michelle tried to cover herself, as a piece of her dress was tied around her mouth. Turning over to cover herself, she lay face down on the floor, as the men kicked and pushed her back and forward playfully laughing. One of the young men then grabbed her hair, lifting her up till she was kneeling, in front of him, as he bent forward whispering in her ear.

"We're going to show what it's like to be fucked by real men." He chuckled, turned on by the fear he saw in her eyes, as she struggled to break free.

"No!" She begged through her gag, sobbing as she wet herself in terror, as the full horror of what they intended to do flooded her mind.

"Look how excited she is Toni she is already wet." The other young man laughed, joined in by the others as her tormentor ripped her bra off showing the others her breasts, as he squeezed them making her moan in pain. Pushing her back onto the floor several of the men lifted her legs while her undies were ripped off exposing her completely. The men impressed, stood silently, their eyes glazed with arousal, some licking their dry lips in anticipation.

Hands swiftly grabbed her arms and legs spreadeagle her on the floor, as the two young men took their clothes off, dropping them where they stood. Michelle's eyes pleaded with them, as shaking her head from side to side indicating no. Seeing her pleading the watching men laughed, yelling encouragement to the young men. Fully aroused they stood over her letting her see them, as the first young man knelt down between her legs, positioning himself. Michelle screaming behind the gag struggled in vain to escape, as he ran his hands along her thighs smiling. Yelling to his men, he told them something in their own language as his men cheered.

Michelle turned her head away unable to watch, giving up hope. Looking at the young man's clothes discarded beside her, she prayed for an end to her pain, when something reflected the light in the clothing. It was the end of a knife protruding from a sheaf. Feeling the men's grip on her hand's ease of as they encouraged her would be rapist; she pulled her right arm free grabbing the knife, thrusting it into the rapist's shoulder. Screaming, he jumped back from her, as she swung the knife cutting the man holding her other hand.

Swinging the knife wildly, the men momentarily confused, released her, as she jumped to her feet. Continuing to wave the knife, she backed away from them, in desperation, she moved to the phone. Pulling off her gag, she picked up the phone dialling emergency, surprised to see the men hadn't tried to stop her. Instead, they stood there laughing, watching her, as her phone failed to dial.

Standing there naked, trembling, Michelle realised they'd cut the phone lines. Sobbing quietly, panic again gripped her, as her body shook violently knowing she was trapped. Feebly holding the knife in front of her, she watched the young man she'd cut on the shoulder pick up a shotgun point it at her.

"No" She moaned, begging for her life, as he pulled the trigger.

The shot was heard clearly at the Blacks van up the road, making Black and the others tense.

"What's going on down there?" Black yelled into his radio, as the people in the house just down from him came out onto the veranda.

"Nick's killed the woman!" Pete replied angrily.

"Shit did Roberts hear the shot?"

"Yeah, he's dropped out of sight. But he's still heading towards us." Pete thought the plan could still work.

"Yeah well, the neighbours heard the shot. I'm sending the Colombians to silence them. You head back up here, leave the killing to our brave friends." Black ordered, sensing the plan was going to hell. The five Colombians along with Black and Rob hopped out of the van. After Black told them about the neighbours, they formed a rough skirmish line and walked towards the house.

"Poor bastards, probably wondering why their phone doesn't work," Black said to Rob, as Pete started up the road towards them, pistol in his hand. At the neighbour's house, Black watched as a young woman came to the front door and waved to the approaching men.

"God she deserves to die for being so stupid!" Rob laughed, as in one smooth motion the young woman lifted an assault rifle to her shoulder. Gunning down the first four men, she then slammed the door shut. Taken aback, Black and Rob stood there, as an old man appeared on the first-floor deck and gunned down the surviving

Colombian. Pete, who was nearly at the van, opened up with his pistol, only to be hammered into the ground by the man's second shot.

"Shit who the hell lives there?" Black yelled, jumping behind the van with Rob, as bullets slammed into it.

"Time to go, boss, we've only got pistols." Rob pointed out.

"Okay you go start the car, I'll cover you," Black answered, as taking aim, he opened fire shooters at the house. As the van engine started, a relieved Black stopped firing and jumped into the passenger seat. He found Rob's head spattered all over the windscreen. Thinking quickly, he leaned across pushing the accelerator with his hand, shoving the car into gear, it jumped forward, accelerating.

Round after round smashed into the side of the van, as taking a quick peek, Black straightened the van onto the road. Opening the driver's door, he pushed out the remains of Rob's body, before sliding into the driver's seat, increasing speed. Making good his escape, Black no longer cared if Roberts lived or died.

That morning John, his wife and Mary, had slept in. Their alarm hadn't woken them, as Black had cut the power. They had instead been awoken by the shot from Steve's house.

"What the hell?" John yelled, recognising the sound of gun fired, he jumped out of bed and ran out onto the veranda.

"It came from Steve's house!" Mary said, standing beside him, as Joan went to the phone.

"The phones and the power are out." She shouted from the bedroom, as John spotted the van.

"Shit Mary, get your weapon, I think we've got company!" John informed her, as five men headed towards their house. When Mary had arrived in Australia, she found living without a weapon unnerving. John retired, had enrolled them both in a local gun club. This gave them both a reason, to have a weapon at home.

"Mary, wait till I open fire, before showing yourself!" John ordered as he grabbed his old hunting rifle, running to the balcony, staying out of sight. Joan kept out of sight, staying with her husband. He was just about to open fire when he heard Mary's weapon erupt downstairs.

"Bugger that girl is headstrong," John told Joan, as he saw the first four men thrown backwards onto the ground. The fifth gunmen stood paralysed wondering what to do. He couldn't have made it easier, as John lined him up and squeezed the trigger, the man exploded away from him. Breaking glass and the whip of a bullet passing close by made John duck.

"There's another man on the road," Joan yelled, as John focusing, spotted him. Leading the target who continued to fire at him, John aimed low at the widest point of his body pulling the trigger, his target dropped with a sickening thud. Looking around for more targets, John concentrated on the van, as Mary came up beside him letting go a full clip.

"Just like the old day's dad!" Mary smiled nervously.

"Keep your head down, and next time I tell you to wait, do it!" John told her, secretly proud of his little girl.

As they reloaded, a man dashed for the driver's side door of the van, jumping in and starting the engine. Another man fired wildly at them from the rear of the van, trying to pin them down. Both ignored the return fire, raising their weapons they both fired at the driver. Seeing a red mist fill the vans front cabin, as the driver disintegrated, they both looked for another target.

Amazingly the van started to move forward taking them by surprise. This forced them to fire again at the van, until rounding a corner they saw the body fall from the driver's side.

"The other guy must have steered from the floor!" Mary concluded as shots rang out from Steve's house hitting their deck.

"I hope Steve and Michelle are okay." John gasped. Looking into Mary's eyes, he saw the truth, as they returned fire from Steve's house.

Hearing the shooting from up the road, Nick and Tony at first thought that their men were wiping out the people next door. But when one of their men reported seeing bodies lying in the street, they became worried.

"We stay here till we get Roberts, they can wait. Just fire at them to keep them busy, we'll take care of them later." Toni smiled, still pumped from his kill.

"Roberts we have your woman, give yourself up!" Nick yelled from the front veranda, gun ready, waiting eagerly for Roberts to show his face.

When Steve heard the shot, his training took over. Adrenalin flooded his system as he moved rapidly towards his home. Trying to work out where the shot had come, he spotted an armed man keeping watch from the deck of his home. This forced him to slow down and think about what he was going to do, as he carefully moved forward. Crawling through the long grass which covered the dunes in front of his home, panic seized him as he passed toys left by his children while playing. Remembering his training, he several deep breathes, before slowly moving towards the deck, sliding underneath it.

Working out there was at least four men, Steve knew he'd needed a diversion. Going to his shed beside the house he grabbed his petrol container and some matches. Crawling back under the house, he upended the container letting the petrol puddle under the lounge area. On the ocean side of the house, the bedroom windows were out of reach, so Steve placed a ladder from under the house, next to the window of his bedroom.

Climbing carefully up, Steve looked down to see the petrol dribbling downhill towards the beach from under the house. Sliding the window open he silently slipped inside, moving carefully to his closet. Finding an old shirt he carefully lit it, throwing it out the window, before moving to the bedroom door. When the petrol ignited, a loud thud resonated from under the house, making the Colombians inside, fire out the windows in panic. Nick had just finished applying a bandage to Toni's shoulder when the thud sounded making them both look at the floor, wondering what was going on.

"Its Roberts he's trying to flush us outside, cover all the windows!" Tony yelled. His men rushed to obey his command, one kicking open Steve's bedroom door and rushing to the window. Surging up from the floor beside his bed, Steve tripped the man, snapping his neck before he had time to scream. Pulling the dead man's pistol from his hand, Steve went to the door and stole a quick look out into the lounge room. He saw two men in the room, one bandaged, near the front veranda and what was left of his wife lay on the floor at their feet.

Rage consumed him as smoke wafted up into the house making visibility difficult. Slipping into the next bedroom Steve choked this man to death, enjoying every second of it, before taking the man's knife. Like a rabid dog devoid of emotion, Steve moved to the third bedroom, killing another man, this time letting him scream, as he slowly cut his throat. Nick and Tony on the veranda and a third Colombian at the kitchen window stopped firing at John's house, as they tried to find out where the scream had come from. Smoke billowing up though the floorboards, forced the three men to back outside onto the veranda, as they looked for their men.

They didn't even hear the shot, which John fired from his house. Toni's chest exploded, showering Nick with blood and guts. Seeing they were distracted, Steve ran out of the smoke, shooting Nick and the last Colombian in their kneecaps, making them both collapse onto the deck screaming. Running forward Steve disarmed them both, before racing back inside. Covering Michelle's body with a window curtain, he dragged her body clear of the flames.

Placing it reverently on the front lawn, Steve looked down at her beautiful face, carefully brushing her hair back into place. Getting up, he went back to the front veranda and the two men.

"Who sent you?" Steve asked, thrusting a knife into Nick's last henchman's neck.

"We'll tell you nothing!" Nick spat out defiantly.

"We'll see." Steve chuckled insanely, as he dragged the henchman forward, severing his head. Nick watched in horror as his man screamed in pain until it turned into a gurgling noise, then stopped. Coming forward Steve grabbed Nick, who by this time had shit himself with fear, dragging his head back.

"Who sent you?"

"My uncle Senor Santini" Nick replied, his eyes glued to the blood-covered knife.

"Where does he live?"

"South of Bogotá, in Colombia," Nick replied scared to death.

"How did you find me?"

"An American named Black, he works for the CIA. He told us where you all lived."

"Did you send men after the others?"

"Yes, they were to attack at the same time at eight in the morning."

"I will need you to go to your uncle with a message."

"And I will be glad to take it."

"Oh I'm sorry, you misunderstood me. For the message, I'll only need your head!" Steve laughed, as Nick felt the blade cut and started screaming.

"My god Steve what have you done?" John moaned, as he approached the front veranda, watching as Steve pick up his two trophies.

"I'll need the use of your freezer John, or else they'll go off," Steve said calmly showing no emotion.

"Steve you're hurt," John said pulling Steve to him, trying to lead him away from the deck.

"They killed Michelle. John, it's my fault!" Steve cried out, as John supporting him, Steve still carrying the heads.

"Drop them, Steve, the police won't understand," John ordered. This time he managed to grab the heads from him, throwing them back into the fire.

"You're right John. This type of thing doesn't seem to work anymore does it?" Steve replied, talking as if in a dream.

In the distance, the sound of sirens could be heard coming down the road. As if sleepwalking, Steve shuffled aimlessly away from his burning home, John supporting him. Coming out of the trance he suddenly straightened up.

"Are my girls okay?" Steve asked as Mary ran towards them. Further up the road the police and ambulance vehicles pulled to the side, letting a fire engine through, before continuing towards Steve's house.

"Mum went to check the school. Michelle would have taken them there earlier." Mary replied, looking around for Michelle, she saw her father's eyes.

"I've got to get to a phone John to warn the others." Steve stammered out, as two police officers approached.

"Your girls are okay Mr Roberts. We saw John's wife Joan on the way here." One of the policemen informed them, as he looked at the body of a woman lying on the grass.

"I need to get to a phone Officer; other members of my unit might be targets!" Steve exclaimed, the need for secrecy gone.

"Okay, you can do it at the station, after that you'll have to answer a few questions. You too John." the Officer said formally this time, as the sad group walked up the road to the police officer's car.

As promised, Steve at the police station was allowed to ring and warn his friends, while John sat down and started telling the police of what had happened. Frantically dialling the number letting it ring four times and hanging up, he then rang again. Steve gazed forlornly at the phone, as the others in the room backed off and gave him some privacy.

"Who is it?" Ali's voice asked cheerfully. Not having heard from any of the team for a while he was looking forward to catching up.

"Ali it's me, Steve!" Steve babbled, trying to control his voice.

"What's wrong Steve?"

"They killed Michelle, Ali" Steve sobbed into the phone.

"What's happened?" Ali asked anger plain to hear, at which time Steve told him of the hit and that they were after them as well having arranged to hit each unit member at 8am.

"I'm so sorry Steve. I'll pass on the warning and come as soon as I can." Ali replied hanging up abruptly, unable to say anything more. Looking out the window, Ali saw the first glimmer of light of a new day approaching. Someone was ever overconfident or stupid he thought, knowing whoever made the decisions to attack at 8 local time wasn't military.

Running into the next room Ali woke Julie, explaining what had happened, his wife burst into tears at her friend's death. Taking only what was necessary, Ali told Julie to take their small child down the road to a friend's house, ordering her to stay there until he came for her. Once she'd left, he rang Cody and Aaron.

After tipping them off, he then called Sukai, knowing it was already too late for him, as it was eight in Japan before Australia. He was surprised when Sukai answered. He found out they had come for him, but he'd been lucky. Sukai lived in a modest house in a suburb of Tokyo. His neighbour who did shift work had a very attractive wife, so in the early hours of the morning, Sukai had climbed over the side fence to keep her company.

While comforting her, he had heard smashing noises from his home. At first, he thought it was a break in. Sneaking a look over the fence, he saw a large group of armed men searching his home. Deciding to stay put, he rang some friends. Since then his house was being watched by some ex-marines, waiting patiently for their return.

"Can you meet me at Steve's place in Australia? I think we're all in trouble?" Ali asked him.

"I'll leave immediately my friend," Sukai answered, hanging up. Looking at his watch, Ali knew the killers would be at his door in just under two hours. Dialling emergency, Ali told the police on duty, that a group of terrorists from his homeland were on their way to kill his family. With his parent's background of living in exile, the Swiss police took it seriously. Telling him to leave immediately, they informed him that a special unit had been dispatched. Ali decided to stay, opening his gun safe he armed himself and waited.

Meanwhile, Aaron and Cody rang each other discussing what to do. Neither had families, but they took the news of Michelle's death personally. Both had been to Steve and Michelle's house many times, they were family. Agreeing they weren't giving in to the enemy, they both prepared for their visitors.

SWITZERLAND

One thing about the Swiss, they loved long-range weapons, Ali thought as he trained his scope on the first of two vans parked opposite his driveway. Looking to the right, Ali saw mixed among the trees and shrubs, the black uniforms of a Swiss police. They'd taken up positions facing the two vehicles. Finger caressing the trigger Ali watched as the doors of the van flew open and twelve men in two groups quickly headed for his front and rear gates. Both groups were just crossing the road, when a police officer with a megaphone called for them to halt and drop their weapons, they froze.

Black's men who knew it was over lowered their weapons. To their horror, the Colombians full of amateur bravado, open fired on the police. Ali shook his head, lowering his weapon knowing it would not be needed. The sound of automatic weapons and the sickening slap of round hitting flesh continued, till none of the hit squad members remained standing. Watching the police move forward, carefully checking each body for any survivors, Ali realised that his days of living here in peace were over. He must now move his family into hiding, far away from here and their peaceful life.

FRANCE

Aaron lived outside Paris, and was next on the timeline. He lived in a converted warehouse. It had only one large double door at the front, the back being against the hill. Stretching a thin wire across his front door, Aaron looked around his house, knowing he would miss it. He then climbed out a side window. Twenty minutes later his uninvited guests arrived across the road, in three cars. Getting out, the twelve men confidently cross the road, weapons ready. Crossing unobserved, Aaron circled around coming up behind their vehicles. At his house, the hit squad started to kick in the front door.

"Won't be long now?" Aaron said to himself, as the twelve men finally broke down his door, ripping the trip wire. This triggered the two kilos of C4 sitting in a bucket of nails just inside the doorway. The explosion was spectacular, better than Aaron had anticipated, as one of their cars flipped over, nearly landed on top of him. Forced into an undignified dive into a ditch, Aaron watched the vehicle continued to roll down the opposite slope.

Getting to his feet, Aaron walked across the road, taking out his knife. Looking around, Aaron cursed angrily, when he realised there was no one left to question.

SCOTLAND

Cody, in Scotland, had the most time to wait. He lived on a lonely, dead-end mountain road one hundred kilometres north of Edinburgh. He loved this spot for its seclusion and outlook. Now it had a bonus. He could sit back and watch them come. As the twelve men drove up the road in a tourist bus, Cody had to admit, that unless he had been warned he'd have been taken entirely by surprise. .

"Keep coming lads!" Cody said out loud, as the bus crawled through a series of bends next to a steep drop. Cody, taking a small transmitter from his pocket, stood up, walking out into the middle of the road. Just as the bus passed a large pile of rock on the hill side of the road, it came to a halt as the driver saw Cody standing there.

"He thinks we're lost!" One of Blacks men said to the others. They all to burst into laughter, as several men prepared their weapons. Cody smiling pointed to the hill, beside the bus. Bewildered Blacks men looked to where Cody pointed. Terror filled them, as they spotted four claymore mines, sitting silently facing them.

"Reverse! Back! Back! Back!" Black's men screamed, as Cody dived to the ground and pressed the transmitter. As each claymore exploded, their loads of four hundred ball bearings erupted, shredding the bus, as it slowly tipped over the edge plunging down the two hundred metre drop. Cody getting to his feet, looked over the edge.

'Well it looks like the quiet life is over' Cody said to himself, as he grabbed his pack and walked briskly down the road heading for town.

PERTH THE FUNERAL

Edward stood with his wife, as she held her brother through the service, surrounded by their friends and family. Michelle's mother and father were there, as well as Michelle's sister and three brothers. Since the attack, Steve was being watched around the clock by an army of Federal Police and Special Forces units who took this attack on Steve personally. It had been considered a terrorist attack by the government and a media blackout had been put in place. The cover story was that several people, mostly tourists, had been killed in a gas explosion on the coast.

As his wife was lowered into the ground, Steve wondered if maybe his two girls should've been here to say goodbye to their mother. The police had advised against it, as they believed the cartel might try again. Steve now lived in a nightmare, too scared to take his girls out in public while anger chewed at him knowing the ones responsible, remained untouched. A squeeze on his shoulder by his sister brought him back to the present. The service was over.

Edward, watching Steve, thought back to that morning. When he'd heard from the police about what had happened, he had wept, wishing he'd arrived back one day earlier. He then had to then tell his wife that her brother's wife was dead and that Steve and the girls were in protective custody. Arriving in Perth the next morning Edward found his sister to be a tower of strength. She helped Steve with everything, from the arrangements for the funeral, to organising where they would all stay. Edward realises what a lucky man he was.

Reaching across to her, Edward gave his wife a reassuring squeeze on the shoulder. Tears flowed down her cheeks, as she helped her brother to his feet, to a waiting car. Suddenly Edward's ear receiver squawked.

"Edward! Four men at two o'clock!" Came a warning as plainclothes agents started to come to life around the cemetery. Looking around for the source of the warning, Edward saw the four men. Approaching the car from the rear were Steve's former unit members, and they looked dangerous.

"They're friendly," Edward replied into his mouthpiece, as Steve reacted instantly to his use of the radio. Turning around swiftly and searching for danger, he saw his friends coming to a stop in front of Steve.

"We're so sorry Steve," was all Ali could say, as tears streamed down his face, the other men hugged Steve, as Edward came closer.

"We're going back to Campbell Barracks, that's where the family and friends are meeting," Edward told them, suspecting what would happen next by their presence.

"Why are they here Steve?" Edward asked softly, as Louise looked at him.

"We've all been targeted Edward, the others have broken contact with their families or moved them into hiding. They've come here to watch my back until I'm ready to go." Steve answered.

"You don't have to go anywhere, Steve. You and the girls can come and stay with us." Louise suggested, scared for her brother.

"You wouldn't be safe with me staying there. Ask Edward, he knows." Steve answered, tears flowing down his face as Louise looked at Edward.

"He's right, my love. These animals won't stop until their honour is restored. And unfortunately, they've got the money and men to do it." Edward replied honestly, ashamed to admit he didn't want Steve near his family.

"I will ask one thing of you sis. I want you to take the girls and look after them till it's safe for me to return."

"Of course we will Steve. We'll raise them like our own. But you don't have to go after them Steve, you can stay here in Australia and let justice take care of them." Tears ran down Edwards checks knowing if Steve left he might never return.

"There is no justice for me Edward. I questioned one of them. Before he died; he said the CIA helped them!"

"He could have been lying Steve?"

"To find just me, I'd have doubts. To find all of us is unbelievable. No, the CIA is involved, I'm sure of it." Steve replied, as the gates to Campbell barracks came into view.

As Michelle's friends and relations paid their respects, Michelle's mum sat with Steve. They watched as Michelle's dad walked outside.

"Will George ever forgive me, Emily?" Steve asked sadly, watching George leave.

"It's hard for him Steve. She was his angel, and he was always worried about what you did in the SAS." Emily replied holding his hand as Steve's two girls came up and sat with their dad and nanna. Outside George sat on the veranda hating this place, everywhere he looked he saw something to do with the army, and it made him livid. Looking up, his eyes blurry with tears, he saw Steve's four friends who were at the wedding, come up beside him.

"Here to see your hero mate!" George growled, trying to strike out at someone, stopping the four men cold.

"That is unfair George. We all loved Michelle, and Steve worshipped your daughter with all his heart!" Ali replied taken aback. "If it weren't for Steve, all of us and our families would be dead right now." Ali continued, as he made to walk passed, George.

"I'm sorry. Ah, your name's Ali isn't it?" George said getting a nod he continued. "I loved my daughter Ali. Its hard she's gone before me." George whispered, tears flowing down his face.

"I am sorry to my friend. They also came after my family as well. The anger is still in me." Ali replied, heading inside to find Steve.

"It makes me so angry that these drug dealers can do this and get away with it." George groaned, fighting his pain.

"They won't get away with it, I can promise you of that!" Sukai answered walking inside, leaving George with his grief.

The afternoon passed swiftly, as Michelle's friends, said their final goodbyes. In groups, they sadly left, most going back to their own lives, all over the country. Leonie, Michelle's younger sister, came to say goodbye, Steve looked up sadly, and his heart missed a beat. Standing there was a young Michelle looking at him. Too shocked to speak Steve sat there as Leonie kissed him on the cheek, saying goodbye and leaving with her family unaware that she had scared him badly.

When all the others were gone, Steve sat with his girls telling them how they would be staying with Louise in Sydney for a while. The girls were devastated by this. They'd just lost their mother, and now their father was not going to be around. All night they clung to their father, not letting him out of their sight. In the end, Louise and Edward had to return home, taking the distraught girls with them.

At the Airport Steve waved to his girls holding back tears, as they boarded their flight. He knew he might never see them again and his hate for those who had caused this atrocity grew in him, burning what was left of his soul. Flanked by his four friends, they hurriedly left the airport and drove to Steve's offices where Steve met with Owen, Warren and Mary and tearfully resigned from his position there.

"You're always welcome to come back," Warren told him.

"It's too dangerous for you all!" Steve replied truthfully, as they all looked at the floor. No one wanted to look him in the eyes and admit they were all a bit scared.

"You've more money than you can spend in twenty lifetimes Steve, we'll look after your share of the business," Owen assured him, hoping he'd be okay.

"I've given my sister access to all my accounts. Make sure she and my girls are okay" Steve said half smiling as he gave them all a hug and left quickly, not looking back.

"Where will he go?" Mary asked, watching Steve and his four friends walked down into the car park.

"Wherever he's going we don't want to know," Owen answered softly as they walked back inside.

"Where to now?" Ali asked Steve, as they drove away.

"Somewhere safe, somewhere where we can plan our next move and see them coming."

"I suggest Mexico City. It's off the radar and in the direction I think we're heading." Cody suggested, getting agreement from the others.

"Right, usual travelling arrangements, we'll meet at Mexico City in four days," Ali ordered as they split up. Ali decide to travel with Steve, the other went their separate ways.

SYDNEY

Edward had been back at work in Sydney for over a week when he was called into his boss's office, something that hadn't happened before.

"Welcome back Edward, that was bad business in Perth, I'm sorry for your families loss."

"Thank you, Sir, it's been hard, especially for Louise's brother's kids. They're staying with us for the moment."

"That what I wanted to talk to you about. The American's have asked for our help. Your brother has been listed as a Rogue mercenary, and we've been asked to assist in finding him. Do you have any idea where he was going?" Glen, his boss asked.

"Rogue mercenary! He used to work for them!"

"We're all friends here Edward. The Americans just want to talk with him, to clear this trouble up." Glen insisted.

"I don't know where he's going, Sir. If I did, I wouldn't tell the yanks I can assure you."

"The Americans are our Allies Edward. If you want to advance in the Federal Police, you'd better play ball!" Glen threatened.

"I'll leave the playing with their balls to you Sir."

PERTH

Back in Perth Mary, Joan and John looked out on the pile of burnt timber that had once been their friend's home.

"Do you think he'll come back?" Joan asked looking down the road.

"I hope so, but knowing Steve, he won't be back till it's safe for everybody," John replied.

"He'll go after them won't he" Mary understood him, and the rage that filled him.

"I hope he gets them all!" Joan said missing Michelle.

"You should never go after someone in anger. It can make you careless and unprofessional." John answered looking out to sea.

"What would you do if it was us?" Mary asked John, watching him.

"I'd do exactly the same as he's doing, but not as well," John replied giving his daughter a smile, as they moved inside.

ARLINGTON CEMETERY WASHINGTON

"What the hell happened?" Brooks angrily asked Black, as he sat down next to him.

"Getting the Colombians involved turned out to be a bad idea." Black answered, deciding beforehand to blame them for everything.

"Did you manage to get any of them?"

"No, only Robert's wife, we lost everyone except the ones that went after Sukai, and me," Black replied glibly.

"Maybe it's time I cleaned shop!"

"Simon, come here!" Black yelled, as one of his men stepped out from behind a hedge carrying a video camera.

"What's this?" Brooks asked defensively, staring at the camera and its implications.

"I thought it prudent to record all our meetings especially the one where you told me to kill Robert's entire unit." Black smiled, knowing he had this bastard. Brooks stood there.

"You need me as much as I need you, Black. Gather some more men and get Robert's and the others, before they come after us!" Brooks then walked off.

"Everything okay boss?" Simon asked, watching Brooks leave.

"It is for the moment, but we'd better find those bastards before they find us!" Black replied wondering, who was the biggest threat.

Warning Santini was the last thing Black wanted to do. Not only had he learned how they intended to kill him and the others after the operation, but the money placed in his account had suddenly disappeared leaving him far from happy.

"I should let Ali's unit cut him down!" Black laughed to himself, as he lifted the phone and dialled. After three rings one of Santini's people answered.

"Who is it?"

"My name is Black. Tell Mr Santini I need to talk with him." Black answered trying to sound friendly, as the man on the other end started talking to someone else in the room.

"So Mr Black you have rung to beg forgiveness for killing my nephews." Santini snarled at Black.

"Your nephews were stupid. They got what was coming to them." Black replied, imagining what Santini was thinking.

"You're a dead man Black!"

"Maybe I am Santini, but my guess is those men your nephews failed to kill will be paying you a visit soon. Just thought I'd ring and give you the good news." Black laughed again, as Santini went into a rage in Spanish, as Black dropped the phone. Laughing for quite some time afterwards, Black wished he could be there to watch when Ali's unit and Santini's people finally went at it. God, it would be great to watch he thought, and he didn't really care who won.

MEXICO CITY

Despite its reputation as one of the most dangerous places on the face of the Earth, Mexico City wasn't such a dangerous place to stay. Especially if you could handle yourself, Ali thought, as he walked through a marketplace picking up some food for tonight's meal. The unit had been here for over a week, staying in a villa, after meeting at the hotel. Ali had rung Julie that day, fulfilling his promise to ring at least once a week. His heart nearly broke when he heard her voice. She lived now with some close friends of his parents who had been in the military in Iran. Like his father, they had left before the new regime took over, and they knew how vital security was these days. Julie tried to sound brave, telling him how much she loved him and that his son missed him, but fear made her voice tremble.

Steve's revelation that the CIA was involved in trying to kill them had shaken the group. Ali knew that going home to his family would be at best fleeting, as sooner or later they would try for them again. Arriving back at the villa, Ali walked past the booby-trapped front door, headed around the back. Making sure no one was following, he carefully stepped over a black tripwire, in the shade of a large tree. Tapping four times on the door before entering, Ali wondered how long they would be able to live with this level of security, without someone being killed.

When the unit had first arrived and found out the CIA was involved, they realised they'd lost one of their main advantages in combat, Intel. Finding another source of information on the Santini Cartel took four days and to say the least, it was a bit unorthodox. Mexico City was a haven for drug cartels. Several of them had distributions centres here. Santini's Cartel was one of the biggest in the city and had a reputation for violence against the police and other cartels. One such group was the Medellin Cartel.

The unit had discovered that it was in a blood vendetta with Santini over the death of its leader's son. Steve, who had been withdrawn since arriving in Mexico, had volunteered to meet with the cartel, in an attempt to gain information on Santini's operation. It was scheduled for tonight, but Ali had doubts about Steve being ready.

"Are you sure you're up to this Steve?" Ali asked.

"I'm fine Ali, it's just the waiting. I'll be better once we get moving."

"Okay Steve, but stay focused on the plan," Ali told him, watching him as he nodded his understanding.

Walking down an alley in the slums of Mexico City in the dark of night was only for the brave or foolhardy. The unit followed Steve in the shadows watching Steve's back, as he walked down the alley looking neither left nor right. Watching him, Ali for the second time that day wondered how sane Steve really was, after what he'd been through. Coming at last to an old warehouse with a flashing fluorescent light outside, Steve went up to the door and banged on it loudly. The door slowly opened, and two men appeared, one pointing a sawn-off shotgun at Steve's stomach.

"What do you want?" the man without the shotgun asked, looking around for anyone else who might be hiding.

"I have a business arrangement for your boss."

"Why would our boss want to see you?" the same man asked with a slight smile on his face.

"I belong to a group who want to kill Santini" Malice radiated from Steve's voice, making both men a little more wary.

"Go away, my friend. It is quite clear Santini has done something to you. You just want to get even, many have offered already." The unarmed man replied, signalling to the man with the shotgun that they were going back inside.

"My group was responsible for the attack on Santini's Cartel several years ago when we killed around seven hundred of his men!" Steve informed them, as the two men at the door halted. After Steve was searched and led inside, he was left in a room with five of Medellin cartel's men, who watched him closely. Don Juan had disappeared into another room, returning five minutes later with an older man.

"Don Juan tells me you claim to be part of a group that attacked Santini's Cartel several years ago. Can you prove it?" the old man asked with a half smile, not believing it.

"With the help of twenty-five marines from a base in Panama, my unit comprising of five Special Forces trained soldiers neutralised Santini's militia group. At the time they were holding villagers hostage in the border region of Colombia and Panama, we were sent there to free them." Steve replied as the men in the room looked at each other, wondering what the gringo had been smoking.

"The press reported Colombian troops aided by Americans did

that!" the old man replied still smiling.

"Do you believe your papers always tell the truth?"

"A good point my friend, if you wait here for few minutes, I will make some enquiries." the old man replied before disappearing back into the adjoining room.

"How did you take care of all the bodies?" one of the men asked, as the other men tried not to laugh.

"We threw them to the sharks" Steve answered emotionlessly, and not one man there doubted him capable of it. Twenty minutes passed slowly as Don Juan asked questions of the raid digging for any discrepancies in Steve story until the old man reappeared.

"I find it hard to believe, but it appears you are telling the truth! "My name is Stefano, why do you want to kill Santini?" Stefano asked death in his eyes.

"He killed my wife!" Steve spat out.

"He killed my son. What do you need?" Stefano whispered his eyes misty.

"We need information on where he is, and what forces he has there."

"You will have it. But I must warn you lately he has increased his armed forces greatly. At first, I thought it was because of me, but now I think it is because you are hunting him." Stefano smiled something he hadn't done for a long time.

After discussing Santini's demise, Stefano suggested Steve's group move to his plantation north of Bogota, where they could plan their attack and select weapons, something they couldn't do here. Seeing Steve's hesitation, Stefano explained that no drugs were anywhere near his home.

"I know we will never be friends, but we share a common enemy. We can help each other. I swear on my son's grave that you will be safe." Stefano said emotionally, Don Juan backing him up.

"I'll have to ask my unit," He was sure they'd agree.

"Good, you can ask them to come in. I guess they're outside watching us?" Stefano chuckled, as his men tensed, watching the door.

"How'd you know?"

"You're professionals! You wouldn't have walked in here unless you thought you'd be able to walk out." Stefano smiled, as Steve went outside to get the others.

The trip down south to Colombia in an old cargo plane was anything but smooth. Stefano had arranged for the unit to travel in one of his own planes, for secrecy. He guaranteed them that it was clean, no drugs, even though the unit guessed it wasn't when it flew north. It was a small two engine Beachcomber popular with businessmen in the sixties for short hops. It had been gutted inside, making room for its special cargo.

Portable seats had been added for their comfort. Unfortunately they hadn't been secured. The first turbulence found the whole unit on the floor, much to the amusement of the pilot. In the end, they'd clung to cargo straps on the walls, sitting on their seat cushions, far from happy.

Arriving at Stefano's airstrip, they were ushered into an old Bedford truck for their covert trip to his home. Staggering out of their hiding place on the back of the truck, it took several minutes for them to straighten up, let alone walk properly, as the unit examined their new hideout. They had to admit it was striking, making the trip more palatable.

"Welcome to my home!" Stefano shouted, from the veranda of a beautiful colonial style home that dominated the countryside, as the unit members stretched and walked towards him. "Your rooms are ready for you, in a bungalow at the rear of this house. It will give you some privacy, but first, join me for a drink." Stefano said happily.

"Thank you, Sir, you are most generous," Ali replied smiling, he felt safe here.

"I am honoured that you came, I thought my son would never be avenged for what they did. Now I have a chance to see a great wrong righted!" Stefano exclaimed, his eyes shining.

"To revenge," Steve whispered, raising his glass his eyes distant.

Unlike the last raid, surprise wouldn't be possible. They figured Santini would have spies in Stefano's ranks, warning him, that they were coming. Santini lived in a building complex, similar to a castle of olden times. There were four separate structures all linked by walls and surrounded, by of all things, a moat. This gave the attackers only one way to enter, and that was over the bridge through a large metal gate.

Surrounding the moat, were Santini's real defences, made up of pillboxes and trenches. The bulk of his forces were deployed in these positions. It was an impressive setup, designed to wear out any attacking force before it even got close to the complex, and if the men outside took too many casualties, they could fall back to the castle complex and wait for reinforcements to arrive.

Santini had nearly two hundred well-trained men in defensive positions around the complex. But his main militia strength of over a thousand men could be called in at a moment's notice, from the surrounding village areas. Stefano's forces were much smaller only about fifty well-trained men with another hundred that he could call on. It appeared his cartel had been taking heavy losses when dealing with Santini. Four nights after arriving Stefano having left them alone to work out their plan, invited them to dine with him and his family.

Ali smiled at the unbelievable situation they were in. Here they were, living with a drug cartel boss, planning to take down another drug cartel, which had been backed by the CIA to kill them, who they used to work for. Dinner was like everything else perfect. The unit all agreed that it was the best place they had ever stayed. The only problem was how their host made his money. The meal was eaten, the women and Stefano's two remaining children left, leaving the men to discuss their business. Also present was Don Juan who had arrived that night bringing twenty extra men to bolster Stefano's forces.

"How is the planning going?" Stefano asked politely.

"Our plan is going well Sir, but we might have to take up your offer of using some of your men," Ali replied, gauging their reaction.

"We can give you half of our men maybe seventy, but that will leave us thin here if you're not successful," Stefano explained, worried at the manpower loss if the plan went wrong.

"That should be sufficient Sir. They'll only be used as a diversion." Ali replied.

"There is another problem my friends. We believe Santini has hired several Cuban military advisors to help with his defences, and he expects you to attack soon." Don Juan informed them.

"It will only help us, Don Juan, our plan calls for them to react as experienced soldiers will," Ali answered.

"Will you capture Santini before killing him?" Stefano asked vengeance in his eyes.

"No Sir, the plan is to kill him and all who stand with him," Ali replied, looking at Steve knowing he wanted to get him himself, something Ali didn't want to see happen.

"That is good enough." Stefano agreed, looking at Don Juan who nodded his agreement. "Are there any special items or weapons you might need?" Stefano asked Ali, who handed him a list silently, watching his reaction as Don Juan came closer to look at the list too.

"My God you're kidding!" Don Juan said shocked after Stefano passed him the list to read.

"I think I get the idea now of what you're going to do, but where do we get those types of weapon?" Stefano asked seriously.

"We have a contact in Singapore, Mr Lou. We think he will be able to supply all our needs." Ali suggested, worried they wouldn't agree.

"We know Mr Lou, he supplies us already, but the cost of these weapons will be high!" Don Juan said worried about the price.

"Well, let's ring him; I'm sure he'll be most helpful," Ali replied as Stefano handed Ali a phone number.

"No matter the cost, this is about family!" Stefano vowed, he and Steve shared the same grief.

SINGAPORE

"What is it nephew, it had better be important!" Mr Lou exploded awoken from his afternoon nap.

"A man called Ali Moustaffer wishes to speak with you. He rang in on a number given to a client in Colombia," His nephew informed him.

"Mr Lou here, how may I help you?" Mr Lou asked politely.

"Good afternoon Mr Lou it is good to hear your voice again, we have a special order for you," Ali replied smiling and then told Mr Lou what they wanted.

"I can obtain all the weapons. The last two weapons will take several days, plus a day to fly them to you. But I must ask, why this type of weapon, and why are you there?"

"One of Mr Stefano's competitors tried to kill one of my friends. We are here to teach them a lesson!" Ali replied.

"Very well. When you are finished there, Mr Moustaffer, I would advise against going near your former employer. He has listed you and your friends, as rogue mercenaries with Interpol. They have been asked to detain you all."

"Thank you for the warning, Mr Lou, you are indeed a good friend."

"Come to Singapore Mr Moustaffer, I have a business proposition for you, which would prove most favourable to both of us. In the meantime, I will send the order as soon as possible. Tell Mr Stefano this order is forty million, payment the usual way, goodbye Mr Moustaffer." Lou said before hanging up. Ali sat there looking at the phone, wondering what Lou wanted them for. He hadn't thought of where they'd go after this operation, but it might prove a wise idea to do so.

"He can supply everything, and it will be here in less than five days," Ali told the group.

"How much?" Don Juan asked, getting a smile from Stefano.

"He wants forty million US dollar. And payment the usual way." Ali replied. Everyone there considered the price.

"Pay it!" Stefano said to Don Juan, as he went out on the veranda to be alone.

"If it cost every cent we had he would have paid it. How can you put a cost on losing family?" Don Juan asked watching his friend leave.

"You can't!" Steve answered leaving as well.

"I am sorry I forgot about your friend's loss." Don Juan replied, embarrassed by what he'd said.

"It's okay Don Juan. He'll soon get a chance to get rid of some of that hate." Cody replied.

The next day the unit started training, honing their skills. None of the unit members had been in action since Afghanistan, so Ali insisted that fitness was paramount in the coming fight. After a week of intensive training, he believed they were fit enough to go into battle. They then decided to train Stefano's militia. Since their role was only as a diversion, weapons' training was what they concentrated on.

As promised, Mr Lou's delivery arrived at Stefano's airstrip, on a huge Russian transport plane. With the help of Stefano's men, all the weapons were unloaded, including the two special ones. Walking across to Stefano's plane, which was an old Hercules transport, Ali wondered what a chequered career it must have had to end up here in Colombia. Approaching the rear of the enormous plane, Ali was impressed by the improvements made inside. It included soundproofing and a large lounge area. There was also space for a Rolls Royce, which always travelled in the plane.

"The roads are not much in South America, I find it better to travel this way when visiting my friends," Stefano admitted as he came up to stand beside Ali.

"We'll have to completely empty the back compartment for this mission. You understand that don't you Sir."

"It will be worth it, I just wish I could go," Stefano replied.

"Its better this way Sir, the men would be demoralised if something happened to you."

"Why do you and your men always address me as Sir, you all know my name?" Stefano asked, knowing it was more than respect.

"We're soldiers Stefano we obey orders. You are supplying us with men and equipment that makes you our superior. You also deal in drugs, which means in the future we won't be friends, it is better that we keep our distance from you." Ali replied watching Stefano stiffen, as he took in Ali's statement.

"You're an honest man Ali, and you're right, we'll never be friends. But until you leave Colombia we are allies." Stefano answered, before leaving.

"Making us more friends," Cody asked, walking up beside Ali.

"Stefano's okay, but his business kills thousands of people. I cannot lie to him and pretend we're friends."

"Your right Ali, but let's wait until we're out of the country before giving him a hard time, okay." Cody smiled.

PAYBACK

Steve wearing a killer suit slowly crawled forward towards the Command bunker on Santini's outer perimeter. It was about seven in the evening, and the sun hadn't completely lost its effect on the countryside giving it a sinister like quality. For the operation to work, Steve knew that this position must be neutralised before full darkness enveloped the area, and the diversion started. Unlike the other positions held by Santini's militia, this one was controlled by well trained Cuban soldiers. They had been hired by Santini to give his men some professional backbone in the expected attack. Steve gave them a lot of respect. He moved closer.

For the last few weeks, Santini's spies had kept him well informed of Stefano's so-called surprise attack, aided by Ali's unit. He had spent a great deal of time and money making sure it would be defeated at the outer perimeter, not in his castle. Not only had he improved the bunkers, in the outer perimeter position, but Santini had also reinforced his walls of the castle, mounting heavy weapons around the entire structure. His Cuban advisers assured him that the only way in was down the front driveway, and nowhere else.

Sitting that afternoon in his office with the four Captains of his militia units and his Cuban advisors, Santini informed them that Stefano's men were on their way and once the attack began he would call in the reserve militia unit from the surrounding areas. By doing this, he hoped to cut off their retreat trapping them between his defences and the militia units coming in from behind. Putting the positions on alert Santini looked around the room expecting excited faces, but the Cubans sat quietly.

"Why the long faces my friends, we will soon have them trapped!" Santini asked excitedly, hoping to finish all his enemies in one bloody battle.

"They're attacking like amateurs, I'd have thought this elite unit would be more professional." one of the Cubans answered looking at the map.

"They're taking their orders from Stefano my friends, and he's no General. Even though I expect there'll be some surprises tonight." Santini answered confidently reassuring the Cubans, as they moved out to the walls to watch the coming battle.

With extreme care, Steve moved silently up a small rut in the ground until he reached the bunkers side. Reaching into his suit he carefully pulled out a satchel charge and placed it against the wall, before pulling the twenty-minute fuse and crawling slowly back the way he'd come. Having only travelled back about half the distance he needed to go, Steve heard the sound of trucks approaching in the distance.

Behind him on the wall Santini, hearing the trucks also, ordered his surrounding militia units to come to his aid. Once Stefano's men had disembarked from the trucks, Ali, Aaron and Sukai guided them forward. This helped keep casualties among the brave soldiers of Stefano's militia to a minimum, as they moved forward fearlessly, towards the enemy positions.

Crawling as fast as possible, Steve realised time was running out, so coming to his feet, he sprinted for the tree line.

"Where did he come from?" One of the Cubans in the bunker yelled while giving instructions to the other bunkers to stop firing wildly and concentrate on moving targets.

"I'm not sure Sergeant." A soldier next to the machine gunner answered.

"We only saw him when he got up. Check outside!" The Sergeant ordered as the bunker exploded, vaporising them all.

When the command bunker exploded into a giant cloud of dust and debris, Stefano's men realised it was the signal to fire their Russian made RPGs into Santini's confused militia positions. Though few casualties were caused, it made Santini's men put their heads down and stopped firing.

"Now!" yelled Ali, as all the men in hearing range hurled smoke bombs towards the enemy positions, while simultaneously firing small smoke canisters from grenade launchers behind the enemy positions. From the wall of the complex, Santini and his Cuban advisors watched the explosion of the command bunker followed by the launching of the smoke grenades.

"They are trying to isolate the positions from each other, so they can attack them one at a time." Carlos the Senior Cuban advisor warned.

"What do you suggest?" Santini asked slightly frightened by these tactics.

"Pull the men back Senor, we can cover the road from the walls. It's the only safe approach to this position, and they'll be slaughtered if they attack down that road." Carlos replied, confident that they had them.

At the sound of a horn from the castle, Santini's men scrambled from their positions, back to the safety of the castle. Once inside the castle, with the steel gates closed, Santini's militia men's confidence was restored. The fact, that except for the loss of the men in command bunkers, they'd received only minor casualties, filled them with confidence as they manned the walls. As the artificial fog continued to swell over the battlefield an eerie silence settled over the castle. The defenders braced themselves for the attack, though except for spasmodic small arms fire, nothing happened.

Ten minutes elapsed as Santini and his advisors waited, scanning the slowly dissipating smoke as the rattle and pounding of feet could be heard getting nearer. Fear gripped Santini's men, as they brought their weapons to the ready, preparing to fire. A voice echoing through the fog, made them hesitate.

"Mr Santini, do not fire, it is Emanuel." A frightened voice sounded through the fog, as shapes began to appear.

"Hold your fire!" Santini yelled, recognising one of his militia officers voices as the men with him visibly relaxed. The smoke rolled away, revealing over two hundred of Santini's reinforcements.

"Where are Stefano's men?" Santini yelled down to his men on the road.

"We do not know Mr Santini we have not seen anyone," Emanuel replied.

"Where are they? Have they run off into the jungle?" Santini asked his advisors.

"I don't understand why would they retreat without attacking?" Carlos asked his second in command, as a plane could be heard approaching.

"Maybe the objective was not to enter the fort, but to get us all inside." Diego, the second Cuban advisor, replied watching the Hercules approach.

"Senor Santini, order everyone out of the complex!" Carlos yelled as fear gripped him.

"Too late!" Diego replied, as two objects dropped from the rear door of the plane and headed earthwards.

Cody sat in the co-pilot's seat looking at the distant fireworks, caused by the attack on the bunkers at Santini's castle. The sky was growing darker, soon the only lights visible on the ground would be the castle complex and the sparkle of gunfire. Looking across at the pilot Cody saw him suddenly talk into his radio, Cody put his headset radio switch on, to hear what was said.

"Ali just called. He said to give them ten minutes then come on in." The Pilot informed him, knowing what was about to happen.

"Right, open the rear door. I'll go back. You signal with the jump light when you want them to go." Cody commanded, undoing his safety belt and heading for the rear of the plane.

'God they look nasty.' Cody thought to himself as he removed the safety pins from the noses of the two black coloured bombs, which sat waiting on the two sleds he had made for them. As the rear ramp door opened behind him, Cody was forced to grab the side rail, as the air rushed out. Clipping himself to a safety harness, Cody, winched the weapons onto the rear door ramp, causing the door to creak dangerously, as the dark void passed by beneath them.

'Napalm, no matter how you put it, was an ugly weapon,' Cody thought as he stood there trying to justify what he was about to do. As the lights came on, usually used for dropping loads of supplies by parachute, Cody without hesitation released the clamps, pushing both bombs out one after the other. Looking at the Castle far below and behind them, Cody wondered how close they'd get to hitting the complex. He and the pilot had only practised this five times and had only hit the target once.

As he watched, a brilliant flash and a visible bubble like a shock wave, radiated up from the surrounding jungle beside the castle showing the first bomb had missed. A split second later a second flash occurred directly in the middle of the castle complex, making Cody forget his early misgivings, and cheer. The realisation of what he had done however sobered him, as he watched the two fireballs expand rapidly.

"Poor bastards!" Cody whispered sadly before he signalled the pilot to close the doors and proceed to the next phase of the mission. Sitting down near the door, Cody looked down to see his hands shaking.

When the first bomb hit the ground, Santini and his men ducked down as napalm burned everything it touched, and for a spit second, they believed they were safe. Unfortunately, Carlos and Diego knew the truth, as they had seen two objects leave the plane. At the same time, they both closed their eyes and prayed, as the second bomb exploded on impact, engulfing the entire complex in liquid fire.

It was said the screams of the dying and the living could be heard twenty kilometres away as napalm splattered over the relief force outside the gates as well. In their panic, they ran into the adjoining fields, causing more fires to erupt as death and destruction rained down on the shattered demoralised men.

Two kilometres away on Santini's own airfield, Ali's unit and the militia waited silently for the Hercules to land. The heat and screams from the castle made them all aware of the murderous attack they had launched. Steve stood on his own, at the side of the airfield, looking in the direction of the castle and feeling the heat from the inferno on his face. Deep down he felt nothing but emptiness.

One of the men who killed his wife was dead, along with who knows how many innocents. Their only crime was being near Santini. Looking over Steve saw the militiamen hastily boarding the Hercules, their faces showing remorse at what they had done. Only hours earlier, they had been bragging about the coming raid and what they would do to the enemy. 'Well, they aren't bragging now.' Steve said to himself, as he stood there watching the fire.

"Time to go Steve," Ali said, watching him as he stood in his killer suit, holding an automatic pistol in his hand.

"Where to?"

"I honestly don't know Steve, but we've all got family out there, including you! So pull yourself together and get over it!" Ali replied angrily, turning and walking towards the plane. Steve stood there for several seconds staring at the Browning pistol until Ali's words slowly penetrated his thoughts. Snapping out of it, he slowly followed Ali.

Onboard the fear of the raid started to dissipate as Stefano's militias finally realised it was over and they were going home. Starting to relax some began to laugh, shouting that it was over and they were heroes. The laughing stopped abruptly, as Steve came up the rear ramp decked out in his killer suit, camouflage paint making his face look inhuman. Cody coming up the ramp behind Steve took the pistol from Steve's hand telling him a take a seat next to him. For the rest of the flight, even though space was limited, a clear space opened up between the unit and the militia, not from respect, but fear.

When the plane landed Stefano, Don Juan and many wives and children of the militia waited for their arrival. Happy to see them home safely they'd prepared a victory feast. Instead, Stefano's men walked out of the plane devoid of emotion, disappearing into the night taking their families with them. Stefano wondered what had happened.

"What is wrong my men they look like they lost not won?" Stefano asked one of his captains, confused.

"It was a slaughter Sir, no one feels like celebrating," he replied, before excusing himself as well, heading home.

"Did you get him?" Stefano asked Steve as he walked past, a killer suit under his arm.

"Yes, he's burning in hell already. Someday I'll see him there!" Steve chuckled, before walking off, leaving Stefano and Don Juan staring after him.

WASHINGTON

Brooks sat at his new desk in his new office, as Director of the CIA. Staring happily out the window which looked towards Washington, he felt victorious. Nothing could touch him today as he bathed in the glow of his sweet victory over Ross Stuart. He even felt some sympathy for Ross, letting him keep his position. The private phone on his desk ringing startled him, but his mood remained happy as he picked it up.

"Brooks here, what is it?"

"It's Black here; I have some information on our friends in Colombia," Black reported.

"Good I hope!"

"Yes and no. It seems our friend Santini and several hundred of his friends and militia, have gone up in smoke. It seems someone dropped a couple of Napalm bombs on them, turning them to mush." Black replied happily, as Brooks looked skywards for planes, before answering.

"How is that good news?"

"Two reasons. One, Santini has been permanently silenced. And two, Roberts and Ali Moustaffer might suspect us, but they can't be sure you gave the order. My men, if he questioned them, only knew that I worked for someone in the CIA, not who." Black replied, smiling to himself.

"You're right. That is good news. As a matter of fact, I had them branded as mercenaries' gone rogue. That means they are hired assassins, everyone will be looking for them."

"That's good! Sooner or later we'll get a sniff of them." Black replied, hanging up.

'And once you've got them, I'll take care of you.' Brooks thought, smiling to himself, as he happily went back to staring out the window.

SINGAPORE DEAL

In the end, as the noose of the worlds law enforcement agencies started to constrict, the unit members fled Mexico. They travelled to the only place where they had a friend if you could call him that. Landing on separate flights and staying in separate hotels, the unit members rendezvoused at one of their first meeting places in Singapore, the Raffles hotel bar.

"Hasn't changed much, since we were here on our first mission, has it?" Cody whispered, downing another beer, something he did quite a lot lately, Ali noticed. Then again the strain showed on all of them since Colombia.

"Mr Lou wants us to meet him at his restaurant around the corner, at eight which is one hour away. Are we all in favour of going?" Ali put forward, as everyone nodded their support.

"Are we just going in blind?" Aaron asked, always suspicious.

"Not completely. I checked our old warehouse; it's still loaded with weapons, so I brought a small one for each of us." Ali replied, passing each of them a cigar-shaped box.

"Thanks, Uncle Ali!" Sukai chuckled, lightening the mood as they all tried to relax.

"Do you think this is wise?" Steve asked, watching the crowd looking for any danger.

"We can't touch our own money it's too dangerous. We have to earn a living doing something. I think Lou wants us for a job." Ali replied, wanting secretly to go home.

"Well if we don't like it, we can walk!" Aaron suggested, getting nods from everyone as they left for the meeting. Once outside they opened their presents, swiftly loading them, before slipping them into their belts or pockets.

"Hey what's the name of his restaurant?" Cody asked.

"The Mystic Dragon," Ali replied smiling.

"How original," Cody grinned, making them all burst into laughter, as they approached the restaurant.

"Good evening gentlemen, I'm so glad you could come." Mr Lou said welcoming them, as the five entered his restaurant looking at the large dragon near the entrance.

"Nice restaurant Mr Lou," Ali replied, as they were herded to a private table upstairs, away from the tourists.

"Yes it is, but the name was picked for the tourists, they expect everything to be like that here," Lou answered with a slight smile. He took the seat at the head of the table, as they all exchanged pleasantries until the meal was completed. It was then Mr Lou became all business and went over his so-called arrangement with them. It appeared a client had reneged on paying for the supplies Mr Lou had sent them, and Mr Lou wanted his money.

"I was over trusting and gave him till after they sorted out their civil war to pay me. Unfortunately, he lost the war, which in most cases would mean they weren't alive. In this case, he'd raided the countries banks and took a sizeable amount of gold with him into exile. I then sent one of my most trusted employees to retrieve my investment from him. He was found floating in the sea." Mr Lou explained, his emotions showing for a second.

"So you want us to retrieve your money?" Ali asked.

"It is too late for that my friends. The client has made me look an easy target, and I cannot allow that or my opposition would soon swallow me." Mr Lou answered clearly not happy.

"We're not assassins Mr Lou," Ali told him.

"I understand that gentlemen. This man hasn't a lot of support and is taking refuge in a Middle Eastern country. If you can seize his funds, he won't be able to pay for protection from his countries new government. They will carry out the punishment for me." Mr Lou replied, smiling at his cleverness.

"That sounds acceptable, but we may have trouble moving through countries at the moment," Ali admitted, worried about travelling.

"I have arranged for several passports for each of you, in the hope, you would accept. They are from different countries, and your pictures are slightly altered from the Interpol photos of you." Mr Lou replied.

"How did you know we would accept, or come here for that matter?" Steve snapped.

"You have nothing to fear, I simply deduced that my offer for employment would be the only one available to you, and I pay well." Mr Lou replied watching Steve cautiously.

"What is the pay?" Cody asked.

"The client owes me five million, I understand he has over ten million in his possession, after the five million is deducted we go halves in what is left. I consider this more than fair." Mr Lou pointed out. They all knew this would be the only offer.

"Okay, we'll do it. Where is he?" Ali asked neutrally.

"Beirut in Lebanon and I can assure you it won't be easy." Mr Lou admitted, before rising and leaving them to discuss it.

"Mr Moustaffer can I see you for a second?" Mr Lou asked from the door, as Ali got up and walked over to him.

"I am concerned about Mr Roberts, he worries me?" Mr Lou asked softly.

"They killed his wife, Mr Lou. It has rattled him a bit that's all." Ali answered, understanding his concern.

"I understand that pain Mr Moustaffer. The envoy I sent was my nephew. Can he be relied upon, is all I ask?" Lou asked, not wanting problems.

"Of course, as time goes by he'll get over it," Ali replied confidently.

"Would you?" Mr Lou asked, before leaving.

It didn't take long for the team to decide to accept the offer, as Mr Lou had said, what other options did they have? Calling Mr Lou back into the room, he, without any ceremony, produced an agreement that Ali signed on behalf of the unit, at which point Mr Lou handed over five sets of beautifully faked passports.

"Good luck gentlemen. I have arranged for a supply of, 'equipment', to be waiting for you in Beirut. When you have completed the mission, please ring me." Mr Lou said before bowing slightly and leaving.

"I for one like the guy, he's got style," Cody admitted smiling.

"I don't trust him," Steve replied softly, watching the door.

"What about me Steve?" Ali asked, challenging him.

"You're my closest friend. Of course, I trust you!"

"Then snap out of it. These dark moods you've been having lately are unacceptable. Get over it, or you won't be going. We can't function properly as a team, with all your hate. Even Mr Lou spotted it!" Ali pointed out, before walking out the door, leaving the others watching Steve silently. Footsteps behind him warned Ali that Steve was following, as he turned to confront him.

"That was unfair back there Ali, I've been through a lot." Steve groaned, close to tears, when suddenly Ali slapped him across the face, shocking him.

"There was a time my friend when surprising you was nearly impossible, now it's easy." He looked into Steve's eyes, he knew he had hit home.

"I just miss her and the girls so badly Ali." Steve choked out. Ali knew Steve was close to breaking.

"I know Steve, but she's gone my friend, and if you can't pull yourself together, you're a danger to your girls and us," Ali informed him, before turning and walking away.

Steve stood there for some time thinking on what Ali had said. In Colombia he had thought of eating a bullet and ending it, that's how low he had felt. Crossing to a park bench Steve flopped down trying to make sense of his life as the pistol dug into his back. Reaching into his belt, he pulled out the pistol and stared at it for some time, before throwing it into the river that bordered the park.

Thinking of the slap, Steve chuckled to himself, knowing Ali was right. Before the attack on his family, no one would have even got close to catching him off guard like Ali just had. He was losing it he realised. Getting to his feet he looked at his watch, it was only eight in the evening in Australia he thought. Hurrying to his hotel room, he quickly dialled his sister's home, happy to get an immediate answer from his sister.

"Hello, who is it?" Louise asked happily, as in the background Steve could hear his girls laughing.

"Hi sis it's me!"

"Steve it's been months, how are you?" Louise asked, a little shaken.

"Better now I've talked to you."

For the next hour, he caught up on what was going on. His two girls excitedly talked to him, telling him about their lives and always asking when he was coming home. Dodging those requests was hard, but as time went by, they gave up asking, happy just to talk with him. In the end, Steve decided to get off the line, saying he was running out of money, when Edward asked to talk with him privately. The sound of 'do we have to' in the background told Steve the girls were gone when Edwards tone changed.

"I don't want to know where you are Steve, but people are looking for you."

"Yes so I've been told, so much for old friends," Steve replied sarcastically.

"Wherever you are now, move immediately!"

"Thanks for the warning Edward, and by the way, we caught up with our Colombian friends."

"Yeah, there are reports someone barbequed a cartel."

"They had it coming!" Steve replied.

"It won't make you feel any better Steve," Edward answered, secretly glad he had got them, but knowing revenge never made you feel better.

"Anyway, thanks for looking after the kids, I hope to see you all soon."

"That would be good, but from now on, short calls only, okay!" Edward insisted, before hanging up. Taking Edwards warning to heart Steve rang down to reception and informed them of a family emergency which meant he had to leave immediately to return home. Arranging to pay the bill and booking a taxi to take him to the airport, he packed. Once at the airport, he hailed another cab and went to a different hotel informing them he had just arrived from Australia and hadn't booked a room. So for an extra large tip, they gladly supplied one.

The next day Steve met the others apologising for his behaviour, which they all laughed off. He could see in their eyes though, that they were all relieved, as together they started to plan the mission.

BEIRUT

"God it's hard to believe this once was one of the most beautiful cities in the world!" Sukai exclaimed, looking out over a city scarred by artillery and fire.

"Keep your head away from the window, there's still sniper activity in this area." Aaron barked, not happy with the location, as Sukai moved away from the window.

"The plan seemed simple back in Singapore, but here it looks shaky to me," Cody admitted, unwrapping some of the supplies Mr Lou had sent. Like usual the weapons were mostly Russian, AK 47's and RPG's, with a couple of American grenades thrown in for good measure.

Opening the final box, Steve was surprised to find military uniforms, in a pattern he hadn't seen before.

"They're Syrian Special Forces uniforms. It appears Syria holds sway here in Lebanon, and since they're protecting our targets, I thought it might help." Ali said checking for his size as the others grabbed a pair each.

The plan was simple, all they had to do was under cover of darkness procure a vehicle and drive to their targets known address. There they would overpower the target's guards, and grab the loot, before driving to the harbour. Once there, they would transfer the loot and themselves to a vessel and make their escape. The boat so far was the only part of the plan in place. Aaron with the help of a large amount of American dollars had convinced the crew of a fishing boat that smuggling was more profitable than fishing.

He had arranged for the trip to take place in five night's time. Unfortunately, that was four days ago, so tonight was the night unless they wanted to swim. Ali, with his Arab appearance, hadn't had any trouble scouting out the enemies hideout. It turned out to be a heavily fortified building, with a large warehouse type front door and no windows on street level.

The rear wasn't much better with bars on all the windows and the steel door bolted from the inside.

"Okay people, any ideas, times running out!" Ali asked, knowing the mission was a bust unless they came up with something.

"I've got one idea, and it's a big one!" Steve replied with a grin, signalling Ali and the others to look out the window. Down into the street, they watched as a self-propelled gun pulled up across the road from their hotel.

"She's a big bastard, isn't she?" Aaron chuckled as the others laughed.

As darkness settled over the city the unmistakable sound of a heavy tracked vehicle could be heard rumbling along the deserted roads. The two guards outside Mohammad Burack's house heard it too, wondering what was going on, as the sound of the vehicle grew louder. Inside Burack sat with four of his former generals studying a map of his beloved country.

"We will need a lot more money than what we have here Sir, to retake the homeland." One of his Generals said honestly, studying the plan to take back their country.

"The Syrians will supply a lot more in return for the uranium. I will give them a permit to mine it, in our country!" the ex-President replied happily.

"What of the Americans and UN forces there at the moment?" another General asked worriedly.

"Like usual they will protest and call meetings, but except for hot air, nothing will happen." the ex-President smiled as his generals laughed. The merriment was interrupted by the sound of the approaching vehicle.

"Someone find out what is making that infernal noise!" the President ordered, annoyed his plans were being interrupted. The sickening sound of a large calibre gun firing was the last thing any of them heard, as the shell impacted with their building, reducing it to rubble.

When the building had come into view, Ali had given Cody the signal to fire. Steve and Sukai at the rear of the vehicle manhandled a shell into the breach of the weapon.

"Sure you know what you're doing?" Steve asked a little worried, as Cody looked through the aperture lining the cross up on the front door. At this range, it was overkill as the door flooded the viewfinder. Signalling he was about to fire, Ali stopped the vehicle, and everyone covered their ears moving away from the weapon to avoid the recoil. The two Syrian guards near the front door stared at them wondering what was going on when the gun fired.

Steve and the others were nearly deafened by the explosion, and so close were they, that the firing and the hitting of the target came almost instantaneously causing debris to rain down upon them and the surrounding area. Stumbling out of the vehicle, Ali led the way into the shattered remains of the house, knowing from Mr Lou, that the strong room was down in the basement. Digging through the rubble, Sukai located the stairs. Sukai and Ali started down; sending Cody and Steve back to the gun, just in case their targets security arrived.

It didn't take Sukai and Ali long to find the strong room or what was left of it. The jail like doors had been half crushed by the explosion giving them a clear entrance. Stacked neatly against the wall, sat twenty boxes each needing two men to carry them. Grabbing one box, Ali and Sukai struggle up the stairs, loading it into the vehicle before heading back for another.

"Can you hurry up I'm double parked!" Cody yelled to them after the tenth trip, as the sound of vehicles could be heard approaching.

"We're stuffed, you two get the others!" Ali gasped out of breath, as Steve and Cody swung down from the vehicle and Ali and Sukai took their places.

"So much for not being assassins," Steve said softly, as they carried a box past the remains of a body.

"You're the one who suggested the big gun remember!" Cody replied, breathing heavily as they slowly carried another box out.

"The next one's the last!" Steve informed Ali, as they pushed another box into the rear of the vehicle, trotting back inside. They'd just enter the building when the stuttering sound of a machine gun opened up behind them.

"Looks like the reinforcements have finally decided to do something." Cody smiled, looking at his watch and working out that it had taken over two hours to load the twenty boxes. The crash of their self-propelled gun firing, not only scared them but rained masonry and debris down onto them as well. Cody and Steve frightened of being buried alive, struggled up what was left of the stairs, carrying the last box, as silence returned to the street outside. The enemy machine gunner, who had started hammering the area, was either dead or beating a retreat out of range from their gun Steve thought, as they emerged onto the street.

Using up their remaining strength, Steve and Cody, with the box between them sprinted for the vehicle. Getting there safely, they climbed inside, as small arms fire erupted again, coming in from all directions. Sukai seeing Cody and Steve were aboard gave Ali the go signal, as he thrust the vehicle into gear moving forward. Accelerating down the street, they all ducked, as bullets danced along the side of the vehicles armour plate. It made an almighty racket, but did little damage, as they swiftly gained speed, racing towards the harbour.

Looking back Steve saw an armoured personnel carrier, nose around a corner from a side road, and increase speed attempting to catch them. Grabbing Cody's arm, Steve pointed at the vehicle behind them.

"Let em come, our gun will turn them into crap!"

"It's a self-propelled gun! It can't turn its barrel around like a tank Cody!" Steve yelled back, as Cody thinking fast grabbed one of the RPG's. Pointing the weapon at the approaching vehicle, Cody squeezed the trigger, and with a small whoosh compared to the gun firing, a rocket sped towards the carrier. Unfortunately, it missed, sailing over it.

"I'll have a go!" Steve yelled grabbing another RPG and firing it. Again it missed, but at least this time it landed in front. It caused a sizable explosion but failed to stop the armoured vehicle.

"Shit you two are hopeless!" Sukai yelled grabbing a third rocket launcher, only to see the carrier turn off. Apparently the driver thought two was enough, making them all burst into laughter.

"Though I walk through the shadow of death I fear no one, for I am the biggest bastard here!" Cody shouted loudly, laughing, as they continued on through the deserted streets, crushing anything that blocked their path beneath the assault guns tracks.

Arriving at the wharf caused pandemonium to break out as people ran in every direction. They all tried to get away from the metal monster heading in their direction at an unstoppable speed. On the fishing boat, the crew too were also about to leave as well. Aaron, producing a revolver, slowed them down considerably until the mobile gun came to a crunching halt beside the pier. With the help of the overwrought boat crew and the unit, except Ali who watched for trouble, the boxes were quickly loaded onto the boat. Then as swiftly as possible, they put to sea, leaving their mayhem behind them.

"Well, that went well!" Sukai smiled, as the boat chugged out to sea at a leisurely pace. Steve was about to agree when a screaming sound made them look back towards land. The scream was followed by a fountain of water rearing up a hundred metres behind the boat.

"Looks like someone notified the shore battery!" Ali mumbled as a distant puff of smoke and another scream sounded the approach of another shell. A fountain went up directly in front of them burying them in water.

"Turn right and follow the coast!" Ali yelled to the captain who spun the wheel and headed along the coast, his eyes wide open with fear. They hadn't turned for more than ten seconds, when a shell screamed down and landed where they would have been if it wasn't for the turn, shaking them badly.

"Good now resume course and turn again the next time they fire," Ali suggested as he looked back towards the shoreline. The game of cat and mouse continued for another hour until they were out of range.

"That was my fault; I didn't know they had a shore battery!" Ali confessed.

"I wouldn't knock yourself out about it, we did make it didn't we?" Steve replied smiling, feeling good.

"Yes we did Steve, but the plan was rough and badly carried out, we're better than that," Ali exclaimed looking at them all, knowing it was more luck at finding the self-propelled gun than anything else.

"Well, Mr Lou will be happy, which for our future security, is a good thing," Sukai added getting agreement from everybody, as they travelled north towards the Turkish coast.

Once ashore, Ali paid the crew of the fishing boat their pay, plus a large bonus for their trouble. Aaron being in charge of transport had hired a small truck to take them and the twenty boxes to the airport, the boxes to be freighted back to Singapore separately. While they waited for Aaron to get the truck, Steve being curious opened one of the boxes. He wanted to be sure that the gold was in there.

At first, he thought the entire box was full of jewellery but digging through it with his hands, he found the bottom half was made up of gold ingots, and the jewels had then been place on top of the bars.

"I think Mr Lou will be more than impressed!" Steve smiled, as the others all came forward to stare at the fortune it contained.

"What's that on your hands?" Ali asked as Steve closed the box revealing a red tinge covering his hands and fingers. Checking Steve's hand swiftly, hoping that some sort of poison hadn't been sprayed on the jewels, Ali realised what the stain was.

"It's dried blood, Steve. From the original owners of the jewellery, I'd say." Ali said softly, throwing Steve a rag, as he desperately to scrub the blood from his hands until all evidence of the stain had gone.

The rest of the trip was spent in silence as the unit members pondered what had happened to the original owners until at last, they reached the Airport. Getting rid of the twenty boxes onto a private plane booked by Mr Lou, the unit quietly boarded a series of international flights. Travelling to different countries, in the end, they all made their way back to Singapore, much relieved to be away from the cargo.

MR LOU'S RESTAURANT

Mr Lou was indeed impressed and sensing their weariness suggested they have some time off, meeting again in four weeks. As the group started to leave, Mr Lou asked Steve to stay a moment, making the others pause.

"While you were away four men appeared at your original hotel before you moved. They were asking questions about you, and they weren't police."

"I rang to check on my kids, they must have bugged my sister's phone."

"We've all rung home Steve, it's just bad luck they got a hit on you," Cody said reassuring him.

"It's funny my brother-in-law Edward came on the line and told me to make the calls short from now on."

"He's a wise man, Mr Roberts if you talk for less than a couple of minutes they can't trace you. Maybe to the country you're in, but not exactly where." Mr Lou replied smiling slightly, showing he knew things they didn't.

"Good advice to us all!" Ali said before continuing. "The best way is to ring when leaving a country. Also get the people you're ringing, and yourselves to use a mobile phone, they're harder to trace!" Ali added, as each made a note to buy a mobile, even if they were quite large to carry.

The years went by swiftly, Mr Lou found them work, and the unit carried out each assignment efficiently. As time passed by the unit slowly went down a slippery slope, not caring what the mission was, as long as they kept alive and their families safe. Over the years that followed there were high points when one of the unit members arranged to visit his family, guarded by the others from a discrete distance. It wasn't perfect, but they got by.

Money was also no object, as Mr Lou, true to his word, banked their share, never deceiving them, and always supplying them with perfectly forged papers. Steve had been home several times to visit. Always arriving suddenly and leaving just as he arrived, but it was better than nothing. Edward was uncomfortable with these visits, knowing the danger it presented to all of them. He always turned a blind eye, pretending not even to notice that Steve's friends were never far away.

At work, Edward knew his not giving up Steve had affected his career. He still caught the bad guys though, which was the main thing to him anyway. Steve's girls made Edward and Louise into a family, something they both loved. It had always been a source of sadness that they couldn't have a family of their own.

Ali had the best set up, as Julie and Peter his son, regularly visited him in Singapore. Supposedly on her way to Australia to visit family, she used Singapore as a stopover point on her way there and when returning. This gave them precious time together. It did make Steve a little jealous, but he was happy for them.

Then everything changed with the raid in Turkey. It was 1996.

THE LABORATORY

It was a hot, humid night in Singapore, which was the norm as the unit members wandered from the Raffles bar down to Mr Lou's restaurant. As usual, the unit met upstairs at Mystic Dragon sitting quietly and a little bored. Years were rolling by and although close friends, everyone needed their space, something they weren't getting. 'We've been together too long,' Ali mumbled to himself, missing his family, as he spotted Mr Lou entering.

"Good evening Gentlemen." Mr Lou said, walking in helped by his daughter Lily, the heir to his empire.

It was one of Mr Lou's great sadness's that he had only three daughters, no son. Lily being the oldest and smartest was his heir. Her sisters had long since married, but Lily loved the business and helped her father run it. She'd never worried much about the opposite sex until she met Sukai. Approaching their table, she formally bowed to each of them, but her eyes always stayed on Sukai. At first, her father had not been impressed with his daughter's boyfriend, being Japanese. He'd accepted him in the end, for two reasons. One he was wealthy and two, more importantly, he was ruthless, a quality needed in the gun running business.

"Good evening Mr Lou." The group answered politely, as Mr Lou sat down.

"As you already know my friends, it's another assignment. This one, unlike the others, is not for profit!" Mr Lou replied softly, his voice sounding strange. Mr Lou laid out a plan of a strange looking building on the table, as the unit gathered round to look at it.

"I give up what is it?" Cody said curiously.

"Some type of lab. Research I guess?" Steve replied distantly, as he study the small rooms interlocked with doors.

"You're close Mr Roberts it is a lab, but not for research, just production." Mr Lou spat out.

"Do they owe you money?" Sukai asked puzzled by Lou's anger.

"No, they don't. What they have done is sullied my name causing me shame!" Mr Lou angrily spat out, as the unit sat there mystified. "They used me to arrange the delivery of certain items, stolen from several governments to their laboratory in Turkey. It implicates me in this murderous adventure at playing God!"

"What are they making there?" Ali asked surprised by Mr Lou's loss of control.

"They're making Biological weapons my friend, and I hate to think where they're going to use them!" Mr Lou replied, worried at the consequences of being connected to these people.

"Who are they anyway?" Steve asked, disgusted that anyone would make such vile weapons.

"My source tells me, that they are a group of Arab terrorists, backed and financed by the Iranians." Mr Lou answered watching Ali.

"I wouldn't care if it was my childhood friends, Mr Lou. Anyone making these weapons is insane." Ali answered, getting a nod from Lou.

"I will be paying for this mission myself gentlemen. I want the place and its contents completely destroyed!" Mr Lou ordered, showing even a gun runner had some morals.

"No Mr Lou, this one is on us. Just arrange papers and supplies, we'll take care of this situation as a favour to you." Ali replied, feeling at last they had a decent mission to carry out.

"Thank you, my friends, I will not forget this gesture," Lou answered his eyes misty with gratitude, before turning and leaving the group to study the plans. 'This operation will not be easy' Steve thought, as he and Ali studied the facilities defences supplied by Mr Lou. Cody, Aaron and Sukai, seeing they weren't needed, had left them to work out the mission, while they went out with Lily, to meet a couple of her friends.

"Most of this complex is underground, looks like it used to be some sort of ammo bunker?" Steve put forward, remembering the bunker in Vietnam where he had to lower the explosives in.

"You could be right Steve. The plan indicates it's been there on the coast for over twenty years until this group purchased it supposedly for storage."

"It does give me an idea though, as there seems only one way in and out."

"What's the idea?"

"Well we don't want anything in there to escape, seems the best idea would be to burn it out," Steve suggested, not wanting to think about the people who would be in there at the time.

"Well we can't drop a Napalm bomb, it wouldn't penetrate the concrete roof!"

"I was thinking of maybe flooding it with an accelerant, then igniting it from a safe distance," Steve replied.

"That would take a lot of fuel, where do we get it?"

"That's the easy part we just steal a fuel tanker. The hard part is making sure no one stops us." Steve smiled studying the perimeter fence and guard post that protected the approach.

"We could do it at night that would cut down on casualties."

"Sounds good Ali, but I've no time for anyone who is working on Bioweapons. I've done some terrible things Ali, but never deliberately against civilians, like these type of weapon will." Steve replied, sensing what Ali was thinking.

Calling it a night Steve left, leaving Ali sitting there. Into the early hours, Ali studied the plan, looking for an alternative idea. Defeated, he realised Steve's plan was the only one that would eliminate all the missions targets in one foul swoop.

Walking home that night, Ali sadly came to the conclusion that he'd had enough, he wanted out of this unending cycle of death.

'This is my last Op's, I'll tell the others when it's finished.' Ali told himself, as he entered his hotel walking slowly to his room.

TURKEY - THE COMPLEX

Lying motionless in the tree line above the complex Ali and Steve, both wearing killer suits, studied the target through their binoculars. There were two guards at the front gate, two hundred metres from the bunker, plus two mobile guards. At the bunker itself, there were two more, one either side of the large steel entry doors, in concrete pillboxes.

"There's no telling what security they have inside Ali. When we do this, we'd better make sure it's done fast."

"I counted at least thirty personnel in there today. I'd say most are security they can't have that many scientists working on a project like this?" Ali replied quietly, a feeling of uneasiness coming over him.

"There's something about the guards too Ali, they're too good for militia. Look at the way they constantly watch the area around them. I'd hazard a guess and say they're soldiers and well trained."

"Your right and there's another thing I nearly missed. They're not stopping to pray like I do Steve, which means they're not Muslims, which the Iranians backed terrorists are!" Ali exclaimed, his gut telling him something was wrong.

"Do you want to scrub the mission?"

"No, it doesn't matter who's in there, we have to stop what they're doing. I'd just like to know what's going on that's all." Ali replied, sensing danger in this operation.

Arriving back to a small house they'd rented, Ali went over the information he and Steve had collected about the target.

"Well, who the hell are they, if they're not this Iranian group?" Cody asked perplexed.

"We're not sure? I rang Mr Lou who too knows nothing about this development." Ali replied neutrally.

"Does it really matter who it is? I think they must be stopped!" Sukai said voicing his opinion.

"Okay, then we'll go in tomorrow night when only the six guards are there, just be careful!" Ali replied going over the plan once more. As they all sat there working on the operation, Ali returned to the subject of the people there.

"It might be wise to take one person from the complex alive, to find out what's going on?" Ali suggested his guts still in knots.

"That's dangerous, but it could be done," Steve replied as it was his job to knock out the six guards.

"Then do it, Steve, my guts tells me we have to know!" Ali exclaimed sounding a bit over the top.

"As long as it keeps your guts are happy." Cody smiled at Ali's superstition, making everyone laugh.

"Get some sleep, you disbelievers. It's going to be a big night." Ali replied smiling, as they all turned in.

THE SURPRISE

Cody and Sukai walked up the road towards the fuel storage depot dressed in overalls and carrying toolboxes, as the guard on the gate fought off sleep.

"What is the problem?" he asked in Turkish, seeing the toolbox.

"There's no problem now!" Sukai said in English, pulling a submachine gun from his toolbox, as the guard's eyes opened wide. Quickly tying up the guard, Cody and Sukai removed all the keys from the rack, before searching the depot for a fuel truck. Finding a tanker, they made sure it was full before they drove cautiously towards the complex.

At the complex Steve moved creped forward, covering the distance between the guard post and the tree line without being seen. It was a moonlit night, allowing Steve to move in silently through the undergrowth, just a shadow to the untrained eye. The two mobile guards had been easy as he and Ali only had to wait till they passed. The fixed gate guards would be a lot harder. Steve inched forward towards the first gate guard, when he became agitated, scanning the surrounding ground searching, as he spoke into his radio.

'Bloody hell' Steve said to himself, he had never been spotted before, but this guy had sensed his approach somehow and it had unnerved him. Having no time left and fearing discovery Steve fired his silenced pistol twice into the guard who had spotted him, then twice into the second guard. The first went straight down, but the second leapt for Steve bringing him down painfully, before trying to draw his knife and finish him. Too shocked to think, Steve grappled with the soldier, until he suddenly went limp. Struggling up, Steve saw Ali cleaning his knife having finished off the guard, before leaning in next to Steve's ear.

"You're losing your touch!" He smiled pointing towards the complex as they moved off.

The experience at the guardhouse had shaken Steve more than Ali realised. Never before had someone got the drop on him. As the two lookout positions near the entrance came into view, Steve moved with more caution hoping this time to approach unseen. Once he'd closed the distance to the entrance another problem arose. The observation windows were a good three metres above the ground. This forced Steve to carefully scale the wall under one window, while watching the adjoining window.

Pulling his silenced pistol from his webbing, Steve slowly edged his way up beside the left window. Taking aim, he looked inside, firing instantly, when the guards head came into view. Climbing in through the window and checking the adjoining hallway, Steve hurriedly closed in on the other guard station. Firing as he entered, the guard dropped noiselessly, and Steve realised too late, that he'd failed to take a prisoner.

Signalling to Ali that the area was secure Steve went back to the front door and opened it just enough to squeeze through before finding a spot in the dark from which to watch the door. Meanwhile, Ali had radioed Cody to bring the tanker in.

"Did you keep one alive?" Ali asked Steve softly, watching the door.

"No sorry Ali, I couldn't take the chance, they were too alert!"

"We were lucky the guards at the gate didn't contact these guards but tried to raise the mobile ones instead, or they'd have been ready for us," Ali replied, showing Steve he was worried by the guard at the gate spotting them.

"Your right, whoever these guys are, they're good!" Steve replied, knowing they'd been lucky.

Inside the complex, unaware of what was going on outside, Rubin and his lab partner Joseph sweating heavily sealed in their airtight suits. Moving to the workstation, they manoeuvred the robotic arms, in the sealed room, placing the harvest of death into the small vial. Ten more times they carried out this exercise until all the deadly harvest had been loaded before the eleven containers were automatically sealed.

"That's all of it, Rubin!"

"Good work Joseph! Now raise the temperature and destroy all the cultures used here to breed these disgusting viruses." Rubin replied, smiling for the first time in ages.

For over a year Joseph and Rubin had been breeding these doomsday viruses perfecting them into weapons. All so someone, somewhere, could hold them over their enemies head, or worse release them. Both scientists were the leaders in biological research in Israel. They had been forced to travel to Turkey, to develop these weapons for the so-called benefit of their country.

"Why Turkey?" Rubin had asked the Army Captain in charge of this assignment, as he was secretly brought here, along with Joseph.

"We set it up, so everyone thinks the Iranians are doing research here. Anything goes wrong, and they'll get the blame!" the Captain had explained smiling, as the two scientists took up residence. For over a year neither man had left this complex, or made a single phone call, such was the secrecy of the project. Tired of the forced detainment, and the ugliness of what they were doing, both men had made a decision to stop. At the start of the day both men had met and put their plan into operation, quietly and efficiently destroying all research and materials, leaving nothing except these eleven vials.

"They're going to be mad Rubin!" Joseph whispered nervously, as he raised the temperature right into the red, as lights flashed on the controls boards above them.

"They have these vials my friend, and that is too much as far as I'm concerned!"

Tucking the vials into a sealed and cushioned briefcase, the men changed out of their Bio suits and started walking towards the front entrance.

"You know the guards won't let us out!" Joseph said nervously as they walked up the final ramp.

"I don't care. They can ring their superiors and get them out of bed, or I'll destroy these last vials!" Rubin replied, meaning it, as the guard post came into sight.

"My God!" Joseph gasped as they saw the body of the first guard shot through the head, lying in a pool of blood. Moving to the second post, they found the guard dead as well.

"These men were paratroops. Whoever did this knew what they were doing." Rubin whispered, looking out the window and seeing the tanker backing up to the door.

"Rubin they're going to torch the whole place!" Joseph stammered fear in his eyes at being burnt alive.

"Well, they don't know we're here. Let's see if we can slip by them." Rubin answered, walking slowly for the front door. Coming up to the door the two scientists found a large pipe had been laid and four men were standing near the tanker, trying to get the pump to work.

"Run for the trees!" Rubin whispered to Joseph, as both men exited the complex unnoticed by the four men.

When the tanker had arrived, Cody and Sukai quickly backed the tanker towards the door finding that its width was too great to reach the actual doors.

"We'll run the hoses the remaining distance!" Cody suggested, as Ali joined them, Steve keeping guard. When the hoses had been laid Cody realised he didn't know how to get the pump to work. Looking at Ali and Sukai for advice both raised their hands indicating neither knew how it worked either. Signalling to Steve who headed over, they explained the situation.

"Just open the tap, it'll flow downhill" Steve smiled in the darkness, at the stupidity of them all standing there trying to work it out.

Up in the tree line Aaron, who had been left to watch for approaching vehicles turned his night sight vision glasses towards the complex watching his four friends standing at the rear of the truck. 'What the hell are they doing?' Aaron said to himself as movement behind them caught his eyes.

"Behind you!" Aaron yelled into his radio, wondering who the two men in white were, as Steve swung around opening fire.

At the back of the truck, Aarons radio call erupted into each mans headset making them all turn, but Steve was by far the fastest, cutting down the running men.

"Where the hell did they come from?" Ali yelled.

"I don't know. There shouldn't be anyone else here, we did a head count!" Steve answered, moving cautiously towards the two men. Turning them over carefully, Steve found one to be dead, but the other who had been shot twice was still alive. Clamping his hand over the wounds, Steve yelled for Cody to bring a first aid kit over.

"Fix him up we'll take him with us. And grab the briefcase!" Ali yelled angrily, knowing he was going against their usual rule of leaving no prisoners.

"What the hell for?" Cody asked wanting to go.

"I want to know what went on here, there's something wrong!" Ali replied before Aaron drove into the complex and they all loaded up and left. An hour later, the timing device did its job, igniting fuel and with a loud whoosh, the complex disintegrated into a million burning fragments.

Four hours later, Rubin awoke feeling clammy. Touching his stomach, he screamed in agony pulling back his hand from his stomach to stop the pain.

"We've given you something for the pain, but it will take a little time to take effect," Ali said in Arabic as the mysterious man lay there. "What is your name?" Ali asked again in Arabic, but still, the man looked at him vaguely.

"I don't think he understands you, Ali!" Aaron whispered, watching the exchange.

"You speak English?" Rubin answered, with his thick Jewish accent as the unit members all stared back shocked.

"What is a Jew doing working with the Iranians?" Ali asked sternly, thinking the man a traitor.

"I work for my government, not the Iranians. The Army was using the Iranians as cover." Rubin replied, knowing this attack was meant for the Arabs.

"You bloody idiots. We thought the Arabs were making Bioweapons!" Cody yelled angrily.

"It was wrong for us to do it too," Rubin answered, before telling them his story, up until when they shot him.

"So this briefcase contains what is left?" Ali asked after Rubin was finished, glad none of Steve's rounds had penetrated the case.

"Please, you must destroy it all!"

"It's what we came here for my friend," Ali answered sadly, as Rubin's eyes closed for the last time.

"What a stuff up!" Cody growled, sounding a little worried.

"Your right, I can't see the Israelis being too happy about this," Steve replied sorry for shooting the man.

"I'm not worried about the Israelis. I'm worried about what do we do with that shit!" Sukai asked sounding scared, his eyes locked on the case.

"It can't survive in heat, as we head back to the Capital we'll drop the vials into a sealed incinerator that should do the trick," Ali replied confidently.

"You sure that's the right thing to do?" Steve asked thinking.

"It's too dangerous to keep!" Cody barked, not sure anyone should have such power.

"I'm just saying someday it might come in handy," Steve answered, wanting to have leverage.

"We'll all sleep on it after we bury our friend here," Ali replied sadly, pondering the advantage of having a weapon like this one, as they wrapped Rubin in a blanket and carried him outside.

AT THE COMPLEX

"They can't have got too far?" Captain Lenca yelled angrily, surveying the damage to the complex.

"They certainly knew what they were doing." A plainclothes companion replied looking around the area.

"I don't understand how they overpowered our six men? They were some of the best men we have."

"I've been up to the tree line, there are signs that several people had been watching, and whoever they were, they all wore combat boots." Jacob, the plain clothed man, informed him.

"Not much to go on!"

"On the contrary, we know they're military and well trained. We know they had Intel on this complex, and they're ruthless. Cutting down Joseph and Rubin by the blood trail shows they usually take no prisoners."

"So this raid was to destroy only, not capture, then where's Rubin?" Lenca asked.

"Hopefully he's dead and lying somewhere in the forest. If they took him, by the loss of blood from his wounds, he would be a liability, so they'll try and question him quickly, before dumping him." Jacob answered sadly, thinking it a sad end for the scientist.

"I can't see it being the Iranians or Hezbollah, they're not good enough!"

"They must have been mercenaries, and very expensive, I'd say." Jacob put forward, writing down his thoughts.

"Have we any people watching the airports?"

"Yes, they'll photograph everyone leaving, for the next few days. Who knows, we might get a hit?" Jacob replied, ordering everyone to pack up and head home, this operation was truly blown.

TEL AVIV ISRAEL

"Welcome back Jacob, how bad is it?" Director David Samuels asked his best investigator in the Mossad.

"Total write-off and we lost two of our leading scientists in the process, plus six good paratroopers!"

"Well, I've got something to cheer you up." Samuels smiled, handing Jacob a file with the photographs of five men.

Reading the file from start to finish, Jacob took in all the information there before looking up, realising he'd been reading it in the director's office while the director sat there.

"God I'm sorry Sir."

"Forget it, Jacob. It's an interesting read isn't it?" Samuel remarked smiling at Jacob's concentration on the file.

"These could be the men we're looking for Sir, but where'd you get this information."

"The CIA sent it to us after we told them one of our camps had been hit by pros," Samuel answered.

"They are certainly capable, any proof they were the ones?"

"We matched two of them at Istanbul Airport three days after the attack! It's too much of a coincidence."

"Any idea where they went?"

"They both headed in different directions, one to England, the other to Russia. From there, they both went on to Singapore, that's where you and twenty of our best men are heading Jacob. Get them, and bring them back if possible!"

SINGAPORE

"I offer you my deepest apologies my friends, I had no idea it was the Israelis!" Mr Lou said sadly, knowing he too had been fooled.

"It wasn't your fault Sir. But I suspect their secret service, will be looking for us." Ali said a little worried.

"Do you think we should split up?" Cody asked sensing trouble.

"No, if they come for us, and I think they will, we're better off staying together!" Steve replied looking around the room.

"I think Mr Roberts is correct, and I for one will be glad to have you close. They will soon work out the Intel came from me, and I'm afraid your air flights, though different, will also bring them here to Singapore." Mr Lou admitted.

"Then let's prepare for the worst Mr Lou. Do you still have that house on Pulau Sakeng?" Ali asked.

"Yes, but its very isolated." Mr Lou answered, not wanting to leave Singapore.

"That will work for us my friend, there we can see them coming, here in Singapore we cannot!" Ali replied as the group hurried away into the night, to gather their belongings from their hotels and move to Mr Lou's home.

PULAU SAKENG

The Island of Pulau Sakeng lies just to the south of Singapore. Except for several warehouses and a large fish growing farm run by a small number of workers, it was deserted. Perched on the only high ground, on the southern end, sat an old fort. It was built in 1905 and used for guarding the sea approaches to Singapore. This was Mr Lou's home and hideout. No one knew how he'd come to purchase it or how much it cost to convert, but it was the ideal place to get away. Sheer cliffs surrounded it, with only one excess point, up a narrow easily defended road.

'It reminds me of home,' Steve thought, as he stared out to sea, remembering his house on the beach.

"I think we're wasting our time Steve. It's been over two months and no sign of the Jews yet!" Cody said breaking the silence, wanting Steve to reassure him.

"We'll know more when Sukai and Aaron get back," Steve said softly, still watching the approach road.

Two days ago Mr Lou, with his daughter Lily had for business reasons returned to Singapore. A major buyer of Mr Lou's equipment had come to town, and Mr Lou had made the decision to meet him. Sukai had volunteered to go with them just in case, even though Mr Lou had his own men there. Aaron had for two reasons also gone. One to keep an eye on Sukai, who was now madly in love with Lily, meaning he was not at his best. The second was to continually keep in touch with Ali, about what was happening.

It was close to six in the morning when Cody and Steve's night watch ended. They slowly crawled down from their position above Mr Lou's house, meeting three of Mr Lou's men, who took over their positions. Changing out of their killer suits, Cody and Steve showered and changed before heading to their rooms for a sleep, when Ali came into view.

"Aaron failed to contact me last night, and I can't raise anyone at Mr Lou's warehouse!" Ali informed them, his face showing a small frown.

"Could be just a problem with the phones" Cody replied, trying to bring some hope into the situation.

"I hope your right Cody, but I don't think so. Anyway get some sleep, I'll put Mr Lou's six men here all on lookout while you two sleep. I'll try to find out what's happening." Ali suggested as Steve and Cody wandered off to bed.

It was just after one in the afternoon when shouting erupted on the driveway, waking Steve from a troubled sleep. Glancing cautiously out his window Steve looked down the road and saw a car racing towards the house. Everyone grabbed a weapon and raced to their prearranged positions. As the car squealed to a stop, two of Mr Lou's men jumped from the vehicle, dragging Aaron out after them. Running downstairs Steve ran into the lounge area to find Aaron laying on a lounge with a gunshot wound to his leg.

"You're lucky Aaron it went right through," Ali told him, examining the wound, before changing the bandage and reapplying a new one.

"I don't feel lucky Ali! They got Sukai and the others!" Aaron sobbed, lapsing in and out of consciousness. With Lou's men's help, Aaron was carefully carried up to his bedroom, where hopefully he would recover. After this, they went back downstairs to talk to Mr Lou's men.

"Do either of you speak English?" Ali asked trying to keep calm.

"I do," One of Mr Lou's men answered, fear in his eyes.

"You're not in any trouble. I just want to know what happened." Ali asked softly, as the man a bit more confidently told them of the past days and what Aaron had told them.

When Mr Lou had returned to his warehouse to meet his client all had gone smoothly, and discussions on price, delivery and types of weapons had all been negotiated. By the second day, Mr Lou had successfully completed his business only needing to sign the contracts the following night. The problem was Mr Lou thought the discussions had gone too well, confiding to Lily and Sukai that something was wrong. Lily assured him he was just overreacting, but they all felt nervous. Unfortunately, Aaron who was on lookout duty on the roof at the time was unaware of Mr Lou's uneasiness, so he hadn't passed it on to Ali.

That night as they waited for Mr Lou's client to arrive and sign the contracts, Aaron again was on duty on the roof and was the first to notice the three cars approaching. Grabbing his radio, he quickly warned Sukai that unlike the other visit where the client had come in one car, this time there were several.

"It might be best for you and your father to move back," Sukai warned Lily, as he signalled to Mr Lou's men to take cover.

"It could just be his financial advisers have accompanied him for the contract signing!" Lily replied nervously picking up on Sukai's unease.

"No Sukai is right, something is wrong!" Mr Lou said solemnly before reaching out and touching his daughter's hand.

"Sukai take my daughter and leave immediately. If nothing is wrong, you can return." Mr Lou ordered, pushing both of them towards the rear of the factory, before returning to stand with his men. Sukai shepherding Lily towards the back door, warned Aaron of his movements. He then yelled to the two guards protecting the back entrance that they were approaching, as the lights went out. Turning a corner, his eyes adjusting to the dark, Sukai saw the back door wide open and the two guards dead beside it.

"Aaron, warn Mr Lou they've come through the back door!" Sukai screamed, into his radio as four black shapes came to life near the door.

"Get back Lily!" Sukai yelled, dragging her back behind some crates as the four black shapes open fired with their silenced pistols. Once around the corner with Lily, Sukai drew his own pistol, changing direction, cannoned into the surprised shadows. Opening fire, he dropped three of them in quick succession and forcing the fourth to skid sideways, jumping behind a crate for cover. Sukai was just about to finish him, when more shadows rushed through the back door, firing as they came. This forced him to retreat back towards Lily, who unfortunately wasn't there.

Lily seeing Sukai bravely attacking the intruders, and knowing she couldn't help him, turned and ran back towards the front of the warehouse, hoping to warn her father. Appearing from the rear of the factory, Lily screamed when she saw her father's body lying with most of his men. Surprised by the scream several shadows that were standing near her father turned at the noise and open fired, spraying the defenceless woman with death. Sukai, still hidden from view, saw Lily shot. Grounding to a halt, he stood frozen by her death.

His training told him that she was dead and to leave. His love for her held him there, as tears filled his eyes. He was just about to go to her, when a hand covered his mouth, pulling him backwards into a row of crates.

"She's gone my friend, we have to leave," Aaron whispered into his ear, dragging his lifeless friend further into the warehouse. Aaron sensing Sukai was recovering removed his hand, as Sukai cried silently, falling to the floor unable to go further.

"They hold both the front and the back doors Sukai. Our best chance is too thin them out a bit, then make a break for it!" Aaron whispered into Sukai's ear. Getting a nod from Sukai, Aaron drew his pistol and crept forward.

"Now I know how Steve felt!" Sukai cried softly, getting a nod from Aaron, as he watched behind them covering Aaron.

"Let's make them pay then shall we!" Aaron replied as he approached an intersection. Turning the corner, Aaron, his gun arm outstretched and ready to fire, went rigid as two shadows came into view. Twice Aaron's gun loudly barked dropping the two men, who moments ago were hunting them. A chug like noise in the darkness knocked Aaron from his feet, as a third shadow moved into sight. Stepping over Aaron, Sukai sent two rounds into the darkness in the general direction of the shooter, hearing a scream after the second shot, signalling a hit. He then dragged Aaron back around the corner.

Retreating a safe distance, Sukai wrapped a piece of rag over Aarons wound to stop the bleeding. Looking both ways making sure they were alone, Sukai made a decision. Pulling forward a large crate, he pushed Aaron behind it, as Aaron sensing what he was up to grabbed him.

"Stay with me Sukai, we can both hide till they're gone!"

"No my friend, without silencers they know where we are every time we fire. I'll lead them away, and then come back for you when it's safe." Sukai replied calmly, hugging his friend. Covering Aaron with another crate, Sukai slowly moved away, into the darkness.

Jacob stood near the rear door looking down at the three dead men.

"I thought these men were the best?"

"They are my friend. But so are the men we're after, remember that!" Captain Lenca replied, signalling to his men to remove the dead men.

"How many were there?" Jacob asked the surviving member of this squad.

"Just one Sir, Japanese I'd say. He came around the corner with a girl and seeing us, retreated back the way he'd come. We were about to give chase when he turned suddenly and dropped the other three members of my squad within the blink of an eye. Would've had me too if I hadn't taken cover!"

"He's right Sir. My second squad entered while he was shooting. We didn't even get close to hitting him!" Sergeant Levi replied from behind Jacob.

"So where is he?" Jacob asked as a scream came from the front of the warehouse.

"Sir the front unit reports that all targets are down including a girl, who came from the rear." The radioman reported to Captain Lenca.

"Tell them one of the main targets is with the girl and to be careful," Lenca whispered to the private, who in turn radioed the front units. Jacob and his men were in the process of taking up positions behind a pile of crates near the rear door when two loud shots followed by two more echoed through the warehouse.

"Must be him, all our weapons are silenced." Sergeant Levi suggested, slightly impressed by their adversaries' survival.

"Sir, three more men are down!" the radioman reported sounding uncertain.

"Tell them to hunt in groups, no splitting up!" Captain Lenca replied angrily, getting edgy. Ten minutes passed, then without any warning, a silhouette glided around the corner and open fired on Jacob's position. Two men went down before anyone had time to react.

"Kill the bastard!" Jacob yelled, as his startled men open fire on the shadow, which instead of hiding, walked straight towards them, firing until his ammo was exhausted.

Who knows how many bullets hit him, as slowly he toppled backwards, hitting the ground. Running forward Jacob kicked his gun away and looked down at the dying man.

"You should not have attacked our base in Turkey, my friend!" Jacob said smugly, staring at the man whose mouth formed a smile.

"Shit we thought it was the Iranians," Sukai answered half smiling. Jacob and Captain Lenca looked at each other.

"Where are the others?" Captain Lenca asked, dismissing Sukai's answer.

"You don't have to look for them. After this, they'll come after you!" Sukai chuckled, seeing some of the shadows near him, look towards the back door expectantly.

"What happened to Professor Rubin from the complex in Turkey?"

Jacob asked, believing this man was telling the truth.

"It was an accident; he and another man ran out of the complex and startled us. They were both shot, Rubin died later. It was lucky we didn't hit the vials he had in his briefcase!" Sukai replied weakly, coughing up blood as Jacob and Lenca faces went white.

"How many vials?" Jacob screamed, getting on his knees to hear the answer.

"I loved Lily, that girl you shot," Sukai replied with tears in his eyes, as he coughed once more and died, leaving Jacobs kneeling there, staring at the dead man. Racing back to the Israeli embassy with their dead and wounded, Jacobs took stock of what they'd learnt.

"Do you think he was telling the truth?" Captain Lenca asked Jacob, as they sat with Sergeant Levi going over the raid.

"We set that complex up to implicate the Iranians by using Mr Lou as a middleman. I believe it worked better than we thought possible." Jacob answered sadly.

"What was in the vials the Jap was talking about?" Levi asked Jacobs, looked at Lenca.

"Let's just say, it'll be Israel's first priority from now on to get them back!" Lenca answered, not saying anymore.

"Yes, I'm afraid we will have to track down the remaining four men and eliminate them all!" Jacob replied sadly.

"We believe they're on Pulau Sakeng at Mr Lou's house. Why don't we go now?" Captain Lenca suggested.

"We have seven dead and one injured, that's nearly half our force. They were killed we believe, by one of these men. Do you really want to go after the other four, Captain?" Jacob's asked, getting agreement from Sergeant Levi.

"It won't matter Jacob, I think the Jap was right. I think they'll come after us." Lenca replied showing a bit of fear, wondering if they would use the vials against Israel.

LOU'S HOME

Ali, Steve and Cody sat quietly, as Mr Lou's man finished telling them what had happened, before leaving with the rest of Mr Lou's men.

"Sukai was a good man!" Cody said his eyes misting up, as he turned away to hide his emotion.

"What are we going to do about it?" Steve asked, angry at his friend's death, and wanting revenge.

"Nothing my friend's, absolutely nothing," Ali replied, looking at the others.

"You're kidding, aren't you?" Steve answered, surprised.

"There's been enough killing Steve. They'll expect us to come after them; we'll let them think it. Our best course of action now is to disappear. Once Aaron is well enough to travel, I'm going!" Ali replied, staring at Steve.

"Then what do we do?" Cody asked softly, still upset at Sukai's death.

"Unfortunately it will be hard, we will all have to separate and disappear, no contact with each other," Ali told them, as the others dejectedly took in this news.

"What if they come after us again?" Cody asked.

"I've no doubt they will, the Jews are relentless in pursuing their enemies, and we must be at the top. Our best chance is to use our Swiss bank accounts set up by Mr Lou and nothing else. When we leave here, it's better for all of us to travel to areas where we can mix in and stay off the radar!" Ali said, knowing they would all miss each other.

"No contact at all?" Steve inquired, hoping there'd be something.

"I have a secure number where Julie and my son are staying. You can ring there once you get settled. After a month I'll be gone from there, so ring before then. I'll then give you another mobile number, so as I travel, you can always get me." Ali replied sadly. He too would miss them.

"Same rules, ring four times hang up and ring again?" Steve asked, feeling a bit better at least having something.

"Maybe in a few years, things will get better?" Cody put forward, trying to lift their spirits.

"Maybe," Ali replied distantly. Steve looked into Ali's eyes and saw the lie.

THE DEPARTURE

Gathering up their gear the four unit members sat quietly on the ferry, crossing back to Singapore for their flights out. It would be the last time the group would be together, and even though the crossing was made in silence, the men felt at ease. As the ferry docked the four got up and with a brief parting nod and a quick handshake, they all shuffled off the boat. Only Cody and Aaron travelled together. They had both decided to stay in Scotland for a while until Aaron had fully recovered. They'd then decide what to do about living out their lives.

Unlike the others, Steve didn't head for the airport. Instead, he wandered down to the docks and boarded a small freighter. It would take him to Darwin in the top end of Australia, where he could disembark no questions asked.

Settling down in his cabin, Steve stared absentmindedly out the small window, as Singapore harbour slowly glided past, along with his life, pondering what to do. He couldn't go near his family, it would only endanger them. No, he thought, the most he could do was to call them occasionally and even then only for a short time.

"God I miss you, Michelle!" Steve cried out, tears filling his eyes, wanting to at least see his two girls, knowing he wouldn't. Pulling a pistol from his bag, he placed the barrel in his mouth. For five minutes Steve sat there silently, the reassuring metallic taste of the gun barrel against his tongue. Taking up the slack on the trigger, he thought how good it would be to see Michelle again and end the pain. Out of the corner of his eye, across the cabin, Steve saw his reflection in the bathroom mirror, and for a split second, he thought he heard his wife's voice.

"Don't let them win Steve." Michelle's voice whispered in his mind, tantalizing him as the pistol slowly dropped from his hand.

"I'll always love you my darling." Steve sobbed, as he rolled in a ball on his bed, not leaving the cabin until Darwin came into sight five days later.

WASHINGTON DC PRESENT DAY

The President sat silently through John Wilson's brief about the Special assault team, created by the CIA. As the implications washed over him, he wished to God that it was another President who had to deal with this mess, not him. John Wilson finished, sat down, his eyes never leaving Brooks, as he sat emotionally void as if he was waiting for a bus.

"What have you got to say for yourself Brooks?" the President asked, bringing Brooks out of his trance.

"Nothing Mr President! His whole story is based on a supposed confession from a terrorist, with a few loose facts thrown in for fun. I deny all involvement!" Brooks replied, looking every bit an innocent man.

"I beg to differ, Don. I think you're in it up to your ears!" Wilson growled, getting a little fed up with Brooks lying.

"Very well, I suggest we put it before a Senate committee, they can decide impartially who's guilty here and who's not!" the President informed them, hoping this move would keep any fallout from his Presidency.

"I think that's the best solution Sir, and I look forward to clearing my name," Brooks replied happily, before excusing himself, leaving John and the President staring after him.

"I hope your right about this John. He seems rather confident that he's in the clear?" the President pointed out.

"There's too much evidence Sir, but I've got to admit he's a cold son of a bitch!" John replied, shaking his head at Brook's bravado.

Don Brook, head of the CIA strode confidently down the hallway from the Oval office radiating power, giving the impression that nothing on earth could touch him. Turning into a restroom at the end of the corridor, Don locked the door then approached the first toilet. Crumbling to his knees, he was violently sick. Flushing the toilet and shaking uncontrollably Don got up and staggered to a hand basin where he washed his mouth out. Spraying water onto his face, he again collapsed back onto the floor, rolling up into a ball and sobbing. 'I should have killed them all in Karachi,' Don chastised himself, punching the wall next to the cubicle. After several minutes had passed, he slowly pulled himself together. Grabbing his mobile phone, he rang a programmed number.

"Black here, what's the problem, Brooks?"

"You blackmailing bastard! Your mistakes have put both our heads on the block!"

"Spit it out, what's wrong?" Black asked, knowing something drastic must have happened to rattle Brooks this much. For the next twenty minutes, Brooks ranted and raved into the phone giving Black a full description of what had happened. In the end, he was practically begging Black for help, something which scared Black more than threats.

"Don, for God sake, pull yourself together. There's no way I'll let Ali reach that Senate committee. Go home now and let me take care of it!"

"Are you sure Black, you know Wilson and his FBI goons are going to keep him well hidden."

"I've got friends there who like money, don't worry, it's my head too, remember," Black answered, hanging up.

Getting to his feet feeling better, Brooks looked in the mirror and combed his hair into place. Putting a couple of mints into his mouth Brooks composed himself. Leaving the restroom, he walked confidently through the White House, even managing along the way to smile at the Secret Service agents, guarding the front door. 'I'll be okay,' Brook thought, feeling better, as his driver brought his car to the front door.

Black, after hanging up, stood staring at the phone for several seconds, before throwing it against the wall angrily.

"God I hate that little scumbag!" Black screamed as the ten men in front of him sniggered, until his face focused on them, bringing the room to a deadly silence. Black outlined what had happened stressing that if Brooks fell, they all would get the chop. This encouraged an immediate discussion of a plan of action to remedy the situation. After three hours of debate, a rough operation for killing Ali began to take shape.

With minor changes, at last Black agreed that it was good enough. The only thing they now needed was the location. That he imagined could be bought easily from one of the many underpaid FBI personnel he knew, who were always short of funds.

Two weeks after the President's meeting with Brooks and Wilson, three black vans entered the grounds of what could only be described as a mansion. Stepping out of one of the vehicle, five men, one shackled, quickly climbed the stairs to the front door and swiftly entered. Once inside and a sweep of the house had been carried out, the group walked up the curved staircase to the first floor. Here the four agents pushed their charge into what was once the main bedroom, locking all doors and windows to the room. Free of their prisoner, Agent Chandler and his team looked out over the grounds impressed by the house and its surrounding property.

"How'd the FBI ever afford to put us up here?" Nigel asked as they all sat themselves down on the expensive furniture that filled the room.

"Didn't you hear, it was seized from some crime family involved with drug trafficking," Bill replied not caring about the house. All he wanted was to go home.

"What are we doing here, with that joker upstairs, that's what I'd like to know?" Ian said rubbing his leg, which was still bandaged from the shooting.

"Didn't you hear, we're heroes now, and since we caught him, they thought it only fair, that we escort him to the trial!" Bill answered sarcastically.

"It's not a trial. It's a Senate committee hearing. After that, he'll be taken care of!" Nigel explained, not impressed with the assignment.

"Waste of time, what difference can his bullshit make. He shot Ian and should rot in jail." Allan replied. He was totally changed from that innocent agent before the shooting.

"I don't know about that, I heard some agents saying Don Brooks could lose his job," Nigel told them.

"Shit he's the head of the CIA isn't he? Bet he's not happy about that." Bill answered, wondering just how much their friend upstairs knew.

"There's something else too!" Ian said hesitantly before continuing. "When I'm near the prisoner, I've noticed he can't look me in the eye as if he's upset that he shot me. Why do you think that is?" Ian asked as the others sat there realising there was more here than met the eye.

"How much backup have we got here?" Bill inquired, looking towards the window.

"Ten Special Op group men are patrolling the perimeter, plus we four inside, we're pretty safe," Nigel assured them, as he too looked towards the windows.

"How about we go talk to our guest! I know we're not supposed to, but I think this joker knows something." Bill whispered as everyone looked towards Nigel.

"Can't hurt and who's to know?" Nigel smiled, as they walked towards the staircase, orders forgotten.

Nigel's team had just reached the staircase when a muffled bang came from the front of the house, out near the front gate, making everyone crouch down. Moving quickly to the windows, Bill and the others scanned the grounds for trouble. Nigel grabbed his radio and asked the FBI agents outside what was going on. An ugly silence settled over the agents, as Nigel's team watched the Special Operations men run to the front gate, before suddenly slowing down and turning around, going back to their assigned areas.

"Relax men the gate guard just radioed in and reported a truck had blown a tyre opposite the gate!" Nigel chuckled, as his team visibly relaxed.

"Shit I thought we were for it!" Bill replied laughing, as the others joined in. Moving up the stairs and unlocking the prisoner's door, Nigel and the others filed in to see their prisoner looking out the window, trying not to show himself.

"Relax camel jockey it was just a truck tyre, most probably made in your country!" Bill said sarcastically as the others smiled.

"Maybe, maybe not," Ali replied distantly staring at the front gate.

"What else would it be?" Nigel scoffed thinking their prisoner was getting a case of the nerves.

"They don't spend much on training you guys do they?" Ali replied, turning around and moving away from the window, as the agents lost their smiles.

"Well if you're so clever what do you think just happened?" Bill asked angrily, having the great urge to flatten this Arab smartarse.

"Could be nothing, or someone might have wanted to know how many men were out there!"

"Your names Ali isn't it, can you tell us what's going on?" Nigel asked politely hoping to defuse the situation.

"I'm sorry I can't Agent Chandler, but I warn you all, there's no way I'll get to that Senate Committee alive!"

"You're full of shit!" Bill laughed, watching Ali closely hoping he'd take a swing. Instead, he laughed too.

"Look I mean none of you any harm, and I apologise for shooting you, my friend," Ali said looking at Ian before continuing. "I thought they'd send a Swat unit not four untrained agents. That was why I shot low."

"You wanted to get caught?" Bill asked worried by the implications.

"Yes my friend, there's more going on here than you could possibly imagine."

"I'll ring Headquarters and tell them what you said," Nigel replied his eyes watching Ali closely.

"They won't believe you Agent Chandler; they'll think I'm just playing with you."

"And that could be true!" Bill replied watching Ali, as Nigel led his team outside onto the landing.

"And don't go outside when it starts, or you'll all die!" Ali yelled sharply, as the door lock clicked behind them.

Downstairs the agents went back to their chairs while Nigel rang Headquarters. He told them of his talk with Ali, before coming into the room and sitting down with an ugly expression on his face.

"Just as he said, they're convinced he's just playing with us."

"I believe him" Allan answered honestly, getting a nod from Ian and then Bill.

"Then what do we do?" Nigel said a bit scared.

"Like he said, stay inside and wait. Remember, he could have made it all up just to scare us." Bill suggested.

"Well, Shit! It's working!" Nigel smiled nervously, looking at his team and feeling the unease.

Out on the main road the truck driver with the assistance of the gate guard had by now changed his tyre and gotten back into his vehicle. Waving goodbye and yelling his thanks to the guard, he drove off. Turning the next corner, he pulled out his mobile phone.

"Black here!" a voice answered on the first ring.

"Its Doug, you were right, they've moved in."

"How many?"

"Looks like ten around the house and the original four agents and our friend inside."

"Good work, get back here, we'll hit them tomorrow night!" Black told him, before cutting the connection. Doug drove on steadily, grinning to himself. 'These Feds won't know what hit them!' He laughed to himself, as turning the corner, he joined the freeway, heading back to base. Five cars back, a motorbike also joined the freeway and cautiously followed him at a distance.

THE ATTACK

Black was taking no chances tonight. He had ten of his own men, plus another fifteen men he'd hired, on 'no questions asked' deal. All ex-military, they knew their stuff, and Black had drummed it into them, no prisoners, no witnesses, no matter what. The attack would be simple, at three in the morning, two vehicles with ten men each would hit the gate and the rear wall behind the house at the same time. Picking off the ten-man detail outside, they'd then hit the house.

Black with five men of his unit would be at his base to monitor the FBI and local enforcement radios, to warn of any interference.

The following night at three in the morning, when the FBI guards were just managing to stay awake, two trucks drove sedately towards their objectives. The men inside silently and professionally, brought their weapons to ready releasing the safety's, as the targets came into sight.

"It's going to be a piece of cake!" Doug said to the driver with a chuckle, as he prepared to take out the gate guard. The night turned into day, as two bright lights ignited on the hills above him. The first, travelled towards them at a terrifying speed, the other headed towards the rear of the house.

"What the!" was all Doug got out, as the rocket hit the front of the truck. Penetrating the cabin, it turned the truck and the ten men inside, into a fireball. At the rear, the same scenario played out as over the countryside two massive explosions rocked the area.

Even though the truck was a good fifty metres from the front gate the guard there was thrown backwards by the explosion and lay alive but unconscious on the driveway. The Special operations group dived to the ground. Fear of the unknown gripped them all, as sending out a mayday, they checked for casualties. Nigel's team, who had been either asleep or watching TV, dropped to the floor and crawled to cover, only lifting their heads after the explosions had died down.

The FBI's special unit members hastily pulled themselves together, and broke into two groups, one heading for the rear while the other checked the front gate. Radioing Nigel's group, the Captain of the Special Op's Group told them to defend the house, while they checked out the explosions. In the dark, Nigel's team lay on the first-floor landing, covering the only staircase. They waited for the coming attack with dread, not sure what to expect.

Ten minutes went by as the sound of sirens both Police and Fire Brigade filled the air. The all-clear was then sounded from the agents outside.

"What the hell happened?" Nigel asked the Captain.

"We're not sure? We've got two truckloads of men, burnt alive near the front and back of the house. They were heavily armed too!" The Captain answered, sounding pleased with the situation. Nigel then told the others what had happened.

"Doesn't make sense?" Bill murmured distantly, before suddenly turning towards the prisoner's room. Running forward, he kicked down the door, looking cautiously around the room.

"Shit he's gone, Nigel!" Bill exclaimed, sounding not too unhappy.

"I don't get it. If he's gone, who are all the dead guys, and who killed them?" Ian asked as the agents hurried downstairs to help the agents outside.

BLACKS BASE

"What's going on? Have you managed to contact them?" Black yelled at one of his men on the radio.

"Nothing Sir, they cut out just as they were about to launch their attack!" The radio operated replied, a little frightened of Black in his present mood.

"I've got something Sir" Shouted the man monitoring the FBI.

"Out with it, Eddie" Black ordered, fearing the worst.

"The FBI agents are reporting two explosions and two trucks on fire!" Eddie replied as the room went quiet.

"It's a setup!" Black whispered, sadly knowing it wasn't over, as an automatic weapon opened up on Black and his men.

Steve walked into the room checking each man, finding Black and one of the men still alive. Pulling his knife out, he cut the throat of the last unfortunate Eddie, before turning to Black. Spitting blood, Black crawled to a chair and pulled himself to a sitting position before looking up defiantly at Steve.

"Well done, I should've known Ali was caught too easily."

"It's taken us a long time to find you, Black!"

"Won't bring your wife or your friends back will it?" Black chuckled, seeing his words hit home, as Steve's knife cut into his leg making him scream.

"Don't worry Black I won't kill you just yet, we've got the whole night ahead of us," Steve whispered in Blacks ear, as he handcuffed Black to the chair, putting a hood over his head. Twenty minutes later, Ali, Cody and Aaron strolled in, coming up and each, in turn, shaking Steve's hand.

"How'd it go at the house?" Steve asked drained by the night's work.

"As to plan, not one of the bastards got out. Where's Black?" Cody asked death in his eyes.

"He bled out. I didn't realise I'd shot him fatally, a pity!" Steve answered, with a faraway look.

"Its most probably better than what we'd planned for him. It would have made the next phase harder." Ali added, glad Steve hadn't had too much time with him.

"About the next stage are you sure it's necessary?" Aaron asked.

"We've got to get them off our backs, killing Brooks won't do that!" Steve answered.

"When's the big march?" Cody asked softly not sure of this plan.

"In about a month's time, we'll see how it goes till then, okay!" Ali suggested, getting agreement from them all.

"Okay, Steve have you got that phone?" Ali asked, as Steve brought it out and tossed it to him.

Back at the house, Nigel was having an uncomfortable talk with his superiors when his phone started ringing.

"Agent Chandler" Nigel answered, glad for a reprieve from his boss.

"Hello Agent Chandler, it's your former prisoner Ali here," Ali answered, hearing the intake of breath from Nigel.

"Ali you shouldn't have left without saying goodbye!" Nigel replied loudly, as his boss and other agents hurriedly grabbed phones, listening in and having the call traced.

"Bloody hell Nigel, I hope I can call you Nigel. You're going to have to practice phone procedure more if you're going to try and keep someone on the line."

"Did you ring for some reason, rather than to insult me?" Nigel replied, his anger just contained, as agents around him smiled at his embarrassment.

"Yes the dead men in the trucks were there to kill me, and all of you in the process. The group I belong to, have been following me on a tracking device I had embedded in my skin."

"You set this all up didn't you?" Nigel replied coldly.

"You are correct Nigel. We figured it was the only way to flush them out in the open, even though I didn't expect to get shot or injure your friend Ian in the process."

"So where are you now?"

"At the enemies' base finishing off the rest of the vermin, who work for Brooks!"

"Look I know you've got your reasons Ali, but this is going to get you killed."

"Many have tried already Nigel, I can assure you," Ali replied, before continuing. "I will leave this phone on so you can find this place. We want to talk to the President. We want him to get the CIA and the Israelis off our backs!" Ali then dropped the phone leaving with his team.

"What the hell's going on here?" Nigel's boss Brett asked, looking confused.

"I think we've been used Sir, to take care of an old grudge," Nigel replied distantly, as the boss stood there thinking.

"I've got the address, Sir! "Allan yelled, from a phone at the far end of the room.

"Nigel, gather your men, you're coming with us. For some strange reason, this sicko bastard likes you, and he may ring again!" Brett explained, as he gathered as many agents as he could, and rushed to the phone traces position.

THE WET SHOP

Looking around the room after Swat had cleared the building, Nigel examined the crime scene and was impressed by the accuracy of the one man they presume, had taken down the six armed men in this room

"These guys don't muck around do they?" Bill said, also studying the site as Allan ran into the room.

"God, what went on here Nigel? The back rooms are full of military equipment and files on foreigners and Americans alike." Allan murmured, spooked by this place.

"It seems we've found a CIA wet shop!" Brett answered sadly, studying some of the folders he had found in the next room.

"What's a wet shop?" Ian asked from the door.

"It's a place the CIA use for their dirty work," Bill answered grimly.

"Did you find anything, useful boss?" Nigel asked, seeing the downcast look on his bosses face.

"Yes, unfortunately. This file is on contacts in the FBI gentlemen. It might be best to seal this room until the Justice Department can investigate." Brett replied, apparently he'd recognised some of those names.

THE WHITE HOUSE

John Wilson and Don Brooks again stood in the Oval Office with the President, both having different opinions on why they were there. Don thought Black had been successful and his troubles were over, John, on the other hand, knew he hadn't been.

"What's going on John?" the President asked with a sense of foreboding.

"It's not good Mr President. Three nights ago, a group tried to assassinate our witness. I have a full news blackout on what happened, Sir." John replied trying to hide what was coming from Don, for as long as possible.

"Has that got something to do with those gas explosions to the east?" the President asked.

"Yes, Mr President."

"Is your witness okay?" Brooks asked smugly, knowing nothing of what was going on and thinking Black had pulled it off.

"Yes he is, but the raiding party of twenty men were completely wiped out!" John replied looking straight at Brooks, seeing the first cracks appearing on his blank face.

"Any casualties?" the President asked, looking shocked.

"No Sir. The FBI did nothing, Sir, they were killed we believe by Ali Moustaffer's unit" Brooks broke down completely.

"You're lying Wilson! Most of them are dead by now, they couldn't be out there!" He screamed, looking towards the window as if he expected them to come through it. The Presidents Secret Service men took station behind Brooks watching him closely.

"Settle down Don, for God's sake you're safe here!" the President shouted, disgusted by Brooks reaction.

"There's more Sir, and it's a lot worse" Wilson exclaimed. Even Brooks stopped babbling to listen. "After they killed the men at the safe house, they located the attackers base which we think was Ali's objective all along. We found six more dead there, including their leader, an ex-Major from Special Forces, named Black." John informed them, a little worried by Brook's appearance.

"You've got to protect me, Mr President!" Brooks sobbed, crumbling to the floor at the Presidents feet, as the Secret Service men came forward, and tried to pick him up.

"Summon the General Staff!" the President ordered before walking up and grabbing Brooks.

"You son of a bitch! Why are they doing this?"

"We tried to terminate them, but it all went wrong. Blacks men killed one of their wives instead." Brooks sobbed as the President let him go.

"My God, what have you done?" The President growled, disgusted at this once invincible man's behaviour.

THE GENERAL STAFF MEETING

When John Wilson walked into the emergency meeting the President had called, he was surprised to see Brooks sitting there silently in the corner.

"Sit down men!" the President ordered, bringing them up to speed on what had happened before asking for questions.

"Why call in the General Staff Sir? This is an internal police, and FBI matter isn't it?" an Admiral asked.

"We believe this group is a highly trained military unit Admiral, we may need some of our best operatives to corner them." the President replied solemnly.

"What do they want?" asked a General, making everyone turn his way.

"General Mosley, why are you here, you're retired aren't you?" the President asked, wondering what this old warrior was doing here.

"The Admiral and I were playing golf when your call came through. When he read out the names of the supposed terrorists, I recognised Steve Robert's name. He thought I might be useful." Mosley said smiling.

"Can you give us a rundown on this man General?" the President asked feeling at last something was going their way.

"Yes Sir, but you're not going to like it," Mosley replied as he told the gathered men and women what they were up against.

When the general had finished, Wilson got up and told what had happened at the Safehouse and later at Blacks base as the room became silent.

"Looks like age hasn't affected their skills," Mosley added.

"General, what were you saying about what they wanted?" Wilson asked.

"Well it's just they haven't killed anyone except their enemies, and it appears they want to meet with us." the General pointed out, glad they'd taken care of Brook's wet squad.

"They killed Americans on American soil General." John Wilson replied, getting a 'who cares' look from the General in return. The President looked at Mosley and was just about to speak when Wilson's phone started to ring. Slightly embarrassed, knowing whatever it was must be urgent, he took the call.

"Mr Wilson its Agent Chandler here. A Steve Roberts, one of Ali's unit members wants to talk with the President!" Nigel explained nervously.

"Well does he now!" John replied, before looking around the room, seeing everyone was watching him.

"What's the problem John?" the President asked as the whole room stared at Wilson.

"One of the terrorists wants to talk to you, Sir."

"Put him through on loudspeaker thank you." the President suggested a slight smile on his lips at the situation. The phone for several seconds crackled, as it was connected to the incoming call.

"Are you there Mr President?" Steve's voice came through loud and clear.

"Yes I am, but how do we know this is Steve Roberts?" the President asked, amused by the situation.

"Ask General Mosley. He knows me as the Ghost." Steve replied as everyone looked at Mosley.

"That's right. It's what the SAS called him." Mosley answered smiling, before continuing. "How are you Steve, I thought you retired and got married."

"Brooks killed my wife. He tried for me and got her instead!"

"I'm sorry Steve I didn't know," Mosley answered his anger clear, as he looked around the room for Brooks.

"Steve, everyone's sorry for what Brooks did, and he will be punished, but what you're doing now is wrong." The President informed him, treading a fine line in talking to a terrorist.

"All we want is to be left alone Sir. Give us a full pardon in writing and get the Israelis off our back and we will walk away!" Steve replied wanting it over.

"Why are the Israelis after you?" the President asked, the situation becoming more complicated by the minute.

"When we were freelancing we wiped out a Bioweapons lab in Turkey. It was sponsored by the Israelis Sir."

"That's not possible Mr Roberts. They signed a treaty with us when they became a State, not to make Bioweapons in exchange for our support!" the President said having read that document not too long ago.

"Was that the same treaty which banned them from making nuclear weapons, Sir?" Steve asked making several people smile and leaving the President fuming.

"We have much to discuss here Mr Roberts. If you could ring us back at the same time tomorrow, we will give you an answer." the President replied, slamming down the phone.

"Get the Israeli Ambassador here now and the rest of you wait here!" the President exploded before marching out of the room. As the others waited for the President's return, lunch was served to a subdued group. John Wilson, after eating, walked across the room, sitting down with General Mosley.

"Are they that good?"

"I've seen this guy in action John, if he's after you, he'll get you. Look at Black, how long did it take them to get him, and he's been in hiding."

"What do you think we should do?"

"Give them the pardon. They deserve it!" Mosley replied when John suddenly jumped.

"What's wrong John?" Mosley asked a little surprised.

"They knew you were here General, even though you're retired. They must be watching the building!"

THE AMBASSADOR

When Jacob Benin first received the call from the American President he smiled, thinking, at last, the Americans would hand over Ali Moustaffer. After all, his superior had made it clear, that that they wanted this man. Entering the White House, he received a cool reception, which surprised him. He knew something bad was coming. Entering the Oval Office diplomacy was forgotten as the Ambassador was pointed to a chair and told to sit and wait. This was something that had not happened before.

Without warning the President walked in, flanked by two secret servicemen, as Jacob started to stand the President signalled him to stay seated.

"Mr President," was all Jacob got out when the President cut him off.

"Mr Ambassador, would you explain why a terrorist that your country wants so badly, just told us he destroyed a Bioweapons lab you set up in Turkey!"

"It's a lie Mr President. We would never do that."

"Then why do your people want them so badly?" the President asked, as Jacob sat there thinking of an answer.

"My government has only informed me that he's responsible for the killing of two of our scientists Sir, which should be enough."

"Well, I want to know what their names were and what fields they worked in Mr Ambassador. You have until tomorrow morning to produce them, good day." The President then left the room, slamming the door.

Jacob upset, slowly got to his feet, as two secret service men escorted him to the front door and to his car. His driver, who was also his countries Head Intelligence Operative in America, listened as Jacob told him of the meeting.

"You won't be getting their names, Jacob!" Benjamin answered as he drove back to the Embassy.

"Why the hell not, it's our chance to discredit this Ali and take him home!" Jacob exclaimed, humiliated by the American President.

"Because it's true my friend and the Americans can never know," Benjamin replied trying to think of a way out, while the Ambassador sat there in shock.

"What do I do then when they ring?"

"Hope they don't, but in the meantime, I'll tell our bosses to lay off Ali and his friends. Somehow they're connected to the Americans, maybe that'll stop more inquiries." Benjamin answered, wondering if it would be enough.

OUTSIDE THE WHITE HOUSE

Across the road in the park, two men played chess innocently, while watching the gates to the White House.

"How'd you think it went?" Cody asked Steve, once he'd put his phone down.

"I'm not sure, I think I embarrassed the President, but he deserved it."

"Shit Steve, you don't care sometimes do you!" Cody grinned, looking around nervously.

"Relax, the phone I rung them on, was rooted through three exchanges. They can't trace us."

"Do you think they believed it was really you?"

"Yes spotting General Mosley going in was just great."

"Yeah, you were lucky there Steve. I heard he'd retired from the General staff." Cody replied, seeing Steve become alert. "What's wrong?" Cody asked looking around as well.

"I didn't know he'd retired. It means he's not usually here, they'll know we're watching the building."

"Split up, I'll meet you back at the house," Cody said softly, as standing and stretching, he walked casually towards the subway. Steve taking a casual looked around, slowly packed up the chess set, before wandering off through the park. Moments after they left, FBI agents closed off the area for one block, stopping everyone who looked suspicious, while agents went over camera surveillance footage for the area, finding nothing.

"Well, it was worth a try!" John said to Mosley when the reports came in.

"You know they're here, that's something!" Mosley replied liking this man, as the President walked back in.

"Gentlemen we do not deal with terrorists. I want these men caught. Brooks do you have descriptions of these men?" The President asked as Brooks sat frozen.

"Brooks answer me!" the President commanded him.

"They'll get us all Sir, don't let them get me!" Brooks screamed like a madman, as he exploded from his chair. The President signalling to his Secret Service men, to have him restrained, before they removed him from the room, as the others remained silent.

"I believe the strain has been too much for Mr Brooks. It might be better if he was stood down Sir." John Wilson suggested, secretly hoping they got the swine for what he'd done.

"Yes, it might be for the best Sir," Ross Stuart, the Deputy Department Head in the CIA replied, as he seated himself in Brook's chair.

"Ross have you got any photos of these men?" the President asked looking the man over.

"I believe all photos and records of the suspects were destroyed, on orders from Mr Brooks Sir. But I'll try to locate some for you." Stuart replied smoothly.

"Sir if I may interrupt. Maybe it would be a good idea to let them go." Mosley suggested, worried by this course of action.

"There's only four of them General, but thank you for your help here today, you may leave now!" All present were surprised at Mosley's dismissal. General Mosley undeterred, got to his feet and with a smile on his face, headed for the door.

"Do you find something funny General?" the President said dangerously, glaring at him.

"I'm sorry Mr President, you just reminded me of someone."

"And who might that be?" the President asked sarcastically.

"Brooks Sir, he was overconfident too." the General smiled, as he disappeared out the door, leaving the President furious.

The next day at the same time, Steve rang Agent Chandler and was put through to the President.

"Mr President, have you made a decision?"

"Yes Mr Roberts, against my advisor's advice, I have decided to give you your pardons and call off the Israelis. In return, your team members will not enter this country again or bear arms for anyone. Is that understood?"

"Yes Sir, we agree to your terms and thank you Sir" Steve replied, choked up that it was finally over.

"I have arranged for two of my men to meet you at the border with Canada near Seattle, in two days time at exactly this time. You will be officially given your pardons and this countries apology for how you were treated. I won't be talking with you again Mr Roberts, so good luck in the future." The President said warmly. Steve was then handed over to an aid to arrange the details. After getting all the arrangements Steve, hanging up excitedly told the others of the President's decision. Overjoyed the remaining members of the unit hugged each other smiling.

"That was easy!" Aaron grinned, happy to be going home in peace at last.

"A little too easy don't you think?" Ali replied.

"He sounded pretty sincere to me!" Steve admitted, also happy it was over.

"You could be right, but one thing I've learned Steve, you can never be too careful. But I want it over too, so this is how we'll do it." Ali put forward, as the unit gathered around and he explained his idea.

"What if something does go wrong?" Aaron asked trying not to jinx's them

"We go back to our original plan," Ali answered, as they all ate in silence, hoping it would go smoothly.

At the White House, the President sat smugly, as John Wilson and Ross Stuart watched on.

"They swallowed it hook, line and sinker!" the President laughed before continuing. "They might have been shit hot soldiers, but they wouldn't make first base in politics gentlemen." the President smiled like a cat with a mouse.

"Of course Mr President the CIA can't help inside America. Are the FBI units up to this?" Stuart asked looking at Wilson, trying to score points.

"No, I'm not taking any chances with these guys. I've contacted the military. They're sending fifty of their best men to handle the rendezvous at the border. No one threatens me!" the President replied.

"I hope your right Sir," John said his guts in knots over this whole setup.

"This is my decision Wilson, you two may leave now." the President ordered, dismissing them and returning to his paperwork. As John walked down the outside hallway, he realised he had gone back to being called by his surname by the President,

"Well, that gratitude didn't last long!" John smiled, as he went back to FBI Headquarters.

DOUBLE CROSS AT THE BORDER

Nigel and Bill sat nervously in the Presidents limousine, borrowed from the White House for this meeting with Ali and his unit. Even though the car was bulletproof, both men felt uncomfortable with this assignment, and both hoped Ali wouldn't turn up. They had been picked simply because they knew what Ali looked like. Their orders were simple; once the terrorists were identified, they were to signal the surrounding troops, who would secure the terrorists by any means possible.

"This sucks Nigel! I feel like a sitting duck!" Bill whispered nervously, his automatic sitting beside him on the seat.

"I think we'll be all right Bill, just don't get out!" Nigel replied as an RV came to a stop fifty metres in front of them on their side of the road. Nigel and Bill sat frozen as they both stared at the RV, which flashed its lights twice.

"Shit that's the signal confirm it with one flash," Nigel ordered Bill, as the RV rolled towards them slowly getting closer.

"Shit, I can't believe they fell for it!" Bill mumbled, the gun now in his hand.

"They must have wanted their pardons badly," Nigel replied, feeling guilty at betraying these men. Without warning, a shot rang out from the surrounding bushland hitting the RV windscreen shattering it. The vehicle turned rapidly, accelerating. It hadn't moved more than five metres when automatic weapons fire erupted from all directions. The RV swerved erratically, as all its tires were shredded, making it grind to a halt.

The deluge of lead continued, until with an ear-splitting roar, the RV burst into a fireball. The explosion engulfed the surrounding area, impacting with the limousine's windscreen, as a cloud of liquid fire swept over the vehicle.

Because it was specially made bulletproof glass, it didn't splinter, protecting the two agents inside. Shocked stupid by the explosions and too frightened to exit the vehicle, the two agents watched in horror, as bullets peppered everything in the area around the RV, including their vehicle. The firefight continued for several minutes, even though the RV had ceased to exist.

As unexpectedly as it started, the firing stopped, as an eerie silence settled over the area. The armies Special Weapons groups, seeing the action was over, excitedly gathered at the remains of the RV. The Major in charge, after taking a few snapshots, saw the two FBI men still sitting in the limo, and came round to the side door. Laughing at the look on the agent's faces, the Major, with the help of his men, forced the passenger door open, which had buckled from the explosion.

"Looks like we got them!" the Major grinned, as his men snapped off more pictures. The FBI forensics team stood shocked at the trampled on crime scene. Bill stumbling to his feet, gun still in hand, walked up to the Major and shoved his gun in his mouth, causing everyone to freeze.

"You stupid fuck! Who said to shoot?" Bill shouted at the Major, as the soldiers stared at the madman with a gun.

"Let him go, Bill, it's done," Nigel said sadly, looking at the burnt remains of the RV, as Bill suddenly pushed the Major backwards and walked away.

BACK AT WASHINGTON

At FBI headquarters John Wilson looked over the report of the attempted arrest, with Nigel's boss Brett. He was shocked that it had got so out of hand.

"Are our men okay?" John Wilson asked worriedly.

"Yes Sir, although they're far from happy with the soldiers opening fire before they identified the suspects."

"Any idea who fired that first shot?" John asked knowing the answer.

"Most probably a sniper, but no one's admitting it!"

"It said in the report, that one of our men shoved a gun in the Majors mouth!" John pointed out.

"Yeah, I'm not sure who it was though?" Brett replied grinning.

"Well under the circumstances it's understandable. Give the two men a well done from me." John answered smiling, as Brett left.

THE WHITEHOUSE

"Well thank God that's over." the President said reading the report and throwing it on his desk.

"We still haven't confirmed the four bodies' identities yet," John replied, always going by the book on these types of incidents.

"They gave the signal before the shooting started John, who else would it be? Let's move on!" the President suggested sternly. John dropped the subject.

"Well next weeks the veterans march Sir, they've asked if you could lend your support," John asked, Ali and the unit forgotten.

"Of course, my Press secretary also suggested to ask a few in for lunch on the rear lawn area, plus maybe a few photos here in the Oval Office." the President answered smiling, thinking of the Presidential elections the following year.

"That sound great Mr President, I'll inform them," John replied glad to leave.

THE MARCH

Randolph Smallwood, the Presidents press secretary, stood watching the President addressing the Veterans. Thanking them for their service to the country, he promised never to forget their sacrifice. In the crowd, people could be seen wiping the odd tear from their eyes, as the President himself stopped to wipe his own eyes.

"God the saps believe it!" Randolph smiled shaking his head. And so they should since he'd written that speech himself he thought proudly. He had to admit this President could really spin it to the crowd and the way his ratings were going he was heading for another term. Of course, that meant Randolph too had a job for another term as well. What would seal the deal was having lunch with some veterans on the lawns of the White House, after some photos inside the Oval Office with the President of course.

The President had already thanked him for the idea, calling him a genius, which had nearly made him laugh. The idea had come to him at a club when listening to some old soldiers. They'd invited him for a few drinks, having seen him with the President. Wanting to help their man get re-elected, they had suggested the President get some real heroes in for a photo shoot from the veteran day march and Randolph had been impressed.

'The poor slobs, the President wouldn't be caught dead with any of them.' Randolph laughed, as he wandered through the crowd of veterans. He was looking for the soldiers he wanted for his special photos with the President. An hour on he was still looking. 'What an ugly old bunch of dropkicks,' Randolph said to himself. 'Surely there's someone here who is photogenic' he thought, as he scanned the veterans looking for that winning shot and finding none. When working out this plan he'd had invited fifty decorated soldiers to visit the White House.

They were now gathered here at the front of the building, but none of them was what he was looking for. Defeated he was just about to give up when his attention was suddenly drawn to a commotion going on near the front gate. A small crowd had gathered, and several cameras were flashing. Going forward he saw the honour guards at the gate snap to attention and present arms, which he'd only seen done when the President walked through.

"What's going on at the gate George?" Randolph asked a Secret

Service agent who was also watching the crowd.

"You see those four old soldiers down near the gate, one in the wheelchair," George answered, with a bit of emotion in his voice, which made Randolph look harder.

"Yeah, what's so special?"

"Two of them have got the Medal of Honour, the guy in the chair and his friend pushing him are both wearing the Navy Cross plus a few others medals. I never thought I'd ever see a Medal of Honour let alone two. That's why the guards went to attention, it's an honour those two men deserve, let alone the other two guys." George replied, getting a little misty as he went forward for a closer look.

Randolph stared at the four soldiers as other soldiers and ordinary people went forward to shake their hands, as the four men proudly headed up the driveway towards the White House. Like the rest of the Veterans, they hoped to maybe get in to see the President, as Randolph smiling, grabbed his phone.

"Mr President, can you hear me?"

"Yes Randolph, what is it?"

"Your next term in office is coming up the front driveway."

After briefing the President about the situation, they found they had a dilemma. There were twice as many veterans there than were invited. There'd been a foul up with the tickets and the Secret Service didn't want to let them in. Calling the Head of Security over, the President wanted an explanation.

"I'm sorry Sir, but I'm not letting that many through. Tickets aside, it would take too long to run them through the metal detectors, as they're all wearing medals!" Watson, the Head of Security informed him.

"Shit they're all over sixty or close to it. What are they going to do, fall on us?" Randolph replied.

"We have these procedures for a reason!" Watson pointed out. He could see they weren't listening

"It's okay Watson, I'll take full responsibility." the President told him firmly, giving Watson no choice.

"Okay Sir, but it's dangerous!"

"Do you think there's enough food?" the President smiled.

"Who cares, they got in didn't they," Randolph replied, laughing with the President.

Watson in the meantime, briefed his security detail, pulling men from the roof to watch the crowds on the lawn. He also arranged for a couple of extra men to accompany the President, who wanted shots taken with four of the Veterans in the Oval Office. Like everyone else the Secret Service agents were impressed by the Medal of Honour holders as they came through the front door, pushing their wheelchair-bound comrade. He appeared to have paid heavily for his medals.

The veterans seeing they were all being allowed in and then spotting the four heroes entering broke into cheering. Even the Secret Service joined in clapping as well. Randolph greeted the men like he was trying for an Oscar, telling them proudly how the President wanted them to see the Oval office. Moved by the gesture, the three standing men thanked Randolph, as the veteran in the chair wiped tears from his eyes.

Watson followed silently behind, hating Randolph for using these brave men as they crowded into the elevator. With three Secret Service men, the Press secretary and the four Vets, it was pretty crowded in the lift. Watson marvelled at what good shape these vets were in.

"Where did you win the medal?" Watson asked the Vet next to him, trying to break the ice.

"Long Tan!" the Vet answered, with a slight accent, that Watson couldn't quite identify. As he looked him straight in the eye, Watson momentarily felt fear. Blinking, Watson looked again and saw nothing to fear in the Vets eyes, coming to the conclusion that his anger with Randolph was making him jumpy. As the lift opened, the group strolled towards the Oval Office. Excusing himself, Watson broke from the group and walked to the Control room, to see how things were going outside.

"How's everything going Dave?" Watson asked as he scanned the monitors checking the crowds.

"Nothing to report here Sir, what did you do with the two Vets with the Medal of Honour?" Dave asked excitedly.

"Watch your screens; they're on their way for photos with the President!"

"Where'd they get the medals?" Dave asked, watching them meet the President.

"I asked one, he said Long Tan."

"Wasn't Long Tan an Australian battle?" Dave replied, thinking

Watson had got it wrong, as Watson froze.

"Shit he's got an Australian accent!" Watson exploded, as he grabbed his communication mike startling Dave.

"Alert, the Vets are impostors!" Watson screamed into his radio, as agents all over the White House looked confused at the hundreds of old soldiers standing there.

In the Oval Office, handshakes had just finished when the two Secret Service guards accompanying the Vets and the two guards with the President, suddenly went for their weapons. The Secret Service agents in the White House privately thought it was a joke, but reacted anyway, as Dave and Watson watched spellbound from the Control room.

All the Secret Service men had to have a great deal of training, to be on the Presidents detail. As they reached for their weapons, the veteran with the Australian accent quickly moved forward. Attacking the closest agent, he grabbed his gun, placing it against the President's head. The other three veterans, including the one in the chair, joined in the scuffle. The struggle stopped when the agents saw the gun at the President's head. Stripping the agents of their weapons, they quickly secured the stunned President and his press secretary to chairs in the middle of the room. One of the veterans with uncanny accuracy, shot out the two cameras in the ceiling, leaving Watson too shocked to react.

As the shots rang out, pandemonium broke out as the people outside cleared the area. Press cameras, set up on the front lawn for happy shots of the veterans, turned towards the White House frantically, looking for the source. Watson coming out of shock, brought all his people up to speed, as agents rushed up onto the first floor. Racing down hallways, the agents moved into position, getting as close as possible to the Oval Office. There they waited silently for the command to storm the room.

Keyed up to attack and breathing heavily, Watson's men looked down the hallway to the oval office, to see the four agents from inside the Office, being pushed out the door blindfolded. Wandering down the corridor aimlessly, the agents there grabbed them and pulled them to safety.

"What do we do Sir?" One agent asked Watson as they stood watching the door to the Oval Office. Watson in the control room looked around, knowing his career was over, and no answer came.

"Stay where you are. We're going to need backup!" Watson replied, picking up his phone.

As time passed, the press on the front lawn were slowly pushed back by local police, who appeared to arrive by the truckload, as the unmistakable sound of choppers could be heard approaching. Landing on the front lawn, black dressed Special Forces soldiers spilt from the bellies of these flying beasts, rushing into the building. It was clear that the situation was desperate. Shocked at first, the watching media exploded to life, broadcasting to every television on the face of the globe, reporting the impossible, that the White House and the President had been taken by terrorists.

Major Matthews watched as one of his men, skilfully manoeuvred the small robot camera around the corner and down the corridor towards the Oval office. He was looking for any obstructions to his coming assault. So far it looked okay until he saw the two objects, sitting silently in the hallway outside the Oval office.

"Shit no!" he said out loud, turning to the people in the room.

"I thought you said they didn't bring any weapons?" Matthews asked Watson, the ex-Head of Security.

"They didn't, they took handguns from my men!" Watson replied, knowing how lame it sounded.

"Then where did the claymores mines come from?" Matthews asked angrily, showing them the screen, knowing an assault would prove costly.

"They must have been under the guy in the wheelchair!"

"Your pathetic Watson, you're relieved," Matthew ordered, pointing to the door, as Watson and most of his team members were dismissed.

"Now what do we do?" One of Matthew's men asked as the phone beside them rang.

"You pick the phone up." Matthews smiled, as he grabbed it. "Who am I speaking to?" Matthews asked.

"It's the man holding your President, so shut up and listen!" Ali growled, he had been waiting for someone to ring him for over ten minutes. "Since you're part of the assault group, think on this. Another two claymores are in here with us, one's on the President body. So he'll be the first to go, when you come through the door, got it!" Ali snapped.

"I hear you, what else?" Matthew's replied.

"Were you one of the Cowboys at Seattle a week ago?" Ali asked.

"Why?" Matthew's replied, this time paying more attention, remembering the FBI agent shoving a gun in his mouth.

"We're the ones you were meant to wipe-out. Instead, you got some gun runners we arranged to meet you there in our place. From now on, we'll talk only to the FBI so contact John Wilson and Agent Nigel Chandler. When they're here, we'll talk again." Ali informed him, hanging up.

"That should get their attention," Ali told the others.

"I think we've got their attention now." Cody smiled, as armoured vehicles pulled up along the fence line and red laser dots crisscrossed the room, as snipers looked for targets.

"Well, we knew after Seattle it was this or nothing!" Steve replied, staring at the President, who hadn't said a word since his capture.

"You're the ones who were after Brooks aren't you?" Randolph asked suddenly, after hearing Ali talk on the phone, as the President's eyes went wide.

"Yes. Your plan didn't work Mr President. We're still alive!" Steve said smiling.

"Not for long my friend." the President replied with a smirk.

"You really amaze me, Mr President, do you think we haven't worked this all out," Ali answered confidently.

"I wouldn't know, but it does amaze me how you managed to get in here though?" the President asked, wondering about that.

"That's easy, ask Randolph! We gave him the idea over a few drinks at a club." Steve replied, seeing the light go on in Randolph's head.

"That was you guys?" Randolph answered stupidly, as the President looked at him with fury in his eyes, making Randolph move away from him.

"None of you will get out of here alive. America doesn't deal with terrorists." the President pointed out, looking every bit a President, as he picked up a paper and began reading. Twenty minutes passed before the phone rang, which Ali picked up.

"Hello?"

"Ali, its agent Chandler here, you seem to be a hard man to kill," Nigel said casually, as the Secret Service agents and FBI team looked on.

"I'm glad you made it out of that car in Seattle Nigel, it's too bad it came to this"

"How did you get out of that one Ali? I thought you'd bought it!" Nigel asked getting looks from everyone, as he went off on a tangent.

"We thought it was too easy, so we talked some gun runners into buying some weapons. We then gave them the location and the signal; your guys did the rest."

"What do you want Ali?" Nigel asked, getting signals to move along from his boss.

"We want to be left alone, for you to call the dogs off!"

"That's going to be hard after this stunt, don't you think?" Nigel replied thinking Ali had lost it.

"We have a strong bargaining chip!"

"Come on Ali, the President isn't that popular," Nigel said, seeing smirks on the agent's faces, but not on Wilsons.

"Who said anything about the President, I'm talking about hundreds of millions of people all over this country!"

"I don't get what you mean Ali," Nigel replied looking around the room, as people shrugged their shoulders not understanding.

"Is John Wilson there Nigel?"

"Yes, he is, why?"

"The Bio lab we destroyed belonging to the Israelis. Did they really think we destroyed everything?" Ali said as Wilson went white as a sheet.

"Oh my God!" Wilson exclaimed alarm on his face, plain for everyone to see.

"I hear your boss in the background there Nigel, so get this straight, we have left small vials in several American cities. If we don't give orders to certain people every week, they have instructions to break those vials. Do you understand?"

"How do we know you're not bluffing?" John Wilson yelled into the phone, grabbing it from Nigel.

"Send Nigel in, we'll give him one for you to examine."

"Okay, he's on his way!" Wilson informed him, before hanging up.

"This is perfect Sir, while Agent Chandlers distracts them, we can rush 'em," Matthew said confidently.

"Are you crazy? What if he breaks a vial, let alone kills the President!" Nigel barked, silencing the room.

"He could be bluffing?" Matthews said, not as sure as before.

"Well let's find out. I'll go get a vial." Nigel replied, sounding more confident than he felt.

Walking down the corridor to the Oval Office, Nigel didn't know who to fear most, the supposed terrorist or the Special Response unit who trained their weapons down the hallway behind him.

"Keep going Nigel we're watching your back." His ear set crackled, not making him feel any better.

"That's what worries me!" Nigel replied nervously, sweat running down his face. Finally reaching the door, he knocked and waited for it to be opened, staring at the claymore mines that sat like silent sentinels on either side of the doorway.

"Who is it?" A happy voice asked, followed by laughter inside the room.

"Agent Chandler," Nigel replied, not getting the joke as the door opened suddenly and the muzzle of a gun faced past him down the hallway.

"Sorry Nigel, but you never know, your Special Ops guys may have tried something stupid," Ali said smiling, as John Wilson and Matthews watched and listened through the devices Nigel was wearing.

"He was waiting for you to try something!" John looked at Matthews and felt the situation slipping away. As they watched Nigel being led into the room and frisked, the camera feed suddenly went dead.

"We'll leave your comm.'s gear working, not your camera," Ali said reassuringly to Nigel, who looked over at the President slightly embarrassed.

"Good afternoon Mr President!" Nigel said sheepishly.

"Not from where I'm sitting son." the President answered, before turning back to a paper he was reading.

"Well, Ali you've really done it this time. There's no way you're walking away from this one!"

"If we go down my friend, we won't be going alone," Ali replied, handing Nigel a small vial.

"I'm sorry for the setup at Seattle. I was only following orders, and they were just supposed to apprehend you guys!" Nigel said as he stood facing these confident middle-aged men.

"Forget it, we've all done things that we'll burn in hell for!" Steve replied, approaching the agent.

"You must be the guy General Mosley called the Ghost," Nigel asked watching Steve closely.

"God I wish I was at the moment." Steve smiled.

"I don't get it you all seem like nice guys. Why are you doing this?" Nigel asked confused.

"We're backed into a corner Agent Chandler. We didn't see any other option other than to die. We just want to stop and be left alone." Steve answered, the others nodding.

"Is there anything else you need?" Nigel asked, knowing he had to go.

"Some food would be good," Cody replied smiling.

"What about women?" Aaron suggested, getting a laugh from the others, as Nigel walked to the door.

"Oh, by the way, try not to drop that vial!" Ali warned, watching as Nigel went to turn the door handle, with the hand he was holding the vial in. This made him hesitate and change hands. "God, you're a classic Nigel!" Ali smiled, as he closed and locked the door.

Back in the control room the vial was packed in a secure container and shipped off to a lab, for it to be analysed. While this was happening, Nigel was pumped for information on the terrorists.

"Interesting that the claymores are outside in the hallway, we might be able to get to them unobserved," Matthew suggested, trying to get something going.

"I don't think so Major, the fourth man in the corner who made a comment about girls was watching a screen. I'd say they've got a camera watching the hallway." Nigel explained, getting a nod of well done from his boss.

"What do you think shrink?" Wilson asked a criminal behaviour expert they had brought in for this situation. He'd been listening in on Nigel's visit to the Oval office.

"We're in big trouble, Sir! These men have nothing to lose. And by the way they can joke at a time like this; I'd hazard a guess and say they are pretty experienced at this kind of thing." The man answered, thinking to himself it might be time to leave.

"Anyone else got an idea?" Wilson asked the people in the room, mostly getting confused looks in return.

"Evacuate all major cities until the vials are located!" Matthews suggested, hoping to take away their edge.

"Are you crazy? This isn't a bomb Major it's a disease that can be carried on the wind. Nowhere is safe!"

"We could agree to their demands, Sir. Let's face it, it would cost us nothing!" Nigel answered softly.

"We don't give in to the demands of terrorists, Agent Chandler. It's a standing order from the President." Wilson replied grimly.

"Who would know Sir?"

"Let's wait for the lab results first okay," Wilson replied before sitting down and ordering a coffee while he thought. After two tension-filled hours, the FBI's infectious diseases labs had analysed the vial and rang.

"So what is it?" John Wilson asked the Chief of research at the lab, Don Williams.

"It's a mutated measles virus, Sir," Don answered his voice sounding strained.

"I've had measles Chief, is that it?" Wilson asked wondering why the Chief of research sounded so alarmed.

"It's been altered, sir. I'd say eighty percent of people who contracted it would die!" Don informed him. Wilson stood there staring around the room at the anxious people watching him.

"Destroy it immediately Don, I want it contained!" Wilson ordered. Getting an okay, he hung up. "I'm afraid it's the real thing men. From now on everyone carries a Bio suit with him at all times!" Wilson ordered, knowing it had gone beyond a simple siege. "And no one calls their families, or leaves this building, is that understood!" Wilson added, not wanting a panic.

Sensing movement, Wilson turned to see the Vice President marched in, accompanied by General Mosley.

"Shit no!" Wilson said out loud, causing everyone to look at the Vice President.

"Good to see you too John." the Vice President smiled at Wilsons remark.

"Sorry about that Sir, you took me by surprise," Wilson answered, embarrassed by his outburst.

The Vice President, unlike the President, was a military man and when this crisis had first occurred, he rung his old friend, General Mosley, to find out what was going on. He had been appalled by the way the situation was being handled.

"By the look on your face Mr Wilson, I guess they're not bluffing?" the Vice President asked, getting an acknowledgement from Wilson

"What do you think Major?" General Mosley asked looking

Matthews over.

"I think we can take them General," Matthew answered confidently.

"Have you looked at their files Major?" Mosley asked dangerously. "Did you know those men in there, once led a team of twenty-five marines and wiped out a force of over seven hundred soldiers?" the General informed him.

"I find that hard to believe Sir!" Matthew replied, standing his ground.

"It's true Major. I was one of those Marines!" the Vice President replied smiling, thinking back to his time in Panama.

The phone rang in the Oval Office and Steve being the closest picked it up.

"Who is it?" Steve asked smiling.

"It Vice President Baker, you're Captain Steve Roberts, formerly of the SAS?" Baker asked, hearing the intake of breath, as Steve lost his smile.

"You know a lot about me, Sir?" Steve answered, not knowing much about the Vice President.

"Can I come over for a talk Captain, with your promise I'll be released afterwards," Baker asked.

"Of course you have my word, but how many are with you?"

"Just me, General Mosley and one Secret Service agent, as my escort," Baker informed him.

"Okay Sir, but no surprises!"

"Who was that?" Ali asked from the window.

"The Vice President, he's coming over for a chat!" Steve answered smiling again, as everyone looked at him as if he was joking.

"You're kidding, aren't you?" the President asked dropping his paper.

THE PLAN

"You can't go, Sir!" John Wilson exploded, grabbing the Vice Presidents arm, before realising who he was grabbing and letting go.

"I'm perfectly safe John. Remain here till I return." Baker ordered him before pointing at Mosley and one of his guards.

"You two are coming with me," Baker ordered, walking out the door and down the corridor past the surprised marines and secret service men. Coming to the Oval Office door, Baker knocked. It was opened by Steve, who came into view, gun ready.

"Mr Vice President, General, it's good to see you!" Steve exclaimed, failing to hide his astonishment.

"What did you think I was lying Captain?" Baker asked a small smile on his lips, as he walked around the room.

"It had entered my mind, Sir."

"It's been a long time Steve, I see everyone's here except the Japanese soldier." the Vice President said, getting strange looks from the unit members by the use of Steve's name.

"You know these terrorists Baker?" the President snarled.

"Yes I do George, and I don't consider them terrorists yet."

"You're Sergeant Baker from the Panama base?" Cody yelled smiling.

"Bingo you got me!" the Vice President replied.

"How did a Sergeant become Vice President?" Ali asked, still off balance by Bakers appearance.

"It was a long hard road gentleman! But you know what they say; Americas the land of dreams!" Baker replied grinning.

"We're sorry it came to this Sir, but we were tired of being hunted," Steve explained his voice showing for the first time how on edge he was.

"How did all this come about Steve?" Baker asked seriously.

"It's a long story Sir" Ali replied.

"Doesn't look like you're going anywhere? You may as well tell me." Baker said as the group sat down.

Secret Service Agent James watched the group from the door, where he had remained. As he stood there, it came to him how quickly he could take these men. In their present state of mind, they were relaxed and talking with the Vice President, their defences down. Moving in a casual friendly way, he got into position to swiftly draw his weapon and fire. He halted when a gun barrel pressed against his head, causing everyone to turn in his direction.

"Are you impressed James?" Baker asked sternly, as Aaron removed the agent's weapon.

"It's our age, Sir. They all think they can take four old men!" Aaron replied smiling, before shoving the agent into a chair, and going back to his monitor.

"Sorry Sir, I just thought that," was all James got out.

"This is why we're in this situation James because everyone overthought, so just sit there and listen!" Baker ordered him. "Please continue Ali," Baker asked as Ali began telling their story.

It took over two hours Ali and then Steve to pour out all that had happened since Fort Bragg, leaving nothing out. Even the President sat spellbound while the story unfolded.

"So Sukai was killed by one of the Israelis hit squads," Baker asked sadly.

"He was a good man!" Aaron choked out.

"For what it's worth, if I'd known the whole story, I would have given you your pardon's." the President said truthfully, looking at his Vice President to show he was telling the truth.

"Unfortunately that was before you threatened us with Bioweapons!" Baker pointed out, showing anger for the first time.

"It was a bluff Sir we only had one vial!" Ali replied, getting shocked looks from the other unit members for revealing it now.

"You've just given away you're advantage!" Mosley told them, surprised.

"So why did you keep one?" the President asked.

"We kept it as a backup and thought about trying this on the Israelis to get them off our backs. It would've meant giving them a sample, and from it, they could have made more." Ali replied, knowing the Americans would have destroyed theirs already.

"So what are we to do now?" Baker asked confused by their honesty.

"It's your call Sir, but the offer still stands. Just let us retire, and we'll go home!" Ali replied, sounding tired

"There's only one solution I can see Sir, they're all going to have to die!" Mosley suggested a small smile on his lips, as he explained his plan to his President.

"Well I can't say I'm happy, but it seems the only way out." the President admitted looking around the room.

"It's perfect Sir. You'll get re-elected for sure!" Randolph practically cheered from the corner, where up till now he had remained, hoping to be overlooked if things went bad.

"Maybe you could shoot one hostage!" Baker suggested staring at Randolph, as the President laughed for the first time that day.

Outside the world's media watched with bated breath. They had been ordered not to broadcast, as the four Special Forces soldiers slid down ropes, outside the Oval office's windows. Inside Major Matthews men silently approached the Oval Office door laying charges. At a prearranged time two explosions sounded, from both the windows and the hallway as the soldiers, night sight goggles in place, stormed the Oval Office. Screams echoed through the watching crowds outside, as the media once again started broadcasting.

Moments later, the shrill of ambulance sirens could be heard approaching, as the front gates to the White House were thrown open, letting the ambulances through. The crowd held its breath, waiting to hear what had happened, as the shooting abated and silence descended.

"The President has been rescued safely!" A loud voice announced from the White House. Cheers rose from the now jubilant crowd that had surged forward, trying to get a look at their President. After several minutes an ambulance started to leave, suddenly stopping near the front gate. A dust-covered President, surrounded by black dressed Special Forces soldiers, stood and waved to the crowd. Cameras drank in the scene and sent it to all corners of the globe.

"God bless America!" the President yelled to the masses, as the crowd erupted cheering for what they saw as a miracle. Shouting the Presidents name the crowd surged forward, trying to be near their President. The Special Forces soldiers were all smiles, as women kissed them and men shook their hands praising them for their bravery. Escorting the president back to the ambulance, he waved again, tears in his eyes, before disappearing down the road, surrounded by his security.

"My god I couldn't have planned it better myself!" Randolph said happily as he watched from inside the White House, getting exasperated looks from all there, including the Vice President.

"Randolph, have you ever been to Alaska?" Vice president Baker asked as Randolph's happy mood evaporated.

At the rear of the White House, General Mosley, James the Secret Service agent and Agent Chandler led four Marines, out to a waiting army van. Hopping in the truck, the men sat silently as James drove out the back gate.

"You know you took a chance telling them you were bluffing!" Mosley remarked, passing around the same flask he'd had in Australia all those years ago.

"It just felt right General, I couldn't lie to Baker. He was a good soldier!" Ali replied.

"Well you shocked me I can tell ya." Cody smiled.

"Do you think they'll honour the agreement?" Steve asked, sobering the group.

"If they go back on it now, they'd have to explain that deception back there, and this President wants to be re-elected. No, I think you can retire Steve, and for what it's worth I hope you all find peace." Mosley answered, showing that he understood their pain and frustration.

"It would be wise not to come back to the States," Nigel said from the front seat as James drove into the Central business area of Washington, making the group lapsed into silence.

"We're sorry for the trouble we've caused you and your team Nigel, but it was, unfortunately, necessary to stop more bloodshed!" Ali replied, knowing a lot of people would never see their side of the story.

"Look I know to get out of this mess someone must think you're worth it, but you killed people here and threatened my country. I can't forgive you for that, no matter what you've done!" Nigel answered angrily, knowing it was his job to bring the lawbreakers to justice, not theirs.

"We respect your opinion Agent, and I can assure you, I will never return unless the President goes back on his word, then all bets are off!" Steve replied as the vehicle slowed. Pulling up near a subway station, Mosley got out with them and shook their hands, saying nothing as the unit members turned to leave.

"Wait" James shouted getting out as well and walking up to Aaron, offering his hand, which Aaron took before they all turned and disappeared into the surrounding crowd. James and the General hopped back in the front with Nigel, as he drove off back towards the White House.

"You're wrong about them Agent, I wish I could tell you what they've done for this country and how we betrayed them, but I can't." General Mosley said quietly, getting a nod from James, who knew everything as well, as they motored along.

"We had them trapped Sir, they couldn't have got away. Why did the President let them go?" Nigel replied defensively.

"You're wrong. They were well prepared to fight their way out. Where did you think those uniforms they were wearing came from?" James replied as he thought how easily they had read him.

"They had planned to detonate the mines and in the confusion help the injured President to the front door pretending to be rescuers. It was so ballsy I think it would have worked." Mosley told him, having gone over it with Ali.

"Maybe, but I was there, and others who would have recognised them!" Nigel replied, not too sure, as his first response would have been to go to the Oval Office.

"Anyway it's over now; best we all put it behind us!" Mosley suggested, glad he could return to retirement, he'd had enough of Washington.

Getting off the subway separately Steve and the others rendezvoused at the house they had rented and had a quiet drink together before saying their goodbyes. Packed up, they all headed out of Washington on their own prearranged transport, promising to all meet in Zurich in six months time. They hoped by then, to have given up hiding and resumed their lives. At the front door, Ali suddenly turned to Steve and embraced him.

"Come with me now to Zurich Steve. Julie and the children can finally meet their uncle!" Ali asked, tears in his eyes, worried for Steve on his own.

"I'm okay Ali. I met someone. I'll bring her with me in three months time." Steve replied seeing Ali's face light up.

"That is good news Steve, but you said nothing?" Ali replied, glad for Steve and wondering why he'd kept it secret.

"I didn't want anyone to know till this business was over," Steve replied, feeling guilty for keeping it from his friend. Ali took in this information nodding his understanding.

"I look forward to meeting her, Steve!" Ali replied honestly, hugging Steve again, before walking away into the night. Looking up, Steve gazed at the night sky, marvelling at the thousands of stars visible tonight. Taking it as a good omen, he grabbed his bags and started walking to the subway. Still cautious he'd decided to hire a car and drive across America, from Washington to LA. This way he could kill some time, making sure it was safe to return home.

"God it'll be great to see the kids again!" Steve thought smiling, hoping they liked Justine, as he boarded a train happy to be just another Aussie tourist, travelling around the USA.

LA INTERNATIONAL AIRPORT

Steve entered the business class lounge and seated himself at a table, trying to keep in check the buoyant mood he found himself in.

'I'm finally able to use my own passport.' Steve said to himself smiling, tasting freedom and for once not bothering to check for danger. Looking around he spotted a smart-looking young woman in a Qantas uniform and signalled to her. Ordered a glass of bourbon, he settled back relaxing. He'd booked a flight to Brisbane where he intended to hire a car and drive south to Ballina and surprise Justine. Then after spending some time with her, they would drive down to Sydney, and she could meet his family.

This would bring his forced exile to an end. Sitting there Steve felt something he hadn't felt for a long time, if ever, peace. The young woman returned, placing his drink and Australian paper next to him.

"Anything else Sir?" the young woman asked politely, waiting while Steve gave her a good tip for her service.

"No that's great and thanks for the paper," Steve replied with a smile, his good mood infectious, as the young woman smiled back with a thank you, before leaving. Sitting there emotions rushing through him, he thumbed his way through the paper catching up on events in Australia. He was excited, looking forward to getting home and being able to travel freely. Maybe, he thought, he could even return to work at Elliot and Fox to resume his career, something he really had enjoyed.

Turning the page over Steve became more alive with every story of home when by chance, he glanced at a story on page three, and his happiness crumbled. 'Young woman murdered in luxury unit in Ballina' read the caption, and beside it was a picture of Justine, taken by Steve, just before he left.

Hypnotised by the photo, his body drained of all colour and emotion, Steve sat paralysed, as tears filled his eyes.

"God, will it ever be over?" He cried out, sobbing uncontrollably as a gut-wrenching pain bent him over in agony, leaving him fighting for breath. The young woman from Qantas, hearing his sobs, hurried to his side wondering what was wrong with the man, who moments before had been so happy.

THE END